The Life, Adventures and
Piracies of the Famous

CAPTAIN
SINGLETON

The Life, Adventures and
Piracies of the Famous

CAPTAIN SINGLETON

DANIEL DEFOE

With an Introduction
by Edward Garnett

WILDSIDE PRESS
Doylestown, Pennsylvania

The Life, Adventures and Piracies
of the Famous Captain Singleton
A publication of

WILDSIDE PRESS
P.O. Box 301
Holicong, PA 18928-0301

www.wildsidepress.com

*A tale which holdeth children from play
and old men from the chimney corner.*
SIR PHILIP SIDNEY

Introduction

By Edward Garnett

*T*hat all Defoe's novels, with the exception of "Robinson Crusoe," should have been covered with the dust of neglect for many generations, is a plain proof of how much fashions in taste affect the popularity of the British classics. It is true that three generations or so ago, Defoe's works were edited by both Sir Walter Scott and Hazlitt, and that this masterly piece of realism, "Captain Singleton," was reprinted a few years back in "The Camelot Classics," but it is safe to say that out of every thousand readers of "Robinson Crusoe" only one or two will have even heard of the "Memoirs of a Cavalier," "Colonel Jack," "Moll Flanders," or "Captain Singleton." It is indeed distressing to think that while many scores of thousands of copies of Lord Lytton's flashy romance, "Paul Clifford," have been devoured by the public, "Captain Singleton" has remained unread and almost forgotten. But the explanation is simple. Defoe's plain and homely realism soon grew to be thought vulgar by people who them-

selves aspired to be refined and genteel. The rapid
spread of popular education, in the middle of last
century, was responsible for a great many aberrations
of taste, and the works of the two most English of
Englishmen, Defoe and Hogarth, were judged to be
hardly fitting for polite society, as we may see from
Lamb's Essay on Hogarth, and from an early edition
of Chambers's "Cyclopaedia of English Literature"
(1843), where we are told: "Nor is it needful to show
how elegant and reflective literature, especially, tends
to moralise, to soften, and to adorn the soul and life
of man." "Unfortunately the taste or *circumstances of
Defoe led him mostly into low life*, and his characters are
such *as we cannot sympathize with*. The whole arcana of
roguery and villany seems to have been open to
him. . . . It might be thought that the good taste which
led Defoe to write in a style of such pure and unpre-
tending English, instead of the inflated manner of
vulgar writers, *would have dictated a more careful selection
of his subjects,* and kept him from wandering so frequently into the low and disgusting purlieus of vice.
But this moral and tasteful discrimination seems to
have been wholly wanting," &c. The 'forties were the
days when critics still talked learnedly of the "noble
style," &c., "the vulgar," of "sinking" or "rising" with
"the subject," the days when Books of Beauty were in
fashion, and Rembrandt's choice of beggars, wrinkled
faces and grey hairs, for his favorite subjects seemed a
low and reprehensible taste in "high art." Though
critics today still ingenuously confound an artist's
subject with his treatment of it, and prefer scenes of
life to be idealized rather than realized by writers, we
have advanced a little since the days of the poet
Montgomery, and it would be difficult now to find
anybody writing so confidently — "Unfortunately the
taste or circumstances of Defoe led him mostly into
low life," however much the critic might believe it. But

let us glance at a few passages in "Captain Singleton," which may show us why Defoe excels as a realist, and why his descriptions of "low life" are artistically as perfect as any descriptions of "higher life" in the works of the English novelists. Take the following description of kidnapping: —

> "The woman pretending to take me up in her arms and kiss me, and play with me, draws the girl a good way from the house, till at last she makes a fine story to the girl, and bids her go back to the maid, and tell her where she was with the child; that a gentlewoman had taken a fancy to the child and was kissing it, but she should not be frightened, or to that purpose; for they were but just there; and so while the girl went, she carried me quite away.

Now here, in a single sentence, Defoe catches for us the whole soul and character of the situation. It *seems* very simple, but it sums up marvelously an exact observation and knowledge of the arts of the gypsy childstealer, of her cunning flattery and brassy boldness, and we can see the simple little girl running back to the house to tell the nurse that a fine lady was kissing the child, and had told her to tell where they were and she should not be frightened, &c.; and this picture again calls up the hue and cry after the kidnappers and the fruitless hopes of the parents. In a word, Defoe has condensed in the eight simple lines of his little scene all that is essential to its living truth; and let the young writer note that it is ever the sign of the master to do in three words, or with three strokes, what the ordinary artist does in thirty. Defoe's imagination is so extraordinarily comprehensive in picking out just those little matter-of-fact details that suggest all the other aspects, and that emphasise the character of the scene or situation, that he makes us believe in the actuality of whatever he is describing. So real, so living in every detail is this apocryphal narrative, in "Captain Singleton," of the crossing of Africa by a body of marooned sailors from the coast of Mozambique to the Gold Coast, that one would firmly believe Defoe was committing to writing the verbal narrative of some adventurer in the flesh, if it were not for certain passages — such as the description of the impossible desert, which proves that Defoe was piecing together his description of an imaginary journey from the geographical records and travelers' tales of his contemporaries, aided perhaps by the confused yarns of some sailor friends. How substantially truthful in spirit and in detail is Defoe's account of Madagascar is proved by the narrative of Robert Drury's "Captivity in Madagascar," published in 1729. The natives themselves, as described intimately by Drury, who lived amongst them for many years, would produce just such an effect as Defoe describes on rough sailors in their perilous position. The method by which Defoe compels us to accept improbabilities, and lulls our critical sense asleep, is well shown in the following passages: —

"Thieving, lying, swearing, forswearing, joined to the most abominable lewdness, was the stated practice of the ship's crew; adding to it, that with the most unsufferable boasts of their own courage, they were, generally speaking, the most complete cowards that I ever met with."

"All the seamen in a body came up to the rail of the quarterdeck, where the captain was walking with some of his officers, and appointing the boatswain to speak for them, he went up, and falling on his knees to the captain, begged of him in the humblest manner possible, to receive the four men on board again, offering to answer for their fidelity, or to have them kept in chains, till they came to Lisbon, and there to be delivered up to justice, rather than, as they said, to have them left, to be murdered by savages, or devoured by wild beasts. It was a great while ere the captain took any notice of them, but when he did, he ordered the boatswain to be seized, and threatened to bring him to the capstan for speaking for them. . . . Upon this severity, one of the seamen, bolder than the rest, but still with all possible respect to the captain, besought his honor, as he called him, that he would give leave to some more of them to go on shore, and die with their companions, or, if possible, to assist them to resist the barbarians."

Now the first passage we have quoted about the cowardice, &c., of the Portuguese crew is not in keeping with the second passage, which shows the men as "wishing to die with their companions"; but so actual is the scene of the seamen "in a body coming up to the rail of the quarterdeck," that we cannot but believe the thing happened so, just as we believe in all the thousand little details of the imaginary narrative of "Robinson Crusoe." This feat of the imagination Defoe strengthens in the most artful manner, by putting in the mouths of his characters various reflections to substantiate the narrative. For example, in the descrip-tion,, of the savages who lined the perilous channel in a half-moon, where the European ship lay, we find the afterthoughts are added so naturally, that they would carry conviction to any judge or jury: —

"They little thought what service they had done

us, and how unwittingly, and by the greatest ignorance, they had made themselves pilots to us, while
we, having not sounded the place, might have been
lost before we were aware. *It is true we might have
sounded our new harbor, before we had ventured out;
but I cannot say for certain, whether we should or not;
for I, for my part, had not the least suspicion of what
our real case was; however, I say, perhaps, before we had
weighed, we should have looked about us a little."*

Turning to the other literary qualities that make
Defoe's novels great, if little read, classics, how delight-
ful are the little satiric touches that add grave weight
to the story. Consider the following: "My good gypsy
mother, for some of her worthy actions, no doubt,
happened in process of time to be hanged, and as this
fell out something too soon for me to be perfected in
the strolling trade," &c. . Every other word here is dryly
satiric, and the large free callousness and careless bru-
tality of Defoe's days with regard to the life of criminals
is conveyed in half a sentence. And what an amount
of shrewd observation is summed up in this one saying:
"Upon these foundations, William said he was satisfied
we might trust them; for, says William, I would as soon
trust a man whose interest binds him to be just to me,
as a man whose principle binds himself." Extremely
subtle is also this remark: *"Why, says I, did you ever know
a pirate repent?* At this he started a little and returned,
At the gallows I have known *one* repent, and I *hope* thou
wilt be the second." The character of William the
Quaker pirate is a masterpiece of shrewd humor. He
is the first Quaker brought into English fiction, and
we know of no other Friend in latter-day fiction to
equal him. Defoe in his inimitable manner has defined
surely and deftly the peculiar characteristics of the sect
in this portrait. On three separate occasions we find

William saving unfortunate natives or defenseless prisoners from the cruel and wicked barbarity of the sailors. For example, the reader will find a most penetrating analysis of the dense stupidity which so often accompanies man's love of bloodshed. The sketch of the second lieutenant, who was for "murdering the negroes to make them tell," when he could not make them even understand what he wanted, is worthy of Tolstoy. We have not space here to dwell upon the scores of passages of similar deep insight which make "Captain Singleton" a most true and vivid commentary on the life of Defoe's times, but we may call special attention to the passage which describe the sale of the negroes to the planters; to the description of the awakening of the conscience of Captain Singleton through terror at the fire-cloud; and to the extraordinarily picturesque conversation between William and the captive Dutchman. Finally, if the reader wishes to taste Defoe's flavor in its perfection let him examine carefully those passages in the concluding twenty pages of the book, wherein Captain Singleton is shown as awakening to the wickedness of his past life, and the admirable dry reasoning of William by which the Quaker prevents him from committing suicide and persuades him to keep his ill-gotten wealth, "with a resolution to do what right with it we are able; and who knows what opportunity Providence may put into our hands. . . . As it is without doubt, our present business is to go to some place of safety, where we may wait His will." How admirable is the passage about William's sister, the widow with four children who kept a little shop in the Minories, and that in which the penitent ex-pirates are shown us as hesitating in Venice for two years before they durst venture to England for fear of the gallows.

"Captain Singleton" was published in 1720, a year after "Robinson Crusoe," when Defoe was fifty-nine.

The following is a list of Defoe's works:

"New Discovery of Old Intrigue" (verse), 1691.
"Character of Dr. Samuel Annesley" (verse), 1697.
"The Pacificator" (verse), 1700.
"True-Born Englishman" (verse), 1701.
"The Mock Mourners" (verse), 1702.
"Reformation of Manners" (verse), 1702.
"New Test of Church of England's Loyalty," 1702.
"Shortest Way with the Dissenters," 1702.
"Ode to the Athenian Society," 1703.
"Enquiry into Acgill's General Translation," 1703.
"More Reformation" (verse), 1703.
"Hymn to the Pillory," 1703.
"The Storm" (Tale), 1704.
"Layman's Sermon on the Late Storm," 1704.
"The Consolidator; or, Memoirs of Sundry Transac-
      tions from the World in the Moon," 1704.
"Elegy on Author of 'True-Born Englishman,'" 1704.
"Hymn to Victory," 1704.
"Giving Alms no Charity," 1704.
"The Dyet of Poland" (verse), 1705.
"Apparition of Mrs. Veal," 1706.
"Sermon on the Filling-up of Dr. Burgess's Meeting-
      house," 1706.
"Jure Divino" (verse), 1706.
"Caledonia" (verse), 1706.
"History of the Union of Great Britain," 1709.
"Short Enquiry into a Late Duel," 1713.
"A General History of Trade," 1713.
"Wars of Charles III.," 1715.
"The Family Instruction" (two eds.), 1715.
"Hymn to the Mob," 1715.
"Memoirs of the Church of Scotland," 1717.

"Life and Death of Count Patkul," 1717.
"Memoirs of Duke of Shrewsbury," 1718.
"Memoirs of Daniel Williams," 1718.
"The Life and Strange Surprising Adventures of Robinson Crusoe, of York, Mariner," 1719.
"The Farther Adventures of Robinson Crusoe," 1719.
"The Dumb Philosopher: or, Great Britain's Wonder," 1719.
"The King of Pirates" (Capt. Avery), 1719.
"Life of Baron de Goertz," 1719.
"Life and Adventures of Duncan Campbell," 1720.
"Mr. Campbell's Pacquet," 1720.
"Memoirs of a Cavalier," 1720.
"Life of Captain Singleton," 1720.
"Serious Reflections during the Life and Surprising Adventures of Robinson Crusoe," 1720.
"The Supernatural Philosopher; or, The Mysteries of Magick," 1720.
Translation of Du Fresnoy's "Compleat Art of Painting" (verse), 1720.
"Moll Flanders," 1722.
"Journal of the Plague Year," 1722.
"Due Preparations for the Plague," 1722.
"Life of Cartouche," 1722.
"History of Colonel Jacque," 1722.
"Religious Courtship," 1722.
"History of Peter the Great," 1723.
"The Highland Rogue" (Rob Roy), 1723.
"The Fortunate Mistress" (Roxana), 1724.
"Narrative of Murders at Calais," 1724.
"Life of John Sheppard," 1724.
"Robberies, Escapes, &c., of John Sheppard," 1724.
"The Great Law of Subordination; or, The Insolence and Insufferable Behavior of Servants in England," 1724.
"A Tour through Great Britain," 1724-6.

"New Voyage Round the World," 1725.

"Account of Jonathan Wild," 1725.

"Account of John Gow," 1725.

"Everybody's Business is Nobody's Business" (on Servants), 1725.

"The Complete English Tradesman," 1725; vol. ii., 1727.

"The Friendly Demon," 1726.

"Mere Nature Delineated" (Peter the Wild Boy), 1726.

"Political History of the Devil," 1726.

"Essay upon Literature and the Original of Letters," 1726.

"History of Discoveries," 1726-7.

"The Protestant Monastery," 1726.

"A System of Magic," 1726.

"Parochial Tyranny," 1727.

"Treatise concerning Use and Abuse of Marriage," 1727.

"Secrets of Invisible World Discovered; or, History and Reality of Apparitions," 1727, 1728.

"A New Family Instructor," 1728.

"Augusta Triumphans," 1728.

"Plan of English Commerce," 1728.

"Second Thoughts are Best" (on Street Robberies), 1728.

"Street Robberies Considered," 1728.

"Humble Proposal to People of England for Increase of Trade, &c.," 1729.

"Preface to R. Dodsley's Poem 'Servitude'" 1729.

"Effectual Scheme for Preventing Street Robberies," 1731.

Besides the above-named publications a large number of further tracts by Defoe are extant, on matters of Politics and Church.

THE LIFE,
ADVENTURES
AND PIRACIES
OF THE
FAMOUS
CAPTAIN
SINGLETON

*A*s it is usual for great persons, whose lives have been remarkable, and whose actions deserve recording to posterity, to insist much upon their originals, give full accounts of their families, and the histories of their ancestors, so, that I may be methodical, I shall do the same, though I can look but a very little way into my pedigree, as you will see presently.

If I may believe the woman whom I was taught to call mother, I was a little boy, of about two years old, very well dressed, had a nursery-maid to attend me, who took me out on a fine summer's evening into the fields towards Islington, as she pretended, to give the child some air; a little girl being with her, of twelve or fourteen years old, that lived in the neighborhood. The maid, whether by appointment or otherwise, meets with a fellow, her sweetheart, as I suppose; he carries her into a public-house, to give her a pot and a cake; and while they were toying in the house the girl plays about, with me in her hand, in the garden and at the door, sometimes in sight, sometimes out of sight, thinking no harm.

At this juncture comes by one of those sort of people who, it seems, made it their business to spirit away little children. This was a hellish trade in those days, and chiefly practiced where they found little children very well dressed, or for bigger children, to sell them to the plantations.

The woman, pretending to take me up in her arms and kiss me, and play with me, draws the girl a good way from the house, till at last she makes a fine story to the girl, and bids her go back to the maid, and tell her where she was with the child; that a gentlewoman had taken a fancy to the child, and was kissing of it, but she should not be frighted, or to that purpose; for they were but just there; and so, while the girl went, she carries me quite away.

From this time, it seems, I was disposed of to a beggar woman that wanted a pretty little child to set out her case; and after that, to a gypsy, under whose government I continued till I was about six years old. And this woman, though I was continually dragged about with her from one part of the country to another, yet never let me want for anything; and I called her mother; though she told me at last she was not my mother, but that she bought me for twelve shillings of another woman, who told her how she came by me, and told her that my name was Bob Singleton, not Robert, but plain Bob; for it seems they never knew by what name I was christened.

It is in vain to reflect here, what a terrible fright the careless hussy was in that lost me; what treatment she received from my justly enraged father and mother, and the horror these must be in at the thoughts of their child being thus carried away; for as I never knew anything of the matter, but just what I have related, nor who my father and mother were, so it would make but a needless digression to talk of it here.

My good gypsy mother, for some of her worthy actions no doubt, happened in process of time to be hanged; and as this fell out something too soon for me to be perfected in the strolling trade, the parish where I was left, which for my life I can't remember, took some care of me, to be sure; for the first thing I can remember of myself afterwards, was, that I went to a parish school, and the minister of the parish used to talk to me to be a good boy; and that, though I was but a poor boy, if I minded my book, and served God, I might make a good man.

I believe I was frequently removed from one town to another, perhaps as the parishes disputed my supposed mother's last settlement. Whether I was so shifted by passes, or otherwise, I know not; but the town where I last was kept, whatever its name was, must be not far off from the seaside; for a master of a ship who took a fancy to me, was the first that brought me to a place not far from Southampton, which I afterwards knew to be Bussleton; and there I attended the carpenters, and such people as were employed in building a ship for him; and when it was done, though I was not above twelve years old, he carried me to sea with him on a voyage to Newfoundland.

I lived well enough, and pleased my master so well that he called me his own boy; and I would have called him father, but he would not allow it, for he had children of his own. I went three or four voyages with him, and grew a great sturdy boy, when, coming home again from the banks of Newfoundland, we were taken by an Algerine rover, or man-of-war; which, if my account stands right, was about the year 1695, for you may be sure I kept no journal.

I was not much concerned at the disaster, though I saw my master, after having been wounded by a splinter in the head during the engagement, very barbarously used by the Turks; I say, I was not much concerned, till, upon some unlucky thing I said, which, as I remember, was about abusing my master, they took me and beat me most unmercifully with a flat stick on the soles of my feet, so that I could neither go or stand for several days together.

But my good fortune was my friend upon this occasion; for, as they were sailing away with our ship in tow as a prize, steering for the Straits, and in sight of the bay of Cadiz, the Turkish rover was attacked by two great Portuguese men-of-war, and taken and carried into Lisbon.

As I was not much concerned at my captivity, not indeed understanding the consequences of it, if it had continued, so I was not suitably sensible of my deliverance; nor, indeed, was it so much a deliverance to me as it would otherwise have been, for my master, who was the only friend I had in the world, died at Lisbon of his wounds; and I being then almost reduced to my primitive state, viz., of starving, had this addition to it, that it was in a foreign country too, where I knew nobody and could not speak a word of their language. However, I fared better here than I had reason to expect; for when all the rest of our men had their liberty to go where they would, I, that knew not whither to go, stayed in the ship for several days, till at length one of the lieutenants seeing me, inquired what that young English dog did there, and why they did not turn him on shore.

I heard him, and partly understood what he meant, though not what he said, and began then to be in a terrible fright; for I knew not where to get a bit of bread; when the pilot of the ship, an old seaman, seeing me look very dull, came to me, and speaking broken English to me, told me I must be gone. "Whither must I go?" said I. "Where you will," said he, "home to your own country, if you will." "How must I go thither?" said I. "Why, have you no friend?" said he. "No," said I, "not in the world, but that dog," pointing to the ship's dog (who, having stolen a piece of meat just before, had brought it close by me, and I had taken it from him, and ate it), "for he has been a good friend, and brought me my dinner."

"Well, well," says he, "you must have your dinner. Will you go with me?" "Yes," says I, "with all my heart." In short, the old pilot took me home with him, and used me tolerably well, though I fared hard enough; and I lived with him about two years, during which time he was soliciting his business, and at length got to be master or pilot under Don Garcia de Pimentesia de Carravallas, captain of a Portuguese galleon or carrack, which was bound to Goa, in the East Indies; and immediately having gotten his commission, put me on board to look after his cabin, in which he had stored himself with abundance of liquors, succades, sugar, spices, and other things, for his accommodation in the voyage, and laid in afterwards a considerable quantity of European goods, fine lace and linen; and also baize, woolen cloth, stuffs, &c., under the pretence of his clothes.

I was too young in the trade to keep any journal of this voyage, though my master, who was, for a Portuguese, a pretty good artist, prompted me to it; but my not understanding the language was one hindrance; at least it served me for an excuse. However, after some time, I began to look into his charts and books; and, as I could write a tolerable hand, understood some Latin, and began to have a little smattering of the Portuguese tongue, so I began to get a superficial knowledge of navigation, but not such as was likely to be sufficient to carry me through a life of adventure, as mine was to be. In short, I learned several material things in this voyage among the Portuguese; I learned particularly to be an arrant thief and a bad sailor; and I think I may say they are the best masters for teaching both these of any nation in the world.

We made our way for the East Indies, by the coast of Brazil; not that it is in the course of sailing the way thither, but our captain, either on his own account, or by the direction of the merchants, went thither first, where at All Saints' Bay, or, as they call it in Portugal, the Rio de Todos los Santos, we delivered near a hundred tons of goods, and took in a considerable quantity of gold, with some chests of sugar, and seventy or eighty great rolls of tobacco, every roll weighing at least a hundredweight.

Here, being lodged on shore by my master's order, I had the charge of the captain's business, he having seen me very diligent for my own master; and in requital for his mistaken confidence, I found means to secure, that is to say, to steal, about twenty moidores out of the gold that was shipped on board by the merchants, and this was my first adventure.

We had a tolerable voyage from hence to the Cape de Bona Speranza; and I was reputed as a mighty diligent servant to my master, and very faithful. I was diligent indeed, but I was very far from honest; however, they thought me honest, which, by the way, was their very great mistake. Upon this very mistake the captain took a particular liking to me, and employed me frequently on his own occasion; and, on the other hand, in recompense for my officious diligence, I received several particular favors from him; particularly, I was, by the captain's command, made a kind of a steward under the ship's steward, for such provisions as the captain demanded for his own table. He had another steward for his private stores besides, but my office concerned only what the captain called for of the ship's stores for his private use.

However, by this means I had opportunity particularly to take care of my master's man, and to furnish myself with sufficient provisions to make me live much better than the other people in the ship; for the captain seldom ordered anything out of the ship's stores, as above, but I snipt some of it for my own share. We arrived at Goa, in the East Indies, in about seven months from Lisbon, and remained there eight more; during which time I had indeed nothing to do, my master being generally on shore, but to learn everything that is wicked among the Portuguese, a nation the most perfidious and the most debauched, the most insolent and cruel, of any that pretend to call themselves Christians, in the world.

Thieving, lying, swearing, forswearing, joined to the most abominable lewdness, was the stated practice of the ship's crew; adding to it, that, with the most insufferable boasts of their own courage, they were, generally speaking, the most complete cowards that I ever met with; and the consequence of their cowardice was evident upon many occasions. However, there was here and there one among them that was not so bad as the rest; and, as my lot fell among them, it made me have the most contemptible thoughts of the rest, as indeed they deserved.

I was exactly fitted for their society indeed; for I had no sense of virtue or religion upon me. I had never heard much of either, except what a good old parson had said to me when I was a child of about eight or nine years old; nay, I was preparing and growing up apace to be as wicked as anybody could be, or perhaps ever was. Fate certainly thus directed my beginning, knowing that I had work which I had to do in the world, which nothing but one hardened against all sense of honesty or religion could go through; and yet, even in this state of original wickedness, I entertained such a settled abhorrence of the abandoned vileness of the Portuguese, that I could not but hate them most heartily from the beginning, and all my life afterwards. They were so brutishly wicked, so base and perfidious, not only to strangers but to one another, so meanly submissive when subjected, so insolent, or barbarous and tyrannical, when superior, that I thought there was something in them that shocked my very nature. Add to this that it is natural to an Englishman to hate a coward, it all joined together to make the devil and a Portuguese equally my aversion.

However, according to the English proverb, he that is shipped with the devil must sail with the devil; I was among them, and I managed myself as well as I could. My master had consented that I should assist the captain in the office, as above; but, as I understood afterwards that the captain allowed my master half a moidore a month for my service, and that he had my name upon the ship's books also, I expected that when the ship came to be paid four months' wages at the Indies, as they, it seems, always do, my master would let me have something for myself.

But I was wrong in my man, for he was none of that kind; he had taken me up as in distress, and his business was to keep me so, and make his market of me as well as he could, which I began to think of after a different manner than I did at first, for at first I thought he had entertained me in mere charity, upon seeing my distressed circumstances, but did not doubt but when he put me on board the ship, I should have some wages for my service.

But he thought, it seems, quite otherwise; and when I procured one to speak to him about it, when the ship was paid at Goa, he flew into the greatest rage imaginable, and called me English dog, young heretic, and threatened to put me into the Inquisition. Indeed, of all the names the four-and-twenty letters could make up, he should not have called me heretic; for as I knew nothing about religion, neither Protestant from Papist, or either of them from a Mahometan, I could never be a heretic. However, it passed but a little, but, as young as I was, I had been carried into the Inquisition, and there, if they had asked me if I was a Protestant or a Catholic, I should have said yes to that which came first. If it had been the Protestant they had asked first, it had certainly made a martyr of me for I did not know what.

But the very priest they carried with them, or chaplain of the ship, as we called him, saved me; for seeing me a boy entirely ignorant of religion, and ready to do or say anything they bid me, he asked me some questions about it, which he found I answered so very simply, that he took it upon him to tell them he would answer for my being a good Catholic, and he hoped he should be the means of saving my soul, and he pleased himself that it was to be a work of merit to him; so he made me as good a Papist as any of them in about a week's time.

I then told him my case about my master; how, it is true, he had taken me up in a miserable case on board a man-of-war at Lisbon; and I was indebted to him for bringing me on board this ship; that if I had been left at Lisbon, I might have starved, and the like; and therefore I was willing to serve him, but that I hoped he would give me some little consideration for my service, or let me know how long he expected I should serve him for nothing.

It was all one; neither the priest nor anyone else could prevail with him, but that I was not his servant but his slave, that he took me in the Algerine, and that I was a Turk, only pretended to be an English boy to get my liberty, and he would carry me to the Inquisition as a Turk.

This frighted me out of my wits, for I had nobody

to vouch for me what I was, or from whence I came; but the good Padre Antonio, for that was his name, cleared me of that part by a way I did not understand; for he came to me one morning with two sailors, and told me they must search me, to bear witness that I was not a Turk. I was amazed at them, and frighted, and did not understand them, nor could I imagine what they intended to do to me. However, stripping me, they were soon satisfied, and Father Antony bade me be easy, for they could all witness that I was no Turk. So I escaped that part of my master's cruelty.

And now I resolved from that time to run away from him if I could, but there was no doing of it there, for there were not ships of any nation in the world in that port, except two or three Persian vessels from Ormus, so that if I had offered to go away from him, he would have had me seized on shore, and brought on board by force; so that I had no remedy but patience. And this he brought to an end too as soon as he could, for after this he began to use me ill, and not only to straiten my provisions, but to beat and torture me in a barbarous manner for every trifle, so that, in a word, my life began to be very miserable.

The violence of this usage of me, and the impossibility of my escape from his hands, set my head a-working upon all sorts of mischief, and in particular I resolved, after studying all other ways to deliver myself, and finding all ineffectual, I say, I resolved to murder him. With this hellish resolution in my head, I spent whole nights and days contriving how to put it in execution, the devil prompting me very warmly to the fact. I was indeed entirely at a loss for the means, for I had neither gun or sword, nor any weapon to assault him with; poison I had my thoughts much upon, but knew not where to get any; or, if I might have got it, I did not know the country word for it, or by what name to ask for it.

In this manner I quitted the fact, intentionally, a hundred and a hundred times; but Providence, either for his sake or for mine, always frustrated my designs, and I could never bring it to pass; so I was obliged to continue in his chains till the ship, having taken in her loading, set sail for Portugal.

I can say nothing here to the manner of our voyage, for, as I said, I kept no journal; but this I can give an account of, that having been once as high as the Cape of Good Hope, as we call it, or Cabo de Bona Speranza, as they call it, we were driven back again by a violent storm from the W.S.W., which held us six days and nights a great way to the eastward, and after that, standing afore the wind for several days more, we at last came to an anchor on the coast of Madagascar.

The storm had been so violent that the ship had received a great deal of damage, and it required some time to repair her; so, standing in nearer the shore, the pilot, my master, brought the ship into a very good harbor, where we rid in twenty-six fathoms water, about half a mile from the shore.

While the ship rode here there happened a most desperate mutiny among the men, upon account of some deficiency in their allowance, which came to that height that they threatened the captain to set him on shore, and go back with the ship to Goa. I wished they would with all my heart, for I was full of mischief in my head, and ready enough to do any. So, though I was but a boy, as they called me, yet I prompted the mischief all I could, and embarked in it so openly, that I escaped very little being hanged in the first and most early part of my life; for the captain had some notice that there was a design laid by some of the company to murder him; and having, partly by money and promises, and partly by threatening and torture, brought two fellows to confess the particulars, and the names of the persons concerned, they were presently apprehended, till, one accusing another, no less than sixteen men were seized and put into irons, whereof I was one.

The captain, who was made desperate by his danger, resolving to clear the ship of his enemies, tried us all, and we were all condemned to die. The manner of his process I was too young to take notice of; but the purser and one of the gunners were hanged immediately, and I expected it with the rest. I do not remember any great concern I was under about it, only that I cried very much, for I knew little then of this world, and nothing at all of the next.

However, the captain contented himself with executing these two, and some of the rest, upon their humble submission and promise of future good behavior, were pardoned; but five were ordered to be set on shore on the island and left there, of which I was one. My master used all his interest with the captain to have me excused, but could not obtain it; for somebody having told him that I was one of them who was singled out to have killed him, when my master desired I might not be set on shore, the captain told him I should stay on board if he desired it, but then I should be hanged, so he might choose for me which he thought best. The captain, it seems, was particularly provoked at my being concerned in the treachery, because of his having been so kind to me, and of his having singled me out to serve him, as I have said above; and this, perhaps, obliged him to give my master such a rough choice, either to set me on shore or to have me hanged on board. And had my master, indeed, known what goodwill I had for him, he would not have been long in choosing for me; for I had certainly determined to do him a mischief the first opportunity I had for it. This was, therefore, a good providence for me to keep me from dipping my hands in blood, and it made me more tender afterwards in matters of blood than I believe I should otherwise have been. But as to my being one of them that was to kill the captain, that I was wronged in, for I was not the person, but it was really one of them that were pardoned, he having the good luck not to have that part discovered.

I was now to enter upon a part of independent life, a thing I was indeed very ill prepared to manage, for I was perfectly loose and dissolute in my behavior, bold and wicked while I was under government, and now perfectly unfit to be trusted with liberty, for I was as ripe for any villainy as a young fellow that had no solid thought ever placed in his mind could be supposed to be. Education, as you have heard, I had none; and all the little scenes of life I had passed through had been full of dangers and desperate circumstances; but I was either so young or so stupid, that I escaped the grief and anxiety of them, for want of having a sense of their tendency and consequences.

This thoughtless, unconcerned temper had one felicity indeed in it, that it made me daring and ready for doing any mischief, and kept off the sorrow which otherwise ought to have attended me when I fell into any mischief; that this stupidity was instead of a happiness to me, for it left my thoughts free to act upon means of escape and deliverance in my distress, however great it might be; whereas my companions in the misery were so sunk by their fear and grief, that they abandoned themselves to the misery of their condition, and gave over all thought but of their perishing and starving, being devoured by wild beasts, murdered, and perhaps eaten by cannibals, and the like.

I was but a young fellow, about seventeen or eighteen; but hearing what was to be my fate, I received it with no appearance of discouragement; but I asked what my master said to it, and being told that he had used his utmost interest to save me, but the captain had answered I should either go on shore or be hanged on board, which he pleased, I then gave over all hope of being received again. I was not very thankful in my thoughts to my master for his soliciting the captain for me, because I knew that what he did was not in kindness to me so much as in kindness to himself; I mean, to preserve the wages which he got for me, which amounted to above six dollars a month, including what the captain allowed him for my particular service to him.

When I understood that my master was so apparently kind, I asked if I might not be admitted to speak with him, and they told me I might, if my master would come down to me, but I could not be allowed to come up to him; so then I desired my master might be spoke to to come to me, and he accordingly came to me. I fell on my knees to him, and begged he would forgive me what I had done to displease him; and indeed the resolution I had taken to murder him lay with some horror upon my mind just at that time, so that I was once just a-going to confess it, and beg him to forgive me, but I kept it in. He told me he had done all he could to obtain my pardon of the captain, but could not and he knew no way for me but to have patience, and submit to my fate; and if they came to speak with any ship of their nation at the Cape, he would endeavor to have them stand in, and fetch us off again, if we might be found.

Then I begged I might have my clothes on shore with me. He told me he was afraid I should have little need of clothes, for he did not see how we could long subsist on the island, and that he had been told that the inhabitants were cannibals or men-eaters (though he had no reason for that suggestion), and we should not be able to live among them. I told him I was not so afraid of that as I was of starving for want of victuals; and as for the inhabitants being cannibals, I believed we should be more likely to eat them than they us, if we could but get at them. But I was mightily concerned, I said, we should have no weapons with us to defend ourselves, and I begged nothing now, but that he would give me a gun and a sword, with a little powder and shot.

He smiled, and said they would signify nothing to us, for it was impossible for us to pretend to preserve our lives among such a populous and desperate nation as the people of this island were. I told him that, however, it would do us this good, for we should not be devoured or destroyed immediately; so I begged hard for the gun. At last he told me he did not know whether the captain would give him leave to give me a gun, and if not, he durst not do it; but he promised to use his interest to obtain it for me, which he did, and the next day he sent me a gun, with some ammunition, but told me the captain would not suffer the ammunition to be given us till we were set all on shore, and till he was just going to set sail. He also sent me the few clothes I had in the ship, which indeed were not many.

Two days after this, we were all carried on shore together; the rest of my fellow-criminals hearing I had a gun, and some powder and shot, solicited for liberty to carry the like with them, which was also granted them; and thus we were set on shore to shift for ourselves.

At our first coming into the island we were terrified exceedingly with the sight of the barbarous people, whose figure was made more terrible to us than it really was by the report we had of them from the seamen;

but when we came to converse with them awhile, we found they were not cannibals, as was reported, or such as would fall immediately upon us and eat us up; but they came and sat down by us, and wondered much at our clothes and arms, and made signs to give us some victuals, such as they had, which was only roots and plants dug out of the ground for the present, but they brought us fowls and flesh afterwards in good plenty.

This encouraged the other four men that were with me very much, for they were quite dejected before; but now they began to be very familiar with them, and made signs, that if they would use us kindly, we would stay and live with them; which they seemed glad of, though they knew little of the necessity we were under to do so, or how much we were afraid of them.

However, upon second thoughts we resolved that we would only stay in that part so long as the ship rid in the bay, and then making them believe we were gone with the ship, we would go and place ourselves, if possible, where there were no inhabitants to be seen, and so live as we could, or perhaps watch for a ship that might be driven upon the coast as we were.

The ship continued a fortnight in the roads, repairing some damage which had been done her in the late storm, and taking in wood and water; and during this time, the boat coming often on shore, the men brought us several refreshments, and the natives believing we only belonged to the ship, were civil enough. We lived in a kind of a tent on the shore, or rather a hut, which we made with the boughs of trees, and sometimes in the night retired to a wood a little out of their way, to let them think we were gone on board the ship. However, we found them barbarous, treacherous, and villainous enough in their nature, only civil from fear, and therefore concluded we should soon fall into their hands when the ship was gone.

The sense of this wrought upon my fellow-sufferers even to distraction; and one of them, being a carpenter, in his mad fit, swam off to the ship in the night, though she lay then a league to sea, and made such pitiful moan to be taken in, that the captain was prevailed with at last to take him in, though they let him lie swimming three hours in the water before he consented to it.

Upon this, and his humble submission, the captain received him, and, in a word, the importunity of this man (who for some time petitioned to be taken in, though they hanged him as soon as they had him) was such as could not be resisted; for, after he had swam so long about the ship, he was not able to reach the shore again; and the captain saw evidently that the man must be taken on board or suffered to drown, and the whole ship's company offering to be bound for him for his good behavior, the captain at last yielded, and he was taken up, but almost dead with his being so long in the water.

When this man was got in, he never left importuning the captain, and all the rest of the officers, in behalf of us that were behind, but to the very last day the captain was inexorable; when, at the time their preparations were making to sail, and orders given to hoist the boats into the ship, all the seamen in a body came up to the rail of the quarterdeck, where the captain was walking with some of his officers, and appointing the boatswain to speak for them, he went up, and falling on his knees to the captain, begged of him, in the humblest manner possible, to receive the four men on board again, offering to answer for their fidelity, or to have them kept in chains till they came to Lisbon, and there to be delivered up to justice, rather than, as they said, to have them left to be murdered by savages, or devoured by wild beasts. It was a great while ere the captain took any notice of them, but when he did, he ordered the boatswain to be seized, and threatened to bring him to the capstan for speaking for them.

Upon this severity, one of the seamen, bolder than the rest, but still with all possible respect to the captain, besought his honor, as he called him, that he would give leave to some more of them to go on shore, and die with their companions, or, if possible, to assist them to resist the barbarians. The captain, rather provoked than cowed with this, came to the barricade of the quarterdeck, and speaking very prudently to the men (for had he spoken roughly, two-thirds of them would have left the ship, if not all of them), he told them, it was for their safety as well as his own that he had been obliged to that severity; that mutiny on board a ship was the same thing as treason in a king's palace, and he could not answer it to his owners and employers to trust the ship and goods committed to his charge with men who had entertained thoughts of the worst and blackest nature; that he wished heartily that it had been anywhere else that they had been set on shore, where they might have been in less hazard from the savages; that, if he had designed they should be destroyed, he could as well have executed them on board as the other two; that he wished it had been in some other part of the world, where he might have delivered them up to the civil justice, or might have left them among Christians; but it was better their lives were put in hazard than his life, and the safety of the ship; and that though he did not know that he had deserved so ill of any of them as that they should leave the ship rather than do their duty, yet if any of them were resolved to do so unless he would consent to take a gang of traitors on board, who, as he had proved before them all, had conspired to murder him, he would not hinder them, nor for the present would he resent their importunity; but, if there was nobody left in the ship but himself, he would never consent to take them on board.

This discourse was delivered so well, was in itself so reasonable, was managed with so much temper, yet so boldly concluded with a negative, that the greatest part of the men were satisfied for the present. However, as it put the men into juntos and cabals, they were not composed for some hours; the wind also slackening towards night, the captain ordered not to weigh till next morning.

The same night twenty-three of the men, among whom was the gunner's mate, the surgeon's assistant, and two carpenters, applying to the chief mate told him, that as the captain had given them leave to go on shore to their comrades, they begged that he would speak to the captain not to take it ill that they were desirous to go and die with their companions; and that they thought they could do no less in such an extremity than go to them; because, if there was any way to save their lives, it was by adding to their numbers, and making them strong enough to assist one another in defending themselves against the savages, till perhaps they might one time or other find means to make their escape, and get to their own country again.

The mate told them, in so many words, that he durst not speak to the captain upon any such design, and was very sorry they had no more respect for him than to desire him to go upon such an errand; but, if they were resolved upon such an enterprise, he would advise them to take the longboat in the morning betimes, and go off, seeing the captain had given them leave, and leave a civil letter behind them to the captain, and to desire him to send his men on shore for the boat, which should be delivered very honestly, and he promised to keep their counsel so long.

Accordingly, an hour before day, those twenty-three men, with every man a firelock and a cutlass, with some pistols, three halberds or half-pikes, and good store of powder and ball, without any provision but about half a hundred of bread, but with all their chests and clothes, tools, instruments, books, &c., embarked themselves so silently, that the captain got no notice of it till they were gotten half the way on shore.

As soon as the captain heard of it he called for the gunner's mate, the chief gunner being at the time sick in his cabin, and ordered to fire at them; but, to his great mortification, the gunner's mate was one of the number, and was gone with them; and indeed it was by this means they got so many arms and so much ammunition. When the captain found how it was, and that there was no help for it, he began to be a little appeased, and made light of it, and called up the men, and spoke kindly to them, and told them he was very well satisfied in the fidelity and ability of those that were now left, and that he would give to them, for their encouragement, to be divided among them, the wages which were due to the men that were gone, and that it was a great satisfaction to him that the ship was free from such a mutinous rabble, who had not the least reason for their discontent.

The men seemed very well satisfied, and particularly the promise of the wages of those who were gone went a great way with them. After this, the letter which was left by the men was given to the captain by his boy, with whom, it seems, the men had left it. The letter was much to the same purpose of what they had said to the mate, and which he declined to say for them, only that at the end of their letter they told the captain that, as they had no dishonest design, so they had taken nothing away with them which was not their own, except some arms and ammunition, such as were absolutely necessary to them, as well for their defense against the savages as to kill fowls or beasts for their food, that they might not perish; and as there were considerable sums due to them for wages, they hoped he would allow the arms and ammunition upon their accounts. They told him that, as to the ship's longboat, which they had taken to bring them on shore, they knew it was necessary to him, and they were very willing to restore it to him, and if he pleased to send for it, it should be very honestly delivered to his men, and not the least injury offered to any of those who came for it, nor the least persuasion or invitation made use of to any of them to stay with them; and, at the bottom of the letter, they very humbly besought him that, for their defense, and for the safety of their lives, he would be pleased to send them a barrel of powder and some ammunition, and give them leave to keep the mast and sail of the boat, that if it was possible for them to make themselves a boat of any kind, they might shift off to sea, to save themselves in such part of the world as their fate should direct them to.

Upon this the captain, who had won much upon the rest of his men by what he had said to them, and was very easy as to the general peace (for it was very true that the most mutinous of the men were gone), came out to the quarterdeck, and, calling the men together, let them know the substance of the letter, and told the men that, however they had not deserved such civility from him, yet he was not willing to expose them more than they were willing to expose themselves; he was inclined to send them some ammunition, and as they had desired but one barrel of powder, he would send them two barrels, and shot, or lead and moulds to make shot, in proportion; and, to let them see that he was civiller to them than they deserved, he ordered a cask of arrack and a great bag of bread to be sent them for subsistence till they should be able to furnish themselves.

The rest of the men applauded the captain's generosity, and every one of them sent us something or other, and about three in the afternoon the pinnace came on shore, and brought us all these things, which we were very glad of, and returned the longboat accordingly; and as to the men that came with the pinnace, as the captain had singled out such men as he knew would not come over to us, so they had positive orders not to bring anyone of us on board again, upon pain of death; and indeed both were so true to our points, that we neither asked them to stay, nor they us to go.

We were now a good troop, being in all twenty-seven men, very well armed, and provided with everything but victuals; we had two carpenters among us, a gunner, and, which was worth all the rest, a surgeon or doctor; that is to say, he was an assistant to a surgeon at Goa, and was entertained as a supernumerary with us. The carpenters had brought all their tools, the doctor all his instruments and medicines, and indeed we had a great deal of baggage, that is to say, on the whole, for some of us had little more than the clothes on our backs, of whom I was one; but I had one thing which none of them had, viz., I had the twenty-two moidores of gold which I had stole at the Brazils, and two pieces of eight. The two pieces of eight I showed, and one moidore, and none of them ever suspected that I had any more money in the world, having been known to be only a poor boy taken up in charity, as you have heard, and used like a slave, and in the worst manner of a slave, by my cruel master the pilot.

It will be easy to imagine we four that were left at first were joyful, nay, even surprised with joy at the coming of the rest, though at first we were frighted, and thought they came to fetch us back to hang us;

but they took ways quickly to satisfy us that they were in the same condition with us, only with this additional circumstance, theirs was voluntary, and ours by force.

The first piece of news they told us after the short history of their coming away was, that our companion was on board, but how he got thither we could not imagine, for he had given us the slip, and we never imagined he could swim so well as to venture off to the ship, which lay at so great a distance; nay, we did not so much as know that he could swim at all, and not thinking anything of what really happened, we thought he must have wandered into the woods and was devoured, or was fallen into the hands of the natives, and was murdered; and these thoughts filled us with fears enough, and of several kinds, about its being some time or other our lot to fall into their hands also. But hearing how he had with much difficulty been received on board the ship again and pardoned, we were much better satisfied than before.

Being now, as I have said, a considerable number of us, and in condition to defend ourselves, the first thing we did was to give everyone his hand that we would not separate from one another upon any occasion whatsoever, but that we would live and die together; that we would kill no food, but that we would distribute it in public; and that we would be in all things guided by the majority, and not insist upon our own resolutions in anything if the majority were against it; that we would appoint a captain among us to be our governor or leader during pleasure; that while he was in office we would obey him without reserve, on pain of death; and that everyone should take turn, but the captain was not to act in any particular thing without advice of the rest, and by the majority.

Having established these rules, we resolved to enter

into some measures for our food, and for conversing with the inhabitants or natives of the island for our supply. As for food, they were at first very useful to us, but we soon grew weary of them, being an ignorant, ravenous, brutish sort of people, even worse than the natives of any other country that we had seen; and we soon found that the principal part of our subsistence was to be had by our guns, shooting of deer and other creatures, and fowls of all other sorts, of which there is abundance.

We found the natives did not disturb or concern themselves much about us; nor did they inquire, or perhaps know, whether we stayed among them or not, much less that our ship was gone quite away, and had cast us off, as was our case; for the next morning, after we had sent back the longboat, the ship stood away to the southeast, and in four hours' time was out of our sight.

The next day two of us went out into the country one way, and two another, to see what kind of a land we were in; and we soon found the country was very pleasant and fruitful, and a convenient place enough to live in; but, as before, inhabited by a parcel of creatures scarce human, or capable of being made social on any account whatsoever.

We found the place full of cattle and provisions; but whether we might venture to take them where we could find them or not, we did not know; and though we were under a necessity to get provisions, yet we were loth to bring down a whole nation of devils upon us at once, and therefore some of our company agreed to try to speak with some of the country, if we could, that we might see what course was to be taken with them. Eleven of our men went on this errand, well armed and furnished for defense. They brought word that they had seen some of the natives, who appeared very civil to them, but very shy and afraid, seeing their guns, for it was easy to perceive that the natives knew what their guns were, and what use they were of.

They made signs to the natives for some food, and they went and fetched several herbs and roots, and some milk; but it was evident they did not design to give it away, but to sell it, making signs to know what our men would give them.

Our men were perplexed at this, for they had nothing to barter; however, one of the men pulled out a knife and showed them, and they were so fond of it that they were ready to go together by the ears for the knife. The seaman seeing that, was willing to make a good market of his knife, and keeping them chaffering about it a good while, some offered him roots, and others milk; at last one offered him a goat for it, which he took. Then another of our men showed them another knife, but they had nothing good enough for that, whereupon one of them made signs that he would go and fetch something; so our men stayed three hours for their return, when they came back and brought him a small-sized, thick, short cow, very fat and good meat, and gave him for his knife.

This was a good market, but our misfortune was we had no merchandise; for our knives were as needful to us as to them, and but that we were in distress for food, and must of necessity have some, these men would not have parted with their knives.

However, in a little time more we found that the woods were full of living creatures, which we might kill for our food, and that without giving offence to them; so that our men went daily out a-hunting, and never failed in killing something or other; for, as to the natives, we had no goods to barter; and for money, all the stock among us would not have subsisted us long. However, we called a general council to see what money we had, and to bring it all together, that it might go as far as possible; and when it came to my turn, I pulled out a moidore and the two dollars I spoke of before.

This moidore I ventured to show, that they might not despise me too much for adding too little to the store, and that they might not pretend to search me; and they were very civil to me, upon the presumption that I had been so faithful to them as not to conceal anything from them.

But our money did us little service, for the people neither knew the value or the use of it, nor could they justly rate the gold in proportion with the silver; so that all our money, which was not much when it was all put together, would go but a little way with us, that is to say, to buy us provisions.

Our next consideration was to get away from this cursed place, and whither to go. When my opinion came to be asked, I told them I would leave that all to them, and I told them I had rather they would let me go into the woods to get them some provisions, than consult with me, for I would agree to whatever they did; but they would not agree to that, for they would not consent that any of us should go into the woods alone; for though we had yet seen no lions or tigers in the woods, we were assured there were many in the island, besides other creatures as dangerous, and perhaps worse, as we afterwards found by our own experience.

We had many adventures in the woods, for our provisions, and often met with wild and terrible beasts, which we could not call by their names; but as they were, like us, seeking their prey, but were themselves good for nothing, so we disturbed them as little as possible.

Our consultations concerning our escape from this place, which, as I have said, we were now upon, ended in this only, that as we had two carpenters among us, and that they had tools almost of all sorts with them, we should try to build us a boat to go off to sea with, and that then, perhaps, we might find our way back to Goa, or land on some more proper place to make our escape. The counsels of this assembly were not of great moment, yet as they seem to be introductory of many more remarkable adventures which happened under my conduct hereabouts many years after, I think this miniature of my future enterprises may not be unpleasant to relate.

To the building of a boat I made no objection, and away they went to work immediately; but as they went on, great difficulties occurred, such as the want of saws to cut our plank; nails, bolts, and spikes, to fasten the timbers; hemp, pitch, and tar, to caulk and pay her seams, and the like. At length, one of the company proposed that, instead of building a bark or sloop, or shallop, or whatever they would call it, which they found was so difficult, they would rather make a large periagua, or canoe, which might be done with great ease.

It was presently objected, that we could never make a canoe large enough to pass the great ocean, which we were to go over to get to the coast of Malabar; that it not only would not bear the sea, but it would never bear the burden, for we were not only twenty-seven men of us, but had a great deal of luggage with us, and must, for our provision, take in a great deal more.

I never proposed to speak in their general consultations before, but finding they were at some loss about what kind of vessel they should make, and how to make it, and what would be fit for our use, and what not, I told them I found they were at a full stop in their counsels of every kind; that it was true we could never pretend to go over to Goa on the coast of Malabar in a canoe, which though we could all get into it, and that it would bear the sea well enough, yet would not hold our provisions, and especially we could not put fresh water enough into it for the voyage; and to make such an adventure would be nothing but mere running into certain destruction, and yet that nevertheless I was for making a canoe.

They answered, that they understood all I had said before well enough, but what I meant by telling them first how dangerous and impossible it was to make our escape in a canoe, and yet then to advise making a canoe, that they could not understand.

To this I answered, that I conceived our business was not to attempt our escape in a canoe, but that, as there were other vessels at sea besides our ship, and that there were few nations that lived on the seashore that were so barbarous, but that they went to sea in some boats or other, our business was to cruise along the coast of the island, which was very long, and to seize upon the first we could get that was better than our own, and so from that to another, till perhaps we might at last get a good ship to carry us wherever we pleased to go.

"Excellent advice," says one of them. "Admirable advice," says another. "Yes, yes," says the third (which was the gunner), "the English dog has given excellent advice; but it is just the way to bring us all to the gallows. The rogue has given us devilish advice, indeed, to go a-thieving, till from a little vessel we came to a great ship, and so we shall turn downright pirates, the end of which is to be hanged."

"You may call us pirates," says another, "if you will, and if we fall into bad hands, we may be used like pirates; but I care not for that, I'll be a pirate, or anything, nay, I'll be hanged for a pirate rather than starve here, therefore I think the advice is very good." And so they cried all, "Let us have a canoe." The gunner, overruled by the rest, submitted; but as we broke up the council, he came to me, takes me by the hand, and, looking into the palm of my hand, and into my face too, very gravely, "My lad," says he, "thou art born to do a world of mischief; thou hast commenced pirate very young; but have a care of the gallows, young man; have a care, I say, for thou wilt be an eminent thief."

I laughed at him, and told him I did not know what I might come to hereafter, but as our case was now, I should make no scruple to take the first ship I came at to get our liberty; I only wished we could see one, and come at her. Just while we were talking, one of our men that was at the door of our hut, told us that the carpenter, who it seems was upon a hill at a distance, cried out, "A sail! a sail!"

We all turned out immediately; but, though it was very clear weather, we could see nothing; but the carpenter continuing to halloo to us, "A sail! a sail!" away we run up the hill, and there we saw a ship plainly; but it was at a very great distance, too far for us to make any signal to her. However, we made a fire upon the hill, with all the wood we could get together, and made as much smoke as possible. The wind was down, and it was almost calm; but as we thought, by a perspective glass which the gunner had in his pocket, her sails were full, and she stood away large with the wind at E.N.E., taking no notice of our signal, but making for the Cape de Bona Speranza; so we had no comfort from her.

We went, therefore, immediately to work about our intended canoe; and, having singled out a very large tree to our minds, we fell to work with her; and having three good axes among us, we got it down, but it was four days' time first, though we worked very hard too. I do not remember what wood it was, or exactly what dimensions, but I remember that it was a very large one, and we were as much encouraged when we launched it, and found it swam upright and steady, as we would have been at another time if we had had a good man-of-war at our command.

She was so very large, that she carried us all very, very easily, and would have carried two or three tons of baggage with us; so that we began to consult about going to sea directly to Goa; but many other considerations checked that thought, especially when we came to look nearer into it; such as want of provisions, and no casks for fresh water; no compass to steer by; no shelter from the breach of the high sea, which would certainly founder us; no defense from the heat of the weather, and the like; so that they all came readily into my project, to cruise about where we were, and see what might offer.

Accordingly, to gratify our fancy, we went one day all out to sea in her together, and we were in a very fair way to have had enough of it; for when she had us all on board, and that we were gotten about half a league to sea, there happening to be a pretty high swell of the sea, though little or no wind, yet she wallowed so in the sea, that we all of us thought she would at last wallow herself bottom up; so we set all to work to get her in nearer the shore, and giving her fresh way in the sea, she swam more steady, and with some hard work we got her under the land again.

We were now at a great loss; the natives were civil enough to us, and came often to discourse with us; one time they brought one whom they showed respect to as a king with them, and they set up a long pole between them and us, with a great tassel of hair hanging, not on the top, but something above the middle of it, adorned with little chains, shells, bits of brass, and the like; and this, we understood afterwards, was a token of amity and friendship; and they brought down to us victuals in abundance, cattle, fowls, herbs, and roots; but we were in the utmost confusion on our side; for we had nothing to buy with, or exchange for; and as to giving us things for nothing they had no notion of that again. As to our money, it was mere trash to them, they had no value for it; so that we were in a fair way to be starved. Had we had but some toys and trinkets, brass chains, baubles, glass beads, or, in a word, the veriest trifles that a shipload of would not have been worth the freight, we might have bought cattle and provisions enough for an army, or to victual a fleet of men-of-war; but for gold or silver we could get nothing.

Upon this we were in a strange consternation. I was but a young fellow, but I was for falling upon them with our firearms, and taking all the cattle from them, and send them to the devil to stop their hunger, rather than be starved ourselves; but I did not consider that this might have brought ten thousand of them down upon us the next day; and though we might have killed a vast number of them, and perhaps have frighted the rest, yet their own desperation, and our small number, would have animated them so that, one time or other, they would have destroyed us all.

In the middle of our consultation, one of our men who had been a kind of a cutler, or worker in iron, started up and asked the carpenter if, among all his tools, he could not help him to a file. "Yes," says the carpenter, "I can, but it is a small one." "The smaller the better," says the other. Upon this he goes to work, and first by heating a piece of an old broken chisel in the fire, and then with the help of his file, he made himself several kinds of tools for his work. Then he takes three or four pieces of eight, and beats them out with a hammer upon a stone, till they were very broad and thin; then he cuts them out into the shape of birds and beasts; he made little chains of them for bracelets and necklaces, and turned them into so many devices of his own head, that it is hardly to be expressed.

When he had for about a fortnight exercised his head and hands at this work, we tried the effect of his ingenuity; and, having another meeting with the natives, were surprised to see the folly of the poor people. For a little bit of silver cut in the shape of a bird, we had two cows, and, which was our loss, if it had been in brass, it had been still of more value. For one of the bracelets made of chain-work, we had as much provision of several sorts, as would fairly have been worth, in England, fifteen or sixteen pounds; and so of all the rest. Thus, that which when it was in coin was not worth sixpence to us, when thus converted into toys and trifles, was worth a hundred times its real value, and purchased for us anything we had occasion for.

In this condition we lived upwards of a year, but all of us began to be very much tired of it, and, whatever came of it, resolved to attempt an escape. We had furnished ourselves with no less than three very good canoes; and as the monsoons, or trade-winds, generally affect that country, blowing in most parts of this island one six months of a year one way, and the other six months another way, we concluded we might be able to bear the sea well enough. But always, when we came to look into it, the want of fresh water was the thing that put us off from such an adventure, for it is a prodigious length, and what no man on earth could be able to perform without water to drink.

Being thus prevailed upon by our own reason to set the thoughts of that voyage aside, we had then but two things before us; one was, to put to sea the other way; viz., west, and go away for the Cape of Good Hope, where, first or last, we should meet with some of our own country ships, or else to put for the mainland of

Africa, and either travel by land, or sail along the coast towards the Red Sea, where we should, first or last, find a ship of some nation or other, that would take us up; or perhaps we might take them up, which, by-the-bye, was the thing that always ran in my head.

It was our ingenious cutler, whom ever after we called silversmith, that proposed this; but the gunner told him, that he had been in the Red Sea in a Malabar sloop, and he knew this, that if we went into the Red Sea, we should either be killed by the wild Arabs, or taken and made slaves of by the Turks; and therefore he was not for going that way.

Upon this I took occasion to put in my vote again. "Why," said I, "do we talk of being killed by the Arabs, or made slaves of by the Turks? Are we not able to board almost any vessel we shall meet with in those seas; and, instead of their taking us, we to take them?" "Well done, pirate," said the gunner (he that had looked in my hand, and told me I should come to the gallows), "I'll say that for him," says he, "he always looks the same way. But I think, of my conscience, it is our only way now." "Don't tell me," says I, "of being a pirate; we must be pirates, or anything, to get fairly out of this cursed place."

In a word, they concluded all, by my advice, that our business was to cruise for anything we could see. "Why then," said I to them, "our first business is to see if the people upon this island have no navigation, and what boats they use; and, if they have any better or bigger than ours, let us take one of them." First, indeed, all our aim was to get, if possible, a boat with a deck and a sail; for then we might have saved our provisions, which otherwise we could not.

We had, to our great good fortune, one sailor among us, who had been assistant to the cook; he told us, that he would find a way how to preserve our beef without cask or pickle; and this he did effectually by curing it in the sun, with the help of saltpetre, of which there was great plenty in the island; so that, before we found any method for our escape, we had dried the flesh of six or seven cows and bullocks, and ten or twelve goats, and it relished so well, that we never gave ourselves the trouble to boil it when we ate it, but either broiled it or ate it dry. But our main difficulty about fresh water still remained; for we had no vessel to put any into, much less to keep any for our going to sea.

But our first voyage being only to coast the island, we resolved to venture, whatever the hazard or consequence of it might be, and in order to preserve as much fresh water as we could, our carpenter made a well athwart the middle of one of our canoes, which he separated from the other parts of the canoe, so as to make it tight to hold the water and covered so as we might step upon it; and this was so large that it held near a hogshead of water very well. I cannot better describe this well than by the same kind which the small fishing-boats in England have to preserve their fish alive in; only that this, instead of having holes to let the salt water in, was made sound every way to keep it out; and it was the first invention, I believe, of its kind for such an use; but necessity is a spur to ingenuity and the mother of invention.

It wanted but a little consultation to resolve now upon our voyage. The first design was only to coast it round the island, as well to see if we could seize upon any vessel fit to embark ourselves in, as also to take hold of any opportunity which might present for our passing over to the main; and therefore our resolution was to go on the inside or west shore of the island, where, at least at one point, the land stretching a great way to the northwest, the distance is not extraordinary great from the island to the coast of Africa.

Such a voyage, and with such a desperate crew, I believe was never made, for it is certain we took the worst side of the island to look for any shipping, especially for shipping of other nations, this being quite out of the way; however, we put to sea, after taking all our provisions and ammunition, bag and baggage, on board; we had made both mast and sail for our two large periaguas, and the other we paddled along as well as we could; but when a gale sprung up, we took her in tow.

We sailed merrily forward for several days, meeting with nothing to interrupt us. We saw several of the natives in small canoes catching fish, and sometimes we endeavored to come near enough to speak with them, but they were always shy and afraid of us, making in for the shore as soon as we attempted it; till one of our company remembered the signal of friendship which the natives made us from the south part of the island, viz., of setting up a long pole, and put us in mind that perhaps it was the same thing to them as a flag of truce to us. So we resolved to try it; and accordingly the next time we saw any of their fishing-boats at sea we put up a pole in our canoe that had no sail, and rowed towards them. As soon as they saw the pole they stayed for us, and as we came nearer paddled towards us; when they came to us they showed themselves very much pleased, and gave us some large fish, of which we did not know the names, but they were very good. It was our misfortune still that we had nothing to give them in return; but our artist, of whom I spoke before, gave them two little thin plates of silver, beaten, as I said before, out of a piece of eight; they were cut in a diamond square, longer one way than the other, and a hole punched at one of the longest corners. This they were so fond of that they made us stay till they had cast their lines and nets again, and gave us as many fish as we cared to have.

All this while we had our eyes upon their boats, viewed them very narrowly, and examined whether any of them were fit for our turn, but they were poor, sorry things; their sail was made of a large mat, only one that was of a piece of cotton stuff fit for little, and their ropes were twisted flags of no strength; so we concluded we were better as we were, and let them alone. We went forward to the north, keeping the coast close on board for twelve days together, and having the wind at east and E.S.E., we made very fresh way. We saw no towns on the shore, but often saw some huts by the waterside upon the rocks, and always abundance of people about them, who we could perceive run together to stare at us.

It was as odd a voyage as ever man went; we were a little fleet of three ships, and an army of between twenty and thirty as dangerous fellows as ever they had amongst them; and had they known what we were, they would have compounded to give us everything we desired to be rid of us.

On the other hand, we were as miserable as nature could well make us to be, for we were upon a voyage and no voyage, we were bound somewhere and no-where; for though we knew what we intended to do, we did really not know what we were doing. We went forward and forward by a northerly course, and as we advanced the heat increased, which began to be intolerable to us, who were on the water, without any covering from heat or wet; besides, we were now in the month of October, or thereabouts, in a southern latitude; and as we went every day nearer the sun, the sun came also every day nearer to us, till at last we found ourselves in the latitude of 20 degrees; and having passed the tropic about five or six days before that, in a few days more the sun would be in the zenith, just over our heads.

Upon these considerations we resolved to seek for a good place to go on shore again, and pitch our tents, till the heat of the weather abated. We had by this time measured half the length of the island, and were come to that part where the shore tending away to the northwest, promised fair to make our passage over to the mainland of Africa much shorter than we expected. But, notwithstanding that, we had good reason to believe it was about 120 leagues.

So, the heats considered, we resolved to take harbor; besides, our provisions were exhausted, and we had not many days' store left. Accordingly, putting in for the shore early in the morning, as we usually did once in three or four days for fresh water, we sat down and considered whether we would go on or take up our standing there; but upon several considerations, too long to repeat here, we did not like the place, so we resolved to go on a few days longer.

After sailing on N.W. by N. with a fresh gale at S.E., about six days, we found, at a great distance, a large promontory or cape of land, pushing out a long way into the sea, and as we were exceeding fond of seeing what was beyond the cape, we resolved to double it before we took into harbor, so we kept on our way, the gale continuing, and yet it was four days more before we reached the cape. But it is not possible to express the discouragement and melancholy that seized us all when we came thither; for when we made the headland of the cape, we were surprised to see the shore fall away on the other side as much as it had advanced on this side, and a great deal more; and that, in short, if we would venture over to the shore of Africa, it must be from hence, for that if we went further, the breadth of the sea still increased, and to what breadth it might increase we knew not.

While we mused upon this discovery, we were surprised with very bad weather, and especially violent
rains, with thunder and lightning, most unusually
terrible to us. In this pickle we run for the shore, and
getting under the lee of the cape, run our frigates into
a little creek, where we saw the land overgrown with
trees, and made all the haste possible to get on shore,
being exceeding wet, and fatigued with the heat, the
thunder, lightning, and rain.

Here we thought our case was very deplorable indeed, and therefore our artist, of whom I have spoken
so often, set up a great cross of wood on the hill which
was within a mile of the headland, with these words,
but in the Portuguese language: —

"Point Desperation. Jesus have mercy."

We set to work immediately to build us some huts,
and to get our clothes dried; and though I was young
and had no skill in such things, yet I shall never forget
the little city we built, for it was no less, and we fortified
it accordingly; and the idea is so fresh in my thought,
that I cannot but give a short description of it.

Our camp was on the south side of a little creek on
the sea, and under the shelter of a steep hill, which lay,
though on the other side of the creek, yet within a
quarter of a mile of us, N.W. by N., and very happily
intercepted the heat of the sun all the after part of the
day. The spot we pitched on had a little fresh water
brook, or a stream running into the creek by us; and
we saw cattle feeding in the plains and low ground east
and to the south of us a great way.

Here we set up twelve little huts like soldiers' tents,
but made of the boughs of trees stuck in the ground,
and bound together on the top with withies, and such
other things as we could get; the creek was our defense
on the north, a little brook on the west, and the south
and east sides were fortified with a bank, which entirely

covered our huts; and being drawn oblique from the northwest to the southeast, made our city a triangle. Behind the bank or line our huts stood, having three other huts behind them at a good distance. In one of these, which was a little one, and stood further off, we put our gunpowder, and nothing else, for fear of danger; in the other, which was bigger, we dressed our victuals, and put all our necessaries; and in the third, which was biggest of all, we ate our dinners, called our councils, and sat and diverted ourselves with such conversation as we had one with another, which was but indifferent truly at that time.

Our correspondence with the natives was absolutely necessary, and our artist the cutler having made abundance of those little diamond-cut squares of silver, with these we made shift to traffic with the black people for what we wanted; for indeed they were pleased wonderfully with them, and thus we got plenty of provisions. At first, and in particular, we got about fifty head of black cattle and goats, and our cook's mate took care to cure them and dry them, salt and preserve them for our grand supply; nor was this hard to do, the salt and saltpetre being very good, and the sun excessively hot; and here we lived about four months.

The southern solstice was over, and the sun gone back towards the equinoctial, when we considered of our next adventure, which was to go over the sea of Zanguebar, as the Portuguese call it, and to land, if possible, upon the continent of Africa.

We talked with many of the natives about it, such as we could make ourselves intelligible to, but all that we could learn from them was, that there was a great land of lions beyond the sea, but that it was a great way off. We knew as well as they that it was a long way, but our people differed mightily about it; some said it was 150 leagues, others not above 100. One of our men, that had a map of the world, showed us by his scale that it was not above eighty leagues. Some said there were islands all the way to touch at, some that there were no islands at all. For my own part, I knew nothing of this matter one way or another, but heard it all without concern, whether it was near or far off; however, this we learned from an old man who was blind and led about by a boy, that if we stayed till the end of August, we should be sure of the wind to be fair and the sea smooth all the voyage.

This was some encouragement; but staying again was very unwelcome news to us, because that then the sun would be returning again to the south, which was what our men were very unwilling to. At last we called a council of our whole body; their debates were too tedious to take notice of, only to note, that when it came to Captain Bob (for so they called me ever since I had taken state upon me before one of their great princes), truly I was on no side; it was not one farthing matter to me, I told them, whether we went or stayed; I had no home, and all the world was alike to me; so I left it entirely to them to determine.

In a word, they saw plainly there was nothing to be done where we were without shipping; that if our business indeed was only to eat and drink, we could not find a better place in the world; but if our business was to get away, and get home into our country, we could not find a worse.

I confess I liked the country wonderfully, and even then had strange notions of coming again to live there; and I used to say to them very often that if I had but a ship of twenty guns, and a sloop, and both well manned, I would not desire a better place in the world to make myself as rich as a king.

But to return to the consultations they were in about going. Upon the whole, it was resolved to venture over for the main; and venture we did, madly enough, indeed, for it was the wrong time of the year to under-take such a voyage in that country; for, as the winds hang easterly all the months from September to March, so they generally hang westerly all the rest of the year, and blew right in our teeth; so that, as soon as we had, with a kind of a land-breeze, stretched over about fifteen or twenty leagues, and, as I may say, just enough to lose ourselves, we found the wind set in a steady fresh gale or breeze from the sea, at west, W.S.W., or S.W. by W., and never further from the west; so that, in a word, we could make nothing of it.

On the other hand, the vessel, such as we had, would not lie close upon a wind; if so, we might have stretched away N.N.W., and have met with a great many islands in our way, as we found afterwards; but we could make nothing of it, though we tried, and by the trying had almost undone us all; for, stretching away to the north, as near the wind as we could, we had forgotten the shape and position of the island of Madagascar itself; how that we came off at the head of a promontory or point of land, that lies about the middle of the island, and that stretches out west a great way into the sea; and that now, being run a matter of forty leagues to the north, the shore of the island fell off again above 200 miles to the east, so that we were by this time in the wide ocean, between the island and the main, and almost 100 leagues from both.

Indeed, as the winds blew fresh at west, as before, we had a smooth sea, and we found it pretty good going before it, and so, taking our smallest canoe in tow, we stood in for the shore with all the sail we could make. This was a terrible adventure, for, if the least gust of wind had come, we had been all lost, our canoes being deep and in no condition to make way in a high sea.

This voyage, however, held us eleven days in all; and

at length, having spent most of our provisions, and every drop of water we had, we spied land, to our great joy, though at the distance of ten or eleven leagues; and as, under the land, the wind came off like a land-breeze, and blew hard against us, we were two days more before we reached the shore, having all that while excessive hot weather, and not a drop of water or any other liquor, except some cordial waters, which one of our company had a little of left in a case of bottles.

This gave us a taste of what we should have done if we had ventured forward with a scant wind and uncertain weather, and gave us a surfeit of our design for the main, at least until we might have some better vessels under us; so we went on shore again, and pitched our camp as before, in as convenient manner as we could, fortifying ourselves against any surprise; but the natives here were exceeding courteous, and much more civil than on the south part of the island; and though we could not understand what they said, or they us, yet we found means to make them understand that we were seafaring men and strangers, and that we were in distress for want of provisions.

The first proof we had of their kindness was, that as soon as they saw us come on shore and begin to make our habitation, one of their captains or kings, for we knew not what to call them, came down with five or six men and some women, and brought us five goats and two young fat steers, and gave them to us for nothing; and when we went to offer them anything, the captain or the king would not let any of them touch it, or take anything of us. About two hours after came another king, or captain, with forty or fifty men after him. We began to be afraid of him, and laid hands upon our weapons; but he perceiving it, caused two men to go before him, carrying two long poles in their hands, which they held upright, as high as they could, which we presently perceived was a signal of peace; and these two poles they set up afterwards, sticking them up in the ground; and when the king and his men came to these two poles, they struck all their lances up in the ground, and came on unarmed, leaving their lances, as also their bows and arrows, behind them.

This was to satisfy us that they were come as friends, and we were glad to see it, for we had no mind to quarrel with them if we could help it. The captain of this gang seeing some of our men making up their huts, and that they did it but bunglingly, he beckoned to some of his men to go and help us. Immediately fifteen or sixteen of them came and mingled among us, and went to work for us; and indeed, they were better workmen than we were, for they run up three or four huts for us in a moment, and much handsomer done than ours.

After this they sent us milk, plantains, pumpkins, and abundance of roots and greens that were very good, and then took their leave, and would not take anything from us that we had. One of our men offered the king or captain of these men a dram, which he drank and was mightily pleased with it, and held out his hand for another, which we gave him; and in a word, after this, he hardly failed coming to us two or three times a week, always bringing us something or other; and one time sent us seven head of black cattle, some of which we cured and dried as before.

And here I cannot but remember one thing, which afterwards stood us in great stead, viz., that the flesh of their goats, and their beef also, but especially the former, when we had dried and cured it, looked red, and ate hard and firm, as dried beef in Holland; they were so pleased with it, and it was such a dainty to them, that at any time after they would trade with us for it, not knowing, or so much as imagining what it was; so that for ten or twelve pounds' weight of smoke-dried beef, they would give us a whole bullock, or cow, or anything else we could desire.

Here we observed two things that were very material to us, even essentially so; first, we found they had a great deal of earthenware here, which they made use of many ways as we did; particularly they had long, deep earthen pots, which they used to sink into the ground, to keep the water which they drunk cool and pleasant; and the other was, that they had larger canoes than their neighbors had.

By this we were prompted to inquire if they had no larger vessels than those we saw there, or if any other of the inhabitants had not such. They signified presently that they had no larger boats than that they showed us; but that on the other side of the island they had larger boats, and that with decks upon them, and large sails; and this made us resolve to coast round the whole island to see them; so we prepared and victualled our canoe for the voyage, and, in a word, went to sea for the third time.

It cost us a month or six weeks' time to perform this voyage, in which time we went on shore several times for water and provisions, and found the natives always very free and courteous; but we were surprised one morning early, being at the extremity of the north-ernmost part of the island, when one of our men cried out, "A sail! a sail!" We presently saw a vessel a great way out at sea; but after we had looked at it with our perspective glasses, and endeavored all we could to make out what it was, we could not tell what to think of it; for it was neither ship, ketch, galley, galliot, or like anything that we had ever seen before; all that we could make of it was, that it went from us, standing out to sea. In a word, we soon lost sight of it, for we were in no condition to chase anything, and we never saw it again; but, by all that we could perceive of it, from what we saw of such things afterwards, it was some Arabian vessel, which had been trading to the coast of Mozambique, or Zanzibar, the same place where we afterwards went, as you shall hear.

I kept no journal of this voyage, nor indeed did I all this while understand anything of navigation, more than the common business of a foremast-man; so I can say nothing to the latitudes or distances of any places we were at, how long we were going, or how far we sailed in a day; but this I remember, that being now come round the island, we sailed up the eastern shore due south, as we had done down the western shore due north before.

Nor do I remember that the natives differed much from one another, either in stature or complexion, or in their manners, their habits, their weapons, or indeed in anything; and yet we could not perceive that they had any intelligence one with another; but they were extremely kind and civil to us on this side, as well as on the other.

We continued our voyage south for many weeks, though with several intervals of going on shore to get provisions and water. At length, coming round a point of land which lay about a league further than ordinary into the sea, we were agreeably surprised with a sight which, no doubt, had been as disagreeable to those concerned, as it was pleasant to us. This was the wreck of an European ship, which had been cast away upon the rocks, which in that place run a great way into the sea.

We could see plainly, at low water, a great deal of the ship lay dry; even at high water, she was not entirely covered; and that at most she did not lie above a league from the shore. It will easily be believed that our curiosity led us, the wind and weather also permitting, to go directly to her, which we did without any difficulty, and presently found that it was a Dutch-built ship, and that she could not have been very long in that condition, a great deal of the upper work of her stern remaining firm, with the mizzen-mast standing. Her stern seemed to be jammed in between two ridges of the rock, and so remained fast, all the fore part of the ship having been beaten to pieces.

We could see nothing to be gotten out of the wreck that was worth our while; but we resolved to go on shore, and stay some time thereabouts, to see if perhaps we might get any light into the story of her; and we were not without hopes that we might hear something more particular about her men, and perhaps find some of them on shore there, in the same condition that we were in, and so might increase our company.

It was a very pleasant sight to us when, coming on shore, we saw all the marks and tokens of a ship-carpenter's yard; as a launch-block and cradles, scaffolds and planks, and pieces of planks, the remains of the building a ship or vessel; and, in a word, a great many things that fairly invited us to go about the same work; and we soon came to understand that the men belonging to the ship that was lost had saved themselves on shore, perhaps in their boat, and had built themselves a barque or sloop, and so were gone to sea again; and, inquiring of the natives which way they went, they pointed to the south and southwest, by which we could easily understand they were gone away to the Cape of Good Hope.

Nobody will imagine we could be so dull as not to gather from hence that we might take the same method for our escape; so we resolved first, in general, that we would try if possible to build us a boat of one kind or other, and go to sea as our fate should direct.

In order to this our first work was to have the two

carpenters search about to see what materials the Dutchmen had left behind them that might be of use; and, in particular, they found one that was very useful, and which I was much employed about, and that was a pitch-kettle, and a little pitch in it.

When we came to set close to this work we found it very laborious and difficult, having but few tools, no ironwork, no cordage, no sails; so that, in short, whatever we built, we were obliged to be our own smiths, rope-makers, sail-makers, and indeed to practice twenty trades that we knew little or nothing of. However, necessity was the spur to invention, and we did many things which before we thought impracticable, that is to say, in our circumstances.

After our two carpenters had resolved upon the dimensions of what they would build, they set us all to work, to go off in our boats and split up the wreck of the old ship, and to bring away everything we could; and particularly that, if possible, we should bring away the mizzen-mast, which was left standing, which with much difficulty we effected, after above twenty days' labor of fourteen of our men.

At the same time we got out a great deal of ironwork, as bolts, spikes, nails, &c., all of which our artist, of whom I have spoken already, who was now grown a very dexterous smith, made us nails and hinges for our rudder, and spikes such as we wanted.

But we wanted an anchor, and if we had had an anchor, we could not have made a cable; so we contented ourselves with making some ropes with the help of the natives, of such stuff as they made their mats of, and with these we made such a kind of cable or tow-line as was sufficient to fasten our vessel to the shore, which we contented ourselves with for that time.

To be short, we spent four months here, and worked very hard too; at the end of which time we launched our frigate, which, in a few words, had many defects, but yet, all things considered, it was as well as we could expect it to be.

In short, it was a kind of sloop, of the burthen of near eighteen or twenty tons; and had we had masts and sails, standing and running rigging, as is usual in such cases, and other conveniences, the vessel might have carried us wherever we could have had a mind to go; but of all the materials we wanted, this was the worst, viz., that we had no tar or pitch to pay the seams and secure the bottom; and though we did what we could, with tallow and oil, to make a mixture to supply that part, yet we could not bring it to answer our end fully; and when we launched her into the water, she was so leaky, and took in the water so fast, that we thought all our labor had been lost, for we had much ado to make her swim; and as for pumps, we had none, nor had we any means to make one.

But at length one of the natives, a black negro-man, showed us a tree, the wood of which being put into the fire, sends forth a liquid that is as glutinous and almost as strong as tar, and of which, by boiling, we made a sort of stuff which served us for pitch, and this answered our end effectually; for we perfectly made our vessel sound and tight, so that we wanted no pitch or tar at all. This secret has stood me in stead upon many occasions since that time in the same place.

Our vessel being thus finished, out of the mizzen-mast of the ship we made a very good mast to her, and fitted our sails to it as well as we could; then we made a rudder and tiller, and, in a word, everything that our present necessity called upon us for; and having victualled her, and put as much fresh water on board as we thought we wanted, or as we knew how to stow (for we were yet without casks), we put to sea with a fair wind.

We had spent near another year in these rambles,

and in this piece of work; for it was now, as our men said, about the beginning of our February, and the sun went from us apace, which was much to our satisfaction, for the heats were exceedingly violent. The wind, as I said, was fair; for, as I have since learned, the winds generally spring up to the eastward, as the sun goes from them to the north.

Our debate now was, which way we should go, and never were men so irresolute; some were for going to the east, and stretching away directly for the coast of Malabar; but others, who considered more seriously the length of that voyage, shook their heads at the proposal, knowing very well that neither our provisions, especially of water, or our vessel, were equal to such a run as that is, of near 2000 miles without any land to touch at in the way.

These men, too, had all along had a great mind to a voyage for the mainland of Africa, where they said we should have a fair cast for our lives, and might be sure to make ourselves rich, which way soever we went, if we were but able to make our way through, whether by sea or by land.

Besides, as the case stood with us, we had not much choice for our way; for, if we had resolved for the east, we were at the wrong season of the year, and must have stayed till April or May before we had gone to sea. At length, as we had the wind at S.E. and E.S.E., and fine promising weather, we came all into the first proposal, and resolved for the coast of Africa; nor were we long in disputing as to our coasting the island which we were upon, for we were now upon the wrong side of the island for the voyage we intended; so we stood away to the north, and, having rounded the cape, we hauled away southward, under the lee of the island, thinking to reach the west point of land, which, as I observed before, runs out so far towards the coast of Africa, as would have shortened our run almost 100 leagues. But when we had sailed about thirty leagues, we found the winds variable under the shore, and right against us, so we concluded to stand over directly, for then we had the wind fair, and our vessel was but very ill fated to lie near the wind, or any way indeed but just before it.

Having resolved upon it, therefore, we put into the shore to furnish ourselves again with fresh water and other provisions, and about the latter end of March, with more courage than discretion, more resolution than judgment, we launched for the main coast of Africa.

As for me, I had no anxieties about it, so that we had but a view of reaching some land or other, I cared not what or where it was to be, having at this time no views of what was before me, nor much thought of what might or might not befall me; but with as little consideration as anyone can be supposed to have at my age, I consented to everything that was proposed, however hazardous the thing itself, however improbable the success.

The voyage, as it was undertaken with a great deal of ignorance and desperation, so really it was not carried on with much resolution or judgment; for we knew no more of the course we were to steer than this, that it was anywhere about the west, within two or three points N. or S., and as we had no compass with us but a little brass pocket compass, which one of our men had more by accident than otherwise, so we could not be very exact in our course.

However, as it pleased God that the wind continued fair at S.E. and by E., we found that N.W. by W., which was right afore it, was as good a course for us as any we could go, and thus we went on.

The voyage was much longer than we expected; our vessel also, which had no sail that was proportioned to her, made but very little way in the sea, and sailed heavily. We had, indeed, no great adventures happened in this voyage, being out of the way of everything that could offer to divert us; and as for seeing any vessel, we had not the least occasion to hail anything in all the voyage; for we saw not one vessel, small or great, the sea we were upon being entirely out of the way of all commerce; for the people of Madagascar knew no more of the shores of Africa than we did, only that there was a country of lions, as they call it, that way.

We had been eight or nine days under sail, with a fair wind, when, to our great joy, one of our men cried out "Land!" We had great reason to be glad of the discovery, for we had not water enough left for above two or three days more, though at a short allowance. However, though it was early in the morning when we discovered it, we made it near night before we reached it, the wind slackening almost to a calm, and our ship being, as I said, a very dull sailer.

We were sadly baulked upon our coming to the land, when we found that, instead of the mainland of Africa, it was only a little island, with no inhabitants upon it, at least none that we could find; nor any cattle, except a few goats, of which we killed three only. However, they served us for fresh meat, and we found very good water; and it was fifteen days more before we reached the main, which, however, at last we arrived at, and which was most essential to us, as we came to it just as all our provisions were spent. Indeed, we may say they were spent first, for we had but a pint of water a day to each man for the last two days. But, to our great joy, we saw the land, though at a great distance, the evening before, and by a pleasant gale in the night were by morning within two leagues of the shore.

We never scrupled going ashore at the first place we came at, though, had we had patience, we might have found a very fine river a little farther north. However, we kept our frigate on float by the help of two great poles, which we fastened into the ground to moor her, like poles; and the little weak ropes, which, as I said, we had made of matting, served us well enough to make the vessel fast.

As soon as we had viewed the country a little, got fresh water, and furnished ourselves with some victuals, which we found very scarce here, we went on board again with our stores. All we got for provision was some fowls that we killed, and a kind of wild buffalo or bull, very small, but good meat; I say, having got these things on board, we resolved to sail along the coast, which lay N.N.E., till we found some creek or river, that we might run up into the country, or some town or people; for we had reason enough to know the place was inhabited, because we several times saw fires in the night, and smoke in the day, every way at a distance from us.

At length we came to a very large bay, and in it several little creeks or rivers emptying themselves into the sea, and we ran boldly into the first creek we came at; where, seeing some huts and wild people about them on the shore, we ran our vessel into a little cove on the north side of the creek, and held up a long pole, with a white bit of cloth on it, for a signal of peace to them. We found they understood us presently, for they came flocking to us, men, women, and children, most of them, of both sexes, stark naked. At first they stood wondering and staring at us, as if we had been monsters, and as if they had been frighted; but we found they inclined to be familiar with us afterwards. The first thing we did to try them, was, we held up our hands to our mouths, as if we were to drink, signifying that we wanted water. This they understood presently, and three of their women and two boys ran away up the land, and came back in about half a quarter of an hour, with several pots, made of earth, pretty enough, and baked, I suppose, in the sun; these they brought us full of water, and set them down near the seashore, and there left them, going back a little, that we might fetch them, which we did.

Some time after this, they brought us roots and herbs, and some fruits which I cannot remember, and gave us; but as we had nothing to give them, we found them not so free as the people in Madagascar were. However, our cutler went to work, and, as he had saved some iron out of the wreck of the ship, he made abundance of toys, birds, dogs, pins, hooks, and rings; and we helped to file them, and make them bright for him, and when we gave them some of these, they brought us all sorts of provisions they had, such as goats, hogs, and cows, and we got victuals enough.

We were now landed upon the continent of Africa, the most desolate, desert, and inhospitable country in the world, even Greenland and Nova Zembla itself not excepted, with this difference only, that even the worst part of it we found inhabited, though, taking the nature and quality of some of the inhabitants, it might have been much better to us if there had been none.

And, to add to the exclamation I am making on the nature of the place, it was here that we took one of the rashest, and wildest, and most desperate resolutions that ever was taken by man, or any number of men, in the world; this was, to travel overland through the heart of the country, from the coast of Mozambique, on the east ocean, to the coast of Angola or Guinea, on the western or Atlantic Ocean, a continent of land of at least 1800 miles, in which journey we had excessive heats to support, unpassable deserts to go over, no carriages, camels, or beasts of any kind to carry our baggage, innumerable numbers of wild and ravenous beasts to encounter with, such as lions, leopards, tigers, lizards, and elephants; we had the equinoctial line to pass under, and, consequently, were in the very center of the torrid zone; we had nations of savages to encounter with, barbarous and brutish to the last degree; hunger and thirst to struggle with, and, in one word, terrors enough to have daunted the stoutest hearts that ever were placed in cases of flesh and blood.

Yet, fearless of all these, we resolved to adventure, and accordingly made such preparations for our journey as the place we were in would allow us, and such as our little experience of the country seemed to dictate to us.

It had been some time already that we had been used to tread barefooted upon the rocks, the gravel, the grass, and the sand on the shore; but as we found the worst thing for our feet was the walking or traveling on the dry burning sands, within the country, so we provided ourselves with a sort of shoes, made of the skins of wild beasts, with the hair inward, and being dried in the sun, the outsides were thick and hard, and would last a great while. In short, as I called them, so I think the term very proper still, we made us gloves for our feet, and we found them very convenient and very comfortable.

We conversed with some of the natives of the country, who were friendly enough. What tongue they spoke I do not yet pretend to know. We talked as far as we could make them understand us, not only about our provisions, but also about our undertaking, and asked them what country lay that way, pointing west with our hands. They told us but little to our purpose, only we thought, by all their discourse, that there were people to be found, of one sort or other, everywhere; that there were many great rivers, many lions and tigers, elephants, and furious wildcats (which in the end we found to be civet cats), and the like.

When we asked them if anyone had ever traveled that way, they told us yes, some had gone to where the sun sleeps, meaning to the west, but they could not tell us who they were. When we asked for some to guide us, they shrunk up their shoulders as Frenchmen do when they are afraid to undertake a thing. When we asked them about the lions and wild creatures, they laughed, and let us know that they would do us no hurt, and directed us to a good way indeed to deal with them, and that was to make some fire, which would always fright them away; and so indeed we found it.

Upon these encouragements we resolved upon our journey, and many considerations put us upon it, which, had the thing itself been practicable, we were not so much to blame for as it might otherwise be supposed; I will name some of them, not to make the account too tedious.

First, we were perfectly destitute of means to work about our own deliverance any other way; we were on shore in a place perfectly remote from all European navigation; so that we could never think of being relieved, and fetched off by any of our own country-men in that part of the world. Secondly, if we had adventured to have sailed on along the coast of Mozambique, and the desolate shores of Africa to the north, till we came to the Red Sea, all we could hope for there was to be taken by the Arabs, and be sold for slaves to the Turks, which to all of us was little better than death. We could not build anything of a vessel that would carry us over the great Arabian Sea to India, nor could we reach the Cape de Bona Speranza, the winds being too variable, and the sea in that latitude too tempestuous; but we all knew, if we could cross this continent of land, we might reach some of the great rivers that run into the Atlantic Ocean; and that, on the banks of any of those rivers, we might there build us canoes which would carry us down, if it were thousands of miles, so that we could want nothing but food, of which we were assured we might kill sufficient with our guns; and to add to the satisfaction of our deliverance, we concluded we might, every one of us, get a quantity of gold, which, if we came safe, would infinitely recompense us for our toil.

I cannot say that in all our consultations I ever began to enter into the weight and merit of any enterprise we went upon till now. My view before was, as I thought, very good, viz., that we should get into the Arabian Gulf, or the mouth of the Red Sea; and waiting for some vessel passing or repassing there, of which there is plenty, have seized upon the first we came at by force, and not only have enriched ourselves with her cargo, but have carried ourselves to what part of the world we had pleased; but when they came to talk to me of a march of 2000 or 3000 miles on foot, of wandering in deserts among lions and tigers, I confess my blood ran chill, and I used all the arguments I could to persuade them against it.

But they were all positive, and I might as well have held my tongue; so I submitted, and told them I would keep to our first law, to be governed by the majority, and we resolved upon our journey. The first thing we did was to take an observation, and see whereabouts in the world we were, which we did, and found we were in the latitude of 12 degrees 35 minutes south of the line. The next thing was to look on the charts, and see the coast of the country we aimed at, which we found to be from 8 to 11 degrees south latitude, if we went for the coast of Angola, or in 12 to 29 degrees north latitude, if we made for the river Niger, and the coast of Guinea.

Our aim was for the coast of Angola, which, by the

charts we had, lying very near the same latitude we were then in, our course thither was due west; and as we were assured we should meet with rivers, we doubted not but that by their help we might ease our journey, especially if we could find means to cross the great lake, or inland sea, which the natives call Coalmucoa, out of which it is said the river Nile has its source or beginning; but we reckoned without our host, as you will see in the sequel of our story.

The next thing we had to consider was, how to carry our baggage, which we were first of all determined not to travel without; neither indeed was it possible for us to do so, for even our ammunition, which was absolutely necessary to us, and on which our subsistence, I mean for food, as well as our safety, and particularly our defense against wild beasts and wild men, depended, — I say, even our ammunition was a load too heavy for us to carry in a country where the heat was such that we should be load enough for ourselves.

We inquired in the country, and found there was no beast of burthen known among them, that is to say, neither horses or mules, or asses, camels, or dromedaries; the only creature they had was a kind of buffalo, or tame bull, such a one as we had killed; and that some of these they had brought so to their hand, that they taught them to go and come with their voices, as they called them to them, or sent them from them; that they made them carry burthens; and particularly that they would swim over rivers and lakes upon them, the creatures swimming very high and strong in the water.

But we understood nothing of the management of guiding such a creature, or how to bind a burthen upon them; and this last part of our consultation puzzled us extremely. At last I proposed a method for them, which, after some consideration, they found very con-

venient; and this was, to quarrel with some of the negro
natives, take ten or twelve of them prisoners, and
binding them as slaves, cause them to travel with us,
and make them carry our baggage; which I alleged
would be convenient and useful many ways as well to
show us the way, as to converse with other natives for
us.

This counsel was not accepted at first, but the natives
soon gave them reason to approve it, and also gave
them an opportunity to put it in practice; for, as our
little traffic with the natives was hitherto upon the
faith of their first kindness, we found some knavery
among them at last; for having bought some cattle of
them for our toys, which, as I said, our cutler had
contrived, one of our men differing with his chapman,
truly they huffed him in their manner, and, keeping
the things he had offered them for the cattle, made
their fellows drive away the cattle before his face, and
laugh at him. Our man crying out loud of this violence, and calling to some of us who were not far off,
the negro he was dealing with threw a lance at him,
which came so true, that, if he had not with great agility
jumped aside, and held up his hand also to turn the
lance as it came, it had struck through his body; and,
as it was, it wounded him in the arm; at which the man,
enraged, took up his fuzee, and shot the negro through
the heart.

The others that were near him, and all those that
were with us at a distance, were so terribly frighted,
first, at the flash of fire; secondly, at the noise; and
thirdly, at seeing their countryman killed, that they
stood like men stupid and amazed, at first, for some
time; but after they were a little recovered from their
fright, one of them, at a good distance from us, set up
a sudden screaming noise, which, it seems, is the noise
they make when they go to fight; and all the rest

understanding what he meant, answered him, and ran together to the place where he was, and we not knowing what it meant, stood still, looking upon one another like a parcel of fools.

But we were presently undeceived; for, in two or three minutes more, we heard the screaming roaring noise go on from one place to another, through all their little towns; nay, even over the creek to the other side; and, on a sudden, we saw a naked multitude running from all parts to the place where the first man began it, as to a rendezvous; and, in less than an hour, I believe there was near 500 of them gotten together, armed some with bows and arrows, but most with lances, which they throw at a good distance, so nicely that they will strike a bird flying.

We had but a very little time for consultation, for the multitude was increasing every moment; and I verily believe, if we had stayed long, they would have been 10,000 together in a little time. We had nothing to do, therefore, but to fly to our ship or bark, where indeed we could have defended ourselves very well, or to advance and try what a volley or two of small shot would do for us.

We resolved immediately upon the latter, depending upon it that the fire and terror of our shot would soon put them to flight; so we drew up all in a line, and marched boldly up to them. They stood ready to meet us, depending, I suppose, to destroy us all with their lances; but before we came near enough for them to throw their lances, we halted, and, standing at a good distance from one another, to stretch our line as far as we could, we gave them a salute with our shot, which, besides what we wounded that we knew not of, knocked sixteen of them down upon the spot, and three more were so lamed, that they fell about twenty or thirty yards from them.

As soon as we had fired, they set up the horridest yell, or howling, partly raised by those that were wounded, and partly by those that pitied and condoled the bodies they saw lie dead, that I never heard anything like it before or since.

We stood stock still after we had fired, to load our guns again, and finding they did not stir from the place we fired among them again; we killed about nine of them at the second fire; but as they did not stand so thick as before, all our men did not fire, seven of us being ordered to reserve our charge, and to advance as soon as the other had fired, while the rest loaded again; of which I shall speak again presently.

As soon as we had fired the second volley, we shouted as loud as we could, and the seven men advanced upon them, and, coming about twenty yards nearer, fired again, and those that were behind having loaded again with all expedition, followed; but when they saw us advance, they ran screaming away as if they were bewitched.

When we came up to the field of battle, we saw a great number of bodies lying upon the ground, many more than we could suppose were killed or wounded; nay, more than we had bullets in our pieces when we fired; and we could not tell what to make of it; but at length we found how it was, viz., that they were frighted out of all manner of sense; nay, I do believe several of those that were really dead, were frighted to death, and had no wound about them.

Of those that were thus frighted, as I have said, several of them, as they recovered themselves, came and worshipped us (taking us for gods or devils, I know not which, nor did it much matter to us): some kneeling, some throwing themselves flat on the ground, made a thousand antic gestures, but all with tokens of the most profound submission. It presently came into my head, that we might now, by the law of arms, take as many prisoners as we would, and make them travel with us, and carry our baggage. As soon as I proposed it, our men were all of my mind; and accordingly we secured about sixty lusty young fellows, and let them know they must go with us; which they seemed very willing to do. But the next question we had among ourselves, was, how we should do to trust them, for we found the people not like those of Madagascar, but fierce, revengeful, and treacherous; for which reason we were sure that we should have no service from them but that of mere slaves; no subjection that would continue any longer than the fear of us was upon them, nor any labor but by violence.

Before I go any farther, I must hint to the reader, that from this time forward I began to enter a little more seriously into the circumstance I was in, and concerned myself more in the conduct of our affairs; for though my comrades were all older men, yet I began to find them void of counsel, or, as I now call it, presence of mind, when they came to the execution of a thing. The first occasion I took to observe this, was in their late engagement with the natives, when, though they had taken a good resolution to attack them and fire upon them, yet, when they had fired the first time, and found that the negroes did not run as they expected, their hearts began to fail, and I am persuaded, if their bark had been near hand, they would every man have run away.

Upon this occasion I began to take upon me a little to hearten them up, and to call upon them to load again, and give them another volley, telling them that I would engage, if they would be ruled by me, I'd make the negroes run fast enough. I found this heartened them, and therefore, when they fired a second time, I desired them to reserve some of their shot for an attempt by itself, as I mentioned above.

Having fired a second time, I was indeed forced to command, as I may call it. "Now, seigniors," said I, "let us give them a cheer." So I opened my throat, and shouted three times, as our English sailors do on like occasions. "And now follow me," said I to the seven that had not fired, "and I'll warrant you we will make work with them," and so it proved indeed; for, as soon as they saw us coming, away they ran, as above.

From this day forward they would call me nothing but Seignior Capitanio; but I told them I would not be called seignior. "Well, then," said the gunner, who spoke good English, "you shall be called Captain Bob;" and so they gave me my title ever after.

Nothing is more certain of the Portuguese than this, take them nationally or personally, if they are animated and heartened up by anybody to go before, and encourage them by example, they will behave well enough; but if they have nothing but their own measures to follow, they sink immediately: these men had certainly fled from a parcel of naked savages, though even by flying they could not have saved their lives, if I had not shouted and hallooed, and rather made sport with the thing than a fight, to keep up their courage.

Nor was there less need of it upon several occasions hereafter; and I do confess I have often wondered how a number of men, who, when they came to the extremity, were so ill supported by their own spirits, had at first courage to propose and to undertake the most desperate and impracticable attempt that ever men went about in the world.

There were indeed two or three indefatigable men among them, by whose courage and industry all the rest were upheld; and indeed those two or three were the managers of them from the beginning; that was the gunner, and that cutler whom I call the artist; and the third, who was pretty well, though not like either of them, was one of the carpenters. These indeed were the life and soul of all the rest, and it was to their courage that all the rest owed the resolution they showed upon any occasion. But when those saw me take a little upon me, as above, they embraced me, and treated me with particular affection ever after.

This gunner was an excellent mathematician, a good scholar, and a complete sailor; and it was in conversing intimately with him that I learned afterwards the grounds of what knowledge I have since had in all the sciences useful for navigation, and particularly in the geographical part of knowledge.

Even in our conversation, finding me eager to understand and learn, he laid the foundation of a general knowledge of things in my mind, gave me just ideas of the form of the earth and of the sea, the situation of countries, the course of rivers, the doctrine of the spheres, the motion of the stars; and, in a word, taught me a kind of system of astronomy, which I afterwards improved.

In an especial manner, he filled my head with aspiring thoughts, and with an earnest desire after learning everything that could be taught me; convincing me, that nothing could qualify me for great undertakings, but a degree of learning superior to what was usual in the race of seamen; he told me, that to be ignorant was to be certain of a mean station in the world, but that knowledge was the first step to preferment. He was always flattering me with my capacity to learn; and though that fed my pride, yet, on the other hand, as I had a secret ambition, which just at that time fed itself in my mind, it prompted in me an insatiable thirst after learning in general, and I resolved, if ever I came back to Europe, and had anything left to purchase it, I would make myself master of all the parts of learning needful to the making of me a complete sailor; but I was not so just to myself afterwards as to do it when I had an opportunity.

But to return to our business; the gunner, when he saw the service I had done in the fight, and heard my proposal for keeping a number of prisoners for our march, and for carrying our baggage, turns to me before them all. "Captain Bob," says he, "I think you must be our leader, for all the success of this enterprise is owing to you." "No, no," said I, "do not compliment me; you shall be our Seignior Capitanio, you shall be general; I am too young for it." So, in short, we all agreed he should be our leader; but he would not accept of it alone, but would have me joined with him; and all the rest agreeing, I was obliged to comply.

The first piece of service they put me upon in this new command was as difficult as any they could think of, and that was to manage the prisoners; which, however, I cheerfully undertook, as you shall hear presently. But the immediate consultation was yet of more consequence; and that was, first, which way we should go; and secondly, how to furnish ourselves for the voyage with provisions.

There was among the prisoners one tall, well-shaped, handsome fellow, to whom the rest seemed to pay great respect, and who, as we understood afterwards, was the son of one of their kings; his father was, it seems, killed at our first volley, and he wounded with a shot in his arm, and with another just on one of his hips or haunches. The shot in his haunch being in a fleshy part, bled much, and he was half dead with the loss of blood. As to the shot in his arm, it had broke his wrist, and he was by both these wounds quite disabled, so that we were once going to turn him away, and let him die; and, if we had, he would have died indeed in a few days more: but, as I found the man had some respect showed him, it presently occurred to my thoughts that we might bring him to be useful to us, and perhaps make him a kind of commander over them. So I caused our surgeon to take him in hand, and gave the poor wretch good words, that is to say, I spoke to him as well as I could by signs, to make him understand that we would make him well again.

This created a new awe in their minds of us, believing that, as we could kill at a distance by something invisible to them (for so our shot was, to be sure), so we could make them well again too. Upon this the young prince (for so we called him afterwards) called six or seven of the savages to him, and said something to them; what it was we know not, but immediately all the seven came to me, and kneeled down to me, holding up their hands, and making signs of entreaty, pointing to the place where one of those lay whom we had killed.

It was a long time before I or any of us could understand them; but one of them ran and lifted up a dead man, pointing to his wound, which was in his eyes, for he was shot into the head at one of his eyes. Then another pointed to the surgeon, and at last we found it out, that the meaning was, that he should heal the prince's father too, who was dead, being shot through the head, as above.

We presently took the hint, and would not say we could not do it, but let them know, the men that were killed were those that had first fallen upon us, and provoked us, and we would by no means make them alive again; and that, if any others did so, we would kill them too, and never let them live any more: but that, if he (the prince) would be willing to go with us, and do as we should direct him, we would not let him die, and would make his arm well. Upon this he bid his men go and fetch a long stick or staff, and lay on the ground. When they brought it, we saw it was an arrow; he took it with his left hand (for his other was lame with the wound), and, pointing up at the sun, broke the arrow in two, and set the point against his breast, and then gave it to me. This was, as I understood afterwards, wishing the sun, whom they worship, might shoot him into the breast with an arrow, if ever he failed to be my friend; and giving the point of the arrow to me was to be a testimony that I was the man he had sworn to: and never was Christian more punctual to an oath than he was to this, for he was a sworn servant to us for many a weary month after that.

When I brought him to the surgeon, he immediately dressed the wound in his haunch or buttock, and found the bullet had only grazed upon the flesh, and passed, as it were, by it, but it was not lodged in the part, so that it was soon healed and well again; but, as to his arm, he found one of the bones broken, which are in the fore-part from the wrist to the elbow; and this he set, and splintered it up, and bound his arm in a sling, hanging it about his neck, and making signs to him that he should not stir it; which he was so strict an observer of, that he set him down, and never moved one way or other but as the surgeon gave him leave.

I took a great deal of pains to acquaint this negro what we intended to do, and what use we intended to make of his men; and particularly to teach him the meaning of what we said, especially to teach him some words, such as yes and no, and what they meant, and to inure him to our way of talking; and he was very willing and apt to learn anything I taught him.

It was easy to let him see that we intended to carry our provision with us from the first day; but he made signs to us to tell us we need not, for we should find provision enough everywhere for forty days. It was very difficult for us to understand how he expressed forty;

for he knew no figures, but some words that they used to one another that they understood it by. At last one of the negroes, by his order, laid forty little stones one by another, to show us how many days we should travel, and find provisions sufficient.

Then I showed him our baggage, which was very heavy, particularly our powder, shot, lead, iron, carpenters' tools, seamen's instruments, cases of bottles, and other lumber. He took some of the things up in his hand to feel the weight, and shook his head at them; so I told our people they must resolve to divide their things into small parcels, and make them portable; and accordingly they did so, by which means we were fain to leave all our chests behind us, which were eleven in number.

Then he made signs to us that he would procure some buffaloes, or young bulls, as I called them, to carry things for us, and made signs, too, that if we were weary, we might be carried too; but that we slighted, only were willing to have the creatures, because, at last, when they could serve us no farther for carriage, we might eat them all up if we had any occasion for them.

I then carried him to our bark, and showed him what things we had here. He seemed amazed at the sight of our bark, having never seen anything of that kind before, for their boats are most wretched things, such as I never saw before, having no head or stern, and being made only of the skins of goats, sewed together with dried guts of goats and sheep, and done over with a kind of slimy stuff like rosin and oil, but of a most nauseous, odious smell; and they are poor miserable things for boats, the worst that any part of the world ever saw; a canoe is an excellent contrivance compared to them.

But to return to our boat. We carried our new prince into it, and helped him over the side, because of his lameness. We made signs to him that his men must carry our goods for us, and showed him what we had; he answered, "Si, Seignior," or, "Yes, sir" (for we had taught him that word and the meaning of it), and taking up a bundle, he made signs to us, that when his arm was well he would carry some for us.

I made signs again to tell him, that if he would make his men carry them, we would not let him carry anything. We had secured all the prisoners in a narrow place, where we had bound them with mat cords, and set up stakes like a palisado round them; so, when we carried the prince on shore, we went with him to them, and made signs to him to ask them if they were willing to go with us to the country of lions. Accordingly he made a long speech to them, and we could understand by it that he told them, if they were willing, they must say, "Si, Seignior," telling them what it signified. They immediately answered, "Si, Seignior," and clapped their hands, looking up to the sun, which, the prince signified to us, was swearing to be faithful. But as soon as they had said so, one of them made a long speech to the prince; and in it we perceived, by his gestures, which were very antic, that they desired something from us, and that they were in great concern about it. So I asked him, as well as I could, what it was they desired of us; he told us by signs that they desired we should clap our hands to the sun (that was, to swear) that we would not kill them, that we would give them chiaruck, that is to say, bread, would not starve them, and would not let the lions eat them. I told him we would promise all that; then he pointed to the sun, and clapped his hands, signing to me that I should do so too, which I did; at which all the prisoners fell flat on the ground, and rising up again, made the oddest, wildest cries that ever I heard.

I think it was the first time in my life that ever any

religious thought affected me; but I could not refrain some reflections, and almost tears, in considering how happy it was that I was not born among such creatures as these, and was not so stupidly ignorant and barbarous; but this soon went off again, and I was not troubled again with any qualms of that sort for a long time after.

When this ceremony was over, our concern was to get some provisions, as well for the present subsistence of our prisoners as ourselves; and making signs to our prince that we were thinking upon that subject, he made signs to me that, if I would let one of the prisoners go to his town, he should bring provisions, and should bring some beasts to carry our baggage. I seemed loth to trust him, and supposing that he would run away, he made great signs of fidelity, and with his own hands tied a rope about his neck, offering me one end of it, intimating that I should hang him if the man did not come again. So I consented, and he gave him abundance of instructions, and sent him away, pointing to the light of the sun, which it seems was to tell him at what time he must be back.

The fellow ran as if he was mad, and held it till he was quite out of sight, by which I supposed he had a great way to go. The next morning, about two hours before the time appointed, the black prince, for so I always called him, beckoning with his hand to me, and hallooing after his manner, desired me to come to him, which I did, when, pointing to a little hill about two miles off, I saw plainly a little drove of cattle, and several people with them; those, he told me by signs, were the man he had sent, and several more with him, and cattle for us.

Accordingly, by the time appointed, he came quite to our huts, and brought with him a great many cows, young runts, about sixteen goats, and four young bulls, taught to carry burthens.

This was a supply of provisions sufficient; as for bread, we were obliged to shift with some roots which we had made use of before. We then began to consider of making some large bags like the soldiers' knapsacks, for their men to carry our baggage in, and to make it easy to them; and the goats being killed, I ordered the skins to be spread in the sun, and they were as dry in two days as could be desired; so we found means to make such little bags as we wanted, and began to divide our baggage into them. When the black prince found what they were for, and how easy they were of carriage when we put them on, he smiled a little, and sent away the man again to fetch skins, and he brought two natives more with him, all loaded with skins better cured than ours, and of other kinds, such as we could not tell what names to give them.

These two men brought the black prince two lances, of the sort they use in their fights, but finer than ordinary, being made of black smooth wood, as fine as ebony, and headed at the point with the end of a long tooth of some creature — we could not tell of what creature; the head was so firm put on, and the tooth so strong, though no bigger than my thumb, and sharp at the end, that I never saw anything like it in anyplace in the world.

The prince would not take them till I gave him leave, but made signs that they should give them to me; however, I gave him leave to take them himself, for I saw evident signs of an honorable just principle in him.

We now prepared for our march, when the prince coming to me, and pointing towards the several quarters of the world, made signs to know which way we intended to go; and when I showed him, pointing to the west, he presently let me know there was a great

river a little further to the north, which was able to
carry our bark many leagues into the country due west.
I presently took the hint, and inquired for the mouth
of the river, which I understood by him was above a
day's march, and, by our estimation, we found it about
seven leagues further. I take this to be the great river
marked by our chart-makers at the northmost part of
the coast of Mozambique, and called there Quilloa.

Consulting thus with ourselves, we resolved to take
the prince, and as many of the prisoners as we could
stow in our frigate, and go about by the bay into the
river; and that eight of us, with our arms, should march
by land to meet them on the river side; for the prince,
carrying us to a rising ground, had showed us the river
very plain, a great way up the country, and in one place
it was not above six miles to it.

It was my lot to march by land, and be captain of
the whole caravan. I had eight of our men with me,
and seven-and-thirty of our prisoners, without any
baggage, for all our luggage was yet on board. We drove
the young bulls with us; nothing was ever so tame, so
willing to work, or carry anything. The negroes would
ride upon them four at a time, and they would go very
willingly. They would eat out of our hand, lick our
feet, and were as tractable as a dog.

We drove with us six or seven cows for food; but our
negroes knew nothing of curing the flesh by salting
and drying it till we showed them the way, and then
they were mighty willing to do so as long as we had
any salt to do it with, and to carry salt a great way too,
after we found we should have no more.

It was an easy march to the river side for us that went
by land, and we came thither in a piece of a day, being,
as above, no more than six English miles; whereas it
was no less than five days before they came to us by
water, the wind in the bay having failed them, and the

way, by reason of a great turn or reach in the river, being about fifty miles about.

We spent this time in a thing which the two strangers, which brought the prince the two lances, put into the head of the prisoners, viz., to make bottles of the goats' skins to carry fresh water in, which it seems they knew we should come to want; and the men did it so dexterously, having dried skins fetched them by those two men, that before our vessel came up, they had every man a pouch like a bladder, to carry fresh water in, hanging over their shoulders by a thong made of other skins, about three inches broad, like the sling of a fuzee.

Our prince, to assure us of the fidelity of the men in this march, had ordered them to be tied two and two by the wrist, as we handcuff prisoners in England; and made them so sensible of the reasonableness of it, that he made them do it themselves, appointing four of them to bind the rest; but we found them so honest, and particularly so obedient to him, that after we were gotten a little further off of their own country, we set them at liberty, though, when he came to us, he would have them tied again, and they continued so a good while.

All the country on the bank of the river was a high land, no marshy swampy ground in it; the verdure good, and abundance of cattle feeding upon it wherever we went, or which way soever we looked; there was not much wood indeed, at least not near us; but further up we saw oak, cedar, and pine trees, some of which were very large.

The river was a fair open channel, about as broad as the Thames below Gravesend, and a strong tide of flood, which we found held us about sixty miles; the channel deep, nor did we find any want of water for a great way. In short, we went merrily up the river with the flood and the wind blowing still fresh at E. and

E.N.E. We stemmed the ebb easily also, especially while the river continued broad and deep; but when we came past the swelling of the tide, and had the natural current of the river to go against, we found it too strong for us, and began to think of quitting our bark; but the prince would by no means agree to that, for, finding we had on board pretty good store of roping made of mats and flags, which I described before, he ordered all the prisoners which were on shore to come and take hold of those ropes, and tow us along by the shore side; and as we hoisted our sail too, to ease them, the men ran along with us at a very great rate.

In this manner the river carried us up, by our computation, near 200 miles, and then it narrowed apace, and was not above as broad as the Thames is at Windsor, or thereabouts; and, after another day, we came to a great waterfall or cataract, enough to fright us, for I believe the whole body of water fell at once perpendicularly down a precipice above sixty foot high, which made noise enough to deprive men of their hearing, and we heard it above ten miles before we came to it.

Here we were at a full stop, and now our prisoners went first on shore; they had worked very hard and very cheerfully, relieving one another, those that were weary being taken into the bark. Had we had canoes or any boats which might have been carried by men's strength we might have gone two hundred miles more up this river in small boats, but our great boat could go no farther.

All this way the country looked green and pleasant, and was full of cattle, and some people we saw, though not many; but this we observed now, that the people did no more understand our prisoners here than we could understand them; being, it seems, of different nations and of different speech. We had yet seen no wild beasts, or, at least, none that came very near us, except two days before we came to the waterfall, when we saw three of the most beautiful leopards that ever were seen, standing upon the bank of the river on the north side, our prisoners being all on the other side of the water. Our gunner espied them first, and ran to fetch his gun, putting a ball extraordinary in it; and coming to me, "Now, Captain Bob," says he, "where is your prince?" So I called him out. "Now," says he, "tell your men not to be afraid; tell them they shall see that thing in his hand speak in fire to one of those beasts, and make it kill itself."

The poor negroes looked as if they had been all going to be killed, notwithstanding what their prince said to them, and stood staring to expect the issue, when on a sudden the gunner fired; and as he was a very good marksman, he shot the creature with two slugs, just in the head. As soon as the leopard felt herself struck, she reared up on her two hind-legs, bolt upright, and throwing her forepaws about in the air, fell backward, growling and struggling, and immediately died; the other two, frighted with the fire and the noise, fled, and were out of sight in an instant.

But the two frighted leopards were not in half the consternation that our prisoners were; four or five of them fell down as if they had been shot; several others fell on their knees, and lifted up their hands to us; whether to worship us, or pray us not to kill them, we did not know; but we made signs to their prince to encourage them, which he did, but it was with much ado that he brought them to their senses. Nay, the prince, notwithstanding all that was said to prepare him for it, yet when the piece went off, he gave a start as if he would have leaped into the river.

When we saw the creature killed, I had a great mind to have the skin of her, and made signs to the prince that he should send some of his men over to take the skin off. As soon as he spoke but a word, four of them, that offered themselves, were untied, and immediately they jumped into the river, and swam over, and went to work with him. The prince having a knife that we gave him, made four wooden knives so clever, that I never saw anything like them in my life; and in less than an hour's time they brought me the skin of the leopard, which was a monstrous great one, for it was from the ears to the tale about seven foot, and near five foot broad on the back, and most admirably spotted all over. The skin of this leopard I brought to London many years after.

We were now all upon a level as to our traveling, being unshipped, for our bark would swim no farther, and she was too heavy to carry on our backs; but as we found the course of the river went a great way farther, we consulted our carpenters whether we could not pull the bark in pieces, and make us three or four small boats to go on with. They told us we might do so, but it would be very long a-doing; and that, when we had done, we had neither pitch or tar to make them sound to keep the water out, or nails to fasten the plank. But one of them told us that as soon as he could come at any large tree near the river, he would make us a canoe or two in a quarter of the time, and which would serve us as well for all the uses we could have any occasion for as a boat; and such, that if we came to any waterfalls, we might take them up, and carry them for a mile or two by land upon our shoulders.

Upon this we gave over the thoughts of our frigate, and hauling her into a little cove or inlet, where a small brook came into the main river, we laid her up for those that came next, and marched forward. We spent indeed two days dividing our baggage, and loading our tame buffaloes and our negroes. Our powder and shot, which was the thing we were most careful of, we ordered thus: — First, the powder we divided into little leather bags, that is to say, bags of dried skins, with the hair inward, that the powder might not grow damp; and then we put those bags into other bags, made of bullocks' skins, very thick and hard, with the hair outward, that no wet might come in; and this succeeded so well, that in the greatest rains we had, whereof some were very violent and very long, we always kept our powder dry. Besides these bags, which held our chief magazine, we divided to everyone a quarter of a pound of powder, and half a pound of shot, to carry always about us; which, as it was enough for our present use, so we were willing to have no weight to carry more than was absolutely necessary, because of the heat.

We kept still on the bank of the river, and for that reason had but very little communication with the people of the country; for, having also our bark stored with plenty of provisions, we had no occasion to look abroad for a supply; but now, when we came to march on foot, we were obliged often to seek out for food. The first place we came to on the river, that gave us any stop, was a little negro town, containing about fifty huts, and there appeared about 400 people, for they all came out to see us, and wonder at us. When our negroes appeared the inhabitants began to fly to arms, thinking there had been enemies coming upon them; but our negroes, though they could not speak their language, made signs to them that they had no weapons, and were tied two and two together as captives, and that there were people behind who came from the sun, and that could kill them all, and make them alive again, if they pleased; but that they would do them no hurt, and came with peace. As soon as they understood this they laid down their lances, and bows and arrows, and came and stuck twelve large stakes in the ground as a token of peace, bowing themselves to us in token of submission. But as soon as they saw white men with beards, that is to say, with mustachios, they ran screaming away, as in a fright.

We kept at a distance from them, not to be too familiar; and when we did appear it was but two or three of us at a time. But our prisoners made them understand that we required some provisions of them; so they brought us some black cattle, for they have abundance of cows and buffaloes all over that side of the country, as also great numbers of deer. Our cutler, who had now a great stock of things of his handiwork, gave them some little knick-knacks, as plates of silver and of iron, cut diamond fashion, and cut into hearts and into rings, and they were mightily pleased. They also brought several fruits and roots, which we did not understand, but our negroes fed heartily on them, and after we had seen them eat them, we did so too.

Having stocked ourselves here with flesh and root as much as we could well carry, we divided the burthens among our negroes, appointing about thirty to forty pounds weight to a man, which we thought indeed was load enough in a hot country; and the negroes did not at all repine at it, but would sometimes help one another when they began to be weary, which did happen now and then, though not often; besides, as most of their luggage was our provision, it lightened every day, like Aesop's basket of bread, till we came to get a recruit. — Note, when we loaded them we untied their hands, and tied them two and two together by one foot.

The third day of our march from this place our chief carpenter desired us to halt, and set up some huts, for he had found out some trees that he liked, and resolved to make us some canoes; for, as he told me, he knew we should have marching enough on foot after we left the river, and he was resolved to go no farther by land than needs must.

We had no sooner given orders for our little camp, and given leave to our negroes to lay down their loads, but they fell to work to build our huts; and though they were tied as above, yet they did it so nimbly as surprised us. Here we set some of the negroes quite at liberty, that is to say, without tying them, having the prince's word passed for their fidelity; and some of these were ordered to help the carpenters, which they did very handily, with a little direction, and others were sent to see whether they could get any provisions near hand; but instead of provisions, three of them came in with two bows and arrows, and five lances. They could not easily make us understand how they came by them, only that they had surprised some negro women, who were in some huts, the men being from home, and they had found the lances and bows in the huts, or houses, the women and children flying away at the sight of them, as from robbers. We seemed very angry at them, and made the prince ask them if they had not killed any of the women or children, making them believe that, if they had killed anybody, we would make them kill themselves too; but they protested their innocence, so we excused them. Then they brought us the bows and arrows and lances; but, at a motion of their black prince, we gave them back the bows and arrows, and gave them leave to go out to see what they could kill for food; and here we gave them the laws of arms, viz., that if any man appeared to assault them, or shoot at them to offer any violence to them, they might kill them; but that they should not offer to kill or hurt any that offered them peace, or laid down their weapons, nor any women or children, upon any occasion whatsoever. These were our articles of war.

These two fellows had not been gone out above three or four hours, but one of them came running to us without his bow and arrows, hallooing and whooping a great while before he came at us, "Okoamo, okoamo!" which, it seems, was, "Help, help!" The rest of the negroes rose up in a hurry, and by twos, as they could, ran forward towards their fellows, to know what the matter was. As for me, I did not understand it, nor any of our people; the prince looked as if something unlucky had fallen out, and some of our men took up their arms to be ready on occasion. But the negroes soon discovered the thing, for we saw four of them presently after coming along with a great load of meat upon their backs. The case was, that the two who went out with their bows and arrows, meeting with a great herd of deer in the plain, had been so nimble as to shoot three of them, and then one of them came running to us for help to fetch them away. This was the first venison we had met with in all our march, and we feasted upon it very plentifully; and this was the first time we began to prevail with our prince to eat his meat dressed our way; after which his men were prevailed with by his example, but before that, they ate most of the flesh they had quite raw.

We wished now we had brought some bows and arrows out with us, which we might have done; and we began to have so much confidence in our negroes, and to be so familiar with them, that we oftentimes let them go, or the greatest part of them, untied, being well assured they would not leave us, and that they did not know what course to take without us; but one thing we resolved not to trust them with, and that was the charging our guns: but they always believed our guns had some heavenly power in them, that would send forth fire and smoke, and speak with a dreadful noise, and kill at a distance whenever we bid them.

In about eight days we finished three canoes, and in them we embarked our white men and our baggage, with our prince, and some of the prisoners. We also found it needful to keep some of ourselves always on shore, not only to manage the negroes, but to defend them from enemies and wild beasts. Abundance of little incidents happened upon this march, which it is impossible to crowd into this account; particularly, we saw more wild beasts now than we did before, some elephants, and two or three lions, none of which kinds we had seen any of before; and we found our negroes were more afraid of them a great deal than we were; principally, because they had no bows and arrows, or lances, which were the particular weapons they were bred up to the exercise of.

But we cured them of their fears by being always ready with our firearms. However, as we were willing to be sparing of our powder, and the killing of any of the creatures now was no advantage to us, seeing their skins were too heavy for us to carry, and their flesh not good to eat, we resolved therefore to keep some of our pieces uncharged and only primed; and causing them to flash in the pan, the beasts, even the lions them-selves, would always start and fly back when they saw it, and immediately march off.

We passed abundance of inhabitants upon this up-per part of the river, and with this observation, that almost every ten miles we came to a separate nation, and every separate nation had a different speech, or else their speech had differing dialects, so that they did not understand one another. They all abounded in cattle, especially on the river-side; and the eighth day of this second navigation we met with a little negro town, where they had growing a sort of corn like rice, which ate very sweet; and, as we got some of it of the people, we made very good cakes of bread of it, and, making a fire, baked them on the ground, after the fire was swept away, very well; so that hitherto we had no want of provisions of any kind that we could desire.

Our negroes towing our canoes, we traveled at a considerable rate, and by our own account could not go less than twenty or twenty-five English miles a day, and the river continuing to be much of the same breadth and very deep all the way, till on the tenth day we came to another cataract; for a ridge of high hills crossing the whole channel of the river, the water came tumbling down the rocks from one stage to another in a strange manner, so that it was a continued link of cataracts from one to another, in the manner of a cascade, only that the falls were sometimes a quarter of a mile from one another, and the noise confused and frightful.

We thought our voyaging was at a full stop now; but three of us, with a couple of our negroes, mounting the hills another way, to view the course of the river, we found a fair channel again after about half a mile's march, and that it was like to hold us a good way further. So we set all hands to work, unloaded our cargo, and hauled our canoes on shore, to see if we could carry them.

Upon examination we found that they were very heavy; but our carpenters, spending but one day's work upon them, hewed away so much of the timber from their outsides as reduced them very much, and yet they were as fit to swim as before. When this was done, ten men with poles took up one of the canoes and made nothing to carry it. So we ordered twenty men to each canoe, that one ten might relieve the other; and thus we carried all our canoes, and launched them into the water again, and then fetched our luggage and loaded it all again into the canoes, and all in an afternoon; and the next morning early we moved forward again. When we had towed about four days more, our gunner, who was our pilot, began to observe that we did not keep our right course so exactly as we ought, the river

winding away a little towards the north, and gave us
notice of it accordingly. However, we were not willing
to lose the advantage of water-carriage, at least not till
we were forced to it; so we jogged on, and the river
served us for about threescore miles further; but then
we found it grew very small and shallow, having passed
the mouths of several little brooks or rivulets which
came into it; and at length it became but a brook itself.

We towed up as far as ever our boats would swim,
and we went two days the farther — having been about
twelve days in this last part of the river — by lightening
the boats and taking our luggage out, which we made
the negroes carry, being willing to ease ourselves as long
as we could; but at the end of these two days, in short,
there was not water enough to swim a London wherry.

We now set forward wholly by land, and without any
expectation of more water-carriage. All our concern for
more water was to be sure to have a supply for our
drinking; and therefore upon every hill that we came
near we clambered up to the highest part to see the
country before us, and to make the best judgment we
could which way to go to keep the lowest grounds, and
as near some stream of water as we could.

The country held verdant, well grown with trees, and
spread with rivers and brooks, and tolerably well with
inhabitants, for about thirty days' march after our
leaving the canoes, during which time things went
pretty well with us; we did not tie ourselves down when
to march and when to halt, but ordered those things
as our convenience and the health and ease of our
people, as well our servants as ourselves, required.

About the middle of this march we came into a low
and plain country, in which we perceived a greater
number of inhabitants than in any other country we
had gone through; but that which was worse for us, we
found them a fierce, barbarous, treacherous people,

and who at first looked upon us as robbers, and gathered themselves in numbers to attack us.

Our men were terrified at them at first, and began to discover an unusual fear, and even our black prince seemed in a great deal of confusion; but I smiled at him, and showing him some of our guns, I asked him if he thought that which killed the spotted cat (for so they called the leopard in their language) could not make a thousand of those naked creatures die at one blow? Then he laughed, and said, yes, he believed it would. "Well, then," said I, "tell your men not to be afraid of these people, for we shall soon give them a taste of what we can do if they pretend to meddle with us." However, we considered we were in the middle of a vast country, and we knew not what numbers of people and nations we might be surrounded with, and, above all, we knew not how much we might stand in need of the friendship of these that we were now among, so that we ordered the negroes to try all the methods they could to make them friends.

Accordingly the two men who had gotten bows and arrows, and two more to whom we gave the prince's two fine lances, went foremost, with five more, having long poles in their hands; and after them ten of our men advanced toward the negro town that was next to us, and we all stood ready to succor them if there should be occasion.

When they came pretty near their houses our negroes hallooed in their screaming way, and called to them as loud as they could. Upon their calling, some of the men came out and answered, and immediately after the whole town, men, women, and children, appeared; our negroes, with their long poles, went forward a little, and stuck them all in the ground, and left them, which in their country was a signal of peace, but the other did not understand the meaning of that. Then the two men with bows laid down their bows and arrows, went forward unarmed, and made signs of peace to them, which at last the other began to understand; so two of their men laid down their bows and arrows, and came towards them. Our men made all the signs of friendship to them that they could think of, putting their hands up to their mouths as a sign that they wanted provisions to eat; and the other pretended to be pleased and friendly, and went back to their fellows and talked with them a while, and they came forward again, and made signs that they would bring some provisions to them before the sun set; and so our men came back again very well satisfied for that time.

But an hour before sunset our men went to them again, just in the same posture as before, and they came according to their appointment, and brought deer's flesh, roots, and the same kind of corn, like rice, which I mentioned above; and our negroes, being furnished with such toys as our cutler had contrived, gave them some of them, which they seemed infinitely pleased with, and promised to bring more provisions the next day.

Accordingly the next day they came again, but our men perceived they were more in number by a great many than before. However, having sent out ten men with firearms to stand ready, and our whole army being in view also, we were not much surprised; nor was the treachery of the enemy so cunningly ordered as in other cases, for they might have surrounded our negroes, which were but nine, under a show of peace; but when they saw our men advance almost as far as the place where they were the day before, the rogues snatched up their bows and arrows and came running upon our men like so many furies, at which our ten men called to the negroes to come back to them, which they did with speed enough at the first word, and stood all behind our men. As they fled, the other advanced, and let fly near a hundred of their arrows at them, by which two of our negroes were wounded, and one we thought had been killed. When they came to the five poles that our men had stuck in the ground, they stood still awhile, and gathering about the poles, looked at them, and handled them, as wondering what they meant. We then, who were drawn up behind all, sent one of our number to our ten men to bid them fire among them while they stood so thick, and to put some small shot into their guns besides the ordinary charge, and to tell them that we would be up with them immediately.

Accordingly they made ready; but by the time they were ready to fire, the black army had left their wandering about the poles, and began to stir as if they would come on, though seeing more men stand at some distance behind our negroes, they could not tell what to make of us; but if they did not understand us before, they understood us less afterwards, for as soon as ever our men found them to begin to move forward they fired among the thickest of them, being about the distance of 120 yards, as near as we could guess.

It is impossible to express the fright, the screaming and yelling of those wretches upon this first volley. We killed six of them, and wounded eleven or twelve, I mean as we knew of; for, as they stood thick, and the small shot, as we called it, scattered among them, we had reason to believe we wounded more that stood farther off, for our small shot was made of bits of lead and bits of iron, heads of nails, and such things as our diligent artificer, the cutler, helped us to.

As to those that were killed and wounded, the other frighted creatures were under the greatest amazement in the world, to think what should hurt them, for they could see nothing but holes made in their bodies they knew not how. Then the fire and noise amazed all their women and children, and frighted them out of their wits, so that they ran staring and howling about like mad creatures.

However, all this did not make them fly, which was what we wanted, nor did we find any of them die as it were with fear, as at first; so we resolved upon a second volley, and then to advance as we did before. Whereupon our reserved men advancing, we resolved to fire only three men at a time, and move forward like an army firing in platoon; so, being all in a line, we fired, first three on the right, then three on the left, and so on; and every time we killed or wounded some of them, but still they did not fly, and yet they were so frighted that they used none of their bows and arrows, or of their lances; and we thought their numbers increased upon our hands, particularly we thought so by the noise. So I called to our men to halt, and bid them pour in one whole volley and then shout, as we did in our first fight, and so run in upon them and knock them down with our muskets.

But they were too wise for that too, for as soon as we had fired a whole volley and shouted, they all ran away, men, women, and children, so fast that in a few moments we could not see one creature of them except some that were wounded and lame, who lay wallowing and screaming here and there upon the ground as they happened to fall.

Upon this we came up to the field of battle, where we found we had killed thirty-seven of them, among which were three women, and had wounded about sixty-four, among which were two women; by wounded I mean such as were so maimed as not to be able to go away, and those our negroes killed afterwards in a cowardly manner in cold blood, for which we were very angry, and threatened to make them go to them if they did so again.

There was no great spoil to be got, for they were all stark naked as they came into the world, men and women together, some of them having feathers stuck in their hair, and others a kind of bracelet about their necks, but nothing else; but our negroes got a booty here, which we were very glad of, and this was the bows and arrows of the vanquished, of which they found more than they knew what to do with, belonging to the killed and wounded men; these we ordered them to pick up, and they were very useful to us afterwards. After the fight, and our negroes had gotten bows and arrows, we sent them out in parties to see what they could get, and they got some provisions; but, which was better than all the rest, they brought us four more young bulls, or buffaloes, that had been brought up to labor and to carry burthens. They knew them, it seems, by the burthens they had carried having galled their backs, for they have no saddles to cover them with in that country.

Those creatures not only eased our negroes, but gave us an opportunity to carry more provisions; and our negroes loaded them very hard at this place with flesh and roots, such as we wanted very much afterwards.

In this town we found a very little young leopard, about two spans high; it was exceeding tame, and purred like a cat when we stroked it with our hands, being, as I suppose, bred up among the negroes like a house-dog. It was our black prince, it seems, who, making his tour among the abandoned houses or huts, found this creature there, and making much of him, and giving a bit or two of flesh to him, the creature followed him like a dog; of which more hereafter.

Among the negroes that were killed in this battle there was one who had a little thin bit or plate of gold, about as big as a sixpence, which hung by a little bit of a twisted gut upon his forehead, by which we supposed he was a man of some eminence among them; but that was not all, for this bit of gold put us upon searching very narrowly if there was not more of it to be had thereabouts, but we found none at all.

From this part of the country we went on for about fifteen days, and then found ourselves obliged to march up a high ridge of mountains, frightful to behold, and the first of the kind that we met with; and having no guide but our little pocket-compass, we had no advantage of information as to which was the best or the worst way, but was obliged to choose by what we saw, and shift as well as we could. We met with several nations of wild and naked people in the plain country before we came to those hills, and we found them much more tractable and friendly than those devils we had been forced to fight with; and though we could learn little from these people, yet we understood by the signs they made that there was a vast desert beyond these hills, and, as our negroes called them, much lion, much spotted cat (so they called the leopard); and they signed to us also that we must carry water with us. At the last of these nations we furnished ourselves with as much provisions as we could possibly carry, not knowing what we had to suffer, or what length we had to go; and, to make our way as familiar to us as possible, I proposed that of the last inhabitants we could find we should make some prisoners and carry them with us for guides over the desert, and to assist us in carrying provision, and, perhaps, in getting it too. The advice was too necessary to be slighted; so finding, by our dumb signs to the inhabitants, that there were some people that dwelt at the foot of the mountains on the other side before we came to the desert itself, we resolved to furnish ourselves with guides by fair means or foul.

Here, by a moderate computation, we concluded ourselves 700 miles from the seacoast where we began. Our black prince was this day set free from the sling his arm hung in, our surgeon having perfectly restored it, and he showed it to his own countrymen quite well, which made them greatly wonder. Also our two negroes began to recover, and their wounds to heal apace, for our surgeon was very skillful in managing their cure.

Having with infinite labor mounted these hills, and coming to a view of the country beyond them, it was indeed enough to astonish as stout a heart as ever was created. It was a vast howling wilderness — not a tree, a river, or a green thing to be seen; for, as far as the eye could look, nothing but a scalding sand, which, as the wind blew, drove about in clouds enough to overwhelm man and beast. Nor could we see any end of it either before us, which was our way, or to the right hand or left; so that truly our men began to be discouraged, and talk of going back again. Nor could we indeed think of venturing over such a horrid place as that before us, in which we saw nothing but present death.

I was as much affected at the sight as any of them; but, for all that, I could not bear the thoughts of going back again. I told them we had marched 700 miles of our way, and it would be worse than death to think of going back again; and that, if they thought the desert was not passable, I thought we should rather change our course, and travel south till we came to the Cape of Good Hope, or north to the country that lay along the Nile, where, perhaps, we might find some way or other over to the west sea; for sure all Africa was not a desert.

Our gunner, who, as I said before, was our guide as to the situation of places, told us that he could not tell what to say to going for the Cape, for it was a monstrous length, being from the place where we now were not less than 1500 miles; and, by his account, we were now come a third part of the way to the coast of Angola, where we should meet the western ocean, and find ways enough for our escape home. On the other hand, he assured us, and showed us a map of it, that, if we went northward, the western shore of Africa went out into the sea above 1000 miles west, so that we should have so much and more land to travel afterwards; which land might, for aught we knew, be as wild, barren, and desert as this. And therefore, upon the whole, he proposed that we should attempt this desert, and perhaps we should not find it so long as we feared; and however, he proposed that we should see how far our provisions would carry us, and, in particular, our water; and we should venture no further than half so far as our water would last; and if we found no end of the desert, we might come safely back again.

This advice was so reasonable that we all approved of it; and accordingly we calculated that we were able to carry provisions for forty-two days, but that we could not carry water for above twenty days, though we were to suppose it to stink, too, before that time expired. So that we concluded that, if we did not come at some water in ten days' time, we would return; but if we found a supply of water, we could then travel twenty-one days; and, if we saw no end of the wilderness in that time, we would return also.

With this regulation of our measures, we descended the mountains, and it was the second day before we quite reached the plain; where, however, to make us amends, we found a fine little rivulet of very good water, abundance of deer, a sort of creature like a hare, but not so nimble, but whose flesh we found very agreeable. But we were deceived in our intelligence, for we found no people; so we got no more prisoners to assist us in carrying our baggage.

The infinite number of deer and other creatures which we saw here, we found was occasioned by the neighborhood of the waste or desert, from whence they retired hither for food and refreshment. We stored ourselves here with flesh and roots of divers kinds, which our negroes understood better than we, and which served us for bread; and with as much water as (by the allowance of a quart a day to a man for our negroes, and three pints a day a man for ourselves, and three quarts a day each for our buffaloes) would serve us twenty days; and thus loaded for a long miserable march, we set forwards, being all sound in health and very cheerful, but not alike strong for so great a fatigue; and, which was our grievance, were without a guide.

In the very first entrance of the waste we were exceedingly discouraged, for we found the sand so deep, and it scalded our feet so much with the heat, that after we had, as I may call it, waded rather than walked through it about seven or eight miles, we were all heartily tired and faint; even the very negroes laid down and panted like creatures that had been pushed beyond their strength.

Here we found the difference of lodging greatly injurious to us; for, as before, we always made us huts to sleep under, which covered us from the night air, which is particularly unwholesome in those hot countries. But we had here no shelter, no lodging, after so hard a march; for here were no trees, no, not a shrub near us; and, which was still more frightful, towards night we began to hear the wolves howl, the lions bellow, and a great many wild asses braying, and other ugly noises which we did not understand.

Upon this we reflected upon our indiscretion, that we had not, at least, brought poles or stakes in our hands, with which we might have, as it were, palisadoed ourselves in for the night, and so we might have slept secure, whatever other inconveniences we suffered. However, we found a way at last to relieve ourselves a little; for first we set up the lances and bows we had, and endeavored to bring the tops of them as near to one another as we could, and so hung our coats on the top of them, which made us a kind of sorry tent. The leopard's skin, and a few other skins we had put together, made us a tolerable covering, and thus we laid down to sleep, and slept very heartily too, for the first night; setting, however, a good watch, being two of our own men with their fuzes, whom we relieved in an hour at first, and two hours afterwards. And it was very well we did this, for they found the wilderness swarmed with raging creatures of all kinds, some of which came directly up to the very enclosure of our tent. But our sentinels were ordered not to alarm us with firing in the night, but to flash in the pan at them, which they did, and found it effectual, for the creatures went off always as soon as they saw it, perhaps with some noise or howling, and pursued such other game as they were upon.

If we were tired with the day's travel, we were all as much tired with the night's lodging. But our black prince told us in the morning he would give us some counsel, and indeed it was very good counsel. He told us we should be all killed if we went on this journey, and through this desert, without some covering for us at night; so he advised us to march back again to a little river-side where we lay the night before, and stay there till we could make us houses, as he called them, to carry with us to lodge in every night. As he began a little to understand our speech, and we very well to understand his signs, we easily knew what he meant, and that we should there make mats (for we remembered that we saw a great deal of matting or bass there, that the natives make mats of) — I say, that we should make large mats there for covering our huts or tents to lodge in at night.

We all approved this advice, and immediately resolved to go back that one day's journey, resolving, though we carried less provisions, we would carry mats with us to cover us in the night. Some of the nimblest of us got back to the river with more ease than we had traveled it the day before; but, as we were not in haste, the rest made a halt, encamped another night, and came to us the next day.

In our return of this day's journey, our men that made two days of it met with a very surprising thing, that gave them some reason to be careful how they parted company again. The case was this: — The second day in the morning, before they had gone half a mile, looking behind them they saw a vast cloud of sand or dust rise in the air, as we see sometimes in the roads in summer when it is very dusty and a large drove of cattle are coming, only very much greater; and they could easily perceive that it came after them; and it came on faster as they went from it. The cloud of sand was so great that they could not see what it was that raised it, and concluded that it was some army of enemies that pursued them; but then considering that they came from the vast uninhabited wilderness, they knew it was impossible any nation or people that way should have intelligence of them or the way of their march; and therefore, if it was an army, it must be of such as they were, traveling that way by accident. On the other hand, as they knew that there were no horses in the country, and that they came on so fast, they concluded that it must be some vast collection of wild beasts, perhaps making to the hill country for food or water, and that they should be all devoured or trampled under foot by their multitude.

Upon this thought, they very prudently observed which way the cloud seemed to point, and they turned a little out of their way to the north, supposing it might pass by them. When they were about a quarter of a mile, they halted to see what it might be. One of the negroes, a nimbler fellow than the rest, went back a little, and came in a few minutes running as fast as the heavy sands would allow, and by signs gave them to know that it was a great herd, or drove, or whatever it might be called, of vast monstrous elephants.

As it was a sight our men had never seen, they were desirous to see it, and yet a little uneasy at the danger too; for though an elephant is a heavy unwieldy creature, yet in the deep sand, which is nothing at all to them, they marched at a great rate, and would soon have tired our people, if they had had far to go, and had been pursued by them.

Our gunner was with them, and had a great mind to have gone close up to one of the outermost of them, and to have clapped his piece to his ear, and to have fired into him, because he had been told no shot would penetrate them; but they all dissuaded him, lest upon the noise they should all turn upon and pursue us; so he was reasoned out of it, and let them pass, which, in our people's circumstances, was certainly the right way.

They were between twenty and thirty in number, but prodigious great ones; and though they often showed our men that they saw them, yet they did not turn out of their way, or take any other notice of them than, as we might say, just to look at them. We that were before saw the cloud of dust they raised, but we had thought it had been our own caravan, and so took no notice; but as they bent their course one point of the compass, or thereabouts, to the southward of the east, and we went due east [? west], they passed by us at some little distance; so that we did not see them, or know anything of them, till evening, when our men came to us and gave us this account of them. However, this was a useful experiment for our future conduct in passing the desert, as you shall hear in its place.

We were now upon our work, and our black prince was head surveyor, for he was an excellent mat-maker himself, and all his men understood it, so that they soon made us near a hundred mats; and as every man, I mean of the negroes, carried one, it was no manner of load, and we did not carry an ounce of provisions the less. The greatest burthen was to carry six long poles, besides some shorter stakes; but the negroes made an advantage of that, for carrying them between two, they made the luggage of provisions which they had to carry so much the lighter, binding it upon two poles, and so made three couple of them. As soon as we saw this, we made a little advantage of it too; for having three or four bags, called bottles (I mean skins to carry water), more than the men could carry, we got them filled, and carried them this way, which was a day's water and more, for our journey.

Having now ended our work, made our mats, and fully recruited our stores of all things necessary, and having made us abundance of small ropes of matting for ordinary use, as we might have occasion, we set forward again, having interrupted our journey eight days in all, upon this affair. To our great comfort, the night before we set out there fell a very violent shower of rain, the effects of which we found in the sand; though the heat of one day dried the surface as much as before, yet it was harder at bottom, not so heavy, and was cooler to our feet, by which means we marched, as we reckoned, about fourteen miles instead of seven, and with much more ease.

When we came to encamp, we had all things ready, for we had fitted our tent, and set it up for trial, where we made it; so that, in less than an hour, we had a large tent raised, with an inner and outer apartment, and two entrances. In one we lay ourselves, in the other our negroes, having light pleasant mats over us, and others at the same time under us. Also we had a little place without all for our buffaloes, for they deserved our care, being very useful to us, besides carrying forage and water for themselves. Their forage was a root, which our black prince directed us to find, not much unlike a parsnip, very moist and nourishing, of which there was plenty wherever we came, this horrid desert excepted.

When we came the next morning to decamp, our negroes took down the tent, and pulled up the stakes; and all was in motion in as little time as it was set up. In this posture we marched eight days, and yet could see no end, no change of our prospect, but all looking as wild and dismal as at the beginning. If there was any alteration, it was that the sand was nowhere so deep and heavy as it was the first three days. This we thought might be because, for six months of the year the winds blowing west (as for the other six they blow constantly east), the sand was driven violently to the side of the desert where we set out, where the mountains lying very high, the easterly monsoons, when they blew, had not the same power to drive it back again; and this was confirmed by our finding the like depth of sand on the farthest extent of the desert to the west.

It was the ninth day of our travel in this wilderness, when we came to the view of a great lake of water; and you may be sure this was a particular satisfaction to us, because we had not water left for above two or three days more, at our shortest allowance; I mean allowing water for our return, if we had been driven to the necessity of it. Our water had served us two days longer than expected, our buffaloes having found, for two or three days, a kind of herb like a broad flat thistle, though without any prickle, spreading on the ground, and growing in the sand, which they ate freely of, and which supplied them for drink as well as forage.

The next day, which was the tenth from our setting out, we came to the edge of this lake, and, very happily for us, we came to it at the south point of it, for to the north we could see no end of it; so we passed by it and traveled three days by the side of it, which was a great comfort to us, because it lightened our burthen, there being no need to carry water when we had it in view. And yet, though here was so much water, we found but very little alteration in the desert; no trees, no grass or herbage, except that thistle, as I called it, and two or three more plants, which we did not understand, of which the desert began to be pretty full.

But as we were refreshed with the neighborhood of this lake of water, so we were now gotten among a prodigious number of ravenous inhabitants, the like whereof, it is most certain, the eye of man never saw; for as I firmly believe that never man nor body of men passed this desert since the flood, so I believe there is not the like collection of fierce, ravenous, and devouring creatures in the world; I mean not in any particular place.

For a day's journey before we came to this lake, and all the three days we were passing by it, and. for six or seven days' march after it, the ground was scattered with elephants' teeth in such a number as is incredible; and as some of them have lain there for some hundreds of years, so, seeing the substance of them scarce ever decays, they may lie there, for aught I know, to the end of time. The size of some of them is, it seems, to those to whom I have reported it, as incredible as the number; and I can assure you there were several so heavy as the strongest man among us could not lift.

As to number, I question not but there are enough to load a thousand sail of the biggest ships in the world, by which I may be understood to mean that the quantity is not to be conceived of; seeing that as they lasted in view for above eighty miles' traveling, so they might continue as far to the right hand, and to the left as far, and many times as far, for aught we knew; for it seems the number of elephants hereabouts is prodigiously great. In one place in particular we saw the head of an elephant, with several teeth in it, but one of the biggest that ever I saw; the flesh was consumed, to be sure, many hundred years before, and all the other bones; but three of our strongest men could not lift this skull and teeth; the great tooth, I believe, weighed at least three hundredweight; and this was particularly remarkable to me, that I observed the whole skull was as good ivory as the teeth, and, I believe, altogether weighed at least six hundredweight; and though I do not know but, by the same rule, all the bones of the elephant may be ivory, yet I think there is this just objection against it from the example before me, that then all the other bones of this elephant would have been there as well as the head.

I proposed to our gunner, that, seeing we had traveled now fourteen days without intermission, and that we had water here for our refreshment, and no want of food yet, nor any fear of it, we should rest our people a little, and see, at the same time, if perhaps we might kill some creatures that were proper for food. The gunner, who had more forecast of that kind than I had, agreed to the proposal, and added, why might we not try to catch some fish out of the lake? The first thing we had before us was to try if we could make any hooks, and this indeed put our artificer to his trumps; however, with some labor and difficulty, he did it, and we catched fresh fish of several kinds. How they came there, none but He that made the lake and all the world knows; for, to be sure, no human hands ever put any in there, or pulled any out before.

We not only catched enough for our present refreshment, but we dried several large fishes, of kinds which I cannot describe, in the sun, by which we lengthened out our provision considerably; for the heat of the sun dried them so effectually without salt that they were perfectly cured, dry, and hard, in one day's time.

We rested ourselves here five days; during which time we had abundance of pleasant adventures with the wild creatures, too many to relate. One of them was very particular, which was a chase between a she-lion, or lioness, and a large deer; and though the deer is naturally a very nimble creature, and she flew by us like the wind, having, perhaps, about 300 yards the start of the lion, yet we found the lion, by her strength, and the goodness of her lungs, got ground of her. They passed by us within about a quarter of a mile, and we had a view of them a great way, when, having given them over, we were surprised, about an hour after, to see them come thundering back again on the other side of us, and then the lion was within thirty or forty yards of her; and both straining to the extremity of their speed, when the deer, coming to the lake, plunged into the water, and swam for her life, as she had before run for it.

The lioness plunged in after her, and swam a little way, but came back again; and when she was got upon the land she set up the most hideous roar that ever I heard in my life, as if done in the rage of having lost her prey.

We walked out morning and evening constantly; the middle of the day we refreshed ourselves under our tent. But one morning early we saw another chase, which more nearly concerned us than the other; for our black prince, walking by the side of the lake, was set upon by a vast, great crocodile, which came out of the lake upon him; and though he was very light of foot, yet it was as much as he could do to get away. He fled amain to us, and the truth is, we did not know what to do, for we were told no bullet would enter her; and we found it so at first, for though three of our men fired at her, yet she did not mind them; but my friend the gunner, a venturous fellow, of a bold heart, and great presence of mind, went up so near as to thrust the muzzle of his piece into her mouth, and fired, but let his piece fall, and ran for it the very moment he had fired it. The creature raged a great while, and spent its fury upon the gun, making marks upon the very iron with its teeth, but after some time fainted and died.

Our negroes spread the banks of the lake all this while for game, and at length killed us three deer, one of them very large, the other two very small. There was water-fowl also in the lake, but we never came near enough to them to shoot any; and as for the desert, we saw no fowls anywhere in it but at the lake.

We likewise killed two or three civet cats; but their flesh is the worst of carrion. We saw abundance of elephants at a distance, and observed they always go in very good company, that is to say, abundance of them together, and always extended in a fair line of battle; and this, they say, is the way they defend themselves from their enemies; for if lions or tigers, wolves or any creatures, attack them, they being drawn in a line, sometimes reaching five or six miles in length, whatever comes in their way is sure to be trod under foot, or beaten in pieces with their trunks, or lifted up in the air with their trunks; so that if a hundred lions or tigers were coming along, if they meet a line of elephants, they will always fly back till they see room to pass by the right hand or the left; and if they did not, it would be impossible for one of them to escape; for the elephant, though a heavy creature, is yet so dexterous and nimble with his trunk, that he will not fail to lift up the heaviest lion, or any other wild creature, and throw him up in the air quite over his back, and then trample him to death with his feet. We saw several lines of battle thus; we saw one so long that indeed there was no end of it to be seen, and I believe there might be 2000 elephants in row or line. They are not beasts of prey, but live upon the herbage of the field, as an ox does; and it is said, that though they are so great a creature, yet that a smaller quantity of forage supplies one of them than will suffice a horse.

The numbers of this kind of creature that are in those parts are inconceivable, as may be gathered from the prodigious quantity of teeth which, as I said, we saw in this vast desert; and indeed we saw a hundred of them to one of any other kind.

One evening we were very much surprised. We were most of us laid down on our mats to sleep, when our watch came running in among us, being frighted with the sudden roaring of some lions just by them, which, it seems, they had not seen, the night being dark, till they were just upon them. There was, as it proved, an old lion and his whole family, for there was the lioness and three young lions, besides the old king, who was a monstrous great one. One of the young ones — who were good, large, well-grown ones too — leaped up upon one of our negroes, who stood sentinel, before he saw him, at which he was heartily frighted, cried out, and ran into the tent. Our other man, who had a gun, had not presence of mind at first to shoot him, but struck him with the butt-end of his piece, which made him whine a little, and then growl at him fearfully; but the fellow retired, and, we being all alarmed, three of our men snatched up their guns, ran to the tent door, where they saw the great old lion by the fire of his eyes, and first fired at him, but, we supposed, missed him, or at least did not kill him; for they went all off, but raised a most hideous roar, which, as if they had called for help, brought down a prodigious number of lions, and other furious creatures, we know not what, about them, for we could not see them; but there was a noise, and yelling and howling, and all sorts of such wilderness music on every side of us, as if all the beasts of the desert were assembled to devour us.

We asked our black prince what we should do with them. "Me go," says he, "and fright them all." So he snatches up two or three of the worst of our mats, and getting one of our men to strike some fire, he hangs the mat up at the end of a pole, and set it on fire, and it blazed abroad a good while; at which the creatures all moved off, for we heard them roar, and make their bellowing noise at a great distance. "Well," says our gunner, "if that will do, we need not burn our mats, which are our beds to lay under us, and our tilting to cover us. Let me alone," says he. So he comes back into our tent, and falls to making some artificial fireworks and the like; and he gave our sentinels some to be ready at hand upon occasion, and particularly he placed a great piece of wild-fire upon the same pole that the mat had been tied to, and set it on fire, and that burned there so long that all the wild creatures left us for that time.

However, we began to be weary of such company; and, to be rid of them, we set forward again two days sooner than we intended. We found now, that though the desert did not end, nor could we see any appearance of it, yet that the earth was pretty full of green stuff of one sort or another, so that our cattle had no want; and secondly, that there were several little rivers which ran into the lake, and so long as the country continued low, we found water sufficient, which eased us very much in our carriage, and we went on still sixteen days more without yet coming to any appearance of better soil. After this we found the country rise a little, and by that we perceived that the water would fail us; so, for fear of the worst, we filled our bladder-bottles with water. We found the country rising gradually thus for three days continually, when, on the sudden, we perceived that, though we had mounted up insensibly, yet that we were on the top of a very high ridge of hills, though not such as at first.

When we came to look down on the other side of the hills, we saw, to the great joy of all our hearts, that the desert was at an end; that the country was clothed with green, abundance of trees, and a large river; and we made no doubt but that we should find people and cattle also; and here, by our gunner's account, who kept our computations, we had marched about 400 miles over this dismal place of horror, having been four-and-thirty days a-doing of it, and consequently were come about 1100 miles of our journey.

We would willingly have descended the hills that night, but it was too late. The next morning we saw everything more plain, and rested ourselves under the shade of some trees, which were now the most refreshing things imaginable to us, who had been scorched above a month without a tree to cover us. We found the country here very pleasant, especially considering that we came from; and we killed some deer here also, which we found very frequent under the cover of the woods. Also we killed a creature like a goat, whose flesh was very good to eat, but it was no goat; we found also a great number of fowls like partridge, but something smaller, and were very tame; so that we lived here very well, but found no people, at least none that would be seen, no, not for several days' journey; and to allay our joy, we were almost every night disturbed with lions and tigers; elephants, indeed, we saw none here.

In three days' march we came to a river, which we saw from the hills, and which we called the Golden River; and we found it ran northward, which was the first stream we had met with that did so. It ran with a very rapid current, and our gunner, pulling out his map, assured me that this was either the river Nile, or run into the great lake out of which the river Nile was said to take its beginning; and he brought out his charts and maps, which, by his instruction, I began to understand very well, and told me he would convince me of it, and indeed he seemed to make it so plain to me that I was of the same opinion.

But I did not enter into the gunner's reason for this inquiry, not in the least, till he went on with it farther, and stated it thus: — "If this is the river Nile, why should not we build some more canoes, and go down this stream, rather than expose ourselves to any more deserts and scorching sands in quest of the sea, which when we are come to, we shall be as much at a loss how to get home as we were at Madagascar?"

The argument was good, had there been no objections in the way of a kind which none of us were capable of answering; but, upon the whole, it was an undertaking of such a nature that every one of us thought it impracticable, and that upon several accounts; and our surgeon, who was himself a good scholar and a man of reading, though not acquainted with the business of sailing, opposed it, and some of his reasons, I remember, were such as these: — First, the length of the way, which both he and the gunner allowed, by the course of the water, and turnings of the river, would be at least 4000 miles. Secondly, the innumerable crocodiles in the river, which we should never be able to escape. Thirdly, the dreadful deserts in the way; and lastly, the approaching rainy season, in which the streams of the Nile would be so furious, and rise so high — spreading far and wide over all the plain country — that we should never be able to know when we were in the channel of the river and when not, and should certainly be cast away, overset, or run aground so often that it would be impossible to proceed by a river so excessively dangerous.

This last reason he made so plain to us that we began to be sensible of it ourselves, so that we agreed to lay that thought aside, and proceed in our first course, westwards towards the sea; but, as if we had been loth to depart, we continued, by way of refreshing ourselves, to loiter two days upon this river, in which time our black prince, who delighted much in wandering up and down, came one evening and brought us several little bits of something, he knew not what, but he found it felt heavy and looked well, and showed it to me as what he thought was some rarity. I took not much notice of it to him, but stepping out and calling the gunner to me I showed it to him, and told him what I thought, viz., that it was certainly gold. He agreed with me in that, and also in what followed, that we would take the black prince out with us the next day, and make him show us where he found it; that if there was any quantity to be found we would tell our company of it, but if there was but little we would keep counsel, and have it to ourselves.

But we forgot to engage the prince in the secret, who innocently told so much to all the rest, as that they guessed what it was, and came to us to see. When we found it was public, we were more concerned to prevent their suspecting that we had any design to conceal it, and openly telling our thoughts of it, we called our artificer, who agreed presently that it was gold; so I proposed that we should all go with the prince to the place where he found it, and if any quantity was to be had, we would lie here some time and see what we could make of it.

Accordingly we went every man of us, for no man was willing to be left behind in a discovery of such a nature. When we came to the place we found it was on the west side of the river, not in the main river, but in another small river or stream which came from the west, and ran into the other at that place. We fell to raking in the sand, and washing it in our hands; and we seldom took up a handful of sand but we washed some little round lumps as big as a pin's head, or sometimes as big as a grape stone, into our hands; and we found, in two or three hours' time, that everyone had got some, so we agreed to leave off, and go to dinner.

While we were eating, it came into my thoughts that while we worked at this rate in a thing of such nicety and consequence, it was ten to one if the gold, which was the make-bait of the world, did not, first or last, set us together by the ears, to break our good articles and our understanding one among another, and perhaps cause us to part companies, or worse; I therefore told them that I was indeed the youngest man in the company, but as they had always allowed me to give my opinion in things, and had sometimes been pleased to follow my advice, so I had something to propose now, which I thought would be for all our advantages, and I believed they would all like it very well. I told them we were in a country where we all knew there was a great deal of gold, and that all the world sent ships thither to get it; that we did not indeed know where it was, and so we might get a great deal, or a little, we did not know whether; but I offered it to them to consider whether it would not be the best way for us, and to preserve the good harmony and friendship that had been always kept among us, and which was so absolutely necessary to our safety, that what we found should be brought together to one common stock, and be equally divided at last, rather than to run the hazard of any difference which might happen among us from anyone's having found more or less than another. I told them, that if we were all upon one bottom we should all apply ourselves heartily to the work; and, besides that, we might then set our negroes all to work for us, and receive equally the fruit of their labor and of our own, and being all exactly alike sharers, there could be no just cause of quarrel or disgust among us.

They all approved the proposal, and everyone jointly swore, and gave their hands to one another, that they would not conceal the least grain of gold from the rest; and consented that if anyone or more should be found to conceal any, all that he had should be taken from him and divided among the rest; and one thing more was added to it by our gunner, from considerations equally good and just, that if anyone of us, by any play, bet, game, or wager, won any money or gold, or the value of any, from another, during our whole voyage, till our return quite to Portugal, he should be obliged by us all to restore it again on the penalty of being disarmed and turned out of the company, and of having no relief from us on any account whatever. This was to prevent wagering and playing for money, which our men were apt to do by several means and at several games, though they had neither cards nor dice.

Having made this wholesome agreement, we went cheerfully to work, and showed our negroes how to work for us; and working up the stream on both sides, and in the bottom of the river, we spent about three weeks' time dabbling in the water; by which time, as it lay all in our way, we had gone about six miles, and not more; and still the higher we went, the more gold we found; till at last, having passed by the side of a hill, we perceived on a sudden that the gold stopped, and that there was not a bit taken up beyond that place. It presently occurred to my mind, that it must then be from the side of that little hill that all the gold we found was worked down.

Upon this, we went back to the hill, and fell to work with that. We found the earth loose, and of a yellowish loamy color, and in some places a white hard kind of stone, which, in describing since to some of our artists, they tell me was the spar which is found by ore, and surrounds it in the mine. However, if it had been all gold, we had no instrument to force it out; so we passed that. But scratching into the loose earth with our fingers, we came to a surprising place, where the earth, for the quantity of two bushels, I believe, or thereabouts, crumbled down with little more than touching it, and apparently showed us that there was a great deal of gold in it. We took it all carefully up, and washing it in the water, the loamy earth washed away, and left the gold dust free in our hands; and that which was more remarkable was, that, when this loose earth was all taken away, and we came to the rock or hard stone, there was not one grain of gold more to be found.

At night we all came together to see what we had got; and it appeared we had found, in that day's heap of earth, about fifty pounds' weight of gold dust, and about thirty-four pounds' weight more in all the rest of our works in the river.

It was a happy kind of disappointment to us, that we found a full stop put to our work; for, had the quantity of gold been ever so small, yet, had any at all come, I do not know when we should have given over; for, having rummaged this place, and not finding the least grain of gold in any other place, or in any of the earth there, except in that loose parcel, we went quite back down the small river again, working it over and over again, as long as we could find anything, how small soever; and we did get six or seven pounds more the second time. Then we went into the first river, and tried it up the stream and down the stream, on the one side and on the other. Up the stream we found nothing, no, not a grain; down the stream we found very little, not above the quantity of half an ounce in two miles' working; so back we came again to the Golden River, as we justly called it, and worked it up the stream and down the stream twice more apiece, and every time we found some gold, and perhaps might have done so if we had stayed there till this time; but the quantity was at last so small, and the work so much the harder, that we agreed by consent to give it over, lest we should fatigue ourselves and our negroes so as to be quite unfit for our journey.

When we had brought all our purchase together, we had in the whole three pounds and a half of gold to a man, share and share alike, according to such a weight and scale as our ingenious cutler made for us to weigh it by, which indeed he did by guess, but which, as he said, he was sure was rather more than less, and so it proved at last; for it was near two ounces more than weight in a pound. Besides this, there was seven or eight pounds' weight left, which we agreed to leave in his hands, to work it into such shapes as we thought fit, to give away to such people as we might yet meet with, from whom we might have occasion to buy provisions, or even to buy friendship, or the like; and particularly we gave about a pound to our black prince, which he hammered and worked by his own indefatigable hand, and some tools our artificer lent him, into little round bits, as round almost as beads, though not exact in shape, and drilling holes through them, put them all upon a string, and wore them about his black neck, and they looked very well there, I assure you; but he was many months a-doing it. And thus ended our first golden adventure.

We now began to discover what we had not troubled our heads much about before, and that was, that, let the country be good or bad that we were in, we could not travel much further for a considerable time. We had been now five months and upwards in our journey, and the seasons began to change; and nature told us, that, being in a climate that had a winter as well as a summer, though of a different kind from what our country produced, we were to expect a wet season, and such as we should not be able to travel in, as well by reason of the rain itself, as of the floods which it would occasion wherever we should come; and though we had been no strangers to those wet seasons in the island of Madagascar, yet we had not thought much of them since we began our travels; for, setting out when the sun was about the solstice, that is, when it was at the greatest northern distance from us, we had found the benefit of it in our travels. But now it drew near us apace, and we found it began to rain; upon which we called another general council, in which we debated our present circumstances, and, in particular, whether we should go forward, or seek for a proper place upon the bank of our Golden River, which had been so lucky to us, to fix our camp for the winter.

Upon the whole, it was resolved to abide where we were; and it was not the least part of our happiness that we did so, as shall appear in its place.

Having resolved upon this, our first measures were to set our negroes to work, to make huts or houses for our habitation, and this they did very dexterously; only that we changed the ground where we at first intended it, thinking, as indeed it happened, that the river might reach it upon any sudden rain. Our camp was like a little town, in which our huts were in the center, having one large one in the center of them also, into which all our particular lodgings opened; so that none of us went into our apartments but through a public tent, where we all ate and drank together, and kept our councils and society; and our carpenters made us tables, benches, and stools in abundance, as many as we could make use of.

We had no need of chimneys, it was hot enough without fire; but yet we found ourselves at last obliged to keep a fire every night upon a particular occasion. For though we had in all other respects a very pleasant and agreeable situation, yet we were rather worse troubled with the unwelcome visits of wild beasts here than in the wilderness itself; for as the deer and other gentle creatures came hither for shelter and food, so the lions and tigers and leopards haunted these places continually for prey.

When first we discovered this we were so uneasy at it that we thought of removing our situation; but after many debates about it we resolved to fortify ourselves in such a manner as not to be in any danger from it; and this our carpenters undertook, who first palisaded our camp quite round with long stakes, for we had wood enough, which stakes were not stuck in one by another like pales, but in an irregular manner; a great multitude of them so placed that they took up near two yards in thickness, some higher, some lower, all sharpened at the top, and about a foot asunder: so that had any creature jumped at them, unless he had gone clean over, which it was very hard to do, he would be hung upon twenty or thirty spikes.

The entrance into this had larger stakes than the rest, so placed before one another as to make three or four short turnings which no four-footed beast bigger than a dog could possibly come in at; and that we might not be attacked by any multitude together, and consequently be alarmed in our sleep, as we had been, or be obliged to waste our ammunition, which we were very chary of, we kept a great fire every night without the entrance of our palisade, having a hut for our two sentinels to stand in free from the rain, just within the entrance, and right against the fire.

To maintain this fire we cut a prodigious deal of wood, and piled it up in a heap to dry, and with the green boughs made a second covering over our huts, so high and thick that it might cast the rain from the first, and keep us effectually dry.

We had scarcely finished all these works but the rain came on so fierce and so continued that we had little time to stir abroad for food, except indeed that our negroes, who wore no clothes, seemed to make nothing of the rain; though to us Europeans, in those hot climates, nothing is more dangerous.

We continued in this posture for four months, that is to say, from the middle of June to the middle of October; for though the rains went off, at least the greatest violence of them, about the equinox, yet, as the sun was then just over our heads, we resolved to stay awhile till it passed a little to the southward.

During our encampment here we had several adventures with the ravenous creatures of that country; and had not our fire been always kept burning, I question much whether all our fence, though we strengthened it afterwards with twelve or fourteen rows of stakes or more, would have kept us secure. It was always in the night that we had the disturbance of them, and sometimes they came in such multitudes that we thought all the lions and tigers, and leopards and wolves of Africa were come together to attack us. One night, being clear moonshine, one of our men being upon the watch, told us that he verily believed he saw ten thousand wild creatures of one sort or another pass by our little camp, and ever as they saw the fire they sheered off, but were sure to howl or roar, or whatever it was, when they were past.

The music of their voices was very far from being pleasant to us, and sometimes would be so very disturbing that we could not sleep for it; and often our sentinels would call us that were awake to come and look at them. It was one windy, tempestuous night, after a rainy day, that we were indeed called up; for such innumerable numbers of devilish creatures came about us that our watch really thought they would attack us. They would not come on the side where the fire was; and though we thought ourselves secure everywhere else, yet we all got up and took to our arms. The moon was near the full, but the air full of flying clouds, and a strange hurricane of wind to add to the terror of the night; when, looking on the back part of our camp, I thought I saw a creature within our fortification, and so indeed he was, except his haunches, for he had taken a running leap, I suppose, and with all his might had thrown himself clear over our palisades, except one strong pile, which stood higher than the rest, and which had caught hold of him, and by his weight he had hanged himself upon it, the spike of the pile running into his hinder haunch or thigh, on the inside; and by that he hung, growling and biting the wood for rage. I snatched up a lance from one of the negroes that stood just by me, and running to him, struck it three or four times into him, and dispatched him, being unwilling to shoot, because I had a mind to have a volley fired among the rest, whom I could see standing without, as thick as a drove of bullocks going to a fair. I immediately called our people out, and showed them the object of terror which I had seen, and, without any further consultation, fired a full volley among them, most of our pieces being loaded with two or three slugs or bullets apiece. It made a horrible clutter among them, and in general they all took to their heels, only that we could observe that some walked off with more gravity and majesty than others, being not so much frighted at the noise and fire; and we could perceive that some were left upon the ground struggling as for life, but we durst not stir out to see what they were.

Indeed they stood so thick, and were so near us, that we could not well miss killing or wounding some of them, and we believed they had certainly the smell of us, and our victuals we had been killing; for we had killed a deer, and three or four of those creatures like goats the day before; and some of the offal had been thrown out behind our camp, and this, we suppose, drew them so much about us; but we avoided it for the future.

Though the creatures fled, yet we heard a frightful roaring all night at the place where they stood, which we supposed was from some that were wounded, and as soon as day came we went out to see what execution we had done. And indeed it was a strange sight; there were three tigers and two wolves quite killed, besides the creature I had killed within our palisade, which seemed to be of an ill-gendered kind, between a tiger and a leopard. Besides this there was a noble old lion alive, but with both his fore-legs broke, so that he could not stir away, and he had almost beat himself to death with struggling all night, and we found that this was the wounded soldier that had roared so loud and given us so much disturbance. Our surgeon, looking at him, smiled. "Now," says he, "if I could be sure this lion would be as grateful to me as one of his majesty's ancestors was to Androcles, the Roman slave, I would certainly set both his legs again and cure him." I had not heard the story of Androcles, so he told it me at large; but as to the surgeon, we told him he had no way to know whether the lion would do so or not, but to cure him first and trust to his honor; but he had no faith, so to dispatch him and put him out of his torment, he shot him in the head and killed him, for which we called him the king-killer ever after.

Our negroes found no less than five of these ravenous creatures wounded and dropped at a distance from our quarters; whereof, one was a wolf, one a fine spotted young leopard, and the other were creatures that we knew not what to call them.

We had several more of these gentlefolks about after that, but no such general rendezvous of them as that was anymore; but this ill effect it had to us, that it frighted the deer and other creatures from our neighborhood, of whose company we were much more desirous, and which were necessary for our subsistence. However, our negroes went out every day a-hunting, as they called it, with bow and arrow, and they scarce ever failed of bringing us home something or other; and particularly we found in this part of the country, after the rains had fallen some time, abundance of wild fowl, such as we have in England, duck, teal, widgeon, etc.; some geese, and some kinds that we had never seen before; and we frequently killed them. Also we catched a great deal of fresh fish out of the river, so that we wanted no provision. If we wanted anything, it was salt to eat with our fresh meat; but we had a little left, and we used it sparingly; for as to our negroes, they could not taste it, nor did they care to eat any meat that was seasoned with it.

The weather began now to clear up, the rains were down, and the floods abated, and the sun, which had passed our zenith, was gone to the southward a good way; so we prepared to go on our way.

It was the 12th of October, or thereabouts, that we began to set forward; and having an easy country to travel in, as well as to supply us with provisions, though still without inhabitants, we made more dispatch, traveling sometimes, as we calculated it, twenty or twenty-five miles a day; nor did we halt anywhere in eleven days' march, one day excepted, which was to make a raft to carry us over a small river, which, having swelled with the rains, was not yet quite down.

When we were past this river, which, by the way, ran to the northward too, we found a great row of hills in our way. We saw, indeed, the country open to the right at a great distance; but, as we kept true to our course, due west, we were not willing to go a great way out of our way, only to shun a, few hills. So we advanced; but we were surprised when, being not quite come to the top, one of our company, who, with two negroes, was got up before us, cried out, "The sea! the sea!" and fell a-dancing and jumping, as signs of joy.

The gunner and I were most surprised at it, because we had but that morning been calculating that we must have yet above 1000 miles on the sea side, and that we could not expect to reach it till another rainy season would be upon us; so that when our man cried out, "The sea," the gunner was angry, and said he was mad.

But we were both in the greatest surprise imaginable, when, coming to the top of the hill, and though it was very high, we saw nothing but water, either before us or to the right hand or the left, being a vast sea, without any bounds but the horizon.

We went down the hill full of confusion of thought, not being able to conceive whereabouts we were or what it must be, seeing by all our charts the sea was yet a vast way off.

It was not above three miles from the hills before we

came to the shore, or water-edge of this sea, and there, to our further surprise, we found the water fresh and pleasant to drink; so that, in short, we knew not what course to take. The sea, as we thought it to be, put a full stop to our journey (I mean westward), for it lay just in the way. Our next question was, which hand to turn to, to the right hand or the left, but this was soon resolved; for, as we knew not the extent of it, we considered that our way, if it had been the sea really, must be on the north, and therefore, if we went to the south now, it must be just so much out of our way at last. So, having spent a good part of the day in our surprise at the thing, and consulting what to do, we set forward to the north.

We traveled upon the shore of this sea full twenty-three days before we could come to any resolution about what it was; at the end of which, early one morning, one of our seamen cried out, "Land!" and it was no false alarm, for we saw plainly the tops of some hills at a very great distance, on the further side of the water, due west; but though this satisfied us that it was not the ocean, but an inland sea or lake, yet we saw no land to the northward, that is to say, no end of it, but were obliged to travel eight days more, and near 100 miles farther, before we came to the end of it, and then we found this lake or sea ended in a very great river which ran N. or N. by E., as the other river had done which I mentioned before.

My friend the gunner, upon examining, said that he believed that he was mistaken before, and that this was the river Nile, but was still of the mind that we were of before, that we should not think of a voyage into Egypt that way; so we resolved upon crossing this river, which, however, was not so easy as before, the river being very rapid and the channel very broad.

It cost us, therefore, a week here to get materials to

waft ourselves and cattle over this river; for though here were stores of trees, yet there was none of any considerable growth sufficient to make a canoe.

During our march on the edge of this bank we met with great fatigue, and therefore traveled a fewer miles in a day than before, there being such a prodigious number of little rivers that came down from the hills on the east side, emptying themselves into this gulf, all which waters were pretty high, the rains having been but newly over.

In the last three days of our travel we met with some inhabitants, but we found they lived upon the little hills and not by the waterside; nor were we a little put to it for food in this march, having killed nothing for four or five days but some fish we caught out of the lake, and that not in such plenty as we found before.

But, to make us some amends, we had no disturbance upon all the shores of this lake from any wild beasts; the only inconveniency of that kind was, that we met an ugly, venomous, deformed kind of a snake or serpent in the wet grounds near the lake, that several times pursued us as if it would attack us; and if we struck or threw anything at it, it would raise itself up and hiss so loud that it might be heard a great way. It had a hellish ugly deformed look and voice, and our men would not be persuaded but it was the devil, only that we did not know what business Satan could have there, where there were no people.

It was very remarkable that we had now traveled 1000 miles without meeting with any people in the heart of the whole continent of Africa, where, to be sure, never man set his foot since the sons of Noah spread themselves over the face of the whole earth. Here also our gunner took an observation with his forestaff, to determine our latitude, and he found now, that having marched about thirty-three days northward, we were in

6 degrees 22 minutes south latitude.

After having with great difficulty got over this river, we came into a strange wild country that began a little to affright us; for though the country was not a desert of dry scalding sand as that was we had passed before, yet it was mountainous, barren, and infinitely full of most furious wild beasts, more than anyplace we had passed yet. There was indeed a kind of coarse herbage on the surface, and now and then a few trees, or rather shrubs. But people we could see none, and we began to be in great suspense about victuals, for we had not killed a deer a great while, but had lived chiefly upon fish and fowl, always by the waterside, both which seemed to fail us now; and we were in the more consternation, because we could not lay in a stock here to proceed upon, as we did before, but were obliged to set out with scarcity, and without any certainty of a supply.

We had, however, no remedy but patience; and having killed some fowls and dried some fish, as much as, with short allowance, we reckoned would last us five days, we resolved to venture, and venture we did; nor was it without cause that we were apprehensive of the danger, for we traveled the five days and met neither with fish nor fowl, nor four-footed beast, whose flesh was fit to eat, and we were in a most dreadful apprehension of being famished to death. On the sixth day we almost fasted, or, as we may say, we ate up all the scraps of what we had left, and at night lay down supperless upon our mats, with heavy hearts, being obliged the eighth day to kill one of our poor faithful servants, the buffaloes that carried our baggage. The flesh of this creature was very good, and so sparingly did we eat of it that it lasted us all three days and a half, and was just spent; and we were on the point of killing another when we saw before us a country that promised better, having high trees and a large river in the middle of it.

This encouraged us, and we quickened our march for the river-side, though with empty stomachs, and very faint and weak; but before we came to this river we had the good hap to meet with some young deer, a thing we had long wished for. In a word, having shot three of them, we came to a full stop to fill our bellies, and never gave the flesh time to cool before we ate it; nay, it was much we could stay to kill it and had not eaten it alive, for we were, in short, almost famished.

Through all that inhospitable country we saw continually lions, tigers, leopards, civet cats, and abundance of kinds of creatures that we did not understand; we saw no elephants, but every now and then we met with an elephant's tooth lying on the ground, and some of them lying, as it were, half buried by the length of time that they had lain there.

When we came to the shore of this river, we found it ran northerly still, as all the rest had done, but with this difference, that as the course of the other rivers were N. by E. or N.N.E., the course of this lay N.W.N.

On the farther bank of this river we saw some sign of inhabitants, but met with none for the first day; but the next day we came into an inhabited country, the people all negroes, and stark naked, without shame, both men and women.

We made signs of friendship to them, and found them a very frank, civil, and friendly sort of people. They came to our negroes without any suspicion, nor did they give us any reason to suspect them of any villainy, as the others had done; we made signs to them that we were hungry, and immediately some naked women ran and fetched us great quantities of roots, and of things like pumpkins, which we made no scruple to eat; and our artificer showed them some of his trinkets that he had made, some of iron, some of silver, but none of gold. They had so much judgment as to choose that of silver before the iron; but when we showed them some gold, we found they did not value it so much as either of the other.

For some of these things they brought us more provisions, and three living creatures as big as calves, but not of that kind; neither did we ever see any of them before; their flesh was very good; and after that they brought us twelve more, and some smaller creatures like hares; all which were very welcome to us, who were indeed at a very great loss for provisions.

We grew very intimate with these people, and indeed they were the civillest and most friendly people that we met with at all, and mightily pleased with us; and, which was very particular, they were much easier to be made to understand our meaning than any we had met with before.

At last we began to inquire our way, pointing to the west. They made us understand easily that we could not go that way, but they pointed to us that we might go northwest, so that we presently understood that there was another lake in our way, which proved to be true; for in two days more we saw it plain, and it held us till we passed the equinoctial line, lying all the way on our left hand, though at a great distance.

Traveling thus northward, our gunner seemed very anxious about our proceedings; for he assured us, and made me sensible of it by the maps which he had been teaching me out of, that when we came into the latitude of six degrees, or thereabouts, north of the line, the land trended away to the west to such a length that we should not come at the sea under a march of above 1500 miles farther westward than the country we desired to go to. I asked him if there were no navigable rivers that we might meet with, which, running into the west ocean, might perhaps carry us down their stream, and then, if it were 1500 miles, or twice 1500 miles, we might do well enough if we could but get provisions.

Here he showed me the maps again, and that there appeared no river whose stream was of any such a length as to do any kindness, till we came perhaps within 200 or 300 miles of the shore, except the Rio Grande, as they call it, which lay farther northward from us, at least 700 miles; and that then he knew not what kind of country it might carry us through; for he said it was his opinion that the heats on the north of the line, even in the same latitude, were violent, and the country more desolate, barren, and barbarous, than those of the south; and that when we came among the negroes in the north part of Africa, next the sea, especially those who had seen and trafficked with the Europeans, such as Dutch, English, Portuguese, Spaniards, etc., they had most of them been so ill-used at some time or other that they would certainly put all the spite they could upon us in mere revenge.

Upon these considerations he advised us that, as soon as we had passed this lake, we should proceed W.S.W., that is to say, a little inclining to the south, and that in time we should meet with the great river Congo, from whence the coast is called Congo, being a little north of Angola, where we intended at first to go.

I asked him if ever he had been on the coast of Congo. He said, yes, he had, but was never on shore there. Then I asked him how we should get from thence to the coast where the European ships came, seeing, if the land trended away west for 1500 miles, we must have all that shore to traverse before we could double the west point of it.

He told me it was ten to one but we should hear of

some European ships to take us in, for that they often visited the coast of Congo and Angola, in trade with the negroes; and that if we could not, yet, if we could but find provisions, we should make our way as well along the seashore as along the river, till we came to the Gold Coast, which, he said, was not above 400 or 500 miles north of Congo, besides the turning of the coast west about 300 more; that shore being in the latitude of six or seven degrees; and that there the English, or Dutch, or French had settlements or factories, perhaps all of them.

I confess I had more mind, all the while he argued, to have gone northward, and shipped ourselves in the Rio Grande, or, as the traders call it, the river Negro or Niger, for I knew that at last it would bring us down to the Cape de Verd, where we were sure of relief; whereas, at the coast we were going to now, we had a prodigious way still to go, either by sea or land, and no certainty which way to get provisions but by force; but for the present I held my tongue, because it was my tutor's opinion.

But when, according to his desire, we came to turn southward, having passed beyond the second great lake, our men began all to be uneasy, and said we were now out of our way for certain, for that we were going farther from home, and that we were indeed far enough off already.

But we had not marched above twelve days more, eight whereof were taken up in rounding the lake, and four more southwest, in order to make for the river Congo, but we were put to another full stop, by entering a country so desolate, so frightful, and so wild, that we knew not what to think or do; for, besides that it appeared as a terrible and boundless desert, having neither woods, trees, rivers, or inhabitants, so even the place where we were was desolate of inhabitants, nor had we any way to gather in a stock of provisions for the passing of this desert, as we did before at our entering the first, unless we had marched back four days to the place where we turned the head of the lake.

Well, notwithstanding this, we ventured; for, to men that had passed such wild places as we had done, nothing could seem too desperate to undertake. We ventured, I say, and the rather because we saw very high mountains in our way at a great distance, and we imagined, wherever there were mountains there would be springs and rivers; where rivers there would be trees and grass; where trees and grass there would be cattle; and where cattle, some kind of inhabitants. At last, in consequence of this speculative philosophy, we entered this waste, having a great heap of roots and plants for our bread, such as the Indians gave us, a very little flesh or salt, and but a little water.

We traveled two days towards those hills, and still they seemed as far off as they did at first, and it was the fifth day before we got to them; indeed, we traveled but softly, for it was excessively hot; and we were much about the very equinoctial line, we hardly knew whether to the south or the north of it.

As we had concluded, that where there were hills there would be springs, so it happened; but we were not only surprised, but really frighted, to find the first spring we came to, and which looked admirably clear and beautiful, to be salt as brine. It was a terrible disappointment to us, and put us under melancholy apprehensions at first; but the gunner, who was of a spirit never discouraged, told us we should not be disturbed at that, but be very thankful, for salt was a bait we stood in as much need of as anything, and there was no question but we should find fresh water as well as salt; and here our surgeon stepped in to encourage us, and told us that if we did not know he would show us a way how to make that salt water fresh, which indeed made us all more cheerful, though we wondered what he meant.

Meantime our men, without bidding, had been seeking about for other springs, and found several; but still they were all salt; from whence we concluded that there was a salt rock or mineral stone in those mountains, and perhaps they might be all of such a substance; but still I wondered by what witchcraft it was that our artist the surgeon would make this salt water turn fresh, and I longed to see the experiment, which was indeed a very odd one; but he went to work with as much assurance as if he had tried it on the very spot before.

He took two of our large mats and sewed them together, and they made a kind of a bag four feet broad, three feet and a half high, and about a foot and a half thick when it was full.

He caused us to fill this bag with dry sand and tread it down as close as we could, not to burst the mats. When thus the bag was full within a foot, he sought some other earth and filled up the rest with it, and still trod all in as hard as he could. When he had done, he made a hole in the upper earth about as broad as the crown of a large hat, or something bigger about, but not so deep, and bade a negro fill it with water, and still as it shrunk away to fill it again, and keep it full. The bag he had placed at first across two pieces of wood, about a foot from the ground; and under it he ordered some of our skins to be spread that would hold water. In about an hour, and not sooner, the water began to come dropping through the bottom of the bag, and, to our great surprise, was perfectly fresh and sweet, and this continued for several hours; but in the end the water began to be a little brackish. When we told him that, "Well, then," said he, "turn the sand out, and fill it again." Whether he did this by way of experiment from his own fancy, or whether he had seen it done before, I do not remember.

The next day we mounted the tops of the hills, where the prospect was indeed astonishing, for as far as the eye could look, south, or west, or northwest, there was nothing to be seen but a vast howling wilderness, with neither tree nor river, nor any green thing. The surface we found, as the part we passed the day before, had a kind of thick moss upon it, of a blackish dead color, but nothing in it that looked like food, either for man or beast.

Had we been stored with provisions to have entered for ten or twenty days upon this wilderness, as we were formerly, and with fresh water, we had hearts good enough to have ventured, though we had been obliged to come back again, for if we went north we did not know but we might meet with the same; but we neither had provisions, neither were we in any place where it was possible to get them. We killed some wild ferine creatures at the foot of these hills; but, except two things, like to nothing that we ever saw before, we met with nothing that was fit to eat. These were creatures that seemed to be between the kind of a buffalo and a deer, but indeed resembled neither; for they had no horns, and had great legs like a cow, with a fine head, and the neck like a deer. We killed also, at several times, a tiger, two young lions, and a wolf; but, God be thanked, we were not so reduced as to eat carrion.

Upon this terrible prospect I renewed my motion of turning northward, and making towards the river Niger or Rio Grande, then to turn west towards the English settlements on the Gold Coast; to which everyone most readily consented, only our gunner, who was indeed our best guide, though he happened to be mistaken at this time. He moved that, as our coast was now northward, so we might slant away northwest, that so, by crossing the country, we might perhaps meet with some other river that run into the Rio Grande northward, or down to the Gold Coast southward, and so both direct our way and shorten the labor; as also because, if any of the country was inhabited and fruitful, we should probably find it upon the shore of the rivers, where alone we could be furnished with provisions.

This was good advice, and too rational not to be taken; but our present business was, what to do to get out of this dreadful place we were in. Behind us was a waste, which had already cost us five days' march, and we had not provisions for five days left to go back again the same way. Before us was nothing but horror, as above; so we resolved, seeing the ridge of the hills we were upon had some appearance of fruitfulness, and that they seemed to lead away to the northward a great way, to keep under the foot of them on the east side, to go on as far as we could, and in the meantime to look diligently out for food.

Accordingly we moved on the next morning; for we had no time to lose, and, to our great comfort, we came in our first morning's march to very good springs of fresh water; and lest we should have a scarcity again, we filled all our bladder bottles and carried it with us. I should also have observed that our surgeon, who made the salt water fresh, took the opportunity of those salt springs, and made us the quantity of three or four pecks of very good salt.

In our third march we found an unexpected supply of food, the hills being full of hares. They were of a kind something different from ours in England, larger and not as swift of foot, but very good meat. We shot several of them, and the little tame leopard, which I told you we took at the negro town that we plundered, hunted them like a dog, and killed us several every day;

but she would eat nothing of them unless we gave it her, which, indeed, in our circumstance, was very obliging. We salted them a little and dried them in the sun whole, and carried a strange parcel along with us. I think it was almost three hundred, for we did not know when we might find any more, either of these or any other food. We continued our course under these hills very comfortably for eight or nine days, when we found, to our great satisfaction, the country beyond us began to look with something of a better countenance. As for the west side of the hills, we never examined it till this day, when three of our company, the rest halting for refreshment, mounted the hills again to satisfy their curiosity, but found it all the same, nor could they see any end of it, no, not to the north, the way we were going; so the tenth day, finding the hills made a turn, and led as it were into the vast desert, we left them and continued our course north, the country being very tolerably full of woods, some waste, but not tediously long, till we came, by our gunner's observation, into the latitude of eight degrees five minutes, which we were nineteen days more in performing.

All this way we found no inhabitants, but abundance of wild ravenous creatures, with which we became so well acquainted now that really we did not much mind them. We saw lions and tigers and leopards every night and morning in abundance; but as they seldom came near us, we let them go about their business: if they offered to come near us, we made false fire with any gun that was uncharged, and they would walk off as soon as they saw the flash.

We made pretty good shift for food all this way; for sometimes we killed hares, sometimes some fowls, but for my life I cannot give names to any of them, except a kind of partridge, and another that was like our turtle. Now and then we began to meet with elephants again in great numbers; those creatures delighted chiefly in the woody part of the country.

This long-continued march fatigued us very much, and two of our men fell sick, indeed, so very sick that we thought they would have died; and one of our negroes died suddenly. Our surgeon said it was an apoplexy, but he wondered at it, he said, for he could never complain of his high feeding. Another of them was very ill; but our surgeon with much ado persuading him, indeed it was almost forcing him to be let blood, he recovered.

We halted here twelve days for the sake of our sick men, and our surgeon persuaded me and three or four more of us to be let blood during the time of rest, which, with other things he gave us, contributed very much to our continued health in so tedious a march and in so hot a climate.

In this march we pitched our matted tents every night, and they were very comfortable to us, though we had trees and woods to shelter us in most places. We thought it very strange that in all this part of the country we yet met with no inhabitants; but the principal reason, as we found afterwards, was, that we, having kept a western course first, and then a northern course, were gotten too much into the middle of the country and among the deserts; whereas the inhabitants are principally found among the rivers, lakes, and lowlands, as well to the southwest as to the north.

What little rivulets we found here were so empty of water, that except some pits, and little more than ordinary pools, there was scarcely any water to be seen in them; and they rather showed that during the rainy months they had a channel, than that they had really running water in them at that time, by which it was easy for us to judge that we had a great way to go; but this was no discouragement so long as we had but

provisions, and some seasonable shelter from the violent heat, which indeed I thought was much greater
now than when the sun was just over our heads.

Our men being recovered, we set forward again, very
well stored with provisions, and water sufficient, and
bending our course a little to the westward of the
north, traveled in hopes of some favorable stream
which might bear a canoe; but we found none till after
twenty days' travel, including eight days' rest; for our
men being weak, we rested very often, especially when
we came to places which were proper for our purpose,
where we found cattle, fowl, or anything to kill for our
food. In those twenty days' march we advanced four
degrees to the northward, besides some meridian distance westward, and we met with abundance of elephants, and with a good number of elephants' teeth
scattered up and down, here and there, in the woody
grounds especially, some of which were very large. But
they were no booty to us; our business was provisions,
and a good passage out of the country; and it had been
much more to our purpose to have found a good fat
deer, and to have killed it for our food, than a hundred
ton of elephants' teeth; and yet, as you shall presently
hear, when we came to begin our passage by water, we
once thought to have built a large canoe, on purpose
to have loaded it with ivory; but this was when we knew
nothing of the rivers, nor knew anything how dangerous and how difficult a passage it was we were likely
to have in them, nor had considered the weight of
carriage to lug them to the rivers where we might
embark.

At the end of twenty days' travel, as above, in the
latitude of three degrees sixteen minutes, we discovered
in a valley, at some distance from us, a pretty tolerable
stream, which we thought deserved the name of a river,
and which ran its course N.N.W., which was just what

we wanted. As we had fixed our thoughts upon our passage by water, we took this for the place to make the experiment, and bent our march directly to the valley.

There was a small thicket of trees just in our way, which we went by, thinking no harm, when on a sudden one of our negroes was dangerously wounded with an arrow shot into his back, slanting between his shoulders. This put us to a full stop; and three of our men, with two negroes, spreading the wood, for it was but a small one, found a negro with a bow, but no arrow, who would have escaped, but our men that discovered him shot him in revenge of the mischief he had done; so we lost the opportunity of taking him prisoner, which, if we had done, and sent him home with good usage, it might have brought others to us in a friendly manner.

Going a little farther, we came to five negro huts or houses, built after a different manner from any we had seen yet; and at the door of one of them lay seven elephants' teeth, piled up against the wall or side of the hut, as if they had been provided against a market. Here were no men, but seven or eight women, and near twenty children. We offered them no incivility of any kind, but gave them everyone a bit of silver beaten out thin, as I observed before, and cut diamond fashion, or in the shape of a bird, at which the women were overjoyed, and brought out to us several sorts of food, which we did not understand, being cakes of a meal made of roots, which they bake in the sun, and which ate very well. We went a little way farther and pitched our camp for that night, not doubting but our civility to the women would produce some good effect when their husbands might come home.

Accordingly, the next morning the women, with eleven men, five young boys, and two good big girls, came to our camp. Before they came quite to us, the women called aloud, and made an odd screaming noise to bring us out; and accordingly we came out, when two of the women, showing us what we had given them, and pointing to the company behind, made such signs as we could easily understand signified friendship. When the men advanced, having bows and arrows, they laid them down on the ground, scraped and threw sand over their heads, and turned round three times with their hands laid up upon the tops of their heads. This, it seems, was a solemn vow of friendship. Upon this we beckoned them with our hands to come nearer; then they sent the boys and girls to us first, which, it seems, was to bring us more cakes of bread and some green herbs to eat, which we received, and took the boys up and kissed them, and the little girls too; then the men came up close to us, and sat them down on the ground, making signs that we should sit down by them, which we did. They said much to one another, but we could not understand them, nor could we find any way to make them understand us, much less whither we were going, or what we wanted, only that we easily made them understand we wanted victuals; whereupon one of the men, casting his eyes about him towards a rising ground that was about half a mile off, started up as if he was frighted, flew to the place where they had laid down their bows and arrows, snatched up a bow and two arrows, and ran like a racehorse to the place. When he came there, he let fly both his arrows, and comes back again to us with the same speed. We, seeing he came with the bow, but without the arrows, were the more inquisitive; but the fellow, saying nothing to us, beckons to one of our negroes to come to him, and we bid him go; so he led him back to the place, where lay a kind of deer, shot with two arrows, but not quite dead, and between them they brought it down to us.

This was for a gift to us, and was very welcome, I assure you, for our stock was low. These people were all stark naked.

The next day there came about a hundred men to us, and women making the same awkward signals of friendship, and dancing, and showing themselves very well pleased, and anything they had they gave us. How the man in the wood came to be so butcherly and rude as to shoot at our men, without making any breach first, we could not imagine; for the people were simple, plain, and inoffensive in all our other conversation with them.

From hence we went down the banks of the little river I mentioned, and where, I found, we should see the whole nation of negroes, but whether friendly to us or not, that we could make no judgment of yet.

The river was no use to us, as to the design of making canoes, a great while; and we traversed the country on the edge of it about five days more, when our carpenters, finding the stream increased, proposed to pitch our tents, and fall to work to make canoes; but after we had begun the work, and cut down two or three trees, and spent five days in the labor, some of our men, wandering further down the river, brought us word that the stream rather decreased than increased, sinking away into the sands, or drying up by the heat of the sun, so that the river appeared not able to carry the least canoe that could be any way useful to us; so we were obliged to give over our enterprise and move on.

In our further prospect this way, we marched three days full west, the country on the north side being extraordinary mountainous, and more parched and dry than any we had seen yet; whereas, in the part which looks due west, we found a pleasant valley running a great way between two great ridges of mountains. The hills looked frightful, being entirely bare of trees or grass, and even white with the dryness of the sand; but in the valley we had trees, grass, and some creatures that were fit for food, and some inhabitants.

We passed by some of their huts or houses, and saw people about them, but they ran up into the hills as soon as they saw us. At the end of this valley we met with a peopled country, and at first it put us to some doubt whether we should go among them, or keep up towards the hills northerly; and as our aim was principally as before, to make our way to the river Niger, we inclined to the latter, pursuing our course by the compass to the N.W. We marched thus without interruption seven days more, when we met with a surprising circumstance much more desolate and disconsolate than our own, and which, in time to come, will scarce seem credible.

We did not much seek the conversing, or acquainting ourselves with the natives of the country, except where we found the want of them for our provision, or their direction for our way; so that, whereas we found the country here begin to be very populous, especially towards our left hand, that is, to the south, we kept at the more distance northerly, still stretching towards the west.

In this tract we found something or other to kill and eat, which always supplied our necessity, though not so well as we were provided in our first setting out; being thus, as it were, pushing to avoid a peopled country, we at last came to a very pleasant, agreeable stream of water, not big enough to be called a river, but running to the N.N.W., which was the very course we desired to go.

On the farthest bank of this brook, we perceived some huts of negroes, not many, and in a little low spot of ground, some maize, or Indian corn, growing, which intimated presently to us, that there were some inhabitants on that side less barbarous than what we had met with in other places where we had been.

As we went forward, our whole caravan being in a body, our negroes, who were in the front, cried out, that they saw a white man! We were not much surprised at first, it being, as we thought, a mistake of the fellows, and asked them what they meant; when one of them stepped to me, and pointing to a hut on the other side of the hill, I was astonished to see a white man indeed, but stark naked, very busy near the door of his hut, and stooping down to the ground with something in his hand, as if he had been at some work; and his back being towards us, he did not see us.

I gave notice to our negroes to make no noise, and waited till some more of our men were come up, to show the sight to them, that they might be sure I was not mistaken; and we were soon satisfied of the truth, for the man, having heard some noise, started up, and looked full at us, as much surprised, to be sure, as we were, but whether with fear or hope, we then knew not.

As he discovered us, so did the rest of the inhabitants belonging to the huts about him, and all crowded together, looking at us at a distance, a little bottom, in which the brook ran, lying between us; the white man, and all the rest, as he told us afterwards, not knowing well whether they should stay or run away. However, it presently came into my thoughts, that if there were white men among them, it would be much easier to make them understand what we meant as to peace or war, than we found it with others; so tying a piece of white rag to the end of a stick, we sent two negroes with it to the bank of the water, carrying the pole up as high as they could; it was presently understood, and two of their men and the white man came to the shore on the other side.

However, as the white man spoke no Portuguese, they could understand nothing of one another but by signs; but our men made the white man understand that they had white men with them too, at which they said the white man laughed. However, to be short, our men came back, and told us they were all good friends, and in about an hour four of our men, two negroes, and the black prince, went to the river-side, where the white man came to them.

They had not been half a quarter of an hour, but a negro came running to me, and told me the white man was Inglese, as he called him; upon which I ran back, eagerly enough, you may be sure, with him, and found, as he said, that he was an Englishman; upon which he embraced me very passionately, the tears running down his face. The first surprise of his seeing us was over before we came, but anyone may conceive it by the brief account he gave us afterwards of his very unhappy circumstances, and of so unexpected a deliverance, such as perhaps never happened to any man in the world, for it was a million to one odds that ever he could have been relieved; nothing but an adventure that never was heard or read of before could have suited his case, unless Heaven, by some miracle that never was to be expected, had acted for him.

He appeared to be a gentleman, not an ordinary-bred fellow, seaman, or laboring man; this showed itself in his behavior in the first moment of our conversing with him, and in spite of all the disadvantages of his miserable circumstances.

He was a middle-aged man, not above thirty-seven or thirty-eight, though his beard was grown exceedingly long, and the hair of his head and face strangely covered him to the middle of his back and breast; he was white, and his skin very fine, though discolored, and in some places blistered, and covered with a brown blackish substance, scurfy, scaly, and hard, which was the effect of the scorching heat of the sun; he was stark naked, and had been so, as he told us, upwards of two years.

He was so exceedingly transported at our meeting with him, that he could scarce enter into any discourse at all with us that day; and when he could get away from us for a little, we saw him walking alone, and showing all the most extravagant tokens of an ungovernable joy; and even afterwards he was never without tears in his eyes for several days, upon the least word spoken by us of his circumstances, or by him of his deliverance.

We found his behavior the most courteous and endearing I ever saw in any man whatever, and most evident tokens of a mannerly, well-bred person appeared in all things he did or said, and our people were exceedingly taken with him. He was a scholar and a mathematician; he could not speak Portuguese indeed, but he spoke Latin to our surgeon, French to another of our men, and Italian to a third.

He had no leisure in his thoughts to ask us whence we came, whither we were going, or who we were; but would have it always as an answer to himself, that to be sure, wherever we were a-going, we came from Heaven, and were sent on purpose to save him from the most wretched condition that ever man was reduced to.

Our men pitching their camp on the bank of a little river opposite to him, he began to inquire what store of provisions we had, and how we proposed to be supplied. When he found that our store was but small, he said he would talk with the natives, and we should have provisions enough; for he said they were the most courteous, good-natured part of the inhabitants in all that part of the country, as we might suppose by his living so safe among them.

The first things this gentleman did for us were indeed of the greatest consequence to us; for, first, he perfectly informed us where we were, and which was the properest course for us to steer; secondly, he put us in the way how to furnish ourselves effectually with provisions; and thirdly, he was our complete interpreter and peacemaker with all the natives, who now began to be very numerous about us, and who were a more fierce and politic people than those we had met with before; not so easily terrified with our arms as those, and not so ignorant as to give their provisions and corn for our little toys, such as, I said before, our artificer made; but as they had frequently traded and conversed with the Europeans on the coast, or with other negro nations that had traded and been concerned with them, they were the less ignorant and the less fearful, and consequently nothing was to be had from them but by exchange for such things as they liked.

This I say of the negro natives, which we soon came among; but as to these poor people that he lived among, they were not much acquainted with things, being at the distance of above 300 miles from the coast; only that they found elephants' teeth upon the hills to the north, which they took and carried about sixty or seventy miles south, where other trading negroes usually met them, and gave them beads, glass, shells, and cowries, for them, such as the English and Dutch and other traders furnish them with from Europe.

We now began to be more familiar with our new acquaintance; and first, though we made but a sorry figure as to clothes ourselves, having neither shoe, or stocking, or glove, or hat among us, and but very few shirts, yet as well as we could we clothed him; and first, our surgeon having scissors and razors, shaved him, and cut his hair; a hat, as I say, we had not in all our stores, but he supplied himself by making himself a cap of a piece of a leopard-skin, most artificially. As for shoes or stockings, he had gone so long without them that he cared not even for the buskins and foot-gloves we wore, which I described above.

As he had been curious to hear the whole story of our travels, and was exceedingly delighted with the relation, so we were no less to know, and pleased with, the account of his circumstances, and the history of his coming to that strange place alone, and in that condition which we found him in, as above. This account of his would indeed be in itself the subject of an agreeable history, and would be as long and diverting as our own, having in it many strange and extraordinary incidents; but we cannot have room here to launch out into so long a digression: the sum of his history was this: —

He had been a factor for the English Guinea Company at Sierra Leone, or some other of their settlements which had been taken by the French, where he had been plundered of all his own effects, as well as of what was entrusted to him by the company. Whether it was that the company did not do him justice in restoring his circumstances, or in further employing him, he quitted their service, and was employed by those called separate traders, and being afterwards out of employ there also, traded on his own account; when, passing unwarily into one of the company's settlements, he was either betrayed into the hands of some of the natives, or, somehow or other, was surprised by them. However, as they did not kill him, he found means to escape from them at that time, and fled to another nation of the natives, who, being enemies to the other, entertained him friendly, and with them he lived some time; but not liking his quarters or his company, he fled

again, and several times changed his landlords: sometimes was carried by force, sometimes hurried by fear,
as circumstances altered with him (the variety of which
deserves a history by itself), till at last he had wandered
beyond all possibility of return, and had taken up his
abode where we found him, where he was well received
by the petty king of the tribe he lived with; and he, in
return, instructed them how to value the product of
their labor, and on what terms to trade with those
negroes who came up to them for teeth.

As he was naked, and had no clothes, so he was naked
of arms for his defense, having neither gun, sword,
staff, or any instrument of war about him, no, not to
guard himself against the attacks of a wild beast, of
which the country was very full. We asked him how he
came to be so entirely abandoned of all concern for
his safety? He answered, that to him, that had so often
wished for death, life was not worth defending; and
that, as he was entirely at the mercy of the negroes, they
had much the more confidence in him, seeing he had
no weapons to hurt them. As for wild beasts, he was
not much concerned about that, for he scarce ever went
from his hut; but if he did, the negro king and his men
went all with him, and they were all armed with bows
and arrows, and lances, with which they would kill any
of the ravenous creatures, lions as well as others; but
that they seldom came abroad in the day; and if the
negroes wander anywhere in the night, they always
build a hut for themselves, and make a fire at the door
of it, which is guard enough.

We inquired of him what we should next do towards
getting to the seaside. He told us we were about one
hundred and twenty English leagues from the coast,
where almost all the European settlements and factories were, and which is called the Gold Coast; but that
there were so many different nations of negroes in the

way, that it was ten to one if we were not either fought with continually, or starved for want of provisions; but that there were two other ways to go, which, if he had had any company to go with him, he had often contrived to make his escape by. The one was to travel full west, which, though it was farther to go, yet was not so full of people, and the people we should find would be so much the civiller to us, or be so much the easier to fight with; or that the other way was, if possible, to get to the Rio Grande, and go down the stream in canoes. We told him, that was the way we had resolved on before we met with him; but then he told us there was a prodigious desert to go over, and as prodigious woods to go through, before we came to it, and that both together were at least twenty days' march for us, travel as hard as we could.

We asked him if there were no horses in the country, or asses, or even bullocks or buffaloes, to make use of in such a journey, and we showed him ours, of which we had but three left. He said no, all the country did not afford anything of that kind.

He told us that in this great wood there were immense numbers of elephants; and upon the desert, great multitudes of lions, lynxes, tigers, leopards, &c.; and that it was to that wood and that desert that the negroes went to get elephants' teeth, where they never failed to find a great number.

We inquired still more, and particularly the way to the Gold Coast, and if there were no rivers to ease us in our carriage; and told him, as to the negroes fighting with us, we were not much concerned at that; nor were we afraid of starving, for if they had any victuals among them, we would have our share of it; and, therefore, if he would venture to show us the way, we would venture to go; and as for himself, we told him we would live and die together — there should not a man of us stir from him.

He told us, with all his heart, if we resolved it, and would venture, we might be assured he would take his fate with us, and he would endeavor to guide us in such a way as we should meet with some friendly savages who would use us well, and perhaps stand by us against some others, who were less tractable; so, in a word, we all resolved to go full south for the Gold Coast.

The next morning he came to us again, and being all met in council, as we may call it, he began to talk very seriously with us, that since we were now come, after a long journey, to a view of the end of our troubles, and had been so obliging to him as to offer to carry him with us, he had been all night revolving in his mind what he and we all might do to make ourselves some amends for all our sorrows; and first, he said, he was to let me know that we were just then in one of the richest parts of the world, though it was really otherwise but a desolate, disconsolate wilderness; "for," says he, "there is not a river but runs gold — not a desert but without ploughing bears a crop of ivory. What mines of gold, what immense stores of gold, those mountains may contain, from whence these rivers come, or the shores which these waters run by, we know not, but may imagine that they must be inconceivably rich, seeing so much is washed down the stream by the water washing the sides of the land, that the quantity suffices all the traders which the European world send thither." We asked him how far they went for it, seeing the ships only trade upon the coast. He told us that the negroes on the coast search the rivers up for the length of 150 or 200 miles, and would be out a month, or two, or three at a time, and always come home sufficiently rewarded; "but," says he, "they never come thus far, and yet hereabouts is as much gold as there." Upon this he told us that he believed he might have gotten a hundred pounds' weight of gold since he came thither, if he had employed himself to look and work for it; but as he knew not what to do with it, and had long since despaired of being ever delivered from the misery he was in, he had entirely omitted it. "For what advantage had it been to me," said he, "or what richer had I been, if I had a ton of gold dust, and lay and wallowed in it? The richness of it," said he, "would not give me one moment's felicity, nor relieve me in the present exigency. Nay," says he, "as you all see, it would not buy me clothes to cover me, or a drop of drink to save me from perishing. It is of no value here," says he; "there are several people among these huts that would weigh gold against a few glass beads or a cockle-shell, and give you a handful of gold-dust for a handful of cowries." N.B. — These are little shells which our children call blackamoors' teeth.

When he had said thus he pulled out a piece of an earthen pot baked hard in the sun. "Here," says he, "is some of the dirt of this country, and if I would I could have got a great deal more;" and, showing it to us, I believe there was in it between two and three pounds weight of gold-dust, of the same kind and color with that we had gotten already, as before. After we had looked at it a while, he told us, smiling, we were his deliverers, and all he had, as well as his life, was ours; and therefore, as this would be of value to us when we came to our own country, so he desired we would accept of it among us; and that was the only time that he had repented that he had picked up no more of it.

I spoke for him, as his interpreter, to my comrades, and in their names thanked him; but, speaking to them in Portuguese, I desired them to defer the acceptance of his kindness to the next morning; and so I did, telling him we would further talk of this part in the morning; so we parted for that time.

When he was gone I found they were all wonderfully affected with his discourse, and with the generosity of his temper, as well as the magnificence of his present, which in another place had been extraordinary. Upon the whole, not to detain you with circumstances, we agreed that, seeing he was now one of our number, and that as we were a relief to him in carrying him out of the dismal condition he was in, so he was equally a relief to us, in being our guide through the rest of the country, our interpreter with the natives, and our director how to manage with the savages, and how to enrich ourselves with the wealth of the country; that, therefore, we would put his gold among our common stock, and everyone should give him as much as would make his up just as much as any single share of our own, and for the future we would take our lot together, taking his solemn engagement to us, as we had before one to another, that we would not conceal the least grain of gold we found one from another.

In the next conference we acquainted him with the adventures of the Golden River, and how we had shared what we got there, so that every man had a larger stock than he for his share; that, therefore, instead of taking any from him, we had resolved everyone to add a little to him. He appeared very glad that we had met with such good success, but would not take a grain from us, till at last, pressing him very hard, he told us, that then he would take it thus: — that, when we came to get any more, he would have so much out of the first as should make him even, and then we would go on as equal adventurers; and thus we agreed.

He then told us he thought it would not be an unprofitable adventure if, before we set forward, and after we had got a stock of provisions, we should make a journey north to the edge of the desert he had told us of, from whence our negroes might bring everyone a large elephant's tooth, and that he would get some more to assist; and that, after a certain length of carriage, they might be conveyed by canoes to the coast, where they would yield a very great profit.

I objected against this on account of our other design we had of getting gold-dust; and that our negroes, who we knew would be faithful to us, would get much more by searching the rivers for gold for us than by lugging a great tooth of a hundred and fifty pounds weight a hundred miles or more, which would be an insufferable labor to them after so hard a journey, and would certainly kill them.

He acquiesced in the justice of this answer, but fain would have had us gone to see the woody part of the hill and the edge of the desert, that we might see how the elephants' teeth lay scattered up and down there; but when we told him the story of what we had seen before, as is said above, he said no more.

We stayed here twelve days, during which time the natives were very obliging to us, and brought us fruits, pompions, and a root like carrots, though of quite another taste, but not unpleasant neither, and some guinea-fowls, whose names we did not know. In short, they brought us plenty of what they had, and we lived very well, and we gave them all such little things as our cutler had made, for he had now a whole bag full of them.

On the thirteenth day we set forward, taking our new gentleman with us. At parting, the negro king sent two savages with a present to him of some dried flesh, but I do not remember what it was, and he gave him again three silver birds which our cutler helped him to, which I assure you was a present for a king.

We traveled now south, a little west, and here we found the first river for above 2000 miles' march, whose waters run south, all the rest running north or west. We followed this river, which was no bigger than a good large brook in England, till it began to increase its water. Every now and then we found our Englishman went down as it were privately to the water, which was to try the land; at length, after a day's march upon this river, he came running up to us with his hands full of sand, and saying, "Look here." Upon looking we found that a good deal of gold lay spangled among the sand of the river. "Now," says he, "I think we may begin to work;" so he divided our negroes into couples and set them to work, to search and wash the sand and ooze in the bottom of the water where it was not deep.

In the first day and a quarter our men all together had gathered a pound and two ounces of gold or thereabouts, and as we found the quantity increased the farther we went, we followed it about three days, till another small rivulet joined the first, and then searching up the stream, we found gold there too; so we pitched our camp in the angle where the rivers joined, and we diverted ourselves, as I may call it, in washing the gold out of the sand of the river, and in getting provisions.

Here we stayed thirteen days more, in which time we had many pleasant adventures with the savages, too long to mention here, and some of them too homely to tell of, for some of our men had made something free with their women, which, had not our new guide made peace for us with one of their men at the price of seven fine bits of silver, which our artificer had cut out into the shapes of lions, and fishes, and birds, and had punched holes to hang them up by (an inestimable treasure), we must have gone to war with them and all their people.

All the while we were busy washing gold-dust out of the rivers, and our negroes the like, our ingenious cutler was hammering and cutting, and he was grown so dexterous by use that he formed all manner of images. He cut out elephants, tigers, civet cats, ostriches, eagles, cranes, fowls, fishes, and indeed whatever he pleased, in thin plates of hammered gold, for his silver and iron were almost all gone.

At one of the towns of these savage nations we were very friendly received by their king, and as he was very much taken with our workman's toys, he sold him an elephant cut out of a gold plate as thin as a sixpence at an extravagant rate. He was so much taken with it that he would not be quiet till he had given him almost a handful of gold-dust, as they call it; I suppose it might weigh three-quarters of a pound; the piece of gold that the elephant was made of might be about the weight of a pistole, rather less than more. Our artist was so honest, though the labor and art were all his own, that he brought all the gold and put it into our common stock; but we had, indeed, no manner of reason in the least to be covetous, for, as our new guide told us, we that were strong enough to defend ourselves, and had time enough to stay (for we were none of us in haste), might in time get together what quantity of gold we pleased, even to an hundred pounds weight each man if we thought fit; and therefore he told us, though he had as much reason to be sick of the country as any of us, yet if we thought to turn our march a little to the southeast, and pitch upon a place proper for our headquarters, we might find provisions plenty enough, and extend ourselves over the country among the rivers for two or three years to the right and left, and we should soon find the advantage of it.

The proposal, however good as to the profitable part of it, suited none of us, for we were all more desirous to get home than to be rich, being tired of the excessive fatigue of above a year's continual wandering among deserts and wild beasts.

However, the tongue of our new acquaintance had a kind of charm in it, and used such arguments, and had so much the power of persuasion, that there was no resisting him. He told us it was preposterous not to take the fruit of all our labors now we were come to the harvest; that we might see the hazard the Europeans run with ships and men, and at great expense, to fetch a little gold, and that we, that were in the center of it, to go away empty-handed was unaccountable; that we were strong enough to fight our way through whole nations, and might make our journey afterward to what part of the coast we pleased, and we should never forgive ourselves when we came to our own country to see we had 500 pistoles in gold, and might as easily have had 5000 or 10,000, or what we pleased; that he was no more covetous than we, but seeing it was in all our powers to retrieve our misfortunes at once, and to make ourselves easy for all our lives, he could not be faithful to us, or grateful for the good we had done him, if he did not let us see the advantage we had in our hands; and he assured us he would make it clear to our own understanding, that we might in two years' time, by good management and by the help of our negroes, gather every man a hundred pounds weight of gold, and get together perhaps two hundred ton of teeth; whereas, if once we pushed on to the coast and separated, we should never be able to see that place again with our eyes, or do anymore than sinners did with heaven, — wish themselves there, but know they can never come at it.

Our surgeon was the first man that yielded to his reasoning, and after him the gunner; and they too, indeed, had a great influence over us, but none of the rest had any mind to stay, nor I neither, I must confess; for I had no notion of a great deal of money, or what to do with myself, or what to do with it if I had it. I thought I had enough already, and all the thoughts I had about disposing of it, if I came to Europe, was only how to spend it as fast as I could, buy me some clothes, and go to sea again to be a drudge for more.

However, he prevailed with us by his good words at last to stay but for six months in the country, and then, if we did resolve to go, he would submit; so at length we yielded to that, and he carried us about fifty English miles southeast, where we found several rivulets of water, which seemed to come all from a great ridge of mountains, which lay to the northeast, and which, by our calculation, must be the beginning that way of the great waste, which we had been forced northward to avoid.

Here we found the country barren enough, but yet we had by his direction plenty of food; for the savages round us, upon giving them some of our toys, as I have so often mentioned, brought us in whatever they had; and here we found some maize, or Indian wheat, which the negro women planted, as we sow seeds in a garden, and immediately our new provider ordered some of our negroes to plant it, and it grew up presently, and by watering it often, we had a crop in less than three months' growth.

As soon as we were settled, and our camp fixed, we fell to the old trade of fishing for gold in the rivers mentioned above, and our English gentleman so well knew how to direct our search, that we scarce ever lost our labor.

One time, having set us to work, he asked if we would give him leave, with four or five negroes, to go out for six or seven days to seek his fortune, and see what he could discover in the country, assuring us whatever he got should be for the public stock. We all gave him our consent, and lent him a gun; and two of our men desiring to go with him, they took then six negroes with them, and two of our buffaloes that came with us the whole journey; they took about eight days' provision of bread with them, but no flesh, except about as much dried flesh as would serve them two days.

They traveled up to the top of the mountains I mentioned just now, where they saw (as our men afterwards vouched it to be) the same desert which we were so justly terrified at when we were on the farther side, and which, by our calculation, could not be less than 300 miles broad and above 600 miles in length, without knowing where it ended.

The journal of their travels is too long to enter upon here. They stayed out two-and-fifty days, when they brought us seventeen pound and something more (for we had no exact weight) of gold-dust, some of it in much larger pieces than any we had found before, besides about fifteen ton of elephants' teeth, which he had, partly by good usage and partly by bad, obliged the savages of the country to fetch, and bring down to him from the mountains, and which he made others bring with him quite down to our camp. Indeed, we wondered what was coming to us when we saw him attended with above 200 negroes; but he soon undeceived us, when he made them all throw down their burdens on a heap at the entrance of our camp.

Besides this, they brought two lions' skins, and five leopards' skins, very large and very fine. He asked our pardon for his long stay, and that he had made no greater a booty, but told us he had one excursion more to make, which he hoped should turn to a better account.

So, having rested himself and rewarded the savages that brought the teeth for him with some bits of silver and iron cut out diamond fashion, and with two shaped like little dogs, he sent them away mightily pleased.

The second journey he went, some more of our men desired to go with him, and they made a troop of ten white men and ten savages, and the two buffaloes to carry their provisions and ammunition. They took the same course, only not exactly the same track, and they stayed thirty-two days only, in which time they killed no less than fifteen leopards, three lions, and several other creatures, and brought us home four-and-twenty pound some ounces of gold-dust, and only six elephants' teeth, but they were very great ones.

Our friend the Englishman showed us that now our time was well bestowed, for in five months which we had stayed here, we had gathered so much gold-dust that, when we came to share it, we had five pound and a quarter to a man, besides what we had before, and besides six or seven pound weight which we had at several times given our artificer to make baubles with. And now we talked of going forward to the coast to put an end to our journey; but our guide laughed at us then. "Nay, you can't go now," says he, "for the rainy season begins next month, and there will be no stirring then." This we found, indeed, reasonable, so we resolved to furnish ourselves with provisions, that we might not be obliged to go abroad too much in the rain, and we spread ourselves some one way and some another, as far as we cared to venture, to get provisions; and our negroes killed us some deer, which we cured as well as we could in the sun, for we had now no salt.

By this time the rainy months were set in, and we could scarce, for above two months, look out of our huts. But that was not all, for the rivers were so swelled with the land-floods, that we scarce knew the little brooks and rivulets from the great navigable rivers. This had been a very good opportunity to have conveyed by water, upon rafts, our elephants' teeth, of

which we had a very great pile; for, as we always gave
the savages some reward for their labor, the very
women would bring us teeth upon every opportunity,
and sometimes a great tooth carried between two; so
that our quantity was increased to about two-and-
twenty ton of teeth.

As soon as the weather proved fair again, he told us
he would not press us to any further stay, since we did
not care whether we got any more gold or no; that we
were indeed the first men he ever met with in his life
that said they had gold enough, and of whom it might
be truly said, that, when it lay under our feet, we would
not stoop to take it up. But, since he had made us a
promise, he would not break it, nor press us to make
any further stay; only he thought he ought to tell us
that now was the time, after the land-flood, when the
greatest quantity of gold was found; and that, if we
stayed but one month, we should see thousands of
savages spread themselves over the whole country to
wash the gold out of the sand, for the European ships
which would come on the coast; that they do it then,
because the rage of the floods always works down a
great deal of gold out of the hills; and, if we took the
advantage to be there before them, we did not know
what extraordinary things we might find.

This was so forcible, and so well argued, that it
appeared in all our faces we were prevailed upon; so
we told him we would all stay: for though it was true
we were all eager to be gone, yet the evident prospect
of so much advantage could not well be resisted; that
he was greatly mistaken, when he suggested that we did
not desire to increase our store of gold, and in that we
were resolved to make the utmost use of the advantage
that was in our hands, and would stay as long as any
gold was to be had, if it was another year.

He could hardly express the joy he was in on this

occasion; and the fair weather coming on, we began, just as he directed, to search about the rivers for more gold. At first we had but little encouragement, and began to be doubtful; but it was very plain that the reason was, the water was not fully fallen, or the rivers reduced to their usual channel; but in a few days we were fully requited, and found much more gold than at first, and in bigger lumps; and one of our men washed out of the sand a piece of gold as big as a small nut, which weighed, by our estimation — for we had no small weights — almost an ounce and a half.

This success made us extremely diligent; and in little more than a month we had altogether gotten near sixty pound weight of gold; but after this, as he told us, we found abundance of the savages, men, women, and children, hunting every river and brook, and even the dry land of the hills for gold; so that we could do nothing like then, compared to what we had done before.

But our artificer found a way to make other people find us in gold without our own labor; for, when these people began to appear, he had a considerable quantity of his toys, birds, beasts, &c., such as before, ready for them; and the English gentleman being the interpreter, he brought the savages to admire them; so our cutler had trade enough, and, to be sure, sold his goods at a monstrous rate; for he would get an ounce of gold, sometimes two, for a bit of silver, perhaps of the value of a groat; nay, if it were iron and if it was of gold, they would not give the more for it; and it was incredible almost to think what a quantity of gold he got that way.

In a word, to bring this happy journey to a conclusion, we increased our stock of gold here, in three months' stay more, to such a degree that, bringing it all to a common stock, in order to share it, we divided almost four pound weight again to every man; and then we set forward for the Gold Coast, to see what method we could find out for our passage into Europe.

There happened several remarkable incidents in this part of our journey, as to how we were, or were not, received friendly by the several nations of savages through which we passed; how we delivered one negro king from captivity, who had been a benefactor to our new guide; and now our guide, in gratitude, by our assistance, restored him to his kingdom, which, perhaps, might contain about 300 subjects; how he entertained us; and how he made his subjects go with our Englishmen, and fetch all our elephants' teeth which we had been obliged to leave behind us, and to carry them for us to the river, the name of which I forgot, where we made rafts, and in eleven days more came down to one of the Dutch settlements on the Gold Coast, where we arrived in perfect health, and to our great satisfaction. As for our cargo of teeth, we sold it to the Dutch factory, and received clothes and other necessaries for ourselves, and such of our negroes as we thought fit to keep with us; and it is to be observed, that we had four pound of gunpowder left when we ended our journey. The negro prince we made perfectly free, clothed him out of our common stock, and gave him a pound and a half of gold for himself, which he knew very well how to manage; and here we all parted after the most friendly manner possible. Our Englishman remained in the Dutch factory some time, and, as I heard afterwards, died there of grief; for he having sent a thousand pounds sterling over to England, by the way of Holland, for his refuge at his return to his friends, the ship was taken by the French and the effects all lost.

The rest of my comrades went away, in a small bark, to the two Portuguese factories, near Gambia, in the latitude of fourteen; and I, with two negroes which I kept with me, went away to Cape Coast Castle, where I got passage for England, and arrived there in September; and thus ended my first harvest of wild oats; the rest were not sowed to so much advantage.

I had neither friend, relation, nor acquaintance in England, though it was my native country; I had consequently no person to trust with what I had, or to counsel me to secure or save it; but, falling into ill company, and trusting the keeper of a public-house in Rotherhithe with a great part of my money, and hastily squandering away the rest, all that great sum, which I got with so much pains and hazard, was gone in little more than two years' time; and, as I even rage in my own thoughts to reflect upon the manner how it was wasted, so I need record no more; the rest merits to be concealed with blushes, for that it was spent in all kinds of folly and wickedness. So this scene of my life may be said to have begun in theft, and ended in luxury; a sad setting-out, and a worse coming home.

About the year —— I began to see the bottom of my stock, and that it was time to think of further adventures; for my spoilers, as I call them, began to let me know, that as my money declined, their respect would ebb with it, and that I had nothing to expect of them further than as I might command it by the force of my money, which, in short, would not go an inch the further for all that had been spent in their favor before.

This shocked me very much, and I conceived a just abhorrence of their ingratitude; but it wore off; nor had I met with any regret at the wasting so glorious a sum of money as I brought to England with me.

I next shipped myself, in an evil hour to be sure, on a voyage to Cadiz, in a ship called the ——, and in the course of our voyage, being on the coast of Spain, was obliged to put into the Groyn, by a strong southwest wind.

Here I fell into company with some masters of mischief; and, among them, one, forwarder than the rest, began an intimate confidence with me, so that we called one another brothers, and communicated all our circumstances to one another. His name was Harris. This fellow came to me one morning, asking me if I would go on shore, and I agreed; so we got the captain's leave for the boat, and went together. When we were together, he asked me if I had a mind for an adventure that might make amends for all past misfortunes. I told him, yes, with all my heart; for I did not care where I went, having nothing to lose, and no one to leave behind me.

He then asked me if I would swear to be secret, and that, if I did not agree to what he proposed, I would nevertheless never betray him. I readily bound myself to that, upon the most solemn imprecations and curses that the devil and both of us could invent.

He told me, then, there was a brave fellow in the other ship, pointing to another English ship which rode in the harbor, who, in concert with some of the men, had resolved to mutiny the next morning, and run away with the ship; and that, if we could get strength enough among our ship's company, we might do the same. I liked the proposal very well, and he got eight of us to join with him, and he told us, that as soon as his friend had begun the work, and was master of the ship, we should be ready to do the like. This was his plot; and I, without the least hesitation, either at the villainy of the fact or the difficulty of performing it, came immediately into the wicked conspiracy, and so it went on among us; but we could not bring our part to perfection.

Accordingly, on the day appointed, his correspondent in the other ship, whose name was Wilmot, began the work, and, having seized the captain's mate and other officers, secured the ship, and gave the signal to us. We were but eleven in our ship, who were in the conspiracy, nor could we get any more that we could trust; so that, leaving the ship, we all took the boat, and went off to join the other.

Having thus left the ship I was in, we were entertained with a great deal of joy by Captain Wilmot and his new gang; and, being well prepared for all manner of roguery, bold, desperate (I mean myself), without the least checks of conscience for what I was entered upon, or for anything I might do, much less with any apprehension of what might be the consequence of it; I say, having thus embarked with this crew, which at last brought me to consort with the most famous pirates of the age, some of whom have ended their journals at the gallows, I think the giving an account of some of my other adventures may be an agreeable piece of story; and this I may venture to say beforehand, upon the word of a pirate, that I shall not be able to recollect the full, no, not by far, of the great variety which has formed one of the most reprobate schemes that ever man was capable to present to the world.

I that was, as I have hinted before, an original thief, and a pirate, even by inclination before, was now in my element, and never undertook anything in my life with more particular satisfaction.

Captain Wilmot (for so we are now to call him) being thus possessed of a ship, and in the manner as you have heard, it may be easily concluded he had nothing to do to stay in the port, or to wait either the attempts that might be made from the shore, or any change that might happen among his men. On the contrary, we weighed anchor the same tide, and stood out to sea, steering away for the Canaries. Our ship had twenty-two guns, but was able to carry thirty; and besides, as she was fitted out for a merchant-ship only, she was not furnished either with ammunition or small-arms sufficient for our design, or for the occasion we might have in case of a fight. So we put into Cadiz, that is to say, we came to an anchor in the bay; and the captain, and one whom we called young Captain Kidd, who was the gunner, [landed,] and some of the men who could best be trusted, among whom was my comrade Harris, who was made second mate, and myself, who was made a lieutenant. Some bales of English goods were proposed to be carried on shore with us for sale, but my comrade, who was a complete fellow at his business, proposed a better way for it; and having been in the town before, told us, in short, that he would buy what powder and bullet, small-arms, or anything else we wanted, on his own word, to be paid for when they came on board, in such English goods as we had there. This was much the best way, and accordingly he and the captain went on shore by themselves, and having made such a bargain as they found for their turn, came away again in two hours' time, and bringing only a butt of wine and five casks of brandy with them, we all went on board again.

The next morning two *barcos longos* came off to us, deeply laden, with five Spaniards on board them, for traffic. Our captain sold them good pennyworths, and they delivered us sixteen barrels of powder, twelve small rundlets of fine powder for our small-arms, sixty muskets, and twelve fusees for the officers; seventeen ton of cannon-ball, fifteen barrels of musket-bullets, with some swords and twenty good pair of pistols. Besides this, they brought thirteen butts of wine (for we, that were now all become gentlemen, scorned to drink the ship's beer), also sixteen puncheons of brandy, with twelve barrels of raisins and twenty chests of lemons;

all which we paid for in English goods; and, over and above, the captain received six hundred pieces of eight in money. They would have come again, but we would stay no longer.

From hence we sailed to the Canaries, and from thence onward to the West Indies, where we committed some depredation upon the Spaniards for provisions, and took some prizes, but none of any great value, while I remained with them, which was not long at that time; for, having taken a Spanish sloop on the coast of Carthagena, my friend made a motion to me, that we should desire Captain Wilmot to put us into the sloop, with a proportion of arms and ammunition, and let us try what we could do; she being much fitter for our business than the great ship, and a better sailer. This he consented to, and we appointed our rendez-vous at Tobago, making an agreement, that whatever was taken by either of our ships should be shared among the ship's company of both; all which we very punctually observed, and joined our ships again, about fifteen months after, at the island of Tobago, as above.

We cruised near two years in those seas, chiefly upon the Spaniards; not that we made any difficulty of taking English ships, or Dutch, or French, if they came in our way; and particularly, Captain Wilmot attacked a New England ship bound from the Madeiras to Jamaica, and another bound from New York to Bar-bados, with provisions; which last was a very happy supply to us. But the reason why we meddled as little with English vessels as we could, was, first, because, if they were ships of any force, we were sure of more resistance from them; and, secondly, because we found the English ships had less booty when taken, for the Spaniards generally had money on board, and that was what we best knew what to do with. Captain Wilmot was, indeed, more particularly cruel when he took any

English vessel, that they might not too soon have advice of him in England; and so the men-of-war have orders to look out for him. But this part I bury in silence for the present.

We increased our stock in these two years considerably, having taken 60,000 pieces of eight in one vessel, and 100,000 in another; and being thus first grown rich, we resolved to be strong too, for we had taken a brigantine built at Virginia, an excellent sea-boat, and a good sailer, and able to carry twelve guns; and a large Spanish frigate-built ship, that sailed incomparably well also, and which afterwards, by the help of good carpenters, we fitted up to carry twenty-eight guns. And now we wanted more hands, so we put away for the Bay of Campeachy, not doubting we should ship as many men there as we pleased; and so we did.

Here we sold the sloop that I was in; and Captain Wilmot keeping his own ship, I took the command of the Spanish frigate as captain, and my comrade Harris as eldest lieutenant, and a bold enterprising fellow he was, as any the world afforded. One culverdine was put into the brigantine, so that we were now three stout ships, well manned, and victualled for twelve months; for we had taken two or three sloops from New England and New York, laden with flour, peas, and barrelled beef and pork, going for Jamaica and Barbados; and for more beef we went on shore on the island of Cuba, where we killed as many black cattle as we pleased, though we had very little salt to cure them.

Out of all the prizes we took here we took their powder and bullet, their small-arms and cutlasses; and as for their men, we always took the surgeon and the carpenter, as persons who were of particular use to us upon many occasions; nor were they always unwilling to go with us, though for their own security, in case of accidents, they might easily pretend they were carried away by force; of which I shall give a pleasant account in the course of my other expeditions.

We had one very merry fellow here, a Quaker, whose name was William Walters, whom we took out of a sloop bound from Pennsylvania to Barbados. He was a surgeon, and they called him doctor; but he was not employed in the sloop as a surgeon, but was going to Barbados to get a berth, as the sailors call it. However, he had all his surgeon's chests on board, and we made him go with us, and take all his implements with him. He was a comic fellow indeed, a man of very good solid sense, and an excellent surgeon; but, what was worth all, very good-humored and pleasant in his conversation, and a bold, stout, brave fellow too, as any we had among us.

I found William, as I thought, not very averse to go along with us, and yet resolved to do it so that it might be apparent he was taken away by force, and to this purpose he comes to me. "Friend," says he, "thou sayest I must go with thee, and it is not in my power to resist thee if I would; but I desire thou wilt oblige the master of the sloop which I am on board to certify under his hand, that I was taken away by force and against my will." And this he said with so much satisfaction in his face, that I could not but understand him. "Aye, aye," says I, "whether it be against your will or no, I'll make him and all the men give you a certificate of it, or I'll take them all along with us, and keep them till they do." So I drew up a certificate myself, wherein I wrote that he was taken away by main force, as a prisoner, by a pirate ship; that they carried away his chest and instruments first, and then bound his hands behind him and forced him into their boat; and this was signed by the master and all his men.

Accordingly I fell a-swearing at him, and called to my men to tie his hands behind him, and so we put him into our boat and carried him away. When I had him on board, I called him to me. "Now, friend," says I, "I have brought you away by force, it is true, but I am not of the opinion I have brought you away so much against your will as they imagine. Come," says I, "you will be a useful man to us, and you shall have very good usage among us." So I unbound his hands, and first ordered all things that belonged to him to be restored to him, and our captain gave him a dram.

"Thou hast dealt friendly by me," says he, "and I will be plain with thee, whether I came willingly to thee or not. I shall make myself as useful to thee as I can, but thou knowest it is not my business to meddle when thou art to fight." "No, no," says the captain, "but you may meddle a little when we share the money." "Those things are useful to furnish a surgeon's chest," says William, and smiled, "but I shall be moderate."

In short, William was a most agreeable companion; but he had the better of us in this part, that if we were taken we were sure to be hanged, and he was sure to escape; and he knew it well enough. But, in short, he was a sprightly fellow, and fitter to be captain than any of us. I shall have often an occasion to speak of him in the rest of the story.

Our cruising so long in these seas began now to be so well known, that not in England only, but in France and Spain, accounts had been made public of our adventures, and many stories told how we murdered the people in cold blood, tying them back to back, and throwing them into the sea; one half of which, how-ever, was not true, though more was done than is fit to speak of here.

The consequence of this, however, was, that several English men-of-war were sent to the West Indies, and were particularly instructed to cruise in the Bay of Mexico, and the Gulf of Florida, and among the Bahama islands, if possible, to attack us. We were not so ignorant of things as not to expect this, after so long a stay in that part of the world; but the first certain account we had of them was at Honduras, when a vessel coming in from Jamaica told us that two English men-of-war were coming directly from Jamaica thither in quest of us. We were indeed as it were embayed, and could not have made the least shift to have got off, if they had come directly to us; but, as it happened, somebody had informed them that we were in the Bay of Campeachy, and they went directly thither, by which we were not only free of them, but were so much to the windward of them, that they could not make any attempt upon us, though they had known we were there.

We took this advantage, and stood away for Carthagena, and from thence with great difficulty beat it up at a distance from under the shore for St. Martha, till we came to the Dutch island of Curacoa, and from thence to the island of Tobago, which, as before, was our rendezvous; which, being a deserted, uninhabited island, we at the same time made use of for a retreat. Here the captain of the brigantine died, and Captain Harris, at that time my lieutenant, took the command of the brigantine.

Here we came to a resolution to go away to the coast of Brazil, and from thence to the Cape of Good Hope, and so for the East Indies; but Captain Harris, as I have said, being now captain of the brigantine, alleged that his ship was too small for so long a voyage, but that, if Captain Wilmot would consent, he would take the hazard of another cruise, and he would follow us in the first ship he could take. So we appointed our rendezvous to be at Madagascar, which was done by my recommendation of the place, and the plenty of provisions to be had there.

Accordingly, he went away from us in an evil hour; for, instead of taking a ship to follow us, he was taken, as I heard afterwards, by an English man-of-war, and being laid in irons, died of mere grief and anger before he came to England. His lieutenant, I have heard, was afterwards executed in England for a pirate; and this was the end of the man who first brought me into this unhappy trade.

We parted from Tobago three days after, bending our course for the coast of Brazil, but had not been at sea above twenty-four hours, when we were separated by a terrible storm, which held three days, with very little abatement or intermission. In this juncture Captain Wilmot happened, unluckily, to be on board my ship, to his great mortification; for we not only lost sight of his ship, but never saw her more till we came to Madagascar, where she was cast away. In short, after having in this tempest lost our fore-topmast, we were forced to put back to the isle of Tobago for shelter, and to repair our damage, which brought us all very near our destruction.

We were no sooner on shore here, and all very busy looking out for a piece of timber for a topmast, but we perceived standing in for the shore an English man-of-war of thirty-six guns. It was a great surprise to us indeed, because we were disabled so much; but, to our great good fortune, we lay pretty snug and close among the high rocks, and the man-of-war did not see us, but stood off again upon his cruise. So we only observed which way she went, and at night, leaving our work, resolved to stand off to sea, steering the contrary way from that which we observed she went; and this, we found, had the desired success, for we saw him no more. We had gotten an old mizzen-topmast on board, which made us a jury fore-topmast for the present; and so we stood away for the isle of Trinidad, where, though there were Spaniards on shore, yet we landed some men with our boat, and cut a very good piece of fir to make us a new topmast, which we got fitted up effectually; and also we got some cattle here to eke out our provisions; and calling a council of war among ourselves, we resolved to quit those seas for the present, and steer away for the coast of Brazil.

The first thing we attempted here was only getting fresh water, but we learnt that there lay the Portuguese fleet at the bay of All Saints, bound for Lisbon, ready to sail, and only waited for a fair wind. This made us lie by, wishing to see them put to sea, and, accordingly as they were with or without convoy, to attack or avoid them.

It sprung up a fresh gale in the evening at S.W. by W., which, being fair for the Portugal fleet, and the weather pleasant and agreeable, we heard the signal given to unmoor, and running in under the island of Si——, we hauled our mainsail and foresail up in the brails, lowered the topsails upon the cap, and clewed them up, that we might lie as snug as we could, expecting their coming out, and the next morning saw the whole fleet come out accordingly, but not at all to our satisfaction, for they consisted of twenty-six sail, and most of them ships of force, as well as burthen, both merchantmen and men-of-war; so, seeing there was no meddling, we lay still where we were also, till the fleet was out of sight, and then stood off and on, in hopes of meeting with further purchase.

It was not long before we saw a sail, and immediately gave her chase; but she proved an excellent sailer, and, standing out to sea, we saw plainly she trusted to her heels — that is to say, to her sails. However, as we were a clean ship, we gained upon her, though slowly, and had we had a day before us, we should certainly have come up with her; but it grew dark apace, and in that case we knew we should lose sight of her.

Our merry Quaker, perceiving us to crowd still after her in the dark, wherein we could not see which way she went, came very dryly to me. "Friend Singleton," says he, "dost thee know what we are a-doing?" Says I, "Yes; why, we are chasing yon ship, are we not?" "And how dost thou know that?" says he, very gravely still. "Nay, that's true," says I again; "we cannot be sure." "Yes, friend," says he, "I think we may be sure that we are running away from her, not chasing her. I am afraid," adds he, "thou art turned Quaker, and hast resolved not to use the hand of power, or art a coward, and art flying from thy enemy."

"What do you mean?" says I (I think I swore at him). "What do you sneer at now? You have always one dry rub or another to give us."

"Nay," says he, "it is plain enough the ship stood off to sea due east, on purpose to lose us, and thou mayest be sure her business does not lie that way; for what should she do at the coast of Africa in this latitude, which should be as far south as Congo or Angola? But as soon as it is dark, that we would lose sight of her, she will tack and stand away west again for the Brazil coast and for the bay, where thou knowest she was going before; and are we not, then, running away from her? I am greatly in hopes, friend," says the dry, gibing creature, "thou wilt turn Quaker, for I see thou art not for fighting."

"Very well, William," says I; "then I shall make an excellent pirate." However, William was in the right, and I apprehended what he meant immediately; and Captain Wilmot, who lay very sick in his cabin, overhearing us, understood him as well as I, and called out to me that William was right, and it was our best way to change our course, and stand away for the bay, where it was ten to one but we should snap her in the morning.

Accordingly we went about-ship, got our larboard tacks on board, set the top-gallant sails, and crowded for the bay of All Saints, where we came to an anchor early in the morning, just out of gunshot of the forts; we furled our sails with rope-yarns, that we might haul home the sheets without going up to loose them, and, lowering our main and fore-yards, looked just as if we had lain there a good while.

In two hours afterwards we saw our game standing in for the bay with all the sail she could make, and she came innocently into our very mouths, for we lay still till we saw her almost within gunshot, when, our foremost gears being stretched fore and aft, we first ran up our yards, and then hauled home the topsail sheets, the rope-yarns that furled them giving way of themselves; the sails were set in a few minutes; at the same time slipping our cable, we came upon her before she could get under way upon the other tack. They were so surprised that they made little or no resistance, but struck after the first broadside.

We were considering what to do with her, when William came to me. "Hark thee, friend," says he, "thou hast made a fine piece of work of it now, hast thou not, to borrow thy neighbor's ship here just at thy neighbor's door, and never ask him leave? Now, dost thou not think there are some men-of-war in the port? Thou hast given them the alarm sufficiently; thou wilt have them upon thy back before night, depend upon it, to ask thee wherefore thou didst so."

"Truly, William," said I, "for aught I know, that may be true; what, then, shall we do next?" Says he, "Thou hast but two things to do: either to go in and take all the rest, or else get thee gone before they come out and take thee; for I see they are hoisting a topmast to yon great ship, in order to put to sea immediately, and they won't be long before they come to talk with thee, and what wilt thou say to them when they ask thee why thou borrowedst their ship without leave?"

As William said, so it was. We could see by our glasses they were all in a hurry, manning and fitting some sloops they had there, and a large man-of-war, and it was plain they would soon be with us. But we were not at a loss what to do; we found the ship we had taken was laden with nothing considerable for our purpose, except some cocoa, some sugar, and twenty barrels of flour; the rest of her cargo was hides; so we took out all we thought fit for our turn, and, among the rest, all her ammunition, great shot, and small-arms, and turned her off. We also took a cable and three anchors she had, which were for our purpose, and some of her sails. She had enough left just to carry her into port, and that was all.

Having done this, we stood on upon the Brazil coast, southward, till we came to the mouth of the river Janeiro. But as we had two days the wind blowing hard at S.E. and S.S.E., we were obliged to come to an anchor under a little island, and wait for a wind. In this time the Portuguese had, it seems, given notice over land to the governor there, that a pirate was upon the coast; so that, when we came in view of the port, we saw two men-of-war riding just without the bar, whereof one, we found, was getting under sail with all possible speed, having slipped her cable on purpose to speak with us; the other was not so forward, but was preparing to follow. In less than an hour they stood both fair after us, with all the sail they could make.

Had not the night come on, William's words had been made good; they would certainly have asked us the question what we did there, for we found the foremost ship gained upon us, especially upon one tack, for we plied away from them to windward; but in the dark losing sight of them, we resolved to change our course and stand away directly for sea, not doubting that we should lose them in the night.

Whether the Portuguese commander guessed we would do so or no, I know not; but in the morning, when the daylight appeared, instead of having lost him, we found him in chase of us about a league astern; only, to our great good fortune, we could see but one of the two. However, this one was a great ship, carried six-and-forty guns, and an admirable sailer, as appeared by her outsailing us; for our ship was an excellent sailer too, as I have said before.

When I found this, I easily saw there was no remedy, but we must engage; and as we knew we could expect no quarter from those scoundrels the Portuguese, a nation I had an original aversion to, I let Captain Wilmot know how it was. The captain, sick as he was, jumped up in the cabin, and would be led out upon the deck (for he was very weak) to see how it was. "Well," says he, "we'll fight them!"

Our men were all in good heart before, but to see the captain so brisk, who had lain ill of a calenture ten or eleven days, gave them double courage, and they went all hands to work to make a clear ship and be ready. William, the Quaker, comes to me with a kind of a smile. "Friend," says he, "what does yon ship follow us for?" "Why," says I, "to fight us, you may be sure." "Well," says he, "and will he come up with us, dost thou think?" "Yes," said I, "you see she will." "Why, then, friend," says the dry wretch, "why dost thou run from her still, when thou seest she will overtake thee? Will it be better for us to be overtaken farther off than here?" "Much as one for that," says I; "why, what would you have us do?" "Do!" says he; "let us not give the poor man more trouble than needs must; let us stay for him and hear what he has to say to us." "He will talk to us in powder and ball," said I. "Very well, then," says he, "if that be his country language, we must talk to him in the same, must we not? or else how shall he understand us?" "Very well, William," says I, "we understand you." And the captain, as ill as he was, called to me, "William's right again," says he; "as good here as a league farther." So he gives a word of command, "Haul up the main-sail; we'll shorten sail for him."

Accordingly we shortened sail, and as we expected her upon our lee-side, we being then upon our starboard tack, brought eighteen of our guns to the larboard side, resolving to give him a broadside that should warm him. It was about half-an-hour before he came up with us, all which time we luffed up, that we might keep the wind of him, by which he was obliged to run up under our lee, as we designed him; when we got him upon our quarter, we edged down, and received the fire of five or six of his guns. By this time you may be sure all our hands were at their quarters, so we clapped our helm hard a-weather, let go the lee-braces of the maintop sail, and laid it a-back, and so our ship fell athwart the Portuguese ship's hawse; then we immediately poured in our broadside, raking them fore and aft, and killed them a great many men.

The Portuguese, we could see, were in the utmost confusion; and not being aware of our design, their ship having fresh way, ran their bowsprit into the fore part of our main shrouds, as that they could not easily get clear of us, and so we lay locked after that manner. The enemy could not bring above five or six guns, besides their small-arms, to bear upon us, while we played our whole broadside upon him.

In the middle of the heat of this fight, as I was very busy upon the quarterdeck, the captain calls to me, for he never stirred from us, "What the devil is friend

William a-doing yonder?" says the captain; "has he any business upon, deck?" I stepped forward, and there was friend William, with two or three stout fellows, lashing the ship's bowsprit fast to our mainmast, for fear they should get away from us; and every now and then he pulled a bottle out of his pocket, and gave the men a dram to encourage them. The shot flew about his ears as thick as may be supposed in such an action, where the Portuguese, to give them their due, fought very briskly, believing at first they were sure of their game, and trusting to their superiority; but there was William, as composed, and in as perfect tranquility as to danger, as if he had been over a bowl of punch, only very busy securing the matter, that a ship of forty-six guns should not run away from a ship of eight-and-twenty.

This work was too hot to hold long; our men behaved bravely: our gunner, a gallant man, shouted below, pouring in his shot at such a rate, that the Portuguese began to slacken their fire; we had dismounted several of their guns by firing in at their forecastle, and raking them, as I said, fore and aft. Presently comes William up to me. "Friend," says he, very calmly, "what dost thou mean? Why dost thou not visit thy neighbor in the ship, the door being open for thee?" I understood him immediately, for our guns had so torn their hull, that we had beat two port-holes into one, and the bulk-head of their steerage was split to pieces, so that they could not retire to their close quarters; so I gave the word immediately to board them. Our second lieutenant, with about thirty men, entered in an instant over the forecastle, followed by some more with the boatswain, and cutting in pieces about twenty-five men that they found upon the deck, and then throwing some grenadoes into the steerage, they entered there also; upon which the Portuguese cried quarter presently, and we mastered the ship, contrary indeed to our own expectation; for we would have compounded with them if they would have sheered off: but laying them athwart the hawse at first, and following our fire furiously, without giving them any time to get clear of us and work their ship; by this means, though they had six-and-forty guns, they were not able to fight above five or six, as I said above, for we beat them immediately from their guns in the forecastle, and killed them abundance of men between decks, so that when we entered they had hardly found men enough to fight us hand to hand upon their deck.

The surprise of joy to hear the Portuguese cry quarter, and see their ancient struck, was so great to our captain, who, as I have said, was reduced very weak with a high fever, that it gave him new life. Nature conquered the distemper, and the fever abated that very night; so that in two or three days he was sensibly better, his strength began to come, and he was able to give his orders effectually in everything that was material, and in about ten days was entirely well and about the ship.

In the meantime I took possession of the Portuguese man-of-war; and Captain Wilmot made me, or rather I made myself, captain of her for the present. About thirty of their seamen took service with us, some of which were French, some Genoese; and we set the rest on shore the next day on a little island on the coast of Brazil, except some wounded men, who were not in a condition to be removed, and whom we were bound to keep on board; but we had an occasion afterwards to dispose of them at the Cape, where, at their own request, we set them on shore.

Captain Wilmot, as soon as the ship was taken, and the prisoners stowed, was for standing in for the river Janeiro again, not doubting but we should meet with the other man-of-war, who, not having been able to find us, and having lost the company of her comrade, would certainly be returned, and might be surprised by the ship we had taken, if we carried Portuguese colors; and our men were all for it.

But our friend William gave us better counsel, for he came to me, "Friend," says he, "I understand the captain is for sailing back to the Rio Janeiro, in hopes to meet with the other ship that was in chase of thee yesterday. Is it true, dost thou intend it?" "Why, yes," says I, "William, pray why not?" "Nay," says he, "thou mayest do so if thou wilt." "Well, I know that too, William," said I, "but the captain is a man will be ruled by reason; what have you to say to it?" "Why," says William gravely, "I only ask what is thy business, and the business of all the people thou hast with thee? Is it not to get money?" "Yes, William, it is so, in our honest way." "And wouldest thou," says he, "rather have money without fighting, or fighting without money? I mean which wouldest thou have by choice, suppose it to be left to thee?" "O William," says I, "the first of the two, to be sure." "Why, then," says he, "what great gain hast thou made of the prize thou hast taken now, though it has cost the lives of thirteen of thy men, besides some hurt? It is true thou hast got the ship and some prisoners; but thou wouldest have had twice the booty in a merchant-ship, with not one quarter of the fighting; and how dost thou know either what force or what number of men may be in the other ship, and what loss thou mayest suffer, and what gain it shall be to thee if thou take her? I think, indeed, thou mayest much better let her alone."

"Why, William, it is true," said I, "and I'll go tell the captain what your opinion is, and bring you word what he says." Accordingly in I went to the captain and told him William's reasons; and the captain was of his mind, that our business was indeed fighting when we could not help it, but that our main affair was money, and that with as few blows as we could. So that adventure was laid aside, and we stood along shore again south for the river De la Plata, expecting some purchase thereabouts; especially we had our eyes upon some of the Spanish ships from Buenos Ayres, which are generally very rich in silver, and one such prize would have done our business. We plied about here, in the latitude of —— south, for near a month, and nothing offered; and here we began to consult what we should do next, for we had come to no resolution yet. Indeed, my design was always for the Cape de Bona Speranza, and so to the East Indies. I had heard some flaming stories of Captain Avery, and the fine things he had done in the Indies, which were doubled and doubled, even ten thousand fold; and from taking a great prize in the Bay of Bengal, where he took a lady, said to be the Great Mogul's daughter, with a great quantity of jewels about her, we had a story told us, that he took a Mogul ship, so the foolish sailors called it, laden with diamonds.

I would fain have had friend William's advice whither we should go, but he always put it off with some quaking quibble or other. In short, he did not care for directing us neither; whether he made a piece of conscience of it, or whether he did not care to venture having it come against him afterwards or no, this I know not; but we concluded at last without him.

We were, however, pretty long in resolving, and hankered about the Rio de la Plata a long time. At last we spied a sail to windward, and it was such a sail as I believe had not been seen in that part of the world a great while. It wanted not that we should give it chase, for it stood directly towards us, as well as they that steered could make it; and even that was more accident of weather than anything else, for if the wind had chopped about anywhere they must have gone with it. I leave any man that is a sailor, or understands anything of a ship, to judge what a figure this ship made when we first saw her, and what we could imagine was the matter with her. Her maintop-mast was come by the board about six foot above the cap, and fell forward, the head of the topgallant-mast hanging in the fore-shrouds by the stay; at the same time the parrel of the mizzen-topsail-yard by some accident giving way, the mizzen-topsail-braces (the standing part of which being fast to the main-topsail shrouds) brought the mizzen-topsail, yard and all, down with it, which spread over part of the quarterdeck like an awning; the fore-topsail was hoisted up two-thirds of the mast, but the sheets were flown; the fore-yard was lowered down upon the forecastle, the sail loose, and part of it hanging overboard. In this manner she came down upon us with the wind quartering. In a word, the figure the whole ship made was the most confounding to men that understood the sea that ever was seen. She had no boat, neither had she any colors out.

When we came near to her, we fired a gun to bring her to. She took no notice of it, nor of us, but came on just as she did before. We fired again, but it was all one. At length we came within pistol-shot of one another, but nobody answered nor appeared; so we began to think that it was a ship gone ashore somewhere in distress, and the men having forsaken her, the high tide had floated her off to sea. Coming nearer to her, we ran up alongside of her so close that we could hear a noise within her, and see the motion of several people through her ports.

Upon this we manned out two boats full of men, and very well armed, and ordered them to board her at the same minute, as near as they could, and to enter one at her fore-chains on the one side, and the other amidships on the other side. As soon as they came to the ship's side, a surprising multitude of black sailors, such as they were, appeared upon deck, and, in short, terrified our men so much that the boat which was to enter her men in the waist stood off again, and durst not board her; and the men that entered out of the other boat, finding the first boat, as they thought, beaten off, and seeing the ship full of men, jumped all back again into their boat, and put off, not knowing what the matter was. Upon this we prepared to pour in a broadside upon her; but our friend William set us to rights again here; for it seems he guessed how it was sooner than we did, and coming up to me (for it was our ship that came up with her), "Friend," says he, "I am of opinion that thou art wrong in this matter, and thy men have been wrong also in their conduct. I'll tell thee how thou shalt take this ship, without making use of those things called guns." "How can that be, William?" said I. "Why," said he, "thou mayest take her with thy helm; thou seest they keep no steerage, and thou seest the condition they are in; board her with thy ship upon her lee quarter, and so enter her from the ship. I am persuaded thou wilt take her without fighting, for there is some mischief has befallen the ship, which we know nothing of."

In a word, it being a smooth sea, and little wind, I took his advice, and laid her aboard. Immediately our men entered the ship, where we found a large ship, with upwards of 600 negroes, men and women, boys and girls, and not one Christian or white man on board.

I was struck with horror at the sight; for immediately I concluded, as was partly the case, that these black devils had got loose, had murdered all the white men, and thrown them into the sea; and I had no sooner told my mind to the men, but the thought so enraged them that I had much ado to keep my men from cutting them all in pieces. But William, with many persuasions, prevailed upon them, by telling them that it was nothing but what, if they were in the negroes' condition, they would do if they could; and that the negroes had really the highest injustice done them, to be sold for slaves without their consent; and that the law of nature dictated it to them; that they ought not to kill them, and that it would be willful murder to do it.

This prevailed with them, and cooled their first heat; so they only knocked down twenty or thirty of them, and the rest ran all down between decks to their first places, believing, as we fancied, that we were their first masters come again.

It was a most unaccountable difficulty we had next; for we could not make them understand one word we said, nor could we understand one word ourselves that they said. We endeavored by signs to ask them whence they came; but they could make nothing of it. We pointed to the great cabin, to the round-house, to the cook-room, then to our faces, to ask if they had no white men on board, and where they were gone; but they could not understand what we meant. On the other hand, they pointed to our boat and to their ship, asking questions as well as they could, and said a thousand things, and expressed themselves with great earnestness; but we could not understand a word of it all, or know what they meant by any of their signs.

We knew very well they must have been taken on board the ship as slaves, and that it must be by some European people too. We could easily see that the ship was a Dutch-built ship, but very much altered, having been built upon, and, as we supposed, in France; for we found two or three French books on board, and afterwards we found clothes, linen, lace, some old shoes, and several other things. We found among the provisions some barrels of Irish beef, some Newfoundland fish, and several other evidences that there had been Christians on board, but saw no remains of them. We found not a sword, gun, pistol, or weapon of any kind, except some cutlasses; and the negroes had hid them below where they lay. We asked them what was become of all the small-arms, pointing to our own and to the places where those belonging to the ship had hung. One of the negroes understood me presently, and beckoned to me to come upon the deck, where, taking my fuzee, which I never let go out of my hand for some time after we had mastered the ship — I say, offering to take hold of it, he made the proper motion of throwing it into the sea; by which I understood, as I did afterwards, that they had thrown all the small-arms, powder, shot, swords, &c., into the sea, believing, as I supposed, those things would kill them, though the men were gone.

After we understood this we made no question but that the ship's crew, having been surprised by these desperate rogues, had gone the same way, and had been thrown overboard also. We looked all over the ship to see if we could find any blood, and we thought we did perceive some in several places; but the heat of the sun, melting the pitch and tar upon the decks, made it impossible for us to discern it exactly, except in the round-house, where we plainly saw that there had been much blood. We found the scuttle open, by which we supposed that the captain and those that were with him had made their retreat into the great cabin, or those in the cabin had made their escape up into the round-house.

But that which confirmed us most of all in what had happened was that, upon further inquiry, we found that there were seven or eight of the negroes very much wounded, two or three of them with shot, whereof one had his leg broken and lay in a miserable condition, the flesh being mortified, and, as our friend William said, in two days more he would have died. William was a most dexterous surgeon, and he showed it in this cure; for though all the surgeons we had on board both our ships (and we had no less than five that called themselves bred surgeons, besides two or three who were pretenders or assistants) — though all these gave their opinions that the negro's leg must be cut off, and that his life could not be saved without it; that the mortification had touched the marrow in the bone, that the tendons were mortified, and that he could never have the use of his leg if it should be cured, William said nothing in general, but that his opinion was otherwise, and that he desired the wound might be searched, and that he would then tell them further. Accordingly he went to work with the leg; and, as he desired that he might have some of the surgeons to assist him, we appointed him two of the ablest of them to help, and all of them to look on, if they thought fit.

William went to work his own way, and some of them pretended to find fault at first. However, he proceeded and searched every part of the leg where he suspected the mortification had touched it; in a word, he cut off a great deal of mortified flesh, in all which the poor fellow felt no pain. William proceeded till he brought the vessels which he had cut to bleed, and the man to cry out; then he reduced the splinters of the bone, and, calling for help, set it, as we call it, and bound it up, and laid the man to rest, who found himself much easier than before.

At the first opening the surgeons began to triumph; the mortification seemed to spread, and a long red streak of blood appeared from the wound upwards to the middle of the man's thigh, and the surgeons told me the man would die in a few hours. I went to look at it, and found William himself under some surprise; but when I asked him how long he thought the poor fellow could live, he looked gravely at me, and said, "As long as thou canst; I am not at all apprehensive of his life," said he, "but I would cure him, if I could, without making a cripple of him." I found he was not just then upon the operation as to his leg, but was mixing up something to give the poor creature, to repel, as I thought, the spreading contagion, and to abate or prevent any feverish temper that might happen in the blood; after which he went to work again, and opened the leg in two places above the wound, cutting out a great deal of mortified flesh, which it seemed was occasioned by the bandage, which had pressed the parts too much; and withal, the blood being at the time in a more than common disposition to mortify, might assist to spread it.

Well, our friend William conquered all this, cleared the spreading mortification, and the red streak went off again, the flesh began to heal, and matter to run; and in a few days the man's spirits began to recover, his pulse beat regular, he had no fever, and gathered strength daily; and, in a word, he was a perfect sound man in about ten weeks, and we kept him amongst us, and made him an able seaman. But to return to the ship: we never could come at a certain information about it, till some of the negroes which we kept on board, and whom we taught to speak English, gave the account of it afterwards, and this maimed man in particular.

We inquired, by all the signs and motions we could imagine, what was become of the people, and yet we could get nothing from them. Our lieutenant was for torturing some of them to make them confess, but William opposed that vehemently; and when he heard it was under consideration he came to me. "Friend," says he, "I make a request to thee not to put any of these poor wretches to torment." "Why, William," said I, "why not? You see they will not give any account of what is become of the white men." "Nay," says William, "do not say so; I suppose they have given thee a full account of every particular of it." "How so?" says I; "pray what are we the wiser for all their jabbering?" "Nay," says William, "that may be thy fault, for aught I know; thou wilt not punish the poor men because they cannot speak English; and perhaps they never heard a word of English before. Now, I may very well suppose that they have given thee a large account of everything; for thou seest with what earnestness, and how long, some of them have talked to thee; and if thou canst not understand their-language, nor they thine, how can they help that? At the best, thou dost but suppose that they have not told thee the whole truth of the story; and, on the contrary, I suppose they have; and how wilt thou decide the question, whether thou art right or whether I am right? Besides, what can they say to thee when thou askest them a question upon the torture, and at the same time they do not understand the question, and thou dost not know whether they say aye or no?"

It is no compliment to my moderation to say I was convinced by these reasons; and yet we had all much ado to keep our second lieutenant from murdering some of them, to make them tell. What if they had told? He did not understand one word of it; but he would not be persuaded but that the negroes must needs understand him when he asked them whether the ship had any boat or no, like ours, and what was become of it.

But there was no remedy but to wait till we made these people understand English, and to adjourn the story till that time. The case was thus: where they were taken on board the ship, that we could never understand, because they never knew the English names which we give to those coasts, or what nation they were who belonged to the ship, because they knew not one tongue from another; but thus far the negro I examined, who was the same whose leg William had cured, told us, that they did not speak the same language as we spoke, nor the same our Portuguese spoke; so that in all probability they must be French or Dutch.

Then he told us that the white men used them barbarously; that they beat them unmercifully; that one of the negro men had a wife and two negro children, one a daughter, about sixteen years old; that a white man abused the negro man's wife, and afterwards his daughter, which, as he said, made all the negro men mad; and that the woman's husband was in a great rage; at which the white man was so provoked that he threatened to kill him; but, in the night, the negro man, being loose, got a great club, by which he made us understand he meant a handspike, and that when the same Frenchman (if it was a Frenchman) came among them again, he began again to abuse the negro man's wife, at which the negro, taking up the handspike, knocked his brains out at one blow; and then taking the key from him with which he usually unlocked the handcuffs which the negroes were fettered with, he set about a hundred of them at liberty, who, getting up upon the deck by the same scuttle that the white men came down, and taking the man's cutlass who was killed, and laying hold of what came next them, they fell upon the men that were upon the deck, and killed them all, and afterwards those they found upon the forecastle; that the captain and his other men, who were in the cabin and the round-house, defended themselves with great courage, and shot out at the loopholes at them, by which he and several other men were wounded, and some killed; but that they broke into the round-house after a long dispute, where they killed two of the white men, but owned that the two white men killed eleven of their men before they could break in; and then the rest, having got down the scuttle into the great cabin, wounded three more of them.

That, after this, the gunner of the ship having secured himself in the gun-room, one of his men hauled up the longboat close under the stern, and putting into her all the arms and ammunition they could come at, got all into the boat, and afterwards took in the captain, and those that were with him, out of the great cabin. When they were all thus embarked, they resolved to lay the ship aboard again, and try to recover it. That they boarded the ship in a desperate manner, and killed at first all that stood in their way; but the negroes being by this time all loose, and having gotten some arms, though they understood nothing of powder and bullet, or guns, yet the men could never master them. However, they lay under the ship's bow, and got out all the men they had left in the cook-room, who had maintained themselves there, notwithstanding all the negroes could do, and with their small-arms killed between thirty and forty of the negroes, but were at last forced to leave them.

They could give me no account whereabouts this was, whether near the coast of Africa, or far off, or how long it was before the ship fell into our hands; only, in general, it was a great while ago, as they called it; and, by all we could learn, it was within two or three days after they had set sail from the coast. They told us that they had killed about thirty of the white men, having knocked them on the head with crows and handspikes, and such things as they could get; and one strong negro killed three of them with an iron crow, after he was shot twice through the body; and that he was afterwards shot through the head by the captain himself at the door of the round-house, which he had split open with the crow; and this we supposed was the occasion of the great quantity of blood which we saw at the round-house door.

The same negro told us that they threw all the powder and shot they could find into the sea, and they would have thrown the great guns into the sea if they could have lifted them. Being asked how they came to have their sails in such a condition, his answer was, "They no understand; they no know what the sails do;" that was, they did not so much as know that it was the sails that made the ship go, or understand what they meant, or what to do with them. When we asked him whither they were going, he said they did not know, but believed they should go home to their own country again. I asked him, in particular, what he thought we were when we first came up with them? He said they were terribly frighted, believing we were the same white men that had gone away in their boats, and were come again in a great ship, with the two boats with them, and expected they would kill them all.

This was the account we got out of them, after we had taught them to speak English, and to understand the names and use of the things belonging to the ship which they had occasion to speak of; and we observed that the fellows were too innocent to dissemble in their relation, and that they all agreed in the particulars, and were always in the same story, which confirmed very much the truth of what they said.

Having taken this ship, our next difficulty was, what to do with the negroes. The Portuguese in the Brazils would have bought them all of us, and been glad of the purchase, if we had not showed ourselves enemies there, and been known for pirates; but, as it was, we durst not go ashore anywhere thereabouts, or treat with any of the planters, because we should raise the whole country upon us; and, if there were any such things as men-of-war in any of their ports, we should be as sure to be attacked by them, and by all the force they had by land or sea.

Nor could we think of any better success if we went northward to our own plantations. One while we determined to carry them all away to Buenos Ayres, and sell them there to the Spaniards; but they were really too many for them to make use of; and to carry them round to the South Seas, which was the only remedy that was left, was so far that we should be no way able to subsist them for so long a voyage.

At last, our old, never-failing friend, William, helped us out again, as he had often done at a dead lift. His proposal was this, that he should go as master of the ship, and about twenty men, such as we could best trust, and attempt to trade privately, upon the coast of Brazil, with the planters, not at the principal ports, because that would not be admitted.

We all agreed to this, and appointed to go away ourselves towards the Rio de la Plata, where we had thought of going before, and to wait for him, not there, but at Port St Pedro, as the Spaniards call it, lying at the mouth of the river which they call Rio Grande, and where the Spaniards had a small fort and a few people, but we believe there was nobody in it.

Here we took up our station, cruising off and on, to see if we could meet any ships going to or coming from the Buenos Ayres or the Rio de la Plata; but we met with nothing worth notice. However, we employed ourselves in things necessary for our going off to sea; for we filled all our water-casks, and got some fish for our present use, to spare as much as possible our ship's stores.

William, in the meantime, went away to the north, and made the land about the Cape de St Thomas; and betwixt that and the isles De Tuberon he found means to trade with the planters for all his negroes, as well the women as the men, and at a very good price too; for William, who spoke Portuguese pretty well, told them a fair story enough, that the ship was in scarcity of provisions, that they were driven a great way out of their way, and indeed, as we say, out of their knowledge, and that they must go up to the northward as far as Jamaica, or sell there upon the coast. This was a very plausible tale, and was easily believed; and, if you observe the manner of the negroes' sailing, and what happened in their voyage, was every word of it true.

By this method, and being true to one another, William passed for what he was — I mean, for a very honest fellow; and by the assistance of one planter, who sent to some of his neighbor planters, and managed the trade among themselves, he got a quick market; for in less than five weeks William sold all his negroes, and at last sold the ship itself, and shipped himself and his twenty men, with two negro boys whom he had left, in a sloop, one of those which the planters used to send on board for the negroes. With this sloop Captain William, as we then called him, came away, and found us at Port St Pedro, in the latitude of 32 degrees 30 minutes south.

Nothing was more surprising to us than to see a sloop come along the coast, carrying Portuguese colors, and come in directly to us, after we were assured he had discovered both our ships. We fired a gun, upon her nearer approach, to bring her to an anchor, but immediately she fired five guns by way of salute, and spread her English ancient. Then we began to guess it was friend William, but wondered what was the meaning of his being in a sloop, whereas we sent him away in a ship of near 300 tons; but he soon let us into the whole history of his management, with which we had a great deal of reason to be very well satisfied. As soon as he had brought the sloop to an anchor, he came aboard of my ship, and there he gave us an account how he began to trade by the help of a Portuguese planter, who lived near the seaside; how he went on shore and went up to the first house he could see, and asked the man of the house to sell him some hogs, pretending at first he only stood in upon the coast to take in fresh water and buy some provisions; and the man not only sold him seven fat hogs, but invited him in, and gave him, and five men he had with him, a very good dinner; and he invited the planter on board his ship, and, in return for his kindness, gave him a negro girl for his wife.

This so obliged the planter that the next morning he sent him on board, in a great luggage-boat, a cow and two sheep, with a chest of sweetmeats and some sugar, and a great bag of tobacco, and invited Captain William on shore again; that, after this, they grew from one kindness to another; that they began to talk about trading for some negroes; and William, pretending it was to do him service, consented to sell him thirty negroes for his private use in his plantation, for which he gave William ready money in gold, at the rate of five-and-thirty moidores per head; but the planter was obliged to use great caution in the bringing them on shore; for which purpose he made William weigh and stand out to sea, and put in again, about fifty miles farther north, where at a little creek he took the negroes on shore at another plantation, being a friend's of his, whom, it seems, he could trust.

This remove brought William into a further intimacy, not only with the first planter, but also with his friends, who desired to have some of the negroes also;

so that, from one to another, they bought so many, till one overgrown planter took 100 negroes, which was all William had left, and sharing them with another planter, that other planter chaffered with William for ship and all, giving him in exchange a very clean, large, well-built sloop of near sixty tons, very well furnished, carrying six guns; but we made her afterwards carry twelve guns. William had 300 moidores of gold, besides the sloop, in payment for the ship; and with this money he stored the sloop as full as she could hold with provisions, especially bread, some pork, and about sixty hogs alive; among the rest, William got eighty barrels of good gunpowder, which was very much for our purpose; and all the provisions which were in the French ship he took out also.

This was a very agreeable account to us, especially when we saw that William had received in gold coined, or by weight, and some Spanish silver, 60,000 pieces of eight, besides a new sloop, and a vast quantity of provisions.

We were very glad of the sloop in particular, and began to consult what we should do, whether we had not best turn off our great Portuguese ship, and stick to our first ship and the sloop, seeing we had scarce men enough for all three, and that the biggest ship was thought too big for our business. However, another dispute, which was now decided, brought the first to a conclusion. The first dispute was, whither we should go. My comrade, as I called him now, that is to say, he that was my captain before we took this Portuguese man-of-war, was for going to the South Seas, and coasting up the west side of America, where we could not fail of making several good prizes upon the Spaniards; and that then, if occasion required it, we might come home by the South Seas to the East Indies, and so go round the globe, as others had done before us.

But my head lay another way. I had been in the East Indies, and had entertained a notion ever since that, if we went thither, we could not fail of making good work of it, and that we might have a safe retreat, and good beef to victual our ship, among my old friends the natives of Zanzibar, on the coast of Mozambique, or the island of St Lawrence. I say, my thoughts lay this way; and I read so many lectures to them all of the advantages they would certainly make of their strength by the prizes they would take in the Gulf of Mocha, or the Red Sea, and on the coast of Malabar, or the Bay of Bengal, that I amazed them.

With these arguments I prevailed on them, and we all resolved to steer away S.E. for the Cape of Good Hope; and, in consequence of this resolution, we concluded to keep the sloop, and sail with all three, not doubting, as I assured them, but we should find men there to make up the number wanting, and if not, we might cast any of them off when we pleased.

We could do no less than make our friend William captain of the sloop which, with such good management, he had brought us. He told us, though with much good manners, he would not command her as a frigate; but, if we would give her to him for his share of the Guinea ship, which we came very honestly by, he would keep us company as a victualler, if we commanded him, as long as he was under the same force that took him away.

We understood him, so gave him the sloop, but upon condition that he should not go from us, and should be entirely under our command. However, William was not so easy as before; and, indeed, as we afterwards wanted the sloop to cruise for purchase, and a right thorough-paced pirate in her, so I was in such pain for William that I could not be without him, for he was my privy counselor and companion upon all occasions; so I put a Scotsman, a bold, enterprising, gallant fellow, into her, named Gordon, and made her carry twelve guns and four petereroes, though, indeed, we wanted men, for we were none of us manned in proportion to our force.

We sailed away for the Cape of Good Hope the beginning of October 1706, and passed by, in sight of the Cape, the 12th of November following, having met with a great deal of bad weather. We saw several merchant-ships in the roads there, as well English as Dutch, whether outward bound or homeward we could not tell; be it what it would, we did not think fit to come to an anchor, not knowing what they might be, or what they might attempt against us, when they knew what we were. However, as we wanted fresh water, we sent the two boats belonging to the Portuguese man-of-war, with all Portuguese seamen or negroes in them, to the watering-place, to take in water; and in the meantime we hung out a Portuguese ancient at sea, and lay by all that night. They knew not what we were, but it seems we passed for anything but really what we was.

Our boats returning the third time loaden, about five o'clock next morning, we thought ourselves sufficiently watered, and stood away to the eastward; but, before our men returned the last time, the wind blowing an easy gale at west, we perceived a boat in the grey of the morning under sail, crowding to come up with us, as if they were afraid we should be gone. We soon found it was an English longboat, and that it was pretty full of men. We could not imagine what the meaning of it should be; but, as it was but a boat, we thought there could be no great harm in it to let them come on board; and if it appeared they came only to inquire who we were, we would give them a full account of our business, by taking them along with us, seeing we wanted men as much as anything. But they saved us the labor of being in doubt how to dispose of them; for it seems our Portuguese seamen, who went for water, had not been so silent at the watering-places as we thought they would have been. But the case, in short, was this: Captain —— (I forbear his name at present, for a particular reason), captain of an East India merchant-ship, bound afterwards for China, had found some reason to be very severe with his men, and had handled some of them very roughly at St Helena; insomuch, that they threatened among themselves to leave the ship the first opportunity, and had long wished for that opportunity. Some of these men, it seems, had met with our boat at the watering-place, and inquiring of one another who we were, and upon what account, whether the Portuguese seamen, by faltering in their account, made them suspect that we were out upon the cruise, or whether they told it in plain English or no (for they all spoke English enough to be understood), but so it was, that as soon as ever the men carried the news on board, that the ships which lay by to the eastward were English, and that they were going upon the *account*, which, by they way, was a sea term for a pirate; I say, as soon as ever they heard it, they went to work, and getting all things ready in the night, their chests and clothes, and whatever else they could, they came away before it was day, and came up with us about seven o'clock.

When they came by the ship's side which I commanded we hailed them in the usual manner, to know what and who they were, and what their business. They answered they were Englishmen, and desired to come on board. We told them they might lay the ship on board, but ordered they should let only one man enter the ship till the captain knew their business, and that he should come without any arms. They said, Aye, with all their hearts.

We presently found their business, and that they desired to go with us; and as for their arms, they desired we would send men on board the boat, and that they would deliver them all to us, which was done. The fellow that came up to me told me how they had been used by their captain, how he had starved the men, and used them like dogs, and that, if the rest of the men knew they should be admitted, he was satisfied two-thirds of them would leave the ship. We found the fellows were very hearty in their resolution, and jolly brisk sailors they were; so I told them I would do nothing without our admiral, that was the captain of the other ship; so I sent my pinnace on board Captain Wilmot, to desire him to come on board. But he was indisposed, and being to leeward, excused his coming, but left it all to me; but before my boat was returned, Captain Wilmot called to me by his speaking-trumpet, which all the men might hear as well as I; thus, calling me by my name, "I hear they are honest fellows; pray tell them they are all welcome, and make them a bowl of punch."

As the men heard it as well as I, there was no need to tell them what the captain said; and, as soon as the trumpet had done, they set up a huzza, that showed us they were very hearty in their coming to us; but we bound them to us by a stronger obligation still after this, for when we came to Madagascar, Captain Wilmot, with consent of all the ship's company, ordered that these men should have as much money given them out of the stock as was due to them for their pay in the ship they had left; and after that we allowed them twenty pieces of eight a man bounty money; and thus we entered them upon shares, as we were all, and brave stout fellows they were, being eighteen in number, whereof two were midshipmen, and one a carpenter.

It was the 28th of November, when, having had some

bad weather, we came to an anchor in the road off St Augustine Bay, at the southwest end of my old acquaintance the isle of Madagascar. We lay here awhile and trafficked with the natives for some good beef; though the weather was so hot that we could not promise ourselves to salt any of it up to keep; but I showed them the way which we practiced before, to salt it first with saltpetre, then cure it by drying it in the sun, which made it eat very agreeably, though not so wholesome for our men, that not agreeing with our way of cooking, viz., boiling with pudding, brewis, &c., and particularly this way, would be too salt, and the fat of the meat be rusty, or dried away so as not to be eaten.

This, however, we could not help, and made ourselves amends by feeding heartily on the fresh beef while we were there, which was excellent, good and fat, every way as tender and as well relished as in England, and thought to be much better to us who had not tasted any in England for so long a time.

Having now for some time remained here, we began to consider that this was not a place for our business; and I, that had some views a particular way of my own, told them that this was not a station for those who looked for purchase; that there were two parts of the island which were particularly proper for our purposes; first, the bay on the east side of the island, and from thence to the island Mauritius, which was the usual way which ships that came from the Malabar coast, or the coast of Coromandel, Fort St George, &c., used to take, and where, if we waited for them, we ought to take our station.

But, on the other hand, as we did not resolve to fall upon the European traders, who were generally ships of force and well manned, and where blows must be looked for; so I had another prospect, which I promised myself would yield equal profit, or perhaps greater, without any of the hazard and difficulty of the former; and this was the Gulf of Mocha, or the Red Sea.

I told them that the trade here was great, the ships rich, and the Strait of Babelmandel narrow; so that there was no doubt but we might cruise so as to let nothing slip our hands, having the seas open from the Red Sea, along the coast of Arabia, to the Persian Gulf, and the Malabar side of the Indies.

I told them what I had observed when I sailed round the island in my former progress; how that, on the northernmost point of the island, there were several very good harbors and roads for our ships; that the natives were even more civil and tractable, if possible, than those where we were, not having been so often ill-treated by European sailors as those had in the south and east sides; and that we might always be sure of a retreat, if we were driven to put in by any necessity, either of enemies or weather.

They were easily convinced of the reasonableness of my scheme; and Captain Wilmot, whom I now called our admiral, though he was at first of the mind to go and lie at the island Mauritius, and wait for some of the European merchant-ships from the road of Coromandel, or the Bay of Bengal, was now of my mind. It is true we were strong enough to have attacked an English East India ship of the greatest force, though some of them were said to carry fifty guns; but I represented to him that we were sure to have blows and blood if we took them; and, after we had done, their loading was not of equal value to us, because we had no room to dispose of their merchandise; and, as our circumstances stood, we had rather have taken one outward-bound East India ship, with her ready cash on board, perhaps to the value of forty or fifty thousand pounds, than three homeward-bound, though their loading would at London be worth three times the money, because we knew not whither to go to dispose of the cargo; whereas the ships from London had abundance of things we knew how to make use of besides their money, such as their stores of provisions and liquors, and great quantities of the like sent to the governors and factories at the English settlements for their use; so that, if we resolved to look for our own country ships, it should be those that were outward-bound, not the London ships homeward.

All these things considered, brought the admiral to be of my mind entirely; so, after taking in water and some fresh provisions where we lay, which was near Cape St Mary, on the southwest corner of the island, we weighed and stood away south, and afterwards S.S.E., to round the island, and in about six days' sail got out of the wake of the island, and steered away north, till we came off Port Dauphin, and then north by east, to the latitude of 13 degrees 40 minutes, which was, in short, just at the farthest part of the island; and the admiral, keeping ahead, made the open sea fair to the west, clear of the whole island; upon which he brought to, and we sent a sloop to stand in round the farthest point north, and coast along the shore, and see for a harbor to put into, which they did, and soon brought us an account that there was a deep bay, with a very good road, and several little islands, under which they found good riding, in ten to seventeen fathom water, and accordingly there we put in.

However, we afterwards found occasion to remove our station, as you shall hear presently. We had now nothing to do but go on shore, and acquaint ourselves a little with the natives, take in fresh water and some fresh provisions, and then to sea again. We found the people very easy to deal with, and some cattle they had; but it being at the extremity of the island, they had not such quantities of cattle here. However, for the present we resolved to appoint this for our place of rendezvous, and go and look out. This was about the latter end of April.

Accordingly we put to sea, and cruised away to the northward, for the Arabian coast. It was a long run, but as the winds generally blow trade from the S. and S.S.E. from May to September, we had good weather; and in about twenty days we made the island of Socotra, lying south from the Arabian coast, and E.S.E. from the mouth of the Gulf of Mocha, or the Red Sea.

Here we took in water, and stood off and on upon the Arabian shore. We had not cruised here above three days, or thereabouts, but I spied a sail, and gave her chase; but when we came up with her, never was such a poor prize chased by pirates that looked for booty, for we found nothing in her but poor, half-naked Turks, going a pilgrimage to Mecca, to the tomb of their prophet Mahomet. The junk that carried them had no one thing worth taking away but a little rice and some coffee, which was all the poor wretches had for their subsistence; so we let them go, for indeed we knew not what to do with them.

The same evening we chased another junk with two masts, and in something better plight to look at than the former. When we came on board we found them upon the same errand, but only that they were people of some better fashion than the other; and here we got some plunder, some Turkish stores, a few diamonds in the ear-drops of five or six persons, some fine Persian carpets, of which they made their saffras to lie upon, and some money; so we let them go also.

We continued here eleven days longer, and saw nothing but now and then a fishing-boat; but the twelfth day of our cruise we spied a ship: indeed I thought at first it had been an English ship, but it appeared to be an European freighted for a voyage from Goa, on the coast of Malabar, to the Red Sea, and was very rich. We chased her, and took her without any fight, though they had some guns on board too, but not many. We found her manned with Portuguese seamen, but under the direction of five merchant Turks, who had hired her on the coast of Malabar of some Portugal merchants, and had laden her with pepper, saltpetre, some spices, and the rest of the loading was chiefly calicoes and wrought silks, some of them very rich.

We took her and carried her to Socotra; but we really knew not what to do with her, for the same reasons as before; for all their goods were of little or no value to us. After some days we found means to let one of the Turkish merchants know, that if he would ransom the ship we would take a sum of money and let them go. He told me that if I would let one of them go on shore for the money they would do it; so we adjusted the value of the cargo at 30,000 ducats. Upon this agreement, we allowed the sloop to carry him on shore, at Dofar, in Arabia, where a rich merchant laid down the money for them, and came off with our sloop; and on payment of the money we very fairly and honestly let them go.

Some days after this we took an Arabian junk, going from the Gulf of Persia to Mocha, with a good quantity of pearl on board. We gutted him of the pearl, which it seems was belonging to some merchants at Mocha, and let him go, for there was nothing else worth our taking.

We continued cruising up and down here till we began to find our provisions grow low, when Captain Wilmot, our admiral, told us it was time to think of going back to the rendezvous; and the rest of the men said the same, being a little weary of beating about for above three months together, and meeting with little or nothing compared to our great expectations; but I was very loth to part with the Red Sea at so cheap a rate, and pressed them to tarry a little longer, which at my instance they did; but three days afterwards, to our great misfortune, understood that, by landing the Turkish merchants at Dofar, we had alarmed the coast as far as the Gulf of Persia, so that no vessel would stir that way, and consequently nothing was to be expected on that side.

I was greatly mortified at this news, and could no longer withstand the importunities of the men to return to Madagascar. However, as the wind continued still to blow at S.S.E. by S., we were obliged to stand away towards the coast of Africa and the Cape Guardafui, the winds being more variable under the shore than in the open sea.

Here we chopped upon a booty which we did not look for, and which made amends for all our waiting; for the very same hour that we made land we spied a large vessel sailing along the shore to the southward. The ship was of Bengal, belonging to the Great Mogul's country, but had on board a Dutch pilot, whose name, if I remember right, was Vandergest, and several European seamen, whereof three were English. She was in no condition to resist us. The rest of her seamen were Indians of the Mogul's subjects, some Malabars and some others. There were five Indian merchants on board, and some Armenians. It seems they had been at Mocha with spices, silks, diamonds, pearls, calico, &c., such goods as the country afforded, and had little on board now but money in pieces of eight, which, by the way, was just what we wanted; and the three English seamen came along with us, and the Dutch pilot would have done so too, but the two Armenian merchants entreated us not to take him, for that he being their pilot, there was none of the men knew how to guide the ship; so, at their request, we refused him; but we made them promise he should not be used ill for being willing to go with us.

We got near 200,000 pieces of eight in this vessel; and, if they said true, there was a Jew of Goa, who intended to have embarked with them, who had 200,000 pieces of eight with him, all his own; but his good fortune, springing out of his ill fortune, hindered him, or he fell sick at Mocha, and could not be ready to travel, which was the saving of his money.

There was none with me at the taking this prize but the sloop, for Captain Wilmot's ship proving leaky, he went away for the rendezvous before us, and arrived there the middle of December; but not liking the port, he left a great cross on shore, with directions written on a plate of lead fixed to it, for us to come after him to the great bays at Mangahelly, where he found a very good harbor; but we learned a piece of news here that kept us from him a great while, which the admiral took offence at; but we stopped his mouth with his share of 200,000 pieces of eight to him and his ship's crew. But the story which interrupted our coming to him was this. Between Mangahelly and another point, called Cape St Sebastian, there came on shore in the night an European ship, and whether by stress of weather or want of a pilot I know not, but the ship stranded and could not be got off.

We lay in the cove or harbor, where, as I have said, our rendezvous was appointed, and had not yet been on shore, so we had not seen the directions our admiral had left for us.

Our friend William, of whom I have said nothing a great while, had a great mind one day to go on shore, and importuned me to let him have a little troop to go with him, for safety, that they might see the country. I was mightily against it for many reasons; but particularly I told him he knew the natives were but savages, and they were very treacherous, and I desired him that he would not go; and, had he gone on much farther, I believe I should have downright refused him, and commanded him not to go.

But, in order to persuade me to let him go, he told me he would give me an account of the reason why he was so importunate. He told me, the last night he had a dream, which was so forcible, and made such an impression upon his mind, that he could not be quiet till he had made the proposal to me to go; and if I refused him, then he thought his dream was significant; and if not, then his dream was at an end.

His dream was, he said, that he went on shore with thirty men, of which the cockswain, he said, was one, upon the island; and that they found a mine of gold, and enriched them all. But this was not the main thing, he said, but that the same morning he had dreamed so, the cockswain came to him just then, and told him that he dreamed he went on shore on the island of Madagascar, and that some men came to him and told him they would show him where he should get a prize which would make them all rich.

These two things put together began to weigh with me a little, though I was never inclined to give any heed to dreams; but William's importunity turned me effectually, for I always put a great deal of stress upon his judgment; so that, in short, I gave them leave to go, but I charged them not to go far off from the seacoast; that, if they were forced down to the seaside upon any occasion, we might perhaps see them, and fetch them off with our boats.

They went away early in the morning, one-and-thirty men of them in number, very well armed, and very stout fellows; they traveled all the day, and at night made us a signal that all was well, from the top of a hill, which we had agreed on, by making a great fire.

Next day they marched down the hill on the other side, inclining towards the seaside, as they had promised, and saw a very pleasant valley before them, with a river in the middle of it, which, a little farther below them, seemed to be big enough to bear small ships; they marched apace towards this river, and were surprised with the noise of a piece going off, which, by the sound, could not be far off. They listened long, but could hear no more; so they went on to the river-side, which was a very fine fresh stream, but widened apace, and they kept on by the banks of it, till, almost at once, it opened or widened into a good large creek or harbor, about five miles from the sea; and that which was still more surprising, as they marched forward, they plainly saw in the mouth of the harbor, or creek, the wreck of a ship.

The tide was up, as we call it, so that it did net appear very much above the water, but, as they made downwards, they found it grow bigger and bigger; and the tide soon after ebbing out, they found it lay dry upon the sands, and appeared to be the wreck of a considerable vessel, larger than could be expected in that country.

After some time, William, taking out his glass to look at it more nearly, was surprised with hearing a musket-shot whistle by him, and immediately after that he heard the gun, and saw the smoke from the other side; upon which our men immediately fired three muskets, to discover, if possible, what or who they were. Upon the noise of these guns, abundance of men came running down to the shore from among the trees; and our men could easily perceive that they were Europeans, though they knew not of what nation; however, our men hallooed to them as loud as they could, and by-and-by they got a long pole, and set it up, and hung a white shirt upon it for a flag of truce.

They on the other side saw it, by the help of their glasses, too, and quickly after our men see a boat launch off from the shore, as they thought, but it was from another creek, it seems; and immediately they came rowing over the creek to our men, carrying also a white flag as a token of truce.

It is not easy to describe the surprise, or joy and satisfaction, that appeared on both sides, to see not only white men, but Englishmen, in a place so remote; but what then must it be when they came to know one another, and to find that they were not only country-men but comrades, and that this was the very ship that Captain Wilmot, our admiral, commanded, and whose company we had lost in the storm at Tobago, after making an agreement to rendezvous at Madagascar!

They had, it seems, got intelligence of us when they came to the south part of the island, and had been a-roving as far as the Gulf of Bengal, when they met Captain Avery, with whom they joined, took several rich prizes, and, amongst the rest, one ship with the Great Mogul's daughter, and an immense treasure in money and jewels; and from thence they came about the coast of Coromandel, and afterwards that of Mala-bar, into the Gulf of Persia, where they also took some prize, and then designed for the south part of Mada-gascar; but the winds blowing hard at S.E. and S.E. by E., they came to the northward of the isle, and being after that separated by a furious tempest from the N.W., they were forced into the mouth of that creek, where they lost their ship. And they told us, also, that they heard that Captain Avery himself had lost his ship also not far off.

When they had thus acquainted one another with their fortunes, the poor overjoyed men were in haste to go back to communicate their joy to their comrades; and, leaving some of their men with ours, the rest went back, and William was so earnest to see them that he and two more went back with them, and there he came to their little camp where they lived. There were about a hundred and sixty men of them in all; they had got their guns on shore, and some ammunition, but a good deal of their powder was spoiled; however, they had raised a fair platform, and mounted twelve pieces of cannon upon it, which was a sufficient defense to them on that side of the sea; and just at the end of the platform they had made a launch and a little yard, and were all hard at work, building another little ship, as I may call it, to go to sea in; but they put a stop to this work upon the news they had of our being come in.

When our men went into their huts, it was surprising, indeed, to see the vast stock of wealth they had got, in gold and silver and jewels, which, however, they told us was a trifle to what Captain Avery had, wherever he was gone.

It was five days we had waited for our men, and no news of them; and indeed I gave them over for lost, but was surprised, after five days' waiting, to see a ship's boat come rowing towards us along shore. What to make of it I could not tell, but was at least better satisfied when our men told me they heard them halloo and saw them wave their caps to us.

In a little time they came quite up to us; and I saw friend William stand up in the boat and make signs to us; so they came on board; but when I saw there were but fifteen of our one-and-thirty men, I asked him what had become of their fellows. "Oh," says William, "they are all very well; and my dream is fully made good, and the cockswain's too."

This made me very impatient to know how the case stood; so he told us the whole story, which indeed surprised us all. The next day we weighed, and stood away southerly to join Captain Wilmot and ship at

Mangahelly, where we found him, as I said, a little chagrined at our stay; but we pacified him afterwards with telling him the history of William's dream, and the consequence of it.

In the meantime the camp of our comrades was so near Mangahelly, that our admiral and I, friend William, and some of the men, resolved to take the sloop and go and see them, and fetch them all, and their goods, bag and baggage, on board our ship, which accordingly we did, and found their camp, their fortifications, the battery of guns they had erected, their treasure, and all the men, just as William had related it; so, after some stay, we took all the men into the sloop, and brought them away with us.

It was some time before we knew what was become of Captain Avery; but after about a month, by the direction of the men who had lost their ship, we sent the sloop to cruise along the shore, to find out, if possible, where they were; and in about a week's cruise our men found them, and particularly that they had lost their ship, as well as our men had lost theirs, and that they were every way in as bad a condition as ours.

It was about ten days before the sloop returned, and Captain Avery with them; and this was the whole force that, as I remember, Captain Avery ever had with him; for now we joined all our companies together, and it stood thus: — We had two ships and a sloop, in which we had 320 men, but much too few to man them as they ought to be, the great Portuguese ship requiring of herself near 400 men to man her completely. As for our lost, but now found comrade, her complement of men was 180, or thereabouts; and Captain Avery had about 300 men with him, whereof he had ten carpenters with him, most of which were taken aboard the prize they had taken; so that, in a word, all the force Avery had at Madagascar, in the year 1699, or thereabouts, amounted to our three ships, for his own was lost, as you have heard; and never had any more than about 1200 men in all.

It was about a month after this that all our crews got together, and as Avery was unshipped, we all agreed to bring our own company into the Portuguese man-of-war and the sloop, and give Captain Avery the Spanish frigate, with all the tackles and furniture, guns and ammunition, for his crew by themselves; for which they, being full of wealth, agreed to give us 40,000 pieces of eight.

It was next considered what course we should take. Captain Avery, to give him his due, proposed our building a little city here, establishing ourselves on shore, with a good fortification and works proper to defend ourselves; and that, as we had wealth enough, and could increase it to what degree we pleased, we should content ourselves to retire here, and bid defiance to the world. But I soon convinced him that this place would be no security to us, if we pretended to carry on our cruising trade; for that then all the nations of Europe, and indeed of that part of the world, would be engaged to root us out; but if we resolved to live there as in retirement, and plant in the country as private men, and give over our trade of pirating, then, indeed, we might plant and settle ourselves where we pleased. But then, I told him, the best way would be to treat with the natives, and buy a tract of land of them farther up the country, seated upon some navigable river, where boats might go up and down for pleasure, but not ships to endanger us; that thus planting the high ground with cattle, such as cows and goats, of which the country also was full, to be sure we might live here as well as any men in the world; and I owned to him I thought it was a good retreat for those that were willing to leave off and lay down, and yet did not care to venture home and be hanged; that is to say, to run the risk of it.

Captain Avery, however he made no positive discovery of his intentions, seemed to me to decline my notion of going up into the country to plant; on the contrary, it was apparent he was of Captain Wilmot's opinion, that they might maintain themselves on shore, and yet carry on their cruising trade too; and upon this they resolved. But, as I afterwards understood, about fifty of their men went up the country, and settled themselves in an inland place as a colony. Whether they are there still or not, I cannot tell, or how many of them are left alive; but it is my opinion they are there still, and that they are considerably increased, for, as I hear, they have got some women among them, though not many; for it seems five Dutch women and three or four little girls were taken by them in a Dutch ship, which they afterwards took going to Mocha; and three of those women, marrying some of these men, went with them to live in their new plantation. But of this I speak only by hearsay.

As we lay here some time, I found our people mightily divided in their notions; some were for going this way, and some that, till at last I began to foresee they would part company, and perhaps we should not have men enough to keep together to man the great ship; so I took Captain Wilmot aside, and began to talk to him about it, but soon perceived that he inclined himself to stay at Madagascar, and having got a vast wealth for his own share, had secret designs of getting home some way or other.

I argued the impossibility of it, and the hazard he would run, either of falling into the hands of thieves and murderers in the Red Sea, who would never let such a treasure as his pass their hands, or of his falling into the hands of the English, Dutch, or French, who would certainly hang him for a pirate. I gave him an account of the voyage I had made from this very place to the continent of Africa, and what a journey it was to travel on foot.

In short, nothing could persuade him, but he would go into the Red Sea with the sloop, and where the children of Israel passed through the sea dry-shod, and, landing there, would travel to Grand Cairo by land, which is not above eighty miles, and from thence he said he could ship himself, by the way of Alexandria, to any part of the world.

I represented the hazard, and indeed the impossibility, of his passing by Mocha and Jiddah without being attacked, if he offered it by force, or plundered, if he went to get leave; and explained the reasons of it so much and so effectually, that, though at last he would not hearken to it himself, none of his men would go with him. They told him they would go anywhere with him to serve him, but that this was running himself and them into certain destruction, without any possibility of avoiding it, or probability of answering his end. The captain took what I said to him quite wrong, and pretended to resent it, and gave me some buccaneer words upon it; but I gave him no return to it but this: that I advised him for his advantage; that if he did not understand it so, it was his fault, not mine; that I did not forbid him to go, nor had I offered to persuade any of the men not to go with him, though it was to their apparent destruction.

However, warm heads are not easily cooled. The captain was so eager that he quitted our company, and, with most part of his crew, went over to Captain Avery, and sorted with his people, taking all the treasure with him, which, by the way, was not very fair in him, we having agreed to share all our gains, whether more or less, whether absent or present.

Our men muttered a little at it, but I pacified them as well as I could, and told them it was easy for us to get as much, if we minded our hits; and Captain Wilmot had set us a very good example; for, by the same rule, the agreement of any further sharing of profits with them was at an end. I took this occasion to put into their heads some part of my further designs, which were, to range over the eastern sea, and see if we could not make ourselves as rich as Mr Avery, who, it was true, had gotten a prodigious deal of money, though not one-half of what was said of it in Europe.

Our men were so pleased with my forward, enterprising temper, that they assured me that they would go with me, one and all, over the whole globe, wherever I would carry them; and as for Captain Wilmot, they would have nothing more to do with him. This came to his ears, and put him into a great rage, so that he threatened, if I came on shore, he would cut my throat.

I had information of it privately, but took no notice of it at all; only I took care not to go unprovided for him, and seldom walked about but in very good company. However, at last Captain Wilmot and I met, and talked over the matter very seriously, and I offered him the sloop to go where he pleased, or, if he was not satisfied with that, I offered to take the sloop and leave him the great ship; but he declined both, and only desired that I would leave him six carpenters, which I had in our ship more than I had need of, to help his men to finish the sloop that was begun before we came thither, by the men that lost their ship. This I consented readily to, and lent him several other hands that were useful to them; and in a little time they built a stout brigantine, able to carry fourteen guns and 200 men.

What measures they took, and how Captain Avery managed afterwards, is too long a story to meddle with here; nor is it any of my business, having my own story still upon my hands.

We lay here, about these several simple disputes, almost five months, when, about the latter end of March, I set sail with the great ship, having in her forty-four guns and 400 men, and the sloop, carrying eighty men. We did not steer to the Malabar coast, and so to the Gulf of Persia, as was first intended, the east monsoons blowing yet too strong, but we kept more under the African coast, where we had the wind variable till we passed the line, and made the Cape Bassa, in the latitude of four degrees ten minutes; from thence, the monsoons beginning to change to the N.E. and N.N.E., we led it away, with the wind large, to the Maldives, a famous ledge of islands, well known by all the sailors who have gone into those parts of the world; and, leaving these islands a little to the south, we made Cape Comorin, the southernmost land of the coast of Malabar, and went round the isle of Ceylon. Here we lay by a while to wait for purchase; and here we saw three large English East India ships going from Bengal, or from Fort St George, homeward for England, or rather for Bombay and Surat, till the trade set in.

We brought to, and hoisting an English ancient and pendant, lay by for them, as if we intended to attack them. They could not tell what to make of us a good while, though they saw our colors; and I believe at first they thought us to be French; but as they came nearer to us, we let them soon see what we were, for we hoisted a black flag, with two cross daggers in it, on our main-top-mast head, which let them see what they were to expect.

We soon found the effects of this; for at first they spread their ancients, and made up to us in a line, as if they would fight us, having the wind off shore, fair enough to have brought them on board us; but when they saw what force we were of, and found we were cruisers of another kind, they stood away from us again, with all the sail they could make. If they had come up, we should have given them an unexpected welcome, but as it was, we had no mind to follow them; so we let them go, for the same reasons which I mentioned before.

But though we let them pass, we did not design to let others go at so easy a price. It was but the next morning that we saw a sail standing round Cape Comorin, and steering, as we thought, the same course with us. We knew not at first what to do with her, because she had the shore on her larboard quarter, and if we offered to chase her, she might put into any port or creek, and escape us; but, to prevent this, we sent the sloop to get in between her and the land. As soon as she saw that, she hauled in to keep the land aboard, and when the sloop stood towards her she made right ashore, with all the canvas she could spread.

The sloop, however, came up with her and engaged her, and found she was a vessel of ten guns, Portuguese built, but in the Dutch traders' hands, and manned by Dutchmen, who were bound from the Gulf of Persia to Batavia, to fetch spices and other goods from thence. The sloop's men took her, and had the rummaging of her before we came up. She had in her some European goods, and a good round sum of money, and some pearl; so that, though we did not go to the gulf for the pearl, the pearl came to us out of the gulf, and we had our share of it. This was a rich ship, and the goods were of very considerable value, besides the money and the pearl.

We had a long consultation here what we should do with the men, for to give them the ship, and let them pursue their voyage to Java, would be to alarm the Dutch factory there, who are by far the strongest in the

Indies, and to make our passage that way impracticable; whereas we resolved to visit that part of the world in our way, but were not willing to pass the great Bay of Bengal, where we hoped for a great deal of purchase; and therefore it behoved us not to be waylaid before we came there, because they knew we must pass by the Straits of Malacca, or those of Sunda; and either way it was very easy to prevent us.

While we were consulting this in the great cabin, the men had had the same debate before the mast; and it seems the majority there were for pickling up the poor Dutchmen among the herrings; in a word, they were for throwing them all into the sea. Poor William, the Quaker, was in great concern about this, and comes directly to me to talk about it. "Hark thee," says William, "what wilt thou do with these Dutchmen that thou hast on board? Thou wilt not let them go, I suppose," says he. "Why," says I, "William, would you advise me to let them go?" "No," says William, "I cannot say it is fit for thee to let them go; that is to say, to go on with their voyage to Batavia, because it is not for thy turn that the Dutch at Batavia should have any knowledge of thy being in these seas." "Well, then," says I to him, "I know no remedy but to throw them overboard. You know, William," says I, "a Dutchman swims like a fish; and all our people here are of the same opinion as well as I." At the same time I resolved it should not be done, but wanted to hear what William would say. He gravely replied, "If all the men in the ship were of that mind, I will never believe that thou wilt be of that mind thyself, for I have heard thee protest against cruelty in all other cases." "Well, William," says I, "that is true; but what then shall we do with them?" "Why," says William, "is there no way but to murder them? I am persuaded thou canst not be in earnest." "No, indeed, William," says I, "I am not in earnest; but they shall not go to Java, no, nor to Ceylon, that is certain." "But," says William, "the men have done thee no injury at all; thou hast taken a great treasure from them; what canst thou pretend to hurt them for?" "Nay, William," says I, "do not talk of that; I have pretence enough, if that be all; my pretence is, to prevent doing me hurt, and that is as necessary a piece of the law of self-preservation as any you can name; but the main thing is, I know not what to do with them, to prevent their prating."

While William and I were talking, the poor Dutchmen were openly condemned to die, as it may be called, by the whole ship's company; and so warm were the men upon it, that they grew very clamorous; and when they heard that William was against it, some of them swore they should die, and if William opposed it, he should drown along with them.

But, as I was resolved to put an end to their cruel project, so I found it was time to take upon me a little, or the bloody humor might grow too strong; so I called the Dutchmen up, and talked a little with them. First, I asked them if they were willing to go with us. Two of them offered it presently; but the rest, which were fourteen, declined it. "Well, then," said I, "where would you go?" They desired they should go to Ceylon. No, I told them I could not allow them to go to any Dutch factory, and told them very plainly the reasons of it, which they could not deny to be just. I let them know also the cruel, bloody measures of our men, but that I had resolved to save them, if possible; and therefore I told them I would set them on shore at some English factory in the Bay of Bengal, or put them on board any English ship I met, after I was past the Straits of Sunda or of Malacca, but not before; for, as to my coming back again, I told them I would run the venture of their Dutch power from Batavia, but I would not have the news come there before me, because it would make all their merchant-ships lay up, and keep out of our way.

It came next into our consideration what we should do with their ship; but this was not long resolving; for there were but two ways, either to set her on fire, or to run her on shore, and we chose the last. So we set her foresail with the tack at the cat-head, and lashed her helm a little to starboard, to answer her head-sail, and so set her agoing, with neither cat or dog in her; and it was not above two hours before we saw her run right ashore upon the coast, a little beyond the Cape Comorin; and away we went round about Ceylon, for the coast of Coromandel.

We sailed along there, not in sight of the shore only, but so near as to see the ships in the road at Fort St David, Fort St George, and at the other factories along that shore, as well as along the coast of Golconda, carrying our English ancient when we came near the Dutch factories, and Dutch colors when we passed by the English factories. We met with little purchase upon this coast, except two small vessels of Golconda, bound across the bay with bales of calicoes and muslins and wrought silks, and fifteen bales of romals, from the bottom of the bay, which were going, on whose account we knew not, to Acheen, and to other ports on the coast of Malacca. We did not inquire to what place in particular; but we let the vessels go, having none but Indians on board.

In the bottom of the bay we met with a great junk belonging to the Mogul's court, with a great many people, passengers as we supposed them to be: it seems they were bound for the river Hooghly or Ganges, and came from Sumatra. This was a prize worth taking indeed; and we got so much gold in her, besides other goods which we did not meddle with — pepper in particular — that it had like to have put an end to our cruise; for almost all my men said we were rich enough, and desired to go back again to Madagascar. But I had other things in my head still, and when I came to talk with them, and set friend William to talk with them, we put such further golden hopes into their heads that we soon prevailed with them to let us go on.

My next design was to leave all the dangerous straits of Malacca, Singapore, and Sunda, where we could expect no great booty, but what we might light on in European ships, which we must fight for; and though we were able to fight, and wanted no courage, even to desperation, yet we were rich too, and resolved to be richer, and took this for our maxim, that while we were sure the wealth we sought was to be had without fighting, we had no occasion to put ourselves to the necessity of fighting for that which would come upon easy terms.

We left, therefore, the Bay of Bengal, and coming to the coast of Sumatra, we put in at a small port, where there was a town, inhabited only by Malays; and here we took in fresh water, and a large quantity of good pork, pickled up and well salted, notwithstanding the heat of the climate, being in the very middle of the torrid zone, viz., in three degrees fifteen minutes north latitude. We also took on board both our vessels forty hogs alive, which served us for fresh provisions, having abundance of food for them, such as the country produced, such as guams, potatoes, and a sort of coarse rice, good for nothing else but to feed the swine. We killed one of these hogs every day, and found them to be excellent meat. We took in also a monstrous quantity of ducks, and cocks and hens, the same kind as we have in England, which we kept for change of provisions; and if I remember right, we had no less than two thousand of them; so that at first we were pestered with them very much, but we soon lessened them by boiling, roasting, stewing, &c., for we never wanted while we had them.

My long-projected design now lay open to me, which was to fall in amongst the Dutch Spice Islands, and see what mischief I could do there. Accordingly, we put out to sea the 12th of August, and passing the line on the 17th, we stood away due south, leaving the Straits of Sunda and the isle of Java on the east, till we came to the latitude of eleven degrees twenty minutes, when we steered east and E.N.E., having easy gales from the W.S.W. till we came among the Moluccas, or Spice Islands.

We passed those seas with less difficulty than in other places, the winds to the south of Java being more variable, and the weather good, though sometimes we met with squally weather and short storms; but when we came in among the Spice Islands themselves we had a share of the monsoons, or trade-winds, and made use of them accordingly.

The infinite number of islands which lie in these seas embarrassed us strangely, and it was with great difficulty that we worked our way through them; then we steered for the north side of the Philippines, when we had a double chance for purchase, viz., either to meet with the Spanish ships from Acapulco, on the coast of New Spain, or we were certain not to fail of finding some ships or junks of China, who, if they came from China, would have a great quantity of goods of value on board, as well as money; or if we took them going back, we should find them laden with nutmegs and cloves from Banda and Ternate, or from some of the other islands.

We were right in our guesses here to a tittle, and we steered directly through a large outlet, which they call a strait, though it be fifteen miles broad, and to an island they call Dammer, and from thence N.N.E. to Banda. Between these islands we met with a Dutch junk, or vessel, going to Amboyna: we took her without much trouble, and I had much ado to prevent our men murdering all the men, as soon as they heard them say they belonged to Amboyna: the reasons I suppose anyone will guess.

We took out of her about sixteen ton of nutmegs, some provisions, and their small-arms, for they had no great guns, and let the ship go: from thence we sailed directly to the Banda Island, or Islands, where we were sure to get more nutmegs if we thought fit. For my part, I would willingly have got more nutmegs, though I had paid for them, but our people abhorred paying for anything; so we got about twelve ton more at several times, most of them from shore, and only a few in a small boat of the natives, which was going to Gilolo. We would have traded openly, but the Dutch, who have made themselves masters of all those islands, forbade the people dealing with us, or any strangers whatever, and kept them so in awe that they durst not do it; so we could indeed have made nothing of it if we had stayed longer, and therefore resolved to be gone for Ternate, and see if we could make up our loading with cloves.

Accordingly we stood away north, but found ourselves so entangled among innumerable islands, and without any pilot that understood the channel and races between them, that we were obliged to give it over, and resolved to go back again to Banda, and see what we could get among the other islands thereabouts.

The first adventure we made here had like to have been fatal to us all, for the sloop, being ahead, made the signal to us for seeing a sail, and afterwards another, and a third, by which we understood she saw three sail; whereupon we made more sail to come up with her, but on a sudden were gotten among some rocks, falling foul upon them in such a manner as frighted us all very heartily; for having, it seems, but just water enough, as it were to an inch, our rudder struck upon the top of a rock, which gave us a terrible shock, and split a great piece off the rudder, and indeed disabled it so that our ship would not steer at all, at least not so as to be depended upon; and we were glad to hand all our sails, except our fore-sail and main-topsail, and with them we stood away to the east, to see if we could find any creek or harbor where we might lay the ship on shore, and repair our rudder; besides, we found the ship herself had received some damage, for she had some little leak near her stern-post, but a great way under water.

By this mischance we lost the advantages, whatever they were, of the three sail of ships, which we afterwards came to hear were small Dutch ships from Batavia, going to Banda and Amboyna, to load spice, and, no doubt, had a good quantity of money on board.

Upon the disaster I have been speaking of you may very well suppose that we came to an anchor as soon as we could, which was upon a small island not far from Banda, where, though the Dutch keep no factory, yet they come at the season to buy nutmegs and mace. We stayed there thirteen days; but there being no place where we could lay the ship on shore, we sent the sloop to cruise among the islands, to look out for a place fit for us. In the meantime we got very good water here, some provisions, roots, and fruits, and a good quantity of nutmegs and mace, which we found ways to trade with the natives for, without the knowledge of their masters, the Dutch.

At length our sloop returned; having found another island where there was a very good harbor, we ran in, and came to an anchor. We immediately unbent all our

sails, sent them ashore upon the island, and set up
seven or eight tents with them; then we unrigged our
top-masts, and cut them down, hoisted all our guns
out, our provisions and loading, and put them ashore
in the tents. With the guns we made two small batteries,
for fear of a surprise, and kept a look-out upon the
hill. When we were all ready, we laid the ship aground
upon a hard sand, the upper end of the harbor, and
shored her up on each side. At low water she lay almost
dry, so we mended her bottom, and stopped the leak,
which was occasioned by straining some of the rudder
irons with the shock which the ship had against the
rock.

Having done this, we also took occasion to clean her
bottom, which, having been at sea so long, was very
foul. The sloop washed and tallowed also, but was
ready before us, and cruised eight or ten days among
the islands, but met with no purchase; so that we began
to be tired of the place, having little to divert us but
the most furious claps of thunder that ever were heard
or read of in the world.

We were in hopes to have met with some purchase
here among the Chinese, who, we had been told, came
to Ternate to trade for cloves, and to the Banda Isles
for nutmegs; and we would have been very glad to have
loaded our galleon, or great ship, with these two sorts
of spice, and have thought it a glorious voyage; but we
found nothing stirring more than what I have said,
except Dutchmen, who, by what means we could not
imagine, had either a jealousy of us or intelligence of
us, and kept themselves close in their ports.

I was once resolved to have made a descent at the
island of Dumas, the place most famous for the best
nutmegs; but friend William, who was always for doing
our business without fighting, dissuaded me from it,
and gave such reasons for it that we could not resist;

particularly the great heats of the season, and of the place, for we were now in the latitude of just half a degree south. But while we were disputing this point we were soon determined by the following accident: — We had a strong gale of wind at S.W. by W., and the ship had fresh way, but a great sea rolling in upon us from the N.E., which we afterwards found was the pouring in of the great ocean east of New Guinea. However, as I said, we stood away large, and made fresh way, when, on the sudden, from a dark cloud which hovered over our heads, came a flash, or rather blast, of lightning, which was so terrible, and quivered so long among us, that not I only, but all our men, thought the ship was on fire. The heat of the flash, or fire, was so sensibly felt in our faces, that some of our men had blisters raised by it on their skins, not immediately, perhaps, by the heat, but by the poisonous or noxious particles which mixed themselves with the matter inflamed. But this was not all; the shock of the air, which the fracture in the clouds made, was such that our ship shook as when a broadside is fired; and her motion being checked, as it were at once, by a repulse superior to the force that gave her way before, the sails all flew back in a moment, and the ship lay, as we might truly say, thunder-struck. As the blast from the cloud was so very near us, it was but a few moments after the flash that the terriblest clap of thunder followed that was ever heard by mortals. I firmly believe a blast of a hundred thousand barrels of gunpowder could not have been greater to our hearing; nay, indeed, to some of our men it took away their hearing.

It is not possible for me to describe, or anyone to conceive, the terror of that minute. Our men were in such a consternation, that not a man on board the ship had presence of mind to apply to the proper duty of a sailor, except friend William; and had he not run very nimbly, and with a composure that I am sure I was not master of, to let go the fore-sheet, set in the weather-brace of the fore-yard, and haul down the top-sails, we had certainly brought all our masts by the board, and perhaps have been overwhelmed in the sea.

As for myself, I must confess my eyes were open to my danger, though not the least to anything of application for remedy. I was all amazement and confusion, and this was the first time that I can say I began to feel the effects of that horror which I know since much more of, upon the just reflection on my former life. I thought myself doomed by Heaven to sink that moment into eternal destruction; and with this peculiar mark of terror, viz., that the vengeance was not executed in the ordinary way of human justice, but that God had taken me into His immediate disposing, and had resolved to be the executer of His own vengeance.

Let them alone describe the confusion I was in who know what was the case of [John] Child, of Shadwell, or Francis Spira. It is impossible to describe it. My soul was all amazement and surprise. I thought myself just sinking into eternity, owning the divine justice of my punishment, but not at all feeling any of the moving, softening tokens of a sincere penitent; afflicted at the punishment, but not at the crime; alarmed at the vengeance, but not terrified at the guilt; having the same gust to the crime, though terrified to the last degree at the thought of the punishment, which I concluded I was just now going to receive.

But perhaps many that read this will be sensible of the thunder and lightning, that may think nothing of the rest, or rather may make a jest of it all; so I say no more of it at this time, but proceed to the story of the voyage. When the amazement was over, and the men began to come to themselves, they fell a-calling for one another, everyone for his friend, or for those he had most respect for; and it was a singular satisfaction to find that nobody was hurt. The next thing was to inquire if the ship had received no damage, when the boatswain, stepping forward, found that part of the head was gone, but not so as to endanger the bowsprit; so we hoisted our top-sails again, hauled aft the fore-sheet, braced the yards, and went our course as before. Nor can I deny but that we were all somewhat like the ship; our first astonishment being a little over, and that we found the ship swim again, we were soon the same irreligious, hardened crew that we were before, and I among the rest.

As we now steered, our course lay N.N.E., and we passed thus, with a fair wind, through the strait or channel between the island of Gilolo and the land of Nova Guinea, when we were soon in the open sea or ocean, on the southeast of the Philippines, being the great Pacific, or South Sea, where it may be said to join itself with the vast Indian Ocean.

As we passed into these seas, steering due north, so we soon crossed the line to the north side, and so sailed on towards Mindanao and Manilla, the chief of the Philippine Islands, without meeting with any purchase till we came to the northward of Manilla, and then our trade began; for here we took three Japanese vessels, though at some distance from Manilla. Two of them had made their market, and were going home with nutmegs, cinnamon, cloves, &c., besides all sorts of European goods, brought with the Spanish ships from Acapulco. They had together eight-and-thirty ton of cloves, and five or six ton of nutmegs, and as much cinnamon. We took the spice, but meddled with very little of the European goods, they being, as we thought, not worth our while; but we were very sorry for it soon after, and therefore grew wiser upon the next occasion.

The third Japanese was the best prize to us; for he

came with money, and a great deal of gold uncoined, to buy such goods as we mentioned above. We eased him of his gold, and did him no other harm, and having no intention to stay long here, we stood away for China.

We were at sea above two months upon this voyage, beating it up against the wind, which blew steadily from the N.E., and within a point or two one way or other; and this indeed was the reason why we met with the more prizes in our voyage.

We were just gotten clear of the Philippines, and we purposed to go to the isle of Formosa, but the wind blew so fresh at N.N.E. that there was no making anything of it, and we were forced to put back to Laconia, the most northerly of those islands. We rode here very secure, and shifted our situation, not in view of any danger, for there was none, but for a better supply of provisions, which we found the people very willing to supply us with.

There lay, while we remained here, three very great galleons, or Spanish ships, from the south seas; whether newly come in or ready to sail we could not understand at first; but as we found the China traders began to load and set forward to the north, we concluded the Spanish ships had newly unloaded their cargo, and these had been buying; so we doubted not but we should meet with purchase in the rest of the voyage, neither, indeed, could we well miss of it.

We stayed here till the beginning of May, when we were told the Chinese traders would set forward; for the northern monsoons end about the latter end of March or beginning of April; so that they are sure of fair winds home. Accordingly we hired some of the country boats, which are very swift sailers, to go and bring us word how affairs stood at Manilla, and when the China junks would sail; and by this intelligence we ordered our matters so well, that three days after we set sail we fell in with no less than eleven of them; out of which, however, having by misfortune of discovering ourselves, taken but three, we contented ourselves and pursued our voyage to Formosa. In these three vessels we took, in short, such a quantity of cloves, nutmegs, cinnamon, and mace, besides silver, that our men began to be of my opinion, — that we were rich enough; and, in short, we had nothing to do now but to consider by what methods to secure the immense treasure we had got.

I was secretly glad to hear that they were of this opinion, for I had long before resolved, if it were possible, to persuade them to think of returning, having fully perfected my first projected design of rummaging among the Spice Islands; and all those prizes, which were exceeding rich at Manilla, was quite beyond my design.

But now I had heard what the men said, and how they thought we were very well, I let them know by friend William, that I intended only to sail to the island of Formosa, where I should find opportunity to turn our spices and Europe goods into ready money, and that then I would tack about for the south, the northern monsoons being perhaps by that time also ready to set in. They all approved of my design, and willingly went forward; because, besides the winds, which would not permit until October to go to the south, I say, besides this, we were now a very deep ship, having near two hundred ton of goods on board, and particularly, some very valuable; the sloop also had a proportion.

With this resolution we went on cheerfully, when, within about twelve days' sail more, we made the island Formosa, at a great distance, but were ourselves shot beyond the southernmost part of the island, being to leeward, and almost upon the coast of China. Here we were a little at a loss, for the English factories were not far off, and we might be obliged to fight some of their ships, if we met with them; which, though we were able enough to do, yet we did not desire it on many accounts, and particularly because we did not think it was our business to have it known who we were, or that such a kind of people as we had been seen on the coast. However, we were obliged to keep to the northward, keeping as good an offing as we could with respect to the coast of China.

We had not sailed long but we chased a small Chinese junk, and having taken her, we found she was bound to the island of Formosa, having no goods on board but some rice and a small quantity of tea; but she had three Chinese merchants in her; and they told us that they were going to meet a large vessel of their country, which came from Tonquin, and lay in a river in Formosa, whose name I forgot; and they were going to the Philippine Islands, with silks, muslins, calicoes, and such goods as are the product of China, and some gold; that their business was to sell their cargo, and buy spices and European goods.

This suited very well with our purpose; so I resolved now that we would leave off being pirates and turn merchants; so we told them what goods we had on board, and that if they would bring their supercargoes or merchants on board, we would trade with them. They were very willing to trade with us, but terribly afraid to trust us; nor was it an unjust fear, for we had plundered them already of what they had. On the other hand, we were as diffident as they, and very uncertain what to do; but William the Quaker put this matter into a way of barter. He came to me and told me he really thought the merchants looked like fair men, that meant honestly. "And besides," says William, "it is their interest to be honest now, for, as they know upon what terms we got the goods we are to truck with them, so they know we can afford good pennyworths; and in the next place, it saves them going the whole voyage, so that the southerly monsoons yet holding, if they traded with us, they could immediately return with their cargo to China;" though, by the way, we afterwards found they intended for Japan; but that was all one, for by this means they saved at least eight months' voyage. Upon these foundations, William said he was satisfied we might trust them; "for," says William, "I would as soon trust a man whose interest binds him to be just to me as a man whose principle binds himself." Upon the whole, William proposed that two of the merchants should be left on board our ship as hostages, and that part of our goods should be loaded in their vessel, and let the third go with it into the port where their ship lay; and when he had delivered the spices, he should bring back such things as it was agreed should be exchanged. This was concluded on, and William the Quaker ventured to go along with them, which, upon my word, I should not have cared to have done, nor was I willing that he should, but he went still upon the notion that it was their interest to treat him friendly.

In the meantime, we came to an anchor under a little island in the latitude of 23 degrees 28 minutes, being just under the northern tropic, and about twenty leagues from the island. Here we lay thirteen days, and began to be very uneasy for my friend William, for they had promised to be back again in four days, which they might very easily have done. However, at the end of thirteen days, we saw three sail coming directly to us, which a little surprised us all at first, not knowing what might be the case; and we began to put ourselves in a posture of defense; but as they came nearer us, we were soon satisfied, for the first vessel was that which

William went in, who carried a flag of truce; and in a few hours they all came to an anchor, and William came on board us with a little boat, with the Chinese merchant in his company, and two other merchants, who seemed to be a kind of brokers for the rest.

Here he gave us an account how civilly he had been used; how they had treated him with all imaginable frankness and openness; that they had not only given him the full value of his spices and other goods which he carried, in gold, by good weight, but had loaded the vessel again with such goods as he knew we were willing to trade for; and that afterwards they had resolved to bring the great ship out of the harbor, to lie where we were, that so we might make what bargain we thought fit; only William said he had promised, in our name, that we should use no violence with them, nor detain any of the vessels after we had done trading with them. I told him we would strive to outdo them in civility, and that we would make good every part of his agreement; in token whereof, I caused a white flag likewise to be spread at the poop of our great ship, which was the signal agreed on.

As to the third vessel which came with them, it was a kind of bark of the country, who, having intelligence of our design to traffic, came off to deal with us, bringing a great deal of gold and some provisions, which at that time we were very glad of.

In short, we traded upon the high seas with these men, and indeed we made a very good market, and yet sold thieves' pennyworths too. We sold here about sixty ton of spice, chiefly cloves and nutmegs, and above two hundred bales of European goods, such as linen and woolen manufactures. We considered we should have occasion for some such things ourselves, and so we kept a good quantity of English stuffs, cloth, baize, &c., for ourselves. I shall not take up any of the little room I have left here with the further particulars of our trade; it is enough to mention, that, except a parcel of tea, and twelve bales of fine China wrought silks, we took nothing in exchange for our goods but gold; so that the sum we took here in that glittering commodity amounted to above fifty thousand ounces good weight.

When we had finished our barter, we restored the hostages, and gave the three merchants about the quantity of twelve hundredweight of nutmegs, and as many of cloves, with a handsome present of European linen and stuff for themselves, as a recompense for what we had taken from them; so we sent them away exceedingly well satisfied.

Here it was that William gave me an account, that while he was on board the Japanese vessel, he met with a kind of religious, or Japan priest, who spoke some words of English to him; and, being very inquisitive to know how he came to learn any of those words, he told him that there was in his country thirteen Englishmen; he called them Englishmen very articulately and distinctly, for he had conversed with them very frequently and freely. He said that they were all that were left of two-and-thirty men, who came on shore on the north side of Japan, being driven upon a great rock in a stormy night, where they lost their ship, and the rest of their men were drowned; that he had persuaded the king of his country to send boats off to the rock or island where the ship was lost, to save the rest of the men, and to bring them on shore, which was done, and they were used very kindly, and had houses built for them, and land given them to plant for provision; and that they lived by themselves.

He said he went frequently among them, to persuade them to worship their god (an idol, I suppose, of their own making), which, he said, they ungratefully refused;

and that therefore the king had once or twice ordered them all to be put to death; but that, as he said, he had prevailed upon the king to spare them, and let them live their own way, as long as they were quiet and peaceable, and did not go about to withdraw others from the worship of the country.

I asked William why he did not inquire from whence they came. "I did," said William; "for how could I but think it strange," said he, "to hear him talk of Englishmen on the north side of Japan?" "Well," said I, "what account did he give of it?" "An account," said William, "that will surprise thee, and all the world after thee, that shall hear of it, and which makes me wish thou wouldst go up to Japan and find them out." "What do you mean?" said I. "Whence could they come?" "Why," says William, "he pulled out a little book, and in it a piece of paper, where it was written, in an Englishman's hand, and in plain English words, thus; and," says William, "I read it myself: — 'We came from Greenland, and from the North Pole.'" This, indeed, was amazing to us all, and more so to those seamen among us who knew anything of the infinite attempts which had been made from Europe, as well by the English as the Dutch, to discover a passage that way into those parts of the world; and as William pressed as earnestly to go on to the north to rescue those poor men, so the ship's company began to incline to it; and, in a word, we all came to this, that we would stand in to the shore of Formosa, to find this priest again, and have a further account of it all from him. Accordingly, the sloop went over; but when they came there, the vessels were very unhappily sailed, and this put an end to our inquiry after them, and perhaps may have disappointed mankind of one of the most noble discoveries that ever was made, or will again be made, in the world, for the good of mankind in general; but so much for that.

William was so uneasy at losing this opportunity, that he pressed us earnestly to go up to Japan to find out these men. He told us that if it was nothing but to recover thirteen honest poor men from a kind of captivity, which they would otherwise never be redeemed from, and where, perhaps, they might, some time or other, be murdered by the barbarous people, in defense of their idolatry, it were very well worth our while, and it would be, in some measure, making amends for the mischiefs we had done in the world; but we, that had no concern upon us for the mischiefs we had done, had much less about any satisfactions to be made for it, so he found that kind of discourse would weigh very little with us. Then he pressed us very earnestly to let him have the sloop to go by himself, and I told him I would not oppose it; but when he came to the sloop none of the men would go with him; for the case was plain, they had all a share in the cargo of the great ship, as well as in thae* of the sloop, and the richness of the cargo was such that they would not leave it by any means; so poor William, much to his mortification, was obliged to give it over. What became of those thirteen men, or whether they are not there still, I can give no account of.

We are now at the end of our cruise; what we had taken was indeed so considerable, that it was not only enough to satisfy the most covetous and the most ambitious minds in the world, but it did indeed satisfy us, and our men declared they did not desire any more. The next motion, therefore, was about going back, and the way by which we should perform the voyage, so as not to be attacked by the Dutch in the Straits of Sunda.

We had pretty well stored ourselves here with provisions, and it being now near the return of the monsoons, we resolved to stand away to the southward; and

---

* Scottish dialect: "those"

not only to keep without the Philippine Islands, that is to say, to the eastward of them, but to keep on to the southward, and see if we could not leave not only the Moluccas, or Spice Islands, behind us, but even Nova Guinea and Nova Hollandia also; and so getting into the variable winds, to the south of the tropic of Capricorn, steer away to the west, over the great Indian Ocean.

This was indeed at first a monstrous voyage in its appearance, and the want of provisions threatened us. William told us in so many words, that it was impossible we could carry provisions enough to subsist us for such a voyage, and especially fresh water; and that, as there would be no land for us to touch at where we could get any supply, it was a madness to undertake it.

But I undertook to remedy this evil, and therefore desired them not to be uneasy at that, for I knew that we might supply ourselves at Mindanao, the most southerly island of the Philippines.

Accordingly, we set sail, having taken all the provisions here that we could get, the 28th of September, the wind veering a little at first from the N.N.W. to the N.E. by E., but afterwards settled about the N.E. and the E.N.E. We were nine weeks in this voyage, having met with several interruptions by the weather, and put in under the lee of a small island in the latitude of 16 degrees 12 minutes, of which we never knew the name, none of our charts having given any account of it: I say, we put in here by reason of a strange tornado or hurricane, which brought us into a great deal of danger. Here we rode about sixteen days, the winds being very tempestuous and the weather uncertain. However, we got some provisions on shore, such as plants and roots, and a few hogs. We believed there were inhabitants on the island, but we saw none of them.

From hence, the weather settling again, we went on

and came to the southernmost part of Mindanao, where we took in fresh water and some cows, but the climate was so hot that we did not attempt to salt up any more than so as to keep a fortnight or three weeks; and away we stood southward, crossing the line, and, leaving Gillolo on the starboard side, we coasted the country they call New Guinea, where, in the latitude of eight degrees south, we put in again for provisions and water, and where we found inhabitants; but they fled from us, and were altogether inconversable. From thence, sailing still southward, we left all behind us that any of our charts and maps took any notice of, and went on till we came to the latitude of seventeen degrees, the wind continuing still northeast.

Here we made land to the westward, which, when we had kept in sight for three days, coasting along the shore for the distance of about four leagues, we began to fear we should find no outlet west, and so should be obliged to go back again, and put in among the Moluccas at last; but at length we found the land break off, and go trending away to the west sea, seeming to be all open to the south and southwest, and a great sea came rolling out of the south, which gave us to understand that there was no land for a great way.

In a word, we kept on our course to the south, a little westerly, till we passed the south tropic, where we found the winds variable; and now we stood away fair west, and held it out for about twenty days, when we discovered land right ahead, and on our larboard bow; we made directly to the shore, being willing to take all advantages now for supplying ourselves with fresh provisions and water, knowing we were now entering on that vast unknown Indian Ocean, perhaps the greatest sea on the globe, having, with very little interruption of islands, a continued sea quite round the globe.

We found a good road here, and some people on

shore; but when we landed, they fled up the country, nor would they hold any correspondence with us, nor come near us, but shot at us several times with arrows as long as lances. We set up white flags for a truce, but they either did not or would not understand it; on the contrary, they shot our flag of truce through several times with their arrows, so that, in a word, we never came near any of them.

We found good water here, though it was something difficult to get at it, but for living creatures we could see none; for the people, if they had any cattle, drove them all away, and showed us nothing but themselves, and that sometimes in a threatening posture, and in number so great, that made us suppose the island to be greater than we first imagined. It is true, they would not come near enough for us to engage with them, at least not openly; but they came near enough for us to see them, and, by the help of our glasses, to see that they were clothed and armed, but their clothes were only about their lower and middle parts; that they had long lances, half pikes, in their hands, besides bows and arrows; that they had great high things on their heads, made, as we believed, of feathers, and which looked something like our grenadiers' caps in England.

When we saw them so shy that they would not come near us, our men began to range over the island, if it was such (for we never surrounded it), to search for cattle, and for any of the Indian plantations, for fruits or plants; but they soon found, to their cost, that they were to use more caution than that came to, and that they were to discover perfectly every bush and every tree before they ventured abroad in the country; for about fourteen of our men going farther than the rest, into a part of the country which seemed to be planted, as they thought, for it did but seem so, only I think it was overgrown with canes, such as we make our cane chairs with — I say, venturing too far, they were suddenly attacked with a shower of arrows from almost every side of them, as they thought, out of the tops of the trees.

They had nothing to do but to fly for it, which, however, they could not resolve on, till five of them were wounded; nor had they escaped so, if one of them had not been so much wiser or thoughtfuller than the rest, as to consider, that though they could not see the enemy, so as to shoot at them, yet perhaps the noise of their shot might terrify them, and that they should rather fire at a venture. Accordingly, ten of them faced about, and fired at random anywhere among the canes.

The noise and the fire not only terrified the enemy, but, as they believed, their shot had luckily hit some of them; for they found not only that the arrows, which came thick among them before, ceased, but they heard the Indians halloo, after their way, to one another, and make a strange noise, more uncouth and inimitably strange than any they had ever heard, more like the howling and barking of wild creatures in the woods than like the voice of men, only that sometimes they seemed to speak words.

They observed also, that this noise of the Indians went farther and farther off, so that they were satisfied the Indians fled away, except on one side, where they heard a doleful groaning and howling, and where it continued a good while, which they supposed was from some or other of them being wounded, and howling by reason of their wounds; or killed, and others howling over them: but our men had enough of making discoveries; so they did not trouble themselves to look farther, but resolved to take this opportunity to retreat. But the worst of their adventure was to come; for as they came back, they passed by a prodigious great trunk of an old tree; what tree it was, they said, they did not know, but it stood like an old decayed oak in a park, where the keepers in England take a stand, as they call it, to shoot a deer; and it stood just under the steep side of a great rock, or hill, that our people could not see what was beyond it.

As they came by this tree, they were of a sudden shot at, from the top of the tree, with seven arrows and three lances, which, to our great grief, killed two of our men, and wounded three more. This was the more surprising, because, being without any defense, and so near the trees, they expected more lances and arrows every moment; nor would flying do them any service, the Indians being, as appeared, very good marksmen. In this extremity, they had happily this presence of mind, viz., to run close to the tree, and stand, as it were, under it; so that those above could not come at, or see them, to throw their lances at them. This succeeded, and gave them time to consider what to do; they knew their enemies and murderers were above; they heard them talk, and those above knew those were below; but they below were obliged to keep close for fear of their lances from above. At length, one of our men, looking a little more strictly than the rest, thought he saw the head of one of the Indians just over a dead limb of the tree, which, it seems, the creature sat upon. One man immediately fired, and levelled his piece so true that the shot went through the fellow's head; and down he fell out of the tree immediately, and came upon the ground with such force, with the height of his fall, that if he had not been killed with the shot, he would certainly have been killed with dashing his body against the ground.

This so frightened them, that, besides the howling noise they made in the tree, our men heard a strange clutter of them in the body of the tree, from whence they concluded they had made the tree hollow, and were got to hide themselves there. Now, had this been the case, they were secure enough from our men, for it was impossible any of our men could get up the tree on the outside, there being no branches to climb by; and, to shoot at the tree, that they tried several times to no purpose, for the tree was so thick that no shot would enter it. They made no doubt, however, but that they had their enemies in a trap, and that a small siege would either bring them down, tree and all, or starve them out; so they resolved to keep their post, and send to us for help. Accordingly, two of them came away to us for more hands, and particularly desired that some of our carpenters might come with tools, to help to cut down the tree, or at least to cut down other wood and set fire to it; and that, they concluded, would not fail to bring them out.

Accordingly, our men went like a little army, and with mighty preparations for an enterprise, the like of which has scarce been ever heard, to form the siege of a great tree. However, when they came there, they found the task difficult enough, for the old trunk was indeed a very great one, and very tall, being at least two-and-twenty feet high, with seven old limbs standing out every way from the top, but decayed, and very few leaves, if any, left on it.

William the Quaker, whose curiosity led him to go among the rest, proposed that they should make a ladder, and get upon the top, and then throw wild-fire into the tree, and smoke them out. Others proposed going back, and getting a great gun out of the ship, which would split the tree in pieces with the iron bullets; others, that they should cut down a great deal of wood, and pile it up round the tree, and set it on fire, and burn the tree, and the Indians in it.

These consultations took up our people no less than two or three days, in all which time they heard nothing

of the supposed garrison within this wooden castle,
nor any noise within. William's project was first gone
about, and a large strong ladder was made, to scale this
wooden tower; and in two or three hours' time it would
have been ready to mount, when, on a sudden, they
heard the noise of the Indians in the body of the tree
again, and a little after, several of them appeared at the
top of the tree, and threw some lances down at our
men; one of which struck one of our seamen a-top of
the shoulder, and gave him such a desperate wound,
that the surgeons not only had a great deal of difficulty
to cure him, but the poor man endured such horrible
torture, that we all said they had better have killed him
outright. However, he was cured at last, though he
never recovered the perfect use of his arm, the lance
having cut some of the tendons on the top of the arm,
near the shoulder, which, as I supposed, performed the
office of motion to the limb before; so that the poor
man was a cripple all the days of his life. But to return
to the desperate rogues in the tree; our men shot at
them, but did not find they had hit them, or any of
them; but as soon as ever they shot at them, they could
hear them huddle down into the trunk of the tree
again, and there, to be sure, they were safe.

Well, however, it was this which put by the project
of William's ladder; for when it was done, who would
venture up among such a troop of bold creatures as
were there, and who, they supposed, were desperate by
their circumstances? And as but one man at a time
could go up, they began to think it would not do; and,
indeed, I was of the opinion (for about this time I was
come to their assistance) that going up the ladder
would not do, unless it was thus, that a man should,
as it were, run just up to the top, and throw some
fireworks into the tree, and come down again; and this
we did two or three times, but found no effect of it. At

last, one of our gunners made a stink-pot, as we called it, being a composition which only smokes, but does not flame or burn; but withal the smoke of it is so thick, and the smell of it so intolerably nauseous, that it is not to be suffered. This he threw into the tree himself, and we waited for the effect of it, but heard or saw nothing all that night or the next day; so we concluded the men within were all smothered; when, on a sudden, the next night we heard them upon the top of the tree again shouting and hallooing like madmen.

We concluded, as anybody would, that this was to call for help, and we resolved to continue our siege; for we were all enraged to see ourselves so baulked by a few wild people, whom we thought we had safe in our clutches; and, indeed, never were there so many concurring circumstances to delude men in any case we had met with. We resolved, however, to try another stink-pot the next night, and our engineer and gunner had got it ready, when, hearing a noise of the enemy on the top of the tree, and in the body of the tree, I was not willing to let the gunner go up the ladder, which, I said, would be but to be certain of being murdered. However, he found a medium for it, and that was to go up a few steps, and, with a long pole in his hand, to throw it in upon the top of the tree, the ladder being standing all this while against the top of the tree; but when the gunner, with his machine at the top of his pole, came to the tree, with three other men to help him, behold the ladder was gone.

This perfectly confounded us; and we now concluded the Indians in the tree had, by this piece of negligence, taken the opportunity, and come all down the ladder, made their escape, and had carried away the ladder with them. I laughed most heartily at my friend William, who, as I said, had the direction of the siege,

and had set up a ladder for the garrison, as we called
them, to get down upon, and run away. But when
daylight came, we were all set to rights again; for there
stood our ladder, hauled up on the top of the tree, with
about half of it in the hollow of the tree, and the other
half upright in the air. Then we began to laugh at the
Indians for fools, that they could not as well have
found their way down by the ladder, and have made
their escape, as to have pulled it up by main strength
into the tree.

We then resolved upon fire, and so to put an end to
the work at once, and burn the tree and its inhabitants
together; and accordingly we went to work to cut wood,
and in a few hours' time we got enough, as we thought,
together; and, piling it up round the bottom of the
tree, we set it on fire, waiting at a distance to see when,
the gentlemen's quarters being too hot for them, they
would come flying out at the top. But we were quite
confounded when, on a sudden, we found the fire all
put out by a great quantity of water thrown upon it.
We then thought the devil must be in them, to be sure.
Says William, "This is certainly the cunningest piece
of Indian engineering that ever was heard of; and there
can be but one thing more to guess at, besides witchcraft and dealing with the devil, which I believe not
one word of," says he; "and that must be, that this is
an artificial tree, or a natural tree artificially made
hollow down into the earth, through root and all; and
that these creatures have an artificial cavity underneath
it, quite into the hill, or a way to go through, and under
the hill, to some other place; and where that other place
is, we know not; but if it be not our own fault, I'll find
the place, and follow them into it, before I am two days
older." He then called the carpenters, to know of them
if they had any large saws that would cut through the
body; and they told him they had no saws that were

long enough, nor could men work into such a monstrous old stump in a great while; but that they would
go to work with it with their axes, and undertake to
cut it down in two days, and stock up the root of it in
two more. But William was for another way, which
proved much better than all this; for he was for silent
work, that, if possible, he might catch some of the
fellows in it. So he sets twelve men to it with large
augers, to bore great holes into the side of the tree, to
go almost through, but not quite through; which holes
were bored without noise, and when they were done he
filled them all with gunpowder, stopping strong plugs,
bolted crossways, into the holes, and then boring a
slanting hole, of a less size, down into the greater hole,
all of which were filled with powder, and at once blown
up. When they took fire, they made such a noise, and
tore and split up the tree in so many places, and in
such a manner, that we could see plainly such another
blast would demolish it; and so it did. Thus at the
second time we could, at two or three places, put our
hands in them, and discovered a cheat, namely, that
there was a cave or hole dug into the earth, from or
through the bottom of the hollow, and that it had
communication with another cave farther in, where we
heard the voices of several of the wild folks, calling and
talking to one another.

When we came thus far we had a great mind to get
at them; and William desired that three men might be
given him with hand-grenadoes; and he promised to
go down first, and boldly he did so; for William, to
give him his due, had the heart of a lion.

They had pistols in their hands, and swords by their
sides; but, as they had taught the Indians before by
their stink-pots, the Indians returned them in their
own kind; for they made such a smoke come up out
of the entrance into the cave or hollow, that William

and his three men were glad to come running out of the cave, and out of the tree too, for mere want of breath; and indeed they were almost stifled.

Never was a fortification so well defended, or assailants so many ways defeated. We were now for giving it over, and particularly I called William, and told him I could not but laugh to see us spinning out our time here for nothing; that I could not imagine what we were doing; that it was certain that the rogues that were in it were cunning to the last degree, and it would vex anybody to be so baulked by a few naked ignorant fellows; but still it was not worth our while to push it any further, nor was there anything that I knew of to be got by the conquest when it was made, so that I thought it high time to give it over.

William acknowledged what I said was just, and that there was nothing but our curiosity to be gratified in this attempt; and though, as he said, he was very desirous to have searched into the thing, yet he would not insist upon it; so we resolved to quit it and come away, which we did. However, William said before we went he would have this satisfaction of them, viz., to burn down the tree and stop up the entrance into the cave. And while doing this the gunner told him he would have one satisfaction of the rogues; and this was, that he would make a mine of it, and see which way it had vent. Upon this he fetched two barrels of powder out of the ships, and placed them in the inside of the hollow of the cave, as far in as he durst go to carry them, and then filling up the mouth of the cave where the tree stood, and ramming it sufficiently hard, leaving only a pipe or touch-hole, he gave fire to it, and stood at a distance to see which way it would operate, when on a sudden he found the force of the powder burst its way out among some bushes on the other side the little hill I mentioned, and that it came roaring out there as out of the mouth of a cannon. Immediately running thither, we saw the effects of the powder.

First, we saw that there was the other mouth of the cave, which the powder had so torn and opened, that the loose earth was so fallen in again that nothing of shape could be discerned; but there we saw what was become of the garrison of the Indians, too, who had given us all this trouble, for some of them had no arms, some no legs, some no head; some lay half buried in the rubbish of the mine — that is to say, in the loose earth that fell in; and, in short, there was a miserable havoc made in them all; for we had good reason to believe not one of them that were in the inside could escape, but rather were shot out of the mouth of the cave, like a bullet out of a gun.

We had now our full satisfaction of the Indians; but, in short, this was a losing voyage, for we had two men killed, one quite crippled, and five more wounded; we spent two barrels of powder, and eleven days' time, and all to get the understanding how to make an Indian mine, or how to keep garrison in a hollow tree; and with this wit, bought at this dear price, we came away, having taken in some fresh water, but got no fresh provisions.

We then considered what we should do to get back again to Madagascar. We were much about the latitude of the Cape of Good Hope, but had such a very long run, and were neither sure of meeting with fair winds nor with any land in the way, that we knew not what to think of it. William was our last resort in this case again, and he was very plain with us. "Friend," says he to Captain Wilmot, "what occasion hast thou to run the venture of starving, merely for the pleasure of saying thou hast been where nobody has been before? There are a great many places nearer home, of which thou mayest say the same thing at less expense. I see no occasion thou hast of keeping thus far south any longer than till you are sure you are to the west end of Java and Sumatra; and then thou mayest stand away north towards Ceylon, and the coast of Coromandel and Madras, where thou mayest get both fresh water and fresh provisions; and to that part it is likely we may hold out well enough with the stores we have already."

This was wholesome advice, and such as was not to be slighted; so we stood away to the west, keeping between the latitude of 31 and 35, and had very good weather and fair winds for about ten days' sail; by which time, by our reckoning, we were clear of the isles, and might run away to the north; and if we did not fall in with Ceylon, we should at least go into the great deep Bay of Bengal.

But we were out in our reckoning a great deal; for, when we had stood due north for about fifteen or sixteen degrees, we met with land again on our starboard bow, about three leagues' distance; so we came to an anchor about half a league from it, and manned out our boats to see what sort of a country it was. We found it a very good one; fresh water easy to come at, but no cattle that we could see, or inhabitants; and we were very shy of searching too far after them, lest we should make such another journey as we did last; so that we let rambling alone, and chose rather to take what we could find, which was only a few wild mangoes, and some plants of several kinds, which we knew not the names of.

We made no stay here, but put to sea again, N.W. by N., but had little wind for a fortnight more, when we made land again; and standing in with the shore, we were surprised to find ourselves on the south shore of Java; and just as we were coming to an anchor we saw a boat, carrying Dutch colors, sailing along-shore. We were not solicitous to speak with them, or any other of their nation, but left it indifferent to our people, when they went on shore, to see the Dutchmen or not to see them; our business was to get provisions, which, indeed, by this time were very short with us.

We resolved to go on shore with our boats in the most convenient place we could find, and to look out a proper harbor to bring the ship into, leaving it to our fate whether we should meet with friends or enemies; resolving, however, not to stay any considerable time, at least not long enough to have expresses sent across the island to Batavia, and for ships to come round from thence to attack us.

We found, according to our desire, a very good harbor, where we rode in seven fathom water, well defended from the weather, whatever might happen; and here we got fresh provisions, such as good hogs and some cows; and that we might lay in a little store, we killed sixteen cows, and pickled and barrelled up the flesh as well as we could be supposed to do in the latitude of eight degrees from the line.

We did all this in about five days, and filled our casks with water; and the last boat was coming off with herbs and roots, we being unmoored, and our fore-topsail loose for sailing, when we spied a large ship to the northward, bearing down directly upon us. We knew not what she might be, but concluded the worst, and made all possible haste to get our anchor up, and get under sail, that we might be in a readiness to see what she had to say to us, for we were under no great concern for one ship, but our notion was, that we should be attacked by three or four together.

By the time we had got up our anchor and the boat was stowed, the ship was within a league of us, and, as we thought, bore down to engage us; so we spread our black flag, or ancient, on the poop, and the bloody flag at the top-masthead, and having made a clear ship, we stretched away to the westward, to get the wind of him.

They had, it seems, quite mistaken us before, expecting nothing of an enemy or a pirate in those seas; and, not doubting but we had been one of their own ships, they seemed to be in some confusion when they found their mistake, so they immediately hauled upon a wind on the other tack, and stood edging in for the shore, towards the easternmost part of the island. Upon this we tacked, and stood after him with all the sail we could, and in two hours came almost within gunshot. Though they crowded all the sail they could lay on, there was no remedy but to engage us, and they soon saw their inequality of force. We fired a gun for them to bring to; so they manned out their boat, and sent to us with a flag of truce. We sent back the boat, but with this answer to the captain, that he had nothing to do but to strike and bring his ship to an anchor under our stern, and come on board us himself, when he should know our demands; but that, however, since he had not yet put us to the trouble of forcing him, which we saw we were able to do, we assured them that the captain should return again in safety, and all his men, and that, supplying us with such things as we should demand, his ship should not be plundered. They went back with this message, and it was some time after they were on board before they struck, which made us begin to think they refused it; so we fired a shot, and in a few minutes more we perceived their boat put off; and as soon as the boat put off the ship struck and came to an anchor, as was directed.

When the captain came on board, we demanded an account of their cargo, which was chiefly bales of goods from Bengal for Bantam. We told them our present want was provisions, which they had no need of, being just at the end of their voyage; and that, if they would send their boat on shore with ours, and procure us six-and-twenty head of black cattle, threescore hogs, a quantity of brandy and arrack, and three hundred bushels of rice, we would let them go free.

As to the rice, they gave us six hundred bushels, which they had actually on board, together with a parcel shipped upon freight. Also, they gave us thirty middling casks of very good arrack, but beef and pork they had none. However, they went on shore with our men, and bought eleven bullocks and fifty hogs, which were pickled up for our occasion; and upon the supplies of provision from shore, we dismissed them and their ship.

We lay here several days before we could furnish ourselves with the provisions agreed for, and some of the men fancied the Dutchmen were contriving our destruction; but they were very honest, and did what they could to furnish the black cattle, but found it impossible to supply so many. So they came and told us ingenuously, that, unless we could stay a while longer, they could get no more oxen or cows than those eleven, with which we were obliged to be satisfied, taking the value of them in other things, rather than stay longer there. On our side, we were punctual with them in observing the conditions we had agreed on; nor would we let any of our men so much as go on board them, or suffer any of their men to come on board us; for, had any of our men gone on board, nobody could have answered for their behavior, any more than if they had been on shore in an enemy's country.

We were now victualled for our voyage; and, as we mattered not purchase, we went merrily on for the coast of Ceylon, where we intended to touch, to get fresh water again, and more provisions; and we had nothing material offered in this part of the voyage, only that we met with contrary winds, and were above a month in the passage.

We put in upon the south coast of the island, desiring to have as little to do with the Dutch as we could; and as the Dutch were lords of the country as to commerce, so they are more so of the seacoast, where they have several forts, and, in particular, have all the cinnamon, which is the trade of that island.

We took in fresh water here, and some provisions, but did not much trouble ourselves about laying in any stores, our beef and hogs, which we got at Java, being not yet all gone by a good deal. We had a little skirmish on shore here with some of the people of the island, some of our men having been a little too familiar with the homely ladies of the country; for homely, indeed, they were, to such a degree, that if our men had not had good stomachs that way, they would scarce have touched any of them.

I could never fully get it out of our men what they did, they were so true to one another in their wickedness, but I understood in the main, that it was some barbarous thing they had done, and that they had like to have paid dear for it, for the men resented it to the last degree, and gathered in such numbers about them, that, had not sixteen more of our men, in another boat, come all in the nick of time, just to rescue our first men, who were but eleven, and so fetch them off by main force, they had been all cut off, the inhabitants being no less than two or three hundred, armed with darts and lances, the usual weapons of the country, and which they are very dexterous at the throwing, even so dexterous that it was scarce credible; and had our men stood to fight them, as some of them were bold enough to talk of, they had been all overwhelmed and killed. As it was, seventeen of our men were wounded, and some of them very dangerously. But they were more frighted than hurt too, for everyone of them gave themselves over for dead men, believing the lances were poisoned. But William was our comfort here too; for, when two of our surgeons were of the same opinion, and told the men foolishly enough that they would die, William cheerfully went to work with them, and cured them all but one, who rather died by drinking some arrack punch than of his wound; the excess of drinking throwing him into a fever.

We had enough of Ceylon, though some of our people were for going ashore again, sixty or seventy men together, to be revenged; but William persuaded them against it; and his reputation was so great among the men, as well as with us that were commanders, that he could influence them more than any of us.

They were mighty warm upon their revenge, and they would go on shore, and destroy five hundred of them. "Well," says William, "and suppose you do, what are you the better?" "Why, then," says one of them, speaking for the rest, "we shall have our satisfaction." "Well, and what will you be the better for that?" says William. They could then say nothing to that. "Then," says William, "if I mistake not, your business is money; now, I desire to know, if you conquer and kill two or three thousand of these poor creatures, they have no money, pray what will you get? They are poor naked wretches; what shall you gain by them? But then," says William, "perhaps, in doing this, you may chance to lose half-a-score of your own company, as it is very probable you may. Pray, what gain is in it? and what account can you give the captain for his lost men?" In short, William argued so effectually, that he convinced them that it was mere murder to do so; and that the men had a right to their own, and that they had no right to take them away; that it was destroying innocent men, who had acted no otherwise than as the laws of nature dictated; and that it would be as much murder to do so, as to meet a man on the highway, and kill him, for the mere sake of it, in cold blood, not regarding whether he had done any wrong to us or no.

These reasons prevailed with them at last, and they were content to go away, and leave them as they found them. In the first skirmish they killed between sixty and seventy men, and wounded a great many more; but they had nothing, and our people got nothing by it, but the loss of one man's life, and the wounding sixteen more, as above.

But another accident brought us to a necessity of further business with these people, and indeed we had like to have put an end to our lives and adventures all at once among them; for, about three days after our putting out to sea from the place where we had that skirmish, we were attacked by a violent storm of wind from the south, or rather a hurricane of wind from all the points southward, for it blew in a most desperate and furious manner from the S.E. to the S.W., one minute at one point, and then instantly turning about again to another point, but with the same violence; nor were we able to work the ship in that condition, so that the ship I was in split three top-sails, and at last brought the main-top-mast by the board; and, in a word, we were once or twice driven right ashore; and one time, had not the wind shifted the very moment it did, we had been dashed in a thousand pieces upon a great ledge of rocks which lay off about half-a-league from the shore; but, as I have said, the wind shifting very often, and at that time coming to the E.S.E., we stretched off, and got above a league more sea-room in half-an-hour. After that, it blew with some fury S.W. by S., then S.W. by W., and put us back again a great way to the eastward of the ledge of rocks, where we found a great opening between the rocks and the land, and endeavored to come to an anchor there, but we found there was no ground fit to anchor in, and that we should lose our anchors, there being nothing but rocks. We stood through the opening, which held about four leagues. The storm continued, and now we found a dreadful foul shore, and knew not what course to take. We looked out very narrowly for some river or creek or bay, where we might run in, and come to an anchor, but found none a great while. At length we saw a great headland lie out far south into the sea, and that to such a length, that, in short, we saw plainly that, if the wind held where it was, we could not weather it, so we ran in as much under the lee of the point as we could, and came to an anchor in about twelve fathom water.

But the wind veering again in the night, and blowing exceedingly hard, our anchors came home, and the ship drove till the rudder struck against the ground; and had the ship gone half her length farther she had been lost, and everyone of us with her. But our sheet-anchor held its own, and we heaved in some of the cable, to get clear of the ground we had struck upon. It was by this only cable that we rode it out all night; and towards morning we thought the wind abated a little; and it was well for us that it was so, for, in spite of what our sheet-anchor did for us, we found the ship fast aground in the morning, to our very great surprise and amazement.

When the tide was out, though the water here ebbed away, the ship lay almost dry upon a bank of hard sand, which never, I suppose, had any ship upon it before. The people of the country came down in great numbers to look at us and gaze, not knowing what we were, but gaping at us as at a great sight or wonder at which they were surprised, and knew not what to do.

I have reason to believe that upon the sight they

immediately sent an account of a ship being there, and of the condition we were in, for the next day there appeared a great man; whether it was their king or no I know not, but he had abundance of men with him, and some with long javelins in their hands as long as half-pikes; and these came all down to the water's edge, and drew up in a very good order, just in our view. They stood near an hour without making any motion; and then there came near twenty of them, with a man before them carrying a white flag. They came forward into the water as high as their waists, the sea not going so high as before, for the wind was abated, and blew off the shore.

The man made a long oration to us, as we could see by his gestures; and we sometimes heard his voice, but knew not one word he said. William, who was always useful to us, I believe was here again the saving of all our lives. The case was this: The fellow, or what I might call him, when his speech was done, gave three great screams (for I know not what else to say they were), then lowered his white flag three times, and then made three motions to us with his arm to come to him.

I acknowledge that I was for manning out the boat and going to them, but William would by no means allow me. He told me we ought to trust nobody; that, if they were barbarians, and under their own government, we might be sure to be all murdered; and, if they were Christians, we should not fare much better, if they knew who we were; that it was the custom of the Malabars to betray all people that they could get into their hands, and that these were some of the same people; and that, if we had any regard to our own safety, we should not go to them by any means. I opposed him a great while, and told him I thought he used to be always right, but that now I thought he was not; that I was no more for running needless risks than he or anyone else; but I thought all nations in the world, even the most savage people, when they held out a flag of peace, kept the offer of peace made by that signal very sacredly; and I gave him several examples of it in the history of my African travels, which I have here gone through in the beginning of this work, and that I could not think these people worse than some of them. And, besides, I told him our case seemed to be such that we must fall into somebody's hands or other, and that we had better fall into their hands by a friendly treaty than by a forced submission, nay, though they had indeed a treacherous design; and therefore I was for a parley with them.

"Well, friend," says William very gravely, "if thou wilt go I cannot help it; I shall only desire to take my last leave of thee at parting, for, depend upon it, thou wilt never see us again. Whether we in the ship may come off any better at last I cannot resolve thee; but this I will answer for, that we will not give up our lives idly, and in cool blood, as thou art going to do; we will at least preserve ourselves as long as we can, and die at last like men, not like fools, trepanned by the wiles of a few barbarians."

William spoke this with so much warmth, and yet with so much assurance of our fate, that I began to think a little of the risk I was going to run. I had no more mind to be murdered than he; and yet I could not for my life be so faint-hearted in the thing as he. Upon which I asked him if he had any knowledge of the place, or had ever been there. He said, No. Then I asked him if he had heard or read anything about the people of this island, and of their way of treating any Christians that had fallen into their hands; and he told me he had heard of one, and he would tell me the story afterward. His name, he said, was Knox, commander of an East India ship, who was driven on shore, just as we were, upon this island of Ceylon, though he could not say it was at the same place, or whereabouts; that he was beguiled by the barbarians, and enticed to come on shore, just as we were invited to do at that time; and that, when they had him, they surrounded him, and eighteen or twenty of his men, and never suffered them to return, but kept them prisoners, or murdered them, he could not tell which; but they were carried away up into the country, separated from one another, and never heard of afterwards, except the captain's son, who miraculously made his escape, after twenty years' slavery.

I had no time then to ask him to give the full story of this Knox, much less to hear him tell it me; but, as it is usual in such cases, when one begins to be a little touched, I turned short with him. "Why then, friend William," said I, "what would you have us do? You see what condition we are in, and what is before us; something must be done, and that immediately." "Why," says William, "I'll tell thee what thou shalt do; first, cause a white flag to be hanged out, as they do to us, and man out the longboat and pinnace with as many men as they can well stow, to handle their arms, and let me go with them, and thou shalt see what we will do. If I miscarry, thou mayest be safe; and I will also tell thee, that if I do miscarry, it shall be my own fault, and thou shalt learn wit by my folly."

I knew not what to reply to him at first; but, after some pause, I said, "William, William, I am as both you should be lost as you are that I should; and if there be any danger, I desire you may no more fall into it than I. Therefore, if you will, let us all keep in the ship, fare alike, and take our fate together."

"No, no," says William, "there's no danger in the method I propose; thou shalt go with me, if thou thinkest fit. If thou pleasest but to follow the measures that I shall resolve on, depend upon it, though we will go off from the ships, we will not a man of us go any nearer them than within call to talk with them. Thou seest they have no boats to come off to us; but," says he, "I rather desire thou wouldst take my advice, and manage the ships as I shall give the signal from the boat, and let us concert that matter together before we go off."

Well, I found William had his measures in his head all laid beforehand, and was not at a loss what to do at all; so I told him he should be captain for this voyage, and we would be all of us under his orders, which I would see observed to a tittle.

Upon this conclusion of our debates, he ordered four-and-twenty men into the longboat, and twelve men into the pinnace, and the sea being now pretty smooth, they went off, being all very well armed. Also he ordered that all the guns of the great ship, on the side which lay next the shore, should be loaded with musket-balls, old nails, stubs, and suchlike pieces of old iron, lead, and anything that came to hand; and that we should prepare to fire as soon as ever we saw them lower the white flag and hoist up a red one in the pinnace.

With these measures fixed between us, they went off towards the shore, William in the pinnace with twelve men, and the longboat coming after him with four-and-twenty more, all stout resolute fellows, and very well armed. They rowed so near the shore as that they might speak to one another, carrying a white flag, as the other did, and offering a parley. The brutes, for such they were, showed themselves very courteous; but finding we could not understand them, they fetched an old Dutchman, who had been their prisoner many years, and set him to speak to us. The sum and substance of his speech was, that the king of the country had sent his general down to know who we were, and what our business was. William stood up in the stern of the pinnace, and told him, that as to that, he, that was an European, by his language and voice, might easily know what we were, and our condition; the ship being aground upon the sand would also tell him that our business there was that of a ship in distress; so William desired to know what they came down for with such a multitude, and with arms and weapons, as if they came to war with us.

He answered, they might have good reason to come down to the shore, the country being alarmed with the appearance of ships of strangers upon the coast; and as our vessels were full of men, and as we had guns and weapons, the king had sent part of his military men, that, in case of any invasion upon the country, they might be ready to defend themselves, whatsoever might be the occasion.

"But," says he, "as you are men in distress, the king has ordered his general, who is here also, to give you all the assistance he can, and to invite you on shore, and receive you with all possible courtesy." Says William, very quick upon him, "Before I give thee an answer to that, I desire thee to tell me what thou art, for by thy speech thou art an European." He answered presently, he was a Dutchman. "That I know well," says William, "by thy speech; but art thou a native Dutchman of Holland, or a native of this country, that has learned Dutch by conversing among the Hollanders, who we know are settled upon this island?"

"No," says the old man, "I am a native of Delft, in the province of Holland, in Europe."

"Well," says William, immediately, "but art thou a Christian or a heathen, or what we call a renegado?"

"I am," says he, "a Christian." And so they went on, in a short dialogue, as follows: —

William. Thou art a Dutchman, and a Christian, thou sayest; pray, art thou a freeman or a servant?

Dutchman. I am a servant to the king here, and in his army.

W. But art thou a volunteer, or a prisoner?

D. Indeed I was a prisoner at first, but am at liberty now, and so am a volunteer.

W. That is to say, being first a prisoner, thou hast liberty to serve them; but art thou so at liberty that thou mayest go away, if thou pleasest, to thine own countrymen?

D. No, I do not say so; my countrymen live a great way off, on the north and east parts of the island, and there is no going to them without the king's express license.

W. Well, and why dost thou not get a license to go away?

D. I have never asked for it.

W. And, I suppose, if thou didst, thou knowest thou couldst not obtain it.

D. I cannot say much as to that; but why do you ask me all these questions?

W. Why, my reason is good; if thou art a Christian and a prisoner, how canst thou consent to be made an instrument to these barbarians, to betray us into their hands, who are thy countrymen and fellow-Christians? Is it not a barbarous thing in thee to do so?

D. How do I go about to betray you? Do I not give you an account how the king invites you to come on shore, and has ordered you to be treated courteously and assisted?

W. As thou art a Christian, though I doubt it much, dost thou believe the king or the general, as thou callest it, means one word of what he says?

D. He promises you by the mouth of his great general.

W. I don't ask thee what he promises, or by whom; but I ask thee this: Canst thou say that thou believest he intends to perform it?

D. How can I answer that? How can I tell what he intends?

W. Thou canst tell what thou believest.

D. I cannot say but he will perform it; I believe he may.

W. Thou art but a double-tongued Christian, I doubt. Come, I'll ask thee another question: Wilt thou say that thou believest it, and that thou wouldst advise me to believe it, and put our lives into their hands upon these promises?

D. I am not to be your adviser.

W. Thou art perhaps afraid to speak thy mind, because thou art in their power. Pray, do any of them understand what thou and I say? Can they speak Dutch?

D. No, not one of them; I have no apprehensions upon that account at all.

W. Why, then, answer me plainly, if thou art a Christian: Is it safe for us to venture upon their words, to put ourselves into their hands, and come on shore?

D. You put it very home to me. Pray let me ask you another question: Are you in any likelihood of getting your ship off, if you refuse it?

W. Yes, yes, we shall get off the ship; now the storm is over we don't fear it.

D. Then I cannot say it is best for you to trust them.

W. Well, it is honestly said.

D. But what shall I say to them?

W. Give them good words, as they give us.

D. What good words?

W. Why, let them tell the king that we are strangers, who were driven on his coast by a great storm; that we thank him very kindly for his offer of civility to us, which, if we are further distressed, we will accept thank-fully; but that at present we have no occasion to come on shore; and besides, that we cannot safely leave the ship in the present condition she is in; but that we are obliged to take care of her, in order to get her off; and expect, in a tide or two more, to get her quite clear, and at an anchor.

D. But he will expect you to come on shore, then, to visit him, and make him some present for his civility.

W. When we have got our ship clear, and stopped the leaks, we will pay our respects to him.

D. Nay, you may as well come to him now as then.

W. Nay, hold, friend; I did not say we would come to him then: you talked of making him a present, that is to pay our respects to him, is it not?

D. Well, but I will tell him that you will come on shore to him when your ship is got off.

W. I have nothing to say to that; you may tell him what you think fit.

D. But he will be in a great rage if I do not.

W. Who will he be in a great rage at?

D. At you.

W. What occasion have we to value that?

D. Why, he will send all his army down against you.

W. And what if they were all here just now? What dost thou suppose they could do to us?

D. He would expect they should burn your ships and bring you all to him.

W. Tell him, if he should try, he may catch a Tartar.

D. He has a world of men.

W. Has he any ships?

D. No, he has no ships.

W. Nor boats?

D. No, nor boats.

W. Why, what then do you think we care for his men? What canst thou do now to us, if thou hadst a hundred thousand with thee?

D. Oh! they might set you on fire.

W. Set us a-firing, thou meanest; that they might indeed; but set us on fire they shall not; they may try, at their peril, and we shall make mad work with your hundred thousand men, if they come within reach of our guns, I assure thee.

D. But what if the king gives you hostages for your safety?

W. Whom can he give but mere slaves and servants like thyself, whose lives he no more values than we an English hound?

D. Whom do you demand for hostages?

W. Himself and your worship.

D. What would you do with him?

W. Do with him as he would do with us — cut his head off.

D. And what would you do with me?

W. Do with thee? We would carry thee home into thine own country; and, though thou deservest the gallows, we would make a man and a Christian of thee again, and not do by thee as thou wouldst have done by us — betray thee to a parcel of merciless, savage pagans, that know no God, nor how to show mercy to man.

D. You put a thought in my head that I will speak to you about tomorrow.

Thus they went away, and William came on board, and gave us a full account of his parley with the old Dutchman, which was very diverting, and to me instructing; for I had abundance of reason to acknowledge William had made a better judgment of things than I.

It was our good fortune to get our ship off that very night, and to bring her to an anchor at about a mile and a half farther out, and in deep water, to our great satisfaction; so that we had no need to fear the Dutch-man's king, with his hundred thousand men; and indeed we had some sport with them the next day, when they came down, a vast prodigious multitude of them, very few less in number, in our imagination, than a hundred thousand, with some elephants; though, if it had been an army of elephants, they could have done us no harm; for we were fairly at our anchor now, and out of their reach. And indeed we thought ourselves more out of their reach than we really were; and it was ten thousand to one that we had not been fast aground again, for the wind blowing off shore, though it made the water smooth where we lay, yet it blew the ebb farther out than usual, and we could easily perceive the sand, which we touched upon before, lay in the shape of a half-moon, and surrounded us with two horns of it, so that we lay in the middle or center of it, as in a round bay, safe just as we were, and in deep water, but present death, as it were, on the right hand and on the left, for the two horns or points of the sand reached out beyond where our ship lay near two miles.

On that part of the sand which lay on our east side, this misguided multitude extended themselves; and being, most of them, not above their knees, or most of them not above ankle-deep in the water, they as it were surrounded us on that side, and on the side of the mainland, and a little way on the other side of the sand, standing in a half-circle, or rather three-fifths of a circle, for about six miles in length. The other horn, or point of the sand, which lay on our west side, being not quite so shallow, they could not extend themselves upon it so far.

They little thought what service they had done us, and how unwittingly, and by the greatest ignorance, they had made themselves pilots to us, while we, having not sounded the place, might have been lost before we were aware. It is true we might have sounded our new harbor before we had ventured out, but I cannot say for certain whether we should or not; for I, for my part, had not the least suspicion of what our real case was; however, I say, perhaps, before we had weighed, we should have looked about us a little. I am sure we ought to have done it; for, besides these armies of human furies, we had a very leaky ship, and all our pumps could hardly keep the water from growing upon us, and our carpenters were overboard, working to find out and stop the wounds we had received, heeling her first on the one side, and then on the other; and it was very diverting to see how, when our men heeled the ship over to the side next the wild army that stood on the east horn of the sand, they were so amazed, between fright and joy, that it put them into a kind of confusion, calling to one another, hallooing and skreeking, in a manner that it is impossible to describe.

While we were doing this, for we were in a great hurry you may be sure, and all hands at work, as well at the stopping our leaks as repairing our rigging and sails, which had received a great deal of damage, and also in rigging a new main-top-mast and the like; — I say, while we were doing all this, we perceived a body of men, of near a thousand, move from that part of the army of the barbarians that lay at the bottom of the sandy bay, and came all along the water's edge, round the sand, till they stood just on our broadside east, and were within about half-a-mile of us. Then we saw the Dutchman come forward nearer to us, and all alone, with his white flag and all his motions, just as before, and there he stood.

Our men had but just brought the ship to rights again as they came up to our broadside, and we had very happily found out and stopped the worst and most dangerous leak that we had, to our very great satisfaction; so I ordered the boats to be hauled up and manned as they were the day before, and William to go as plenipotentiary. I would have gone myself if I had understood Dutch, but as I did not, it was to no purpose, for I should be able to know nothing of what was said but from him at second-hand, which might be done as well afterwards. All the instructions I pretended to give William was, if possible, to get the old Dutchman away, and, if he could, to make him come on board.

Well, William went just as before, and when he came within about sixty or seventy yards of the shore, he held up his white flag as the Dutchman did, and turning the boat's broadside to the shore, and his men lying upon their oars, the parley or dialogue began again thus: —

William. Well, friend, what dost thou say to us now?

Dutchman. I come of the same mild errand as I did yesterday.

W. What! dost thou pretend to come of a mild errand with all these people at thy back, and all the foolish weapons of war they bring with them? Prithee, what dost thou mean?

D. The king hastens us to invite the captain and all his men to come on shore, and has ordered all his men to show them all the civility they can.

W. Well, and are all those men come to invite us ashore?

D. They will do you no hurt, if you will come on shore peaceably.

W. Well, and what dost thou think they can do to us, if we will not?

D. I would not have them do you any hurt then, neither.

W. But prithee, friend, do not make thyself fool and

knave too. Dost not thou know that we are out of fear
of all thy army, and out of danger of all that they can
do? What makes thee act so simply as well as so knav-
ishly?

D. Why, you may think yourselves safer than you
are; you do not know what they may do to you. I can
assure you they are able to do you a great deal of harm,
and perhaps burn your ship.

W. Suppose that were true, as I am sure it is false;
you see we have more ships to carry us off (pointing
to the sloop).

[N.B. — Just at this time we discovered the sloop
standing towards us from the east, along the shore, at
about the distance of two leagues, which was to our
particular satisfaction, she having been missing thirteen days.]

D. We do not value that; if you had ten ships, you
dare not come on shore, with all the men you have, in
a hostile way; we are too many for you.

W. Thou dost not, even in that, speak as thou meanest; and we may give thee a trial of our hands when
our friends come up to us, for thou hearest they have
discovered us.

[Just then the sloop fired five guns, which was to get
news of us, for they did not see us.]

D. Yes, I hear they fire; but I hope your ship will not
fire again; for, if they do, our general will take it for
breaking the truce, and will make the army let fly a
shower of arrows at you in the boat.

W. Thou mayest be sure the ship will fire that the
other ship may hear them, but not with ball. If thy
general knows no better, he may begin when he will;
but thou mayest be sure we will return it to his cost.

D. What must I do, then?

W. Do! Why, go to him, and tell him of it beforehand, then; and let him know that the ship firing is

not at him nor his men; and then come again, and tell us what he says.

D. No; I will send to him, which will do as well.

W. Do as thou wilt, but I believe thou hadst better go thyself; for if our men fire first, I suppose he will be in a great wrath, and it may be at thee; for, as to his wrath at us, we tell thee beforehand we value it not.

D. You slight them too much; you know not what they may do.

W. Thou makest as if these poor savage wretches could do mighty things: prithee, let us see what you can all do, we value it not; thou mayest set down thy flag of truce when thou pleasest, and begin.

D. I had rather make a truce, and have you all part friends.

W. Thou art a deceitful rogue thyself, for it is plain thou knowest these people would only persuade us on shore to entrap and surprise us; and yet thou that art a Christian, as thou callest thyself, would have us come on shore and put our lives into their hands who know nothing that belongs to compassion, good usage, or good manners. How canst thou be such a villain?

D. How can you call me so? What have I done to you, and what would you have me do?

W. Not act like a traitor, but like one that was once a Christian, and would have been so still, if you had not been a Dutchman.

D. I know not what to do, not I. I wish I were from them; they are a bloody people.

W. Prithee, make no difficulty of what thou shouldst do. Canst thou swim?

D. Yes, I can swim; but if I should attempt to swim off to you, I should have a thousand arrows and javelins sticking in me before I should get to your boat.

W. I'll bring the boat close to thee, and take thee on board in spite of them all. We will give them but one volley, and I'll engage they will all run away from thee.

D. You are mistaken in them, I assure you; they would immediately come all running down to the shore, and shoot fire-arrows at you, and set your boat and ship and all on fire about your ears.

W. We will venture that if thou wilt come off.

D. Will you use me honorably when I am among you?

W. I'll give thee my word for it, if thou provest honest.

D. Will you not make me a prisoner?

W. I will be thy surety, body for body, that thou shalt be a free man, and go whither thou wilt, though I own to thee thou dost not deserve it.

Just at this time our ship fired three guns to answer the sloop and let her know we saw her, who immediately, we perceived, understood it, and stood directly for the place. But it is impossible to express the confusion and filthy vile noise, the hurry and universal disorder, that was among that vast multitude of people upon our firing off three guns. They immediately all repaired to their arms, as I may call it; for to say they put themselves into order would be saying nothing.

Upon the word of command, then, they advanced all in a body to the seaside, and resolving to give us one volley of their fire-arms (for such they were), immediately they saluted us with a hundred thousand of their fire-arrows, everyone carrying a little bag of cloth dipped in brimstone, or some such thing, which, flying through the air, had nothing to hinder it taking fire as it flew, and it generally did so.

I cannot say but this method of attacking us, by a way we had no notion of, might give us at first some little surprise, for the number was so great at first, that we were not altogether without apprehensions that they might unluckily set our ship on fire, so that

William resolved immediately to row on board, and persuade us all to weigh and stand out to sea; but there was no time for it, for they immediately let fly a volley at the boat, and at the ship, from all parts of the vast crowd of people which stood near the shore. Nor did they fire, as I may call it, all at once, and so leave off; but their arrows being soon notched upon their bows, they kept continually shooting, so that the air was full of flame.

I could not say whether they set their cotton rag on fire before they shot the arrow, for I did not perceive they had fire with them, which, however, it seems they had. The arrow, besides the fire it carried with it, had a head, or a peg, as we call it, of bone; and some of sharp flint stone; and some few of a metal, too soft in itself for metal, but hard enough to cause it to enter, if it were a plank, so as to stick where it fell.

William and his men had notice sufficient to lie close behind their waste-boards, which, for this very purpose, they had made so high that they could easily sink themselves behind them, so as to defend themselves from anything that came point-blank (as we call it) or upon a line; but for what might fall perpendicularly out of the air they had no guard, but took the hazard of that. At first they made as if they would row away, but before they went they gave a volley of their fire-arms, firing at those which stood with the Dutchman; but William ordered them to be sure to take their aim at others, so as to miss him, and they did so.

There was no calling to them now, for the noise was so great among them that they could hear nobody, but our men boldly rowed in nearer to them, for they were at first driven a little off, and when they came nearer, they fired a second volley, which put the fellows into great confusion, and we could see from the ship that several of them were killed or wounded.

We thought this was a very unequal fight, and therefore we made a signal to our men to row away, that we might have a little of the sport as well as they; but the arrows flew so thick upon them, being so near the shore, that they could not sit to their oars, so they spread a little of their sail, thinking they might sail along the shore, and lie behind their waste-board; but the sail had not been spread six minutes till it had five hundred fire-arrows shot into it and through it, and at length set it fairly on fire; nor were our men quite out of the danger of its setting the boat on fire, and this made them paddle and shove the boat away as well as they could, as they lay, to get farther off.

By this time they had left us a fair mark at the whole savage army; and as we had sheered the ship as near to them as we could, we fired among the thickest of them six or seven times, five guns at a time, with shot, old iron, musket-bullets, &c.

We could easily see that we made havoc among them, and killed and wounded abundance of them, and that they were in a great surprise at it; but yet they never offered to stir, and all this while their fire-arrows flew as thick as before.

At last, on a sudden their arrows stopped, and the old Dutchman came running down to the waterside all alone, with his white flag, as before, waving it as high as he could, and making signals to our boat to come to him again.

William did not care at first to go near him, but the man continuing to make signals to him to come, at last William went; and the Dutchman told him that he had been with the general, who was much mollified by the slaughter of his men, and that now he could have anything of him.

"Anything!" says William; "what have we to do with him? Let him go about his business, and carry his men out of gunshot, can't he?"

"Why," says the Dutchman, "but he dares not stir, nor see the king's face; unless some of your men come on shore, he will certainly put him to death."

"Why, then," says William, "he is a dead man; for if it were to save his life, and the lives of all the crowd that is with him, he shall never have one of us in his power. But I'll tell thee," said William, "how thou shalt cheat him, and gain thy own liberty too, if thou hast any mind to see thy own country again, and art not turned savage, and grown fond of living all thy days among heathens and savages."

"I would be glad to do it with all my heart," says he; "but if I should offer to swim off to you now, though they are so far from me, they shoot so true that they would kill me before I got half-way."

"But," says William, "I'll tell thee how thou shalt come with his consent. Go to him, and tell him I have offered to carry you on board, to try if you could persuade the captain to come on shore, and that I would not hinder him if he was willing to venture."

The Dutchman seemed in a rapture at the very first word. "I'll do it," says he; "I am persuaded he will give me leave to come."

Away he runs, as if he had a glad message to carry, and tells the general that William had promised, if he would go on board the ship with him, he would persuade the captain to return with him. The general was fool enough to give him orders to go, and charged him not to come back without the captain; which he readily promised, and very honestly might.

So they took him in, and brought him on board, and he was as good as his word to them, for he never went back to them any more; and the sloop being come to the mouth of the inlet where we lay, we weighed and set sail; but, as we went out, being pretty near the shore, we fired three guns, as it were among them, but without any shot, for it was of no use to us to hurt any more of them. After we had fired, we gave them a cheer, as the seamen call it; that is to say, we hallooed, at them, by way of triumph, and so carried off their ambassador. How it fared with their general, we know nothing of that.

This passage, when I related it to a friend of mine, after my return from those rambles, agreed so well with his relation of what happened to one Mr Knox, an English captain, who some time ago was decoyed on shore by these people, that it could not but be very much to my satisfaction to think what mischief we had all escaped; and I think it cannot but be very profitable to record the other story (which is but short) with my own, to show whoever reads this what it was I avoided, and prevent their falling into the like, if they have to do with the perfidious people of Ceylon. The relation is as follows: —

The island of Ceylon being inhabited for the greatest part by barbarians, which will not allow any trade or commerce with any European nation, and inaccessible by any travelers, it will be convenient to relate the occasion how the author of this story happened to go into this island, and what opportunities he had of being fully acquainted with the people, their laws and customs, that so we may the better depend upon the account, and value it as it deserves, for the rarity as well as the truth of it; and both these the author gives us a brief relation of in this manner. His words are as follows:

In the year 1657, the *Anne* frigate, of London, Captain Robert Knox, commander, on the 21st day of January, set sail out of the Downs, in the service of the honorable East India Company of England, bound for Fort St George, upon the coast of Coromandel, to trade for one year from port to port in India; which having performed, as he was lading his goods to return for England, being in the road of Masulipatam, on the 19th of November 1659, there happened such a mighty storm, that in it several ships were cast away, and he was forced to cut his mainmast by the board, which so disabled the ship, that he could not proceed in his voyage; whereupon Cottiar, in the island of Ceylon, being a very commodious bay, fit for her present distress, Thomas Chambers, Esq., since Sir Thomas Chambers, the agent at Fort St George, ordered that the ship should take in some cloth and India merchants belonging to Porto Novo, who might trade there while she lay to set her mast, and repair the other damages sustained by the storm. At her first coming thither, after the Indian merchants were set ashore, the captain and his men were very jealous of the people of that place, by reason the English never had any commerce or dealing with them; but after they had been there twenty days, going ashore and returning again at pleasure, without any molestation, they began to lay aside all suspicious thoughts of the people that dwelt thereabouts, who had kindly entertained them for their money.

By this time the king of the country had notice of their arrival, and, not being acquainted with their intents, he sent down a dissauva, or general, with an army, to them, who immediately sent a messenger to the captain on board, to desire him to come ashore to him, pretending a letter from the king. The captain saluted the message with firing of guns, and ordered his son, Robert Knox, and Mr John Loveland, merchant of the ship, to go ashore, and wait on him. When they were come before him, he demanded who they were, and how long they should stay. They told him they were Englishmen, and not to stay above twenty or thirty days, and desired permission to trade in his Majesty's port. His answer was, that the king was glad to hear the English were come into his country, and had commanded him to assist them as they should desire, and had sent a letter to be delivered to none but the captain himself. They were then twelve miles from the seaside, and therefore replied, that the captain could not leave his ship to come so far; but if he pleased to go down to the seaside, the captain would wait on him to receive the letter; whereupon the dissauva desired them to stay that day, and on the morrow he would go with them; which, rather than displease him in so small a matter, they consented to. In the evening the dissauva sent a present to the captain of cattle and fruits, &c., which, being carried all night by the messengers, was delivered to him in the morning, who told him withal that his men were coming down with the dissauva, and desired his company on shore against his coming, having a letter from the king to deliver into his own hand. The captain, mistrusting nothing, came on shore with his boat, and, sitting under a tamarind tree, waited for the dissauva. In the meantime the native soldiers privately surrounded him and the seven men he had with him, and seizing them, carried them to meet the dissauva, bearing the captain on a hammock on their shoulders.

The next day the longboat's crew, not knowing what had happened, came on shore to cut down a tree to make cheeks for the mainmast, and were made prisoners after the same manner, though with more violence, because they were more rough with them, and made resistance; yet they were not brought to the captain and his company, but quartered in another house in the same town.

The dissauva having thus gotten two boats and eighteen men, his next care was to gain the ship; and to that end, telling the captain that he and his men were only detained because the king intended to send letters and a present to the English nation by him, desired he would send some men on board his ship to order her to stay; and because the ship was in danger of being fired by the Dutch if she stayed long in the bay, to bring her up the river. The captain did not approve of the advice, but did not dare to own his dislike; so he sent his son with the order, but with a solemn conjuration to return again, which he accordingly did, bringing a letter from the company in the ship, that they would not obey the captain, nor any other, in this matter, but were resolved to stand on their own defense. This letter satisfied the dissauva, who thereupon gave the captain leave to write for what he would have brought from the ship, pretending that he had not the king's order to release them, though it would suddenly come.

The captain seeing he was held in suspense, and the season of the year spending for the ship to proceed on her voyage to some place, sent order to Mr John Burford, the chief mate, to take charge of the ship, and set sail to Porto Novo, from whence they came, and there to follow the agent's order.

And now began that long and sad captivity they all along feared. The ship being gone, the dissauva was called up to the king, and they were kept under guards a while, till a special order came from the king to part them, and put one in a town, for the conveniency of their maintenance, which the king ordered to be at the charge of the country. On September 16, 1660, the captain and his son were placed in a town called Bonder Coswat, in the country of Hotcurly [? Hewarrisse Korle], distant from the city of Kandy northward thirty miles, and from the rest of the English a full day's journey. Here they had their provisions brought them twice a day, without money, as much as they could eat, and as good as the country yielded. The situation of the place was very pleasant and commodious; but that year that part of the land was very sickly by agues and fevers, of which many died. The captain and his son after some time were visited with the common distemper, and the captain, being also loaded with grief for his deplorable condition, languished more than three months, and then died, February 9, 1661.

Robert Knox, his son, was now left desolate, sick, and in captivity, having none to comfort him but God, who is the Father of the fatherless, and hears the groans of such as are in captivity; being alone to enter upon a long scene of misery and calamity; oppressed with weakness of body and grief of soul for the loss of his father, and the remediless trouble that he was like to endure; and the first instance of it was in the burial of his father, for he sent his black boy to the people of the town, to desire their assistance, because they understood not their language; but they sent him only a rope, to drag him by the neck into the woods, and told him that they would offer him no other help, unless he would pay for it. This barbarous answer increased his trouble for his father's death, that now he was like to lie unburied, and be made a prey to the wild beasts in the woods; for the ground was very hard, and they had not tools to dig with, and so it was impossible for them to bury him; and having a small matter of money left him, viz., a pagoda and a gold ring, he hired a man, and so buried him in as decent a manner as their condition would permit.

His dead father being thus removed out of his sight, but his ague continuing, he was reduced very low, partly by sorrow and partly by his disease. All the comfort he had was to go into the wood and fields

with a book, either the "Practice of Piety" or Mr
Rogers's "Seven Treatises," which were the only two
books he had, and meditate and read, and sometimes
pray; in which his anguish made him often invert
Elijah's petition, — that he might die, because his life
was a burden to him. God, though He was pleased to
prolong his life, yet He found a way to lighten his grief,
by removing his ague, and granting him a desire which
above all things was acceptable to him. He had read
his two books over so often that he had both almost
by heart; and though they were both pious and good
writings, yet he longed for the truth from the original
fountain, and thought it his greatest unhappiness that
he had not a Bible, and did believe that he should never
see one again; but, contrary to his expectation, God
brought him one after this manner. As he was fishing
one day with his black boy, to catch some fish to relieve
his hunger, an old man passed by them, and asked his
boy whether his master could read; and when the boy
had answered yes, he told him that he had gotten a
book from the Portuguese, when they left Colombo;
and, if his master pleased, he would sell it him. The
boy told his master, who bade him go and see what
book it was. The boy having served the English some
time, knew the book, and as soon as he got it into his
hand, came running to him, calling out before he came
to him, "It is the Bible!" The words startled him, and
he flung down his angle to meet him, and, finding it
was true, was mightily rejoiced to see it; but he was
afraid he should not have enough to purchase it,
though he was resolved to part with all the money he
had, which was but one pagoda, to buy it; but his black
boy persuading him to slight it, and leave it to him to
buy it, he at length obtained it for a knit cap.

This accident he could not but look upon as a great
miracle, that God should bestow upon him such an

extraordinary blessing, and bring him a Bible in his own native language, in such a remote part of the world, where His name was not known, and where it was never heard of that an Englishman had ever been before. The enjoyment of this mercy was a great comfort to him in captivity, and though he wanted no bodily convenience that the country did afford; for the king, immediately after his father's death, had sent an express order to the people of the towns, that they should be kind to him, and give him good victuals; and after he had been some time in the country, and understood the language, he got him good conveniences, as a house and gardens; and falling to husbandry, God so prospered him, that he had plenty, not only for himself, but to lend others; which being, according to the custom of the country, at 50 per cent. a year, much enriched him: he had also goats, which served him for mutton, and hogs and hens. Notwithstanding this, I say, for he lived as fine as any of their noblemen, he could not so far forget his native country as to be contented to dwell in a strange land, where there was to him a famine of God's word and sacraments, the want of which made all other things to be of little value to him; therefore, as he made it his daily and fervent prayer to God, in His good time, to restore him to both, so, at length, he, with one Stephen Rutland, who had lived with him two years before, resolved to make their escape, and, about the year 1673, meditated all secret ways to compass it. They had before taken up a way of peddling about the country, and buying tobacco, pepper, garlic, combs, and all sorts of iron ware, and carried them into those parts of the country where they wanted them; and now, to promote their design, as they went with their commodities from place to place, they discoursed with the country people (for they could now speak their language well) concerning the ways and inhabitants, where the isle was thinnest and fullest inhabited, where and how the watches lay from one country to another, and what commodities were proper for them to carry into all parts; pretending that they would furnish themselves with such wares as the respective places wanted. None doubted but what they did was upon the account of trade, because Mr Knox was so well seated, and could not be supposed to leave such an estate, by traveling northward, because that part of the land was least inhabited; and so, furnishing themselves with such wares as were vendible in those parts, they set forth, and steered their course towards the north part of the islands, knowing very little of the ways, which were generally intricate and perplexed, because they have no public roads, but a multitude of little paths from one town to another, and those often changing; and for white men to inquire about the ways was very dangerous, because the people would presently suspect their design.

At this time they traveled from Conde Uda as far as the country of Nuwarakalawiya, which is the furthermost part of the king's dominions, and about three days' journey from their dwelling. They were very thankful to Providence that they had passed all difficulties so far, but yet they durst not go any farther, because they had no wares left to traffic with; and it being the first time they had been absent so long from home, they feared the townsmen would come after them to seek for them; and so they returned home, and went eight or ten times into those parts with their wares, till they became well acquainted both with the people and the paths.

In these parts Mr Knox met his black boy, whom he had turned away divers years before. He had now got a wife and children, and was very poor; but being acquainted with these quarters, he not only took directions of him, but agreed with him, for a good reward, to conduct him and his companions to the Dutch. He gladly undertook it, and a time was appointed between them; but Mr Knox being disabled by a grievous pain, which seized him on his right side, and held him five days that he could not travel, this appointment proved in vain; for though he went as soon as he was well, his guide was gone into another country about his business, and they durst not at that time venture to run away without him.

These attempts took up eight or nine years, various accidents hindering their designs, but most commonly the dry weather, because they feared in the woods they should be starved with thirst, all the country being in such a condition almost four or five years together for lack of rain.

On September 22, 1679, they set forth again, furnished with knives and small axes for their defense, because they could carry them privately and send all sorts of wares to sell as formerly, and all necessary provisions, the moon being twenty-seven days old, that they might have light to run away by, to try what success God Almighty would now give them in seeking their liberty. Their first stage was to Anuradhapoora, in the way to which lay a wilderness, called Parraoth Mocolane, full of wild elephants, tigers, and bears; and because it is the utmost confines of the king's dominions, there is always a watch kept.

In the middle of the way they heard that the governor's officers of these parts were out to gather up the king's revenues and duties, to send them up to the city; which put them into no small fear, lest, finding them, they should send them back again; whereupon they withdrew to the western parts of Ecpoulpot, and sat down to knitting till they heard the officers were gone. As soon as they were departed, they went onwards of their journey, having got a good parcel of cotton-yarn to knit caps with, and having kept their wares, as they pretended, to exchange for dried flesh, which was sold only in those lower parts. Their way lay necessarily through the governor's yard at Kalluvilla, who dwells there on purpose to examine all that go and come. This greatly distressed them, because he would easily suspect they were out of their bounds, being captives; however, they went resolutely to his house, and meeting him, presented him with a small parcel of tobacco and betel; and, showing him their wares, told him they came to get dried flesh to carry back with them. The governor did not suspect them, but told them he was sorry they came in so dry a time, when no deer were to be catched, but if some rain fell, he would soon supply them. This answer pleased them, and they seemed contented to stay; and accordingly, abiding with him two or three days, and no rain falling, they presented the governor with five or six charges of gunpowder, which is a rarity among them; and leaving a bundle at his house, they desired him to shoot them some deer, while they made a step to Anuradhapoora. Here also they were put in a great fright by the coming of certain soldiers from the king to the governor, to give him orders to set a secure guard at the watches, that no suspicious persons might pass, which, though it was only intended to prevent the flight of the relations of certain nobles whom the king had clapped up, yet they feared they might wonder to see white men here, and so send them back again; but God so ordered it that they were very kind to them and left them to their business, and so they got safe to Anuradhapoora. Their pretence was dried flesh, though they knew there was none to be had; but their real business was to search the way down to the Dutch, which they stayed three days to do; but finding that in the way to Jaffnapatam, which is one of the Dutch ports, there was a watch which could hardly be passed, and other inconveniences not surmountable, they resolved to go back, and take the river Malwatta Oya, which they had before judged would be a probable guide to lead them to the sea; and, that they might not be pursued, left Anuradhapoora just at night, when the people never travel for fear of wild beasts, on Sunday, October 12, being stored with all things needful for their journey, viz., ten days' provision, a basin to boil their provision in, two calabashes to fetch water in, and two great tallipat leaves for tents, with jaggery, sweetmeats, tobacco, betel, tinder-boxes, and a deerskin for shoes, to keep their feet from thorns, because to them they chiefly trusted. Being come to the river, they struck into the woods, and kept by the side of it; yet not going on the sand (lest their footsteps should be discerned), unless forced, and then going backwards.

Being gotten a good way into the wood, it began to rain; wherefore they erected their tents, made a fire, and refreshed themselves against the rising of the moon, which was then eighteen days old; and having tied deerskins about their feet, and eased themselves of their wares, they proceeded on their journey. When they had traveled three or four hours with difficulty, because the moon gave but little light among the thick trees, they found an elephant in their way before them, and because they could not scare him away, they were forced to stay till morning; and so they kindled a fire, and took a pipe of tobacco. By the light they could not discern that ever anybody had been there, nothing being to be seen but woods; and so they were in great hopes that they were past all danger, being beyond all inhabitants; but they were mistaken, for the river winding northward, brought them into the midst of a parcel of towns, called Tissea Wava, where, being in danger of being seen, they were under a mighty terror; for had the people found them, they would have beat them, and sent them up to the king; and, to avoid it, they crept into a hollow tree, and sat there in mud and wet till it began to grow dark, and then betaking themselves to their legs, traveled till the darkness of night stopped them. They heard voices behind them, and feared it was somebody in pursuit of them; but at length, discerning it was only an hallooing to keep the wild beasts out of the corn, they pitched their tents by the river, and having boiled rice and roasted meat for their suppers, and satisfied their hunger, they committed themselves to God's keeping, and laid them down to sleep.

The next morning, to prevent the worst, they got up early and hastened on their journey; and though they were now got out of all danger of the tame Chiangulays, they were in great danger of the wild ones, of whom those woods were full; and though they saw their tents, yet they were all gone, since the rains had fallen, from the river into the woods; and so God kept them from that danger, for, had they met the wild men, they had been shot.

Thus they traveled from morning till night several days, through bushes and thorns, which made their arms and shoulders, which were naked, all of a gore blood. They often met with bears, hogs, deer, and wild buffaloes; but they all ran away as soon as they saw them. The river was exceedingly full of alligators; in the evening they used to pitch their tents, and make great fires both before and behind them, to affright the wild beasts; and though they heard the voices of all sorts, they saw none.

On Thursday, at noon, they crossed the river Coronda [? Kannadera Oya], which parts the country of the Malabars from the king's, and on Friday, about

nine or ten in the morning, came among the inhabitants, of whom they were as much afraid as of the
Chiangulays before; for, though the Wanniounay, or
prince of this people, payeth tribute to the Dutch out
of fear, yet he is better affected to the King of Kandy,
and, if he had took them, would have sent them up to
their old master; but not knowing any way to escape,
they kept on their journey by the river-side by day,
because the woods were not to be traveled by night for
thorns and wild beasts, who came down then to the
river to drink. In all the Malabar country they met with
only two Brahmins, who treated them very civilly; and
for their money, one of them conducted them till they
came into the territories of the Dutch, and out of all
danger of the King of Kandy, which did not a little
rejoice them; but yet they were in no small trouble how
to find the way out of the woods, till a Malabar, for
the lucre of a knife, conducted them to a Dutch town,
where they found guides to conduct them from town
to town, till they came to the fort called Aripo, where
they arrived Saturday, October 18, 1679, and there
thankfully adored God's wonderful providence, in
thus completing their deliverance from a long captivity
of nineteen years and six months.

I come now back to my own history, which grows
near a conclusion, as to the travels I took in this part
of the world. We were now at sea, and we stood away
to the north for a while, to try if we could get a market
for our spice, for we were very rich in nutmegs, but we
ill knew what to do with them; we durst not go upon
the English coast, or, to speak more properly, among
the English factories to trade; not that we were afraid
to fight any two ships they had, and, besides that, we
knew that, as they had no letters of marque, or of
reprisals from the government, so it was none of their
business to act offensively, no, not though we were

pirates. Indeed, if we had made any attempt upon them, they might have justified themselves in joining together to resist, and assisting one another to defend themselves; but to go out of their business to attack a pirate ship of almost fifty guns, as we were, it was plain that it was none of their business, and consequently it was none of our concern, so we did not trouble ourselves about it; but, on the other hand, it was none of our business to be seen among them, and to have the news of us carried from one factory to another, so that whatever design we might be upon at another time, we should be sure to be prevented and discovered. Much less had we any occasion to be seen among any of the Dutch factories upon the coast of Malabar; for, being fully laden with the spices which we had, in the sense of their trade, plundered them of, it would have told them what we were, and all that we had been doing; and they would, no doubt, have concerned themselves all manner of ways to have fallen upon us.

The only way we had for it was to stand away for Goa, and trade, if we could, for our spices, with the Portuguese factory there. Accordingly, we sailed almost thither, for we had made land two days before, and being in the latitude of Goa, were standing in fair for Margaon, on the head of Salsat, at the going up to Goa, when I called to the men at the helm to bring the ship to, and bid the pilot go away N.N.W., till we came out of sight of the shore, when William and I called a council, as we used to do upon emergencies, what course we should take to trade there and not be discovered; and we concluded at length that we would not go thither at all, but that William, with such trusty fellows only as could be depended upon, should go in the sloop to Surat, which was still farther northward, and trade there as merchants with such of the English factory as they could find to be for their turn.

To carry this with the more caution, and so as not to be suspected, we agreed to take out all her guns, and put such men into her, and no other, as would promise us not to desire or offer to go on shore, or to enter into any talk or conversation with any that might come on board; and, to finish the disguise to our mind, William documented two of our men, one a surgeon, as he himself was, and the other, a ready-witted fellow, an old sailor, that had been a pilot upon the coast of New England, and was an excellent mimic; these two William dressed up like two Quakers, and made them talk like such. The old pilot he made go captain of the sloop, and the surgeon for doctor, as he was, and himself supercargo. In this figure, and the sloop all plain, no curled work upon her (indeed she had not much before), and no guns to be seen, away he went for Surat.

I should, indeed, have observed, that we went, some days before we parted, to a small sandy island close under the shore, where there was a good cove of deep water, like a road, and out of sight of any of the factories, which are here very thick upon the coast. Here we shifted the loading of the sloop, and put into her such things only as we had a mind to dispose of there, which was indeed little but nutmegs and cloves, but chiefly the former; and from thence William and his two Quakers, with about eighteen men in the sloop, went away to Surat, and came to an anchor at a distance from the factory.

William used such caution that he found means to go on shore himself, and the doctor, as he called him, in a boat which came on board them to sell fish, rowed with only Indians of the country, which boat he afterwards hired to carry him on board again. It was not long that they were on shore, but that they found means to get acquaintance with some Englishmen, who, though they lived there, and perhaps were the company's servants at first, yet appeared then to be traders for themselves, in whatever coast business especially came in their way; and the doctor was made the first to pick acquaintance; so he recommended his friend, the supercargo, till, by degrees, the merchants were as fond of the bargain as our men were of the merchants, only that the cargo was a little too much for them.

However, this did not prove a difficulty long with them, for the next day they brought two more merchants, English also, into their bargain, and, as William could perceive by their discourse, they resolved, if they bought them, to carry them to the Gulf of Persia upon their own accounts. William took the hint, and, as he told me afterwards, concluded we might carry them there as well as they. But this was not William's present business; he had here no less than three-and-thirty ton of nuts and eighteen ton of cloves. There was a good quantity of mace among the nutmegs, but we did not stand to make much allowance. In short, they bargained, and the merchants, who would gladly have bought sloop and all, gave William directions, and two men for pilots, to go to a creek about six leagues from the factory, where they brought boats, and unloaded the whole cargo, and paid William very honestly for it; the whole parcel amounting, in money, to about thirty-five thousand pieces of eight, besides some goods of value, which William was content to take, and two large diamonds, worth about three hundred pounds sterling.

When they paid the money, William invited them on board the sloop, where they came; and the merry old Quaker diverted them exceedingly with his talk, and "thee'd" them and "thou'd" them till he made them so drunk that they could not go on shore for that night.

They would fain have known who our people were, and whence they came; but not a man in the sloop would answer them to any question they asked, but in such a manner as let them think themselves bantered and jested with. However, in discourse, William said they were able men for any cargo we could have brought them, and that they would have bought twice as much spice if we had had it. He ordered the merry captain to tell them that they had another sloop that lay at Margaon, and that had a great quantity of spice on board also; and that, if it was not sold when he went back (for that thither he was bound), he would bring her up.

Their new chaps were so eager, that they would have bargained with the old captain beforehand. "Nay, friend," said he, "I will not trade with thee unsight and unseen; neither do I know whether the master of the sloop may not have sold his loading already to some merchants of Salsat; but if he has not when I come to him, I think to bring him up to thee."

The doctor had his employment all this while, as well as William and the old captain, for he went on shore several times a day in the Indian boat, and brought fresh provisions for the sloop, which the men had need enough of. He brought, in particular, seventeen large casks of arrack, as big as butts, besides smaller quantities, a quantity of rice, and abundance of fruits, mangoes, pompions, and such things, with fowls and fish. He never came on board but he was deep laden; for, in short, he bought for the ship as well as for themselves; and, particularly, they half-loaded the ship with rice and arrack, with some hogs, and six or seven cows, alive; and thus, being well victualled, and having directions for coming again, they returned to us.

William was always the lucky welcome messenger to

us, but never more welcome to us than now; for where we had thrust in the ship, we could get nothing, except a few mangoes and roots, being not willing to make any steps into the country, or make ourselves known till we had news of our sloop; and indeed our men's patience was almost tired, for it was seventeen days that William spent upon this enterprise, and well bestowed too.

When he came back we had another conference upon the subject of trade, namely, whether we should send the best of our spices, and other goods we had in the ship, to Surat, or whether we should go up to the Gulf of Persia ourselves, where it was probable we might sell them as well as the English merchants of Surat. William was for going ourselves, which, by the way, was from the good, frugal, merchantlike temper of the man, who was for the best of everything; but here I overruled William, which I very seldom took upon me to do; but I told him, that, considering our circumstances, it was much better for us to sell all our cargoes here, though we made but half-price of them, than to go with them to the Gulf of Persia, where we should run a greater risk, and where people would be much more curious and inquisitive into things than they were here, and where it would not be so easy to manage them, seeing they traded freely and openly there, not by stealth, as those men seemed to do; and, besides, if they suspected anything, it would be much more difficult for us to retreat, except by mere force, than here, where we were upon the high sea as it were, and could be gone whenever we pleased, without any disguise, or, indeed, without the least appearance of being pursued, none knowing where to look for us.

My apprehensions prevailed with William, whether my reasons did or no, and he submitted; and we resolved to try another ship's loading to the same merchants. The main business was to consider how to get off that circumstance that had exposed them to the English merchants, namely that it was our other sloop; but this the old Quaker pilot undertook; for being, as I said, an excellent mimic himself, it was the easier for him to dress up the sloop in new clothes; and first, he put on all the carved work he had taken off before; her stern, which was painted of a dumb white or dun color before, all flat, was now all lacquered and blue, and I know not how many gay figures in it; as to her quarter, the carpenters made her a neat little gallery on either side; she had twelve guns put into her, and some petereroes upon her gunnel, none of which were there before; and to finish her new habit or appearance, and make her change complete, he ordered her sails to be altered; and as she sailed before with a half-sprit, like a yacht, she sailed now with square-sail and mizzen-mast, like a ketch; so that, in a word, she was a perfect cheat, disguised in everything that a stranger could be supposed to take any notice of that had never had but one view, for they had been but once on board.

In this mean figure the sloop returned; she had a new man put into her for captain, one we knew how to trust; and the old pilot appearing only as a passenger, the doctor and William acting as the supercargoes, by a formal procuration from one Captain Singleton, and all things ordered in form.

We had a complete loading for the sloop; for, besides a very great quantity of nutmegs and cloves, mace, and some cinnamon, she had on board some goods which we took in as we lay about the Philippine Islands, while we waited as looking for purchase.

William made no difficulty of selling this cargo also, and in about twenty days returned again, freighted with all necessary provisions for our voyage, and for a long time; and, as I say, we had a great deal of other goods:

he brought us back about three-and-thirty thousand pieces of eight, and some diamonds, which, though William did not pretend to much skill in, yet he made shift to act so as not to be imposed upon, the merchants he had to deal with, too, being very fair men.

They had no difficulty at all with these merchants, for the prospect they had of gain made them not at all inquisitive, nor did they make the least discovery of the sloop; and as to the selling them spices which were fetched so far from thence, it seems it was not so much a novelty there as we believed, for the Portuguese had frequently vessels which came from Macao in China, who brought spices, which they bought of the Chinese traders, who again frequently dealt among the Dutch Spice Islands, and received spices in exchange for such goods as they carried from China.

This might be called, indeed, the only trading voyage we had made; and now we were really very rich, and it came now naturally before us to consider whither we should go next. Our proper delivery port, as we ought to have called it, was at Madagascar, in the Bay of Mangahelly; but William took me by myself into the cabin of the sloop one day, and told me he wanted to talk seriously with me a little; so we shut ourselves in, and William began with me.

"Wilt thou give me leave," says William, "to talk plainly with thee upon thy present circumstances, and thy future prospect of living? and wilt thou promise, on thy word, to take nothing ill of me?"

"With all my heart," said I. "William, I have always found your advice good, and your designs have not only been well laid, but your counsel has been very lucky to us; and, therefore, say what you will, I promise you I will not take it ill."

"But that is not all my demand," says William; "if thou dost not like what I am going to propose to thee, thou shalt promise me not to make it public among the men."

"I will not, William," says I, "upon my word;" and swore to him, too, very heartily.

"Why, then," says William, "I have but one thing more to article with thee about, and that is, that thou wilt consent that if thou dost not approve of it for thyself, thou wilt yet consent that I shall put so much of it in practice as relates to myself and my new comrade doctor, so that it be nothing to thy detriment and loss."

"In anything," says I, "William, but leaving me, I will; but I cannot part with you upon any terms whatever."

"Well," says William, "I am not designing to part from thee, unless it is thy own doing. But assure me in all these points, and I will tell my mind freely."

So I promised him everything he desired of me in the solemnest manner possible, and so seriously and frankly withal, that William made no scruple to open his mind to me.

"Why, then, in the first place," says William, "shall I ask thee if thou dost not think thou and all thy men are rich enough, and have really gotten as much wealth together (by whatsoever way it has been gotten, that is not the question) as we all know what to do with?"

"Why, truly, William," said I, "thou art pretty right; I think we have had pretty good luck."

"Well, then," says William, "I would ask whether, if thou hast gotten enough, thou hast any thought of leaving off this trade; for most people leave off trading when they are satisfied of getting, and are rich enough; for nobody trades for the sake of trading; much less do men rob for the sake of thieving."

"Well, William," says I, "now I perceive what it is thou art driving at. I warrant you," says I, "you begin to hanker after home."

"Why, truly," says William, "thou hast said it, and so I hope thou dost too. It is natural for most men that are abroad to desire to come home again at last, especially when they are grown rich, and when they are (as thou ownest thyself to be) rich enough, and so rich as they know not what to do with more if they had it."

"Well, William," said I, "but now you think you have laid your preliminary at first so home that I should have nothing to say; that is, that when I had got money enough, it would be natural to think of going home. But you have not explained what you mean by home, and there you and I shall differ. Why, man, I am at home; here is my habitation; I never had any other in my lifetime; I was a kind of charity school boy; so that I can have no desire of going anywhere for being rich or poor, for I have nowhere to go."

"Why," says William, looking a little confused, "art not thou an Englishman?"

"Yes," says I, "I think so: you see I speak English; but I came out of England a child, and never was in it but once since I was a man; and then I was cheated and imposed upon, and used so ill that I care not if I never see it more."

"Why, hast thou no relations or friends there?" says he; "no acquaintance — none that thou hast any kindness or any remains of respect for?"

"Not I, William," said I; "no more than I have in the court of the Great Mogul."

"Nor any kindness for the country where thou wast born?" says William.

"Not I, any more than for the island of Madagascar, nor so much neither; for that has been a fortunate island to me more than once, as thou knowest, William," said I.

William was quite stunned at my discourse, and held

his peace; and I said to him, "Go on, William; what hast thou to say farther? for I hear you have some project in your head," says I; "come, let's have it out."

"Nay," says William, "thou hast put me to silence, and all I had to say is overthrown; all my projects are come to nothing, and gone."

"Well, but, William," said I, "let me hear what they were; for though it is so that what I have to aim at does not look your way, and though I have no relation, no friend, no acquaintance in England, yet I do not say I like this roving, cruising life so well as never to give it over. Let me hear if thou canst propose to me anything beyond it."

"Certainly, friend," says William, very gravely, "there is something beyond it;" and lifting up his hands, he seemed very much affected, and I thought I saw tears stand in his eyes; but I, that was too hardened a wretch to be moved with these things, laughed at him. "What!" says I, "you mean death, I warrant you: don't you? That is beyond this trade. Why, when it comes, it comes; then we are all provided for."

"Aye," says William, "that is true; but it would be better that some things were thought on before that came."

"Thought on!" says I; "what signifies thinking of it? To think of death is to die, and to be always thinking of it is to be all one's life long a-dying. It is time enough to think of it when it comes."

You will easily believe I was well qualified for a pirate that could talk thus. But let me leave it upon record, for the remark of other hardened rogues like myself, — my conscience gave me a pang that I never felt before when I said, "What signifies thinking of it?" and told me I should one day think of these words with a sad heart; but the time of my reflection was not yet come; so I went on.

Says William very seriously, "I must tell thee, friend, I am sorry to hear thee talk so. They that never think of dying, often die without thinking of it."

I carried on the jesting way a while farther, and said, "Prithee, do not talk of dying; how do we know we shall ever die?" and began to laugh.

"I need not answer thee to that," says William; "it is not my place to reprove thee, who art commander over me here; but I would rather thou wouldst talk otherwise of death; it is a coarse thing."

"Say anything to me, William," said I; "I will take it kindly." I began now to be very much moved at his discourse.

Says William (tears running down his face), "It is because men live as if they were never to die, that so many die before they know how to live. But it was not death that I meant when I said that there was something to be thought of beyond this way of living."

"Why, William," said I, "what was that?"

"It was repentance," says he.

"Why," says I, "did you ever know a pirate repent?"

At this he startled a little, and returned, "At the gallows I have [known] one before, and I hope thou wilt be the second."

He spoke this very affectionately, with an appearance of concern for me.

"Well, William," says I, "I thank you; and I am not so senseless of these things, perhaps, as I make myself seem to be. But come, let me hear your proposal."

"My proposal," says William, "is for thy good as well as my own. We may put an end to this kind of life, and repent; and I think the fairest occasion offers for both, at this very time, that ever did, or ever will, or, indeed, can happen again."

"Look you, William," says I; "let me have your proposal for putting an end to our present way of living first, for that is the case before us, and you and I will talk of the other afterwards. I am not so insensible," said I, "as you may think me to be. But let us get out of this hellish condition we are in first."

"Nay," says William, "thou art in the right there; we must never talk of repenting while we continue pirates."

"Well," says I, "William, that's what I meant; for if we must not reform, as well as be sorry for what is done, I have no notion what repentance means; indeed, at best I know little of the matter; but the nature of the thing seems to tell me that the first step we have to take is to break off this wretched course; and I'll begin there with you, with all my heart."

I could see by his countenance that William was thoroughly pleased with the offer; and if he had tears in-his eyes before, he had more now; but it was from quite a different passion; for he was so swallowed up with joy he could not speak.

"Come, William," says I, "thou showest me plain enough thou hast an honest meaning; dost thou think it practicable for us to put an end to our unhappy way of living here, and get off?"

"Yes," says he, "I think it very practicable for me; whether it is for thee or no, that will depend upon thyself."

"Well," says I, "I give you my word, that as I have commanded you all along, from the time I first took you on board, so you shall command me from this hour, and everything you direct me I'll do."

"Wilt thou leave it all to me? Dost thou say this freely?"

"Yes, William," said I, "freely; and I'll perform it faithfully."

"Why, then," says William, "my scheme is this: We are now at the mouth of the Gulf of Persia; we have sold so much of our cargo here at Surat, that we have money enough; send me away for Bassorah with the sloop, laden with the China goods we have on board, which will make another good cargo, and I'll warrant thee I'll find means, among the English and Dutch merchants there, to lodge a quantity of goods and money also as a merchant, so as we will be able to have recourse to it again upon any occasion, and when I come home we will contrive the rest; and, in the meantime, do you bring the ship's crew to take a resolution to go to Madagascar as soon as I return."

I told him I thought he need not go so far as Bassorah, but might run into Gombroon, or to Ormuz, and pretend the same business.

"No," says he, "I cannot act with the same freedom there, because the Company's factories are there, and I may be laid hold of there on pretence of interloping."

"Well, but," said I, "you may go to Ormuz, then; for I am loth to part with you so long as to go to the bottom of the Persian Gulf." He returned, that I should leave it to him to do as he should see cause.

We had taken a large sum of money at Surat, so that we had near a hundred thousand pounds in money at our command, but on board the great ship we had still a great deal more.

I ordered him publicly to keep the money on board which he had, and to buy up with it a quantity of ammunition, if he could get it, and so to furnish us for new exploits; and, in the meantime, I resolved to get a quantity of gold and some jewels, which I had on board the great ship, and place them so that I might carry them off without notice as soon as he came back; and so, according to William's directions, I left him to go the voyage, and I went on board the great ship, in which we had indeed an immense treasure.

We waited no less than two months for William's

return, and indeed I began to be very uneasy about William, sometimes thinking he had abandoned me, and that he might have used the same artifice to have engaged the other men to comply with him, and so they were gone away together; and it was but three days before his return that I was just upon the point of resolving to go away to Madagascar, and give him over; but the old surgeon, who mimicked the Quaker and passed for the master of the sloop at Surat, persuaded me against that, for which good advice and apparent faithfulness in what he had been trusted with, I made him a party to my design, and he proved very honest.

At length William came back, to our inexpressible joy, and brought a great many necessary things with him; as, particularly, he brought sixty barrels of powder, some iron shot, and about thirty ton of lead; also he brought a great deal of provisions; and, in a word, William gave me a public account of his voyage, in the hearing of whoever happened to be upon the quarterdeck, that no suspicions might be found about us.

After all was done, William moved that he might go up again, and that I would go with him; named several things which we had on board that he could not sell there; and, particularly, told us he had been obliged to leave several things there, the caravans being not come in; and that he had engaged to come back again with goods.

This was what I wanted. The men were eager for his going, and particularly because he told them they might load the sloop back with rice and provisions; but I seemed backward to going, when the old surgeon stood up and persuaded me to go, and with many arguments pressed me to it; as, particularly, if I did not go, there would be no order, and several of the men might drop away, and perhaps betray all the rest; and that they should not think it safe for the sloop to go again if I did not go; and to urge me to it, he offered himself to go with me.

Upon these considerations I seemed to be overpersuaded to go, and all the company seemed to be better satisfied when I had consented; and, accordingly, we took all the powder, lead, and iron out of the sloop into the great ship, and all the other things that were for the ship's use, and put in some bales of spices and casks or frails of cloves, in all about seven ton, and some other goods, among the bales of which I had conveyed all my private treasure, which, I assure you, was of no small value, and away I went.

At going off I called a council of all the officers in the ship to consider in what place they should wait for me, and how long, and we appointed the ship to stay eight-and-twenty days at a little island on the Arabian side of the Gulf, and that, if the sloop did not come in that time, they should sail to another island to the west of that place, and wait there fifteen days more, and that then, if the sloop did not come, they should conclude some accident must have happened, and the rendezvous should be at Madagascar.

Being thus resolved, we left the ship, which both William and I, and the surgeon, never intended to see any more. We steered directly for the Gulf, and through to Bassorah, or Balsara. This city of Balsara lies at some distance from the place where our sloop lay, and the river not being very safe, and we but ill acquainted with it, having but an ordinary pilot, we went on shore at a village where some merchants live, and which is very populous, for the sake of small vessels riding there.

Here we stayed and traded three or four days, landing all our bales and spices, and indeed the whole cargo that was of any considerable value, which we chose to do rather than go up immediately to Balsara till the project we had laid was put in execution.

After we had bought several goods, and were preparing to buy several others, the boat being on shore with twelve men, myself, William, the surgeon, and one fourth man, whom we had singled out, we contrived to send a Turk just at the dusk of the evening with a letter to the boatswain, and giving the fellow a charge to run with all possible speed, we stood at a small distance to observe the event. The contents of the letter were thus written by the old doctor: —

"BOATSWAIN THOMAS, —

"We are all betrayed. For God's sake make off with the boat, and get on board, or you are all lost. The captain, William the Quaker, and George the reformade are seized and carried away: I am escaped and hid, but cannot stir out; if I do I am a dead man. As soon as you are on board cut or slip, and make sail for your lives. Adieu.

"— R.S."

We stood undiscovered, as above, it being the dusk of the evening, and saw the Turk deliver the letter, and in three minutes we saw all the men hurry into the boat and put off, and no sooner were they on board than they took the hint, as we supposed, for the next morning they were out of sight, and we never heard tale or tidings of them since.

We were now in a good place, and in very good circumstances, for we passed for merchants of Persia.

It is not material to record here what a mass of ill-gotten wealth we had got together: it will be more to the purpose to tell you that I began to be sensible of the crime of getting of it in such a manner as I had done; that I had very little satisfaction in the possession of it; and, as I told William, I had no expectation of keeping it, nor much desire; but, as I said to him one day walking out into the fields near the town of Bassorah, so I depended upon it that it would be the case, which you will hear presently.

We were perfectly secured at Bassorah, by having frighted away the rogues, our comrades; and we had nothing to do but to consider how to convert our treasure into things proper to make us look like merchants, as we were now to be, and not like freebooters, as we really had been.

We happened very opportunely here upon a Dutchman, who had traveled from Bengal to Agra, the capital city of the Great Mogul, and from thence was come to the coast of Malabar by land, and got shipping, somehow or other, up the Gulf; and we found his design was to go up the great river to Bagdad or Babylon, and so, by the caravan, to Aleppo and Scanderoon. As William spoke Dutch, and was of an agreeable, insinuating behavior, he soon got acquainted with this Dutchman, and discovering our circumstances to one another, we found he had considerable effects with him; and that he had traded long in that country, and was making homeward to his own country; and that he had servants with him; one an Armenian, whom he had taught to speak Dutch, and who had something of his own, but had a mind to travel into Europe; and the other a Dutch sailor, whom he had picked up by his fancy, and reposed a great trust in him, and a very honest fellow he was.

This Dutchman was very glad of an acquaintance, because he soon found that we directed our thoughts to Europe also; and as he found we were encumbered with goods only (for we let him know nothing of our money), he readily offered us his assistance to dispose of as many of them as the place we were in would put off, and his advice what to do with the rest.

While this was doing, William and I consulted what

to do with ourselves and what we had; and first, we resolved we would never talk seriously of our measures but in the open fields, where we were sure nobody could hear; so every evening, when the sun began to decline and the air to be moderate we walked out, sometimes this way, sometimes that, to consult of our affairs.

I should have observed that we had new clothed ourselves here, after the Persian manner, with long vests of silk, a gown or robe of English crimson cloth, very fine and handsome, and had let our beards grow so after the Persian manner that we passed for Persian merchants, in view only, though, by the way, we could not understand or speak one word of the language of Persia, or indeed of any other but English and Dutch; and of the latter I understood very little.

However, the Dutchman supplied all this for us; and as we had resolved to keep ourselves as retired as we could, though there were several English merchants upon the place, yet we never acquainted ourselves with one of them, or exchanged a word with them; by which means we prevented their inquiry of us now, or their giving any intelligence of us, if any news of our landing here should happen to come, which, it was easy for us to know, was possible enough, if any of our comrades fell into bad hands, or by many accidents which we could not foresee.

It was during my being here, for here we stayed near two months, that I grew very thoughtful about my circumstances; not as to the danger, neither indeed were we in any, but were entirely concealed and unsuspected; but I really began to have other thoughts of myself, and of the world, than ever I had before.

William had struck so deep into my unthinking temper with hinting to me that there was something beyond all this; that the present time was the time of enjoyment, but that the time of account approached; that the work that remained was gentler than the labor past, viz., repentance, and that it was high time to think of it; — I say these, and such thoughts as these, engrossed my hours, and, in a word, I grew very sad.

As to the wealth I had, which was immensely great, it was all like dirt under my feet; I had no value for it, no peace in the possession of it, no great concern about me for the leaving of it.

William had perceived my thoughts to be troubled and my mind heavy and oppressed for some time; and one evening, in one of our cool walks, I began with him about the leaving our effects. William was a wise and wary man, and indeed all the prudentials of my conduct had for a long time been owing to his advice, and so now all the methods for preserving our effects, and even ourselves, lay upon him; and he had been telling me of some of the measures he had been taking for our making homeward, and for the security of our wealth, when I took him very short. "Why, William," says I, "dost thou think we shall ever be able to reach Europe with all this cargo that we have about us?"

"Aye," says William, "without doubt, as well as other merchants with theirs, as long as it is not publicly known what quantity or of what value our cargo consists."

"Why, William," says I, smiling, "do you think that if there is a God above, as you have so long been telling me there is, and that we must give an account to Him, — I say, do you think, if He be a righteous Judge, He will let us escape thus with the plunder, as we may call it, of so many innocent people, nay, I might say nations, and not call us to an account for it before we can get to Europe, where we pretend to enjoy it?"

William appeared struck and surprised at the question, and made no answer for a great while; and I repeated the question, adding that it was not to be expected.

After a little pause, says William, "Thou hast started a very weighty question, and I can make no positive answer to it; but I will state it thus: first, it is true that, if we consider the justice of God, we have no reason to expect any protection; but as the ordinary ways of Providence are out of the common road of human affairs, so we may hope for mercy still upon our repentance, and we know not how good He may be to us; so we are to act as if we rather depended upon the last, I mean the merciful part, than claimed the first, which must produce nothing but judgment and vengeance."

"But hark ye, William," says I, "the nature of repentance, as you have hinted once to me, included reformation; and we can never reform; how, then, can we repent?"

"Why can we never reform?" says William.

"Because," said I, "we cannot restore what we have taken away by rapine and spoil."

"It is true," says William, "we never can do that, for we can never come to the knowledge of the owners."

"But what, then, must be done with our wealth," said I, "the effects of plunder and rapine? If we keep it, we continue to be robbers and thieves; and if we quit it we cannot do justice with it, for we cannot restore it to the right owners."

"Nay," says William, "the answer to it is short. To quit what we have, and do it here, is to throw it away to those who have no claim to it, and to divest ourselves of it, but to do no right with it; whereas we ought to keep it carefully together, with a resolution to do what right with it we are able; and who knows what opportunity Providence may put into our hands to do justice, at least, to some of those we have injured? So we ought, at least, to leave it to Him and go on. As it is, without doubt our present business is to go to some place of safety, where we may wait His will."

This resolution of William was very satisfying to me indeed, as, the truth is, all he said, and at all times, was solid and good; and had not William thus, as it were, quieted my mind, I think, verily, I was so alarmed at the just reason I had to expect vengeance from Heaven upon me for my ill-gotten wealth, that I should have run away from it as the devil's goods, that I had nothing to do with, that did not belong to me, and that I had no right to keep, and was in certain danger of being destroyed for.

However, William settled my mind to more prudent steps than these, and I concluded that I ought, however, to proceed to a place of safety, and leave the event to God Almighty's mercy. But this I must leave upon record, that I had from this time no joy of the wealth I had got. I looked upon it all as stolen, and so indeed the greatest part of it was. I looked upon it as a hoard of other men's goods, which I had robbed the innocent owners of, and which I ought, in a word, to be hanged for here, and damned for hereafter. And now, indeed, I began sincerely to hate myself for a dog; a wretch that had been a thief and a murderer; a wretch that was in a condition which nobody was ever in; for I had robbed, and though I had the wealth by me, yet it was impossible I should ever make any restitution; and upon this account it ran in my head that I could never repent, for that repentance could not be sincere without restitution, and therefore must of necessity be damned. There was no room for me to escape. I went about with my heart full of these thoughts, little better than a distracted fellow; in short, running headlong into the dreadfullest despair, and premeditating nothing but how to rid myself out of the world; and, indeed, the devil, if such things are of the devil's immediate doing, followed his work very close with me, and nothing lay upon my mind for several days but to shoot myself into the head with my pistol.

I was all this while in a vagrant life, among infidels, Turks, pagans, and such sort of people. I had no minister, no Christian to converse with but poor William. He was my ghostly father or confessor, and he was all the comfort I had. As for my knowledge of religion, you have heard my history. You may suppose I had not much; and as for the Word of God, I do not remember that I ever read a chapter in the Bible in my lifetime. I was little Bob at Bussleton, and went to school to learn my Testament.

However, it pleased God to make William the Quaker everything to me. Upon this occasion, I took him out one evening, as usual, and hurried him away into the fields with me, in more haste than ordinary; and there, in short, I told him the perplexity of my mind, and under what terrible temptations of the devil I had been; that I must shoot myself, for I could not support the weight and terror that was upon me.

"Shoot yourself!" says William; "why, what will that do for you?"

"Why," says I, "it will put an end to a miserable life."

"Well," says William, "are you satisfied the next will be better?"

"No, no," says I; "much worse, to be sure."

"Why, then," says he, "shooting yourself is the devil's motion, no doubt; for it is the devil of a reason, that, because thou art in an ill case, therefore thou must put thyself into a worse."

This shocked my reason indeed. "Well, but," says I, "there is no bearing the miserable condition I am in."

"Very well," says William; "but it seems there is some bearing a worse condition; and so you will shoot yourself, that you may be past remedy?"

"I am past remedy already," says I.

"How do you know that?" says he.

"I am satisfied of it," said I.

"Well," says he, "but you are not sure; so you will shoot yourself to make it certain; for though on this side death you cannot be sure you will be damned at all, yet the moment you step on the other side of time you are sure of it; for when it is done, it is not to be said then that you will be, but that you are damned."

"Well, but," says William, as if he had been between jest and earnest, "pray, what didst thou dream of last night?"

"Why," said I, "I had frightful dreams all night; and, particularly, I dreamed that the devil came for me, and asked me what my name was; and I told him. Then he asked me what trade I was. 'Trade?' says I; 'I am a thief, a rogue, by my calling: I am a pirate and a murderer, and ought to be hanged.' 'Aye, aye,' says the devil, 'so you do; and you are the man I looked for, and therefore come along with me.' At which I was most horribly frighted, and cried out so that it waked me; and I have been in horrible agony ever since."

"Very well," says William; "come, give me the pistol thou talkedst of just now."

"Why," says I, "what will you do with it?"

"Do with it!" says William. "Why, thou needest not shoot thyself; I shall be obliged to do it for thee. Why, thou wilt destroy us all."

"What do you mean, William?" said I.

"Mean!" said he; "nay, what didst thou mean, to cry out aloud in thy sleep, 'I am a thief, a pirate, a murderer, and ought to be hanged'? Why, thou wilt ruin us all. 'Twas well the Dutchman did not understand English. In short, I must shoot thee, to save my own life. Come, come," says he, "give me thy pistol."

I confess this terrified me again another way, and I began to be sensible that, if anybody had been near me to understand English, I had been undone. The thought of shooting myself forsook me from that time; and I turned to William, "You disorder me extremely, William," said I; "why, I am never safe, nor is it safe to keep me company. What shall I do? I shall betray you all."

"Come, come, friend Bob," says he, "I'll put an end to it all, if you will take my advice."

"How's that?" said I.

"Why, only," says he, "that the next time thou talkest with the devil, thou wilt talk a little softlier, or we shall be all undone, and you too."

This frighted me, I must confess, and allayed a great deal of the trouble of mind I was in. But William, after he had done jesting with me, entered upon a very long and serious discourse with me about the nature of my circumstances, and about repentance; that it ought to be attended, indeed, with a deep abhorrence of the crime that I had to charge myself with; but that to despair of God's mercy was no part of repentance, but putting myself into the condition of the devil; indeed, that I must apply myself with a sincere, humble confession of my crime, to ask pardon of God, whom I had offended, and cast myself upon His mercy, resolving to be willing to make restitution, if ever it should please God to put it in my power, even to the utmost of what I had in the world. And this, he told me, was the method which he had resolved upon himself; and in this, he told me, he had found comfort.

I had a great deal of satisfaction in William's discourse, and it quieted me very much; but William was very anxious ever after about my talking in my sleep, and took care to lie with me always himself, and to keep me from lodging in any house where so much as a word of English was understood.

However, there was not the like occasion afterward; for I was much more composed in my mind, and resolved for the future to live a quite different life from what I had done. As to the wealth I had, I looked upon it as nothing; I resolved to set it apart to any such opportunity of doing justice as God should put into my hand; and the miraculous opportunity I had afterwards of applying some parts of it to preserve a ruined family, whom I had plundered, may be worth reading, if I have room for it in this account.

With these resolutions I began to be restored to some degree of quiet in my mind; and having, after almost three months' stay at Bassorah, disposed of some goods, but having a great quantity left, we hired boats according to the Dutchman's direction, and went up to Bagdad, or Babylon, on the river Tigris, or rather Euphrates. We had a very considerable cargo of goods with us, and therefore made a great figure there, and were received with respect. We had, in particular, two-and-forty bales of Indian stuffs of sundry sorts, silks, muslins, and fine chintz; we had fifteen bales of very fine China silks, and seventy packs or bales of spices, particularly cloves and nutmegs, with other goods. We were bid money here for our cloves, but the Dutchman advised us not to part with them, and told us we should get a better price at Aleppo, or in the Levant; so we prepared for the caravan.

We concealed our having any gold or pearls as much as we could, and therefore sold three or four bales of China silks and Indian calicoes, to raise money to buy camels and to pay the customs which are taken at several places, and for our provisions over the deserts.

I traveled this journey, careless to the last degree of my goods or wealth, believing that, as I came by it all by rapine and violence, God would direct that it should be taken from me again in the same manner; and, indeed, I think I might say I was very willing it should be so. But, as I had a merciful Protector above me, so I had a most faithful steward, counselor, partner, or whatever I might call him, who was my guide, my pilot, my governor, my everything, and took care both of me and of all we had; and though he had never been in any of these parts of the world, yet he took the care of all upon him; and in about nine-and-fifty days we arrived from Bassorah, at the mouth of the river Tigris or Euphrates, through the desert, and through Aleppo to Alexandria, or, as we call it, Scanderoon, in the Levant.

Here William and I, and the other two, our faithful comrades, debated what we should do; and here William and I resolved to separate from the other two, they resolving to go with the Dutchman into Holland, by the means of some Dutch ship which lay then in the road. William and I told them we resolved to go and settle in the Morea, which then belonged to the Venetians.

It is true we acted wisely in it not to let them know whither we went, seeing we had resolved to separate; but we took our old doctor's directions how to write to him in Holland, and in England, that we might have intelligence from him on occasion, and promised to give him an account how to write to us, which we afterwards did, as may in time be made out.

We stayed here some time after they were gone, till at length, not being thoroughly resolved whither to go till then, a Venetian ship touched at Cyprus, and put in at Scanderoon to look for freight home. We took the hint, and bargaining for our passage, and the freight of our goods, we embarked for Venice, where, in two-and-twenty days, we arrived safe, with all our treasure, and with such a cargo, take our goods and our money and our jewels together, as, I believed, was never brought into the city by two single men, since the state of Venice had a being.

We kept ourselves here *incognito* for a great while, passing for two Armenian merchants still, as we had done before; and by this time we had gotten so much of the Persian and Armenian jargon, which they talked at Bassorah and Bagdad, and everywhere that we came in the country, as was sufficient to make us able to talk to one another, so as not to be understood by anybody, though sometimes hardly by ourselves.

Here we converted all our effects into money, settled our abode as for a considerable time, and William and I, maintaining an inviolable friendship and fidelity to one another, lived like two brothers; we neither had or sought any separate interest; we conversed seriously and gravely, and upon the subject of our repentance continually; we never changed, that is to say, so as to leave off our Armenian garbs; and we were called, at Venice, the two Grecians.

I had been two or three times going to give a detail of our wealth, but it will appear incredible, and we had the greatest difficulty in the world how to conceal it, being justly apprehensive lest we might be assassinated in that country for our treasure. At length William told me he began to think now that he must never see England any more, and that indeed he did not much concern himself about it; but seeing we had gained so great wealth, and he had some poor relations in England, if I was willing, he would write to know if they were living, and to know what condition they were in, and if he found such of them were alive as he had some thoughts about, he would, with my consent, send them something to better their condition.

I consented most willingly; and accordingly William wrote to a sister and an uncle, and in about five weeks' time received an answer from them both, directed to himself, under cover of a hard Armenian name that he had given himself, viz., Signore Constantine Alexion of Ispahan, at Venice.

It was a very moving letter he received from his sister, who, after the most passionate expressions of joy to hear he was alive, seeing she had long ago had an account that he was murdered by the pirates in the West Indies, entreats him to let her know what circumstances he was in; tells him she was not in any capacity to do anything considerable for him, but that he should be welcome to her with all her heart; that she was left a widow, with four children, but kept a little shop in the Minories, by which she made shift to maintain her family; and that she had sent him five pounds, lest he should want money, in a strange country, to bring him home.

I could see the letter brought tears out of his eyes as he read it; and, indeed, when he showed it to me, and the little bill for five pounds, upon an English merchant in Venice, it brought tears out of my eyes too.

After we had been both affected sufficiently with the tenderness and kindness of this letter, he turns to me; says he, "What shall I do for this poor woman?" I mused a while; at last says I, "I will tell you what you shall do for her. She has sent you five pounds, and she has four children, and herself, that is five; such a sum, from a poor woman in her circumstances, is as much as five thousand pounds is to us; you shall send her a bill of exchange for five thousand pounds English money, and bid her conceal her surprise at it till she hears from you again; but bid her leave off her shop, and go and take a house somewhere in the country, not far off from London, and stay there, in a moderate figure, till she hears from you again."

"Now," says William, "I perceive by it that you have

some thoughts of venturing into England."

"Indeed, William," said I, "you mistake me; but it presently occurred to me that you should venture, for what have you done that you may not be seen there? Why should I desire to keep you from your relations, purely to keep me company?"

William looked very affectionately upon me. "Nay," says he, "we have embarked together so long, and come together so far, I am resolved I will never part with thee as long as I live, go where thou wilt, or stay where thou wilt; and as for my sister," said William, "I cannot send her such a sum of money, for whose is all this money we have? It is most of it thine."

"No, William," said I, "there is not a penny of it mine but what is yours too, and I won't have anything but an equal share with you, and therefore you shall send it to her; if not, I will send it."

"Why," says William, "it will make the poor woman distracted; she will be so surprised she will go out of her wits."

"Well," said I, "William, you may do it prudently; send her a bill backed of a hundred pounds, and bid her expect more in a post or two, and that you will send her enough to live on without keeping shop, and then send her more."

Accordingly William sent her a very kind letter, with a bill upon a merchant in London for a hundred and sixty pounds, and bid her comfort herself with the hope that he should be able in a little time to send her more. About ten days after, he sent her another bill of five hundred and forty pounds; and a post or two after, another for three hundred pounds, making in all a thousand pounds; and told her he would send her sufficient to leave off her shop, and directed her to take a house as above.

He waited then till he received an answer to all the

three letters, with an account that she had received the money, and, which I did not expect, that she had not let any other acquaintance know that she had received a shilling from anybody, or so much as that he was alive, and would not till she had heard again.

When he showed me this letter, "Well, William," said I, "this woman is fit to be trusted with life or anything; send her the rest of the five thousand pounds, and I'll venture to England with you, to this woman's house, whenever you will."

In a word, we sent her five thousand pounds in good bills; and she received them very punctually, and in a little time sent her brother word that she had pretended to her uncle that she was sickly and could not carry on the trade any longer, and that she had taken a large house about four miles from London, under pretence of letting lodgings for her livelihood; and, in short, intimated as if she understood that he intended to come over to be *incognito,* assuring him he should be as retired as he pleased.

This was opening the very door for us that we thought had been effectually shut for this life; and, in a word, we resolved to venture, but to keep ourselves entirely concealed, both as to name and every other circumstance; and accordingly William sent his sister word how kindly he took her prudent steps, and that she had guessed right that he desired to be retired, and that he obliged her not to increase her figure, but live private, till she might perhaps see him.

He was going to send the letter away. "Come, William," said I, "you shan't send her an empty letter; tell her you have a friend coming with you that must be as retired as yourself, and I'll send her five thousand pounds more."

So, in short, we made this poor woman's family rich; and yet, when it came to the point, my heart failed me, and I durst not venture; and for William, he would not stir without me; and so we stayed about two years after this, considering what we should do.

You may think, perhaps, that I was very prodigal of my ill-gotten goods, thus to load a stranger with my bounty, and give a gift like a prince to one that had been able to merit nothing of me, or indeed know me; but my condition ought to be considered in this case; though I had money to profusion, yet I was perfectly destitute of a friend in the world, to have the least obligation or assistance from, or knew not either where to dispose or trust anything I had while I lived, or whom to give it to if I died.

When I had reflected upon the manner of my getting of it, I was sometimes for giving it all to charitable uses, as a debt due to mankind, though I was no Roman Catholic, and not at all of the opinion that it would purchase me any repose to my soul; but I thought, as it was got by a general plunder, and which I could make no satisfaction for, it was due to the community, and I ought to distribute it for the general good. But still I was at a loss how, and where, and by whom to settle this charity, not daring to go home to my own country, lest some of my comrades, strolled home, should see and detect me, and for the very spoil of my money, or the purchase of his own pardon, betray and expose me to an untimely end.

Being thus destitute, I say, of a friend, I pitched thus upon William's sister; the kind step of hers to her brother, whom she thought to be in distress, signifying a generous mind and a charitable disposition; and having resolved to make her the object of my first bounty, I did not doubt but I should purchase something of a refuge for myself, and a kind of a center, to which I should tend in my future actions; for really a man that has a subsistence, and no residence, no place that has a magnetic influence upon his affections, is in one of the most odd, uneasy conditions in the world, nor is it in the power of all his money to make it up to him.

It was, as I told you, two years and upwards that we remained at Venice and thereabout, in the greatest hesitation imaginable, irresolute and unfixed to the last degree. William's sister importuned us daily to come to England, and wondered we should not dare to trust her, whom we had to such a degree obliged to be faithful; and in a manner lamented her being suspected by us.

At last I began to incline; and I said to William, "Come, brother William," said I (forever since our discourse at Bassorah I called him brother), "if you will agree to two or three things with me, I'll go home to England with all my heart."

Says William, "Let me know what they are."

"Why, first," says I, "you shall not disclose yourself to any of your relations in England but your sister — no, not one; secondly, we will not shave off our mustachios or beards" (for we had all along worn our beards after the Grecian manner), "nor leave off our long vests, that we may pass for Grecians and foreigners; thirdly, that we shall never speak English in public before anybody, your sister excepted; fourthly, that we will always live together and pass for brothers."

William said he would agree to them all with all his heart, but that the not speaking English would be the hardest, but he would do his best for that too; so, in a word, we agreed to go from Venice to Naples, where we converted a large sum of money into bales of silk, left a large sum in a merchant's hands at Venice, and another considerable sum at Naples, and took bills of exchange for a great deal too; and yet we came with such a cargo to London as few American merchants had done for some years, for we loaded in two ships seventy-three bales of thrown silk, besides thirteen bales of wrought silks, from the duchy of Milan, shipped at Genoa, with all which I arrived safely; and some time after I married my faithful protectress, William's sister, with whom I am much more happy than I deserve.

And now, having so plainly told you that I am come to England, after I have so boldly owned what life I have led abroad, it is time to leave off, and say no more for the present, lest some should be willing to inquire too nicely after your old friend CAPTAIN BOB.

Printed in the United States
16106LVS00001B/544

9 781592 244263